C0-GMH-600

WALKER'S ISLAND

Smithville Public Library
507 Main Street
Smithville, Texas 78957
512-237-3282 ext 6

K. J. Radebaugh

Illustrated by Jenn Spurlock

Copyright © 2008 by K. J. Radebaugh
Cover illustration: *Raymond and Dolly, November 1866*
© Jenn Spurlock
ISBN 1-434-83046-2

All Rights Reserved.
This book or parts thereof may not be reproduced in any form without written permission of the author.

This is a work of fiction. The names, characters, and incidents are all figments of the author's imagination, with the exception of historical figures and events, which are treated in a fictional manner.

To my traveling companions,
Michael and Sam

Part I

April 1865 – November 1866

Jessie's Chicken House

Chapter One

Raymond Pennell and Everett Asbell led the unit down the wagon track to the Bennett farm. The track wound past clumps of pine and palmetto, now shady and cool, now bright and warm, the spring air breezy and sweet and busy with insects and birds. Raymond didn't care about any of that. He had orders to watch the road for signs of mounted horses, one of which was rumored to be shod. Raymond believed in the horses the way he believed in haunts. They were nightmares ridden by bogeymen, monsters that vanished with daybreak. No one could convince him otherwise. The stories were too terrible to be true. Still, there was little else to do, so he watched the road.

The sandy ruts were hard-packed with last night's rain, and marked by nothing more menacing than the passage of wildlife. Raymond noted sign as it appeared, but did not dwell on it. Thinking about game made his stomach growl.

He looked sideways at Everett. The older man was running his thumb up and down the notched poplar stick in his hand. It was his April 1865 stick, and so far he'd cut twenty-eight notches in it, one for each day of the month, up through yesterday. Today was April 29, and tonight, just before he went to sleep, Everett would notch it into the stick. He had more poplar sticks in his pack, one for each month he'd been in the army. When he got back to Tallahassee, Everett said, he was going to set the sticks on fire and watch the war go up in flames. He didn't know what he was going to do after that. The flames were as far as he could see.

Suddenly, Everett yelped and disappeared from view. Raymond dropped to the ground and peered through the grass. Everett was face down between the ruts, mumbling. Raymond laughed. "What're you doing, Everett?" he asked. "Praying?"

"Gopher hole," Everett said. He rolled over on his back with his spectacles in one hand and the stick in the other. Raymond sat up and rested his elbows on his knees. The rest of the unit caught up and shuffled to a halt. Billy Baxter flung himself into the high grass beside Everett. Dolly Baxter let his pack slide to the ground and took his hat off to rub the top of his head. He'd developed a bald spot over the summer and it worried him no end. Frowning, he put his hat back on.

"So what are we doing?" he asked.

"Taking a break," Raymond said.

"Taking a break, my butt," Vancey said. "Everett's gone and fell down again. Why don't you leave them sticks alone, Everett, and watch where you're going for a change?"

Everett rubbed the dirt off his spectacles and put them back on. "Pardon me, Vancey?" he asked. "Were you saying something?" He squinted at Vancey as if he had come on something peculiar and not very nice. It was a look Everett had perfected over time, and it was not lost on anyone. Even Lucas Walker, as broad and solid as a live oak tree and just about as smart, knew when Everett had insulted Vancey. Lucas studied Vancey now, a big grin on his face, clearly hoping for an outburst. Vancey turned red and looked as if he might oblige.

"That's enough," Fitz said. "It's like traveling with a pack of dogs, sometimes, the way y'all fight."

Wallace Turner sat down next to Raymond and pulled a chunk of wood and a knife out of his pack. Wallace carved a woman's torso every day - from neck to mid-thigh, never more than ten inches high, but anatomically correct in every way - that he slept with every night, only to throw it away the next morning and begin another. Billy once asked him how come they never had a head, or any arms or legs. Wallace said he wasn't interested in those parts. They were mostly extra, he said, and more trouble than they were worth, especially the head.

"There's something peculiar hereabouts," he said.

Hebron Wilkes sent a stream of spit into one of the ruts, knocking a fly off a pile of rabbit droppings. "You talking about the chimney smoke?" he asked.

"What chimney smoke?" Raymond asked.

"That's right," Wallace said. "I don't like it."

"Most likely everything is all right," Lucas said.

"We'll see," Fitz said. "Let's keep moving."

They started walking again, Raymond and Everett still in front. As was his wont when he was nervous or scared, Everett started saying the stick in his hand, thumbing the notches and telling on one long, sad note all that had happened on each day, the trivial and the significant given equal emphasis. His words flowed through Raymond's mind like a stream of tepid water, so that he forgot the road and his assignment, and started thinking, instead, about the gate at the road's end that opened into Beely's place. Beely was dust dry with hard times and widowhood. But she was kind, too, in a rough way, and a good cook. Raymond followed his hunger past the gate, into the yard full of children and dogs and flowers blooming by the front door, into the clean house, to the meal set out on the kitchen table, a dinner of smother-fried rabbit, coontie gravy, sweet potatoes, and corn pone, with buttermilk to drink if the cow had freshened, and spring water if it had not. Raymond smacked his lips and pushed Everett away when the older man grabbed his arm. "Leave me be, Everett," he said. "I'm..."

"Look yonder, Raymond," Everett said.

Raymond followed Everett's finger. The picture in his mind blinked away. Coming onto the road from a side trail not ten feet ahead was a confusion of hoof prints. They sorted into at least six horses, maybe eight, headed down the road to the Bennett farm. One of them was shod.

"Sweet Jesus," Everett whispered.

No such prayer came to Raymond's lips. He opened his mouth and smelled his own breath. It stank. One by one, the others stopped, forming a line across the road that none of them would pass. Even Fitz seemed paralyzed.

Ben pushed forward and knelt down beside the tracks. He traced an imprint of the horseshoe with one finger. "They must have come through after the rain last night," he said. "No later than sunrise, anyway." He filled the track with sand and smoothed it over, erasing it, then stood up. "They've already been to Beely's, I reckon."

"We may as well turn back!" Vancey cried. "We can't make no difference there, not now." He lowered his voice. "Let's go," he urged. "Let's get out of here."

"Go where?" Ben demanded. "Where will you hide that this won't find you?" He kicked savagely at the tracks. When he spoke next, his voice was calm. "Do as you choose," he said. "I'm going to the farm." After a moment, the others followed.

Around the curve of an oak thicket the road straightened. Ahead of them was the gate to the Bennett property. It was open. Beely liked the gate kept shut. She was as particular about that as she was about the cleanliness of her floors. Raymond looked beyond the gate, to the house sitting quiet in its empty yard. There were no children, no dogs, and still no chimney smoke. Beely should have been fixing dinner by now, and her hounds should have caught their scent and come to investigate. He tried to remember how many children there were - five or six, at least - and twice that many dogs, one of them as bad a catch dog as any Raymond had ever seen. Beely always had to call him off before they could enter the gate. The dog, a liver-colored cur, was nowhere to be seen.

Lucas Walker was the last man through the gate. He stopped in the opening and called out after the rest of them. "Most likely everything's all right," he said. The others just kept walking. Lucas raised his voice. "I said, most likely everything is all right."

Raymond heard the panic rising in Lucas's voice. He stopped where he was, along with everyone else.

"Shut the gate, Lucas," Ben said.

Lucas shut the gate. No one moved until he caught up, and they all walked to the house together.

It was deserted. Breakfast sat uneaten on the table. Flies crawled over the food. There was mud on the floor. Beely, the cleanest and neatest of women, had left her kitchen a mess.

"This ain't good," Hebron said.

Ben led them through the house. There were no bodies, no blood, nothing torn up. Even the beds were undisturbed. Just an abandoned meal on the table and mud on the floor. They walked out the back door, across the kitchen garden to the barn. A cow stood in the milking parlor, teats grotesquely swollen, horns bloody where she'd tried to pull free of the stanchion. Fitz turned her loose, and she buried her nose in a trough half-filled with water.

"She'll probably founder," Wallace said.

"Probably," Fitz said.

Raymond climbed the ladder to the loft. It was empty. He opened the hay door and looked out over the farm. There was a small pasture behind the barn, bordered by a creek on the west side, woods on the east and north. Buzzards flew above it in tight spirals. "Ben," he said.

"What?"

"There's something laying on the ground over yonder."

It was Beely's youngest child, a girl about six years old. Her dress was torn from neck to hem, and fanned out on each side of her naked body like wings. What had been done to her was more than Raymond's mind could grasp. The girl's eyes moved from face to face with a remote, untouchable expression. Lucas whimpered. Billy turned into Dolly's arms.

"Good God," Hebron said. "Who would do such a thing?"

Everett knelt down beside her. The little girl just looked at him. He took hold of the edges of her dress and pulled them together over her white chest, as flat as a boy's. Everett took the bedroll off his pack, shook it out, and tucked it around her.

"I'm taking you home with me to Tallahassee," he said. "I've got two little girls about your age. They're almost as pretty as you are. The three of you will have tea parties and play dress up. Everything will be fine. You'll forget all this. I promise." The girl smiled.

Fitz stepped away from them and faced the trees. "Bastards!" he yelled.

The word echoed back and forth between the creek and the trees. A rifle cracked. Fitz dropped on top of the child, a neat black hole in the center of his forehead. When Everett pushed his body away, the little girl was dead, too.

They ran. Sometimes they stumbled and fell, and when they did, they flailed upwards again and ran some more. They ran pursued by the roar and sob of their own breath and the pounding of their own blood, with the taste of that blood in their throats. Vancey was the surest of foot and the fastest, so that the others ended up following him, first to the house, then to the edge of the woods behind the house, then down a game trail so narrow they had to go single file. Finally he stopped running to dig a hole, burrowing under fallen branches, brush, and leaf mold. The others did the same, trying to be as quiet as the spiders and scorpions whose hiding places they shared.

Time passed. Raymond's nerves sang shrill as cicadas, then died away to a tremulous silence. His stomach was empty, but he felt no hunger. A stick poked him in the side, and an insect stung his leg, but he did not move. Finally, he grew tired enough to rest his head on his arms. He fell into a waking sleep that rode the current of his breath until it joined the creek and flowed away, past the cold ground beneath him, past Beely's farm, past the raiders and Lieutenant Fitz and the war, all the way back to the beginning.

He'd left home July of 1860, apprenticed by his father to a cow hunter for a ten dollar gold piece and a jug of whiskey. Raymond was eleven at the time, tall for his age, heavy-boned and spare-fleshed, with big hands and feet and good teeth. He had a slow, drawling manner of speech, listened more than he talked, and seldom reviewed a judgment once he'd made it. He was good with livestock and even better with his hands, and found it easier to get along with people than not. And while he didn't know much about hunting cattle, he knew he could learn whatever he needed to know.

A year later, he could hunt and drive cattle with the best of them, and having fulfilled the terms of his apprenticeship, went to work for a rancher named Jacob Summerlin. Raymond was making board and five dollars a month, and would have thought himself in high cotton were it not for Vancey Adams. Vancey was so good-looking he was almost pretty, and a born bully. He put rabbit pills in Raymond's coffee, saltpeter in his beans, and sandspurs in his bedroll. He embarrassed him in front of other cow hunters and shamed him in front of strangers. He even beat him up one time, breaking some ribs and bruising Raymond's mouth so bad he couldn't eat for a week. Raymond had a score with Vancey Adams. All he needed was an opportunity to settle it.

In August of 1861, Jacob Summerlin's cow crews gathered in Baldwin, Florida with herds from all over the state for shipment to Confederate troops further north. Cattle bawled, dogs barked, men shouted, cow whips cracked like rifle shots, and a boy could hardly make himself heard through the commotion. Raymond went looking for the paymaster's office, and along the way ran into Vancey Adams, who was tormenting the Baxter brothers.

The brothers' reputations had preceded them to Baldwin. Dolly was the same age as Raymond, but short-legged and thick-bodied, with black hair and eyes of an unusual cobalt blue. Stories of violence surrounded him, and the cow whip he used – a twelve-foot extension of his arm - lent them credence. Ten-year-old Billy was as friendly as his brother was cold, and the only person in the world, it was said, who could make Dolly Baxter smile.

Like Raymond, Vancey had already heard of the brothers. He was particularly interested in the younger boy's affliction. Billy Baxter couldn't hold his water when he laughed. Most anything could bring it on – a joke, somebody tripping or passing gas – because most anything made Billy laugh, and if he laughed hard enough, he wet his pants. He couldn't help it. Then he'd cry, and that was funny, too. And when that happened, a man could laugh as hard as he wanted to, so long as he was ready for a fight, because mister, if you laughed when Billy Baxter pissed his drawers, Dolly Baxter was coming to you, make no mistake about it. The fights he'd waged on his brother's behalf were the stuff of legend, and there was not a man on their crew who had not borne the marks of Dolly's fists and left his own on Dolly in return. Back on the trail, these pleasures had given way to boredom. But this was Baldwin, where a whole new audience was waiting to be entertained. All it needed was somebody to get it started.

Vancey had taken that honor on himself. He walked around the cornered boys like a barker at a fair, drawing a crowd with his mockery until there must have been twenty men in the audience. Then he snatched Billy up, tickled him until he wet his pants, and set him back down in front of his brother. Billy's eyes filled with tears, and he began to weep.

Vancey laughed. He leaned over, slapped his hands on his knees, and guffawed. And when he did, Dolly Baxter jumped on him. The fury of that attack inspired Raymond to join it, and Billy came right behind him. The three boys climbed Vancey Adams like a tall pine tree, punching and kicking and gouging all the way. Together, they beat the pretty off his face and the laughter out of his belly and reduced twenty chortling, backslapping cracker cow hunters to respectful silence punctuated by a single, but admiring, "Sheeeyit." Only Raymond never heard that word of commendation, because Dolly was smiling at him. Raymond smiled back, and their friendship was born. That exchange was as good as a handshake on a contract, and the two of them would honor it as best they could for the rest of their lives.

The next day, Jacob Summerlin put Raymond, Vancey, the Baxter brothers, and three other men on a crew under a foreman named Ben Monroe. Ben did not tolerate meanness, so while Vancey was no more courteous than he'd been before, he was certainly more cautious. And if, now and then, he seemed a little too quiet, and rubbed his now misshapen nose a little too hard, he gave the boys little reason to think it had anything to do with them.

Ben and his crew rode the length and breadth of peninsular Florida for the next two years, exempt from military service for the duration of Summerlin's contract with the Confederate Army. Summerlin had begun supplying beef in 1861, and by December of '62 had shipped some twenty-five thousand head of cattle to Georgia, South Carolina, and Alabama. He was paid ten dollars a head in Confederate script, which he exchanged for Confederate bonds. But when southern banks refused to exchange the bonds for gold, Summerlin terminated his contract. Ben Monroe and his crew continued hunting cattle in Summerlin's employ, so sure of the world and their place in it that none of them – man or boy – were as mindful of their lost exemption as they should have been.

Carelessness took them too far north in September 1863. Ben split his crew up southeast of Brooksville. Jeb Duncan, Duval Bedford, and Hiram Young turned east, followed by Hiram's yellow cur dog. Ben, Vancey, and the three boys headed west, and had picked up ten head by that afternoon. They drove them directly into the sights of one Confederate Lieutenant Fitz, who drew his revolver and shot their lead cow between the eyes.

Vancey was offended by Fitz's action and threatened retribution, until Fitz cocked the revolver a second time and aimed it at his flattened nose. When Ben arrived a few seconds later, Vancey looked to him for help. Raymond and the Baxter brothers looked at Ben, too, expecting rescue. But Ben couldn't even rescue himself. All five horses bore Summerlin's brand on their left shoulder. The cow hunters could admit they rode for him and be conscripted into the Confederate Army, or deny it, and be hanged for horse theft. It just wasn't all that hard a choice to make.

Fitz marched his ragtag unit of men and boys up and down the coast with such single-minded intensity and to so little effect that Raymond and Dolly decided he was crazy. The war had largely abandoned Florida by this time, so instead of fighting, they chased rumors and false alarms and searched gutted farms for starving livestock, or gathered on porch steps and listened to rambling stories of the war, or sat down to meals cooked by the likes of Beely Bennett and ate like civilized men. Every now and then, they'd stumble on a Union patrol and exchange shots. The unit lost a man that way – his name was Gabe Wilson – just three days after the cow hunters' conscription. Raymond dreamed about Gabe's death for weeks, and Lucas Walker had still not recovered. Since then, they'd exchanged fire with the enemy exactly six times, with no apparent damage to either side.

They heard about the raiders for the first time in January of 1865, Confederate renegades that robbed travelers and stole their horses. Then the stories got worse: bodies mutilated and burned, houses and barns ransacked and torched or mysteriously deserted. And just last week, they themselves had come upon a murdered Union soldier, his half-naked body hanging upside down from a tree by a rope around his ankles, his pants and boots in a pile on the ground beneath him. Ben wanted to bury him, but hearing horses approach they ran, instead, fearing raiders and Yankees both. Vancey snatched up the clothes on his way and later tried them on. The pants fit him just right, but only Raymond could wear the boots. Vancey insisted he take them, and even Ben agreed that they were no longer of any use to the dead soldier. So Raymond kept the boots and wore them and was glad for them despite where they came from, because they were well made and comfortable, and still in one piece.

And they were still comfortable and whole even after the terrible things he'd seen this day, even though his arm was asleep and his leg was itching and Vancey was kicking dirt in his face and saying, "Get up. They're not coming. We're safe." And whether that was true or not, Raymond crawled out from his hiding place to take stock of his surroundings and the future.

Chapter Two

They were standing on the edge of a small clearing in a bay head. The creek turned a corner here so that there was water, though it was too dangerous for a fire. They ate hard tack washed down with water and stood, or sat on their bedrolls and whispered among themselves, alert for signs of pursuit. All was quiet, though, and their voices grew louder, though still muted.

"What do we do now?" Everett asked. His small face was wrinkled like a dried apple, and he held his April stick close to his chest. He seemed smaller than he'd been earlier in the day, as though he were shrinking.

"I'm leaving," Marshall said. "Heading home. To Tallahassee."

"When are you going to do that, Marshall?" Everett asked.

"First light," Marshall said. "You coming with me?"

"I don't know," Everett said. "Are we done?"

"I am," Marshall said.

"What about you, Ben?" Everett asked. "Are you done?"

"Yes," Ben said. "I'm going home now." Raymond looked around the clearing and beyond it, through the trees. The light was failing. It would be dark within the hour.

"Right now?' he asked.

"First light," Ben said.

"Can we come with you?' Billy asked.

"Yes."

"What about you, Hebron?" Everett asked.

"I'm going home, Everett," Hebron said. He pointed toward the west. "There it is. Gulf Hammock. So close I can almost smell it.""

"What's it smell like?" Billy asked.

"Smoked mullet and corn liquor," Hebron said.

"I want some," Billy said.

"You come with me and you can have it," Hebron said. "All you can hold."

"I guess I'll go with Ben," Billy said. "Thank you for the invite, though."

"Anytime, young Billy," Hebron said. "Anytime."

"What about you, Vancey?" Everett asked.

"What business is it of yours?' Vancey asked.

"I was just wondering," Everett said.

"I ain't decided yet," Vancey said. "Right now I'm hungry. I've a mind to find something to eat."

"You won't find it in the dark," Ben said. "Best you stay here until dawn, anyway. Let us get some distance on this place before you go making a lot of noise."

"I ain't got to take orders from you," Vancey said. "I ain't got to do what I'm told, not anymore. I can do what I want." The truth of what he said stirred like a shift in the weather. There was no arguing with it.

"What about me?" Lucas asked. "Where will I go?"

"You'll go home, Lucas," Ben said. "Like the rest of us."

"Where is home?" Lucas asked.

"The Cedar Keys," Hebron said. "You can go with me for awhile. I'll point you in the right direction when it's time."

"I don't want to go to the Cedar Keys," Lucas said. "I don't want that home."

"Where do you want to go, Lucas?" Ben asked.

"With you," Lucas said.

"All right, Lucas," Ben said

"You won't change your mind," Lucas said.

"No," Ben said. "I won't change my mind."

"All right," Lucas said. "Ben says I'm going with him, Everett."

"That's fine, Lucas," Everett said. He paused. "I reckon I'll go with you, then, Marshall."

"That's fine, Everett," Marshall said. "Come morning, you and me, we'll head north, Hebron will go west, and the rest of them will go south." He took the carving out of his backpack and stretched out on his bedroll. "I guess I'll sleep for a while. Somebody else get first watch, they can wake me up in an hour or so. I'm pretty tired right now."

"I'm taking the watch," Vancey said, and walked into the trees until he was no more than a shadow in the failing light.

Raymond put his blanket down and stretched out, not to sleep – the image of Fitz and the little girl were too sharp in his mind for that – but simply to rest, to loosen the tendons and muscles that pulled in his neck and shoulders like cables. Dolly sat down next to him and Billy got between them. The three of them spoke in whispers.

"Why don't we go now?" Billy asked.

"Because it'll be dark soon," Dolly said. "We'd get lost."

"We're already lost," Billy said.

"We'd get more lost. Be quiet. Let Ben figure it out."

"First light," Raymond said. "We'll head south. Ben will go home to his family and we'll go to Summerlin's. It's simple."

"I want to go now," Billy said.

"Be quiet," Dolly said. "You can't..."

"LIEUTENANT FIIIIIITZ! SOMEBODY HEEELP! LIEUTENANT FIIIITZ!"

"Not now, Lucas," Dolly muttered. "Not now." But it was going to be now, all the same, and every one of them knew it.

The cow hunters had first encountered Lucas Walker's bizarre outbursts the night Gabe Wilson was killed. The skirmish itself was bad enough, what with all the bullets flying around. But the aftermath was worse, because it took Gabe a long, hard time to die and he wasn't quiet about it. Billy couldn't keep anything on his stomach afterwards, and the rest of them felt puny and sad. But they felt a whole lot worse later that night when Lucas wailed into the hushed night, "IT COULD HAVE BEEN ONE OF US!" Raymond had come straight up off the ground with the hair standing up on the back of his neck as Lucas shouted all the ways they could have died that day, and probably would have, had Gabe not done it for them. He went on and on until Vancey shrieked, "Shut him the hell up!" But the lieutenant had said there was no shutting Lucas up once he started. They would just have to wait him out.

Since that time, Raymond had come to pity Lucas, but tonight he cussed him under his breath. Here they were, mere hours away from safety and the return of sanity, and Lucas had to go crazy on them and tell the whole damn world where they were.

"We're going to die!" Lucas shrieked. "They're going to shoot us! You saw what they did to that little girl! What if they do that to us?"

"Not tonight, Walker!" Vancey yelled. "Quit that howling before I come over there and do it for you!"

"We're leaving tomorrow morning, Lucas," Billy said. "With Ben. Remember? He said so. He said you can go with him."

"I'm afraid to go home," Lucas wailed.

"You aren't going home," Dolly said. "You're going to the island. You're going there with Ben. Then everything will be all right. Ain't that right, Ben?"

"There's nothing right," Lucas moaned. "Not anywhere, not even there."

"Ben?" Hebron's voice was gritty.

"What?" Ben asked.

"I'm fixing to shoot him."

"Your powder's gone."

"Then I'll club him to death," Hebron snapped. He sounded to Raymond like he meant it.

Lucas kept on crying. "Every place is the same," he said. "Dead, gone, burned up. Everything is dead, the cows and the horses, the deer and the turkeys, everything…"

Billy got up and moved away. Raymond could hear him retching. Dolly muttered a curse. Finally, Ben spoke. He sounded like an old man.

"Lucas," he said. "Lucas."

"What if we go there and it's gone, Ben?" Lucas cried. "What will we do?"

"It's there," Ben said. "It's all there. There's some things can't nobody hurt."

"They can hurt it. They can hurt anything."

"No, they can't," Ben said. "They can't touch it, and here's why…"

And though it was now full dark and he couldn't see them, Raymond knew that Ben had moved over next to Lucas, to pat his shoulder and tell him about an island far to the south that was waiting for him, the only words in the world with the power to comfort Lucas Walker.

The story of the island began the night Gabe Wilson died. Ben had treated Lucas like one of his own children, telling him stories of scrub cattle, marsh ponies, and cow dogs, and the adventures he'd had in their company. He described the great river of grass that flowed from Lake Okeechobee to the sea, and the broad grazing lands along the Caloosahatchee, thick with cattle and game. Lucas was already quiet and listening, as was Raymond, when Ben mentioned an island he and his crew had once seen, that crowned the headwaters of the Locknahatchee River.

Raymond remembered the island well. They'd crossed it in February when the water was low and the cattle they were driving had grazed the marsh grasses to the ground. Hundreds of thousands of ducks – canvasbacks, teal, wood ducks, black ducks, and mallards – covered the marsh and lakes. They'd taken to the air in mass flight when the herd approached, darkening the sky like the black, tarry smoke of a pitch pine fire, the beat of their wings like thunder over Raymond's head. The drovers watered the herd and their horses and continued on, knowing from experience that when the rains returned, the land they rode across would disappear, swallowed by the water that crept beyond the boundaries of lakes and marsh and swamp to make an island of the hammock to the west.

The hammock was cut down the middle by a deep, swift creek. Live oaks grew there so great in girth that three men as big as Lucas himself could not join hands around them, and the fronds of cabbage palms bent over sandy trails littered with leaves and filtered sunlight, where wolves and panthers pursued deer and wild cattle. Great flocks of little green Carolina parakeets nested in the trees, fox squirrels as big as cats, with golden bellies and huge brown eyes, buried stores of acorns for the hogs to dig up again, and raccoons slipped eggs and hatchlings from their nests. And always, the hammock was alive with sounds – shrieks and twitters, rustles, hoots, and howls – as the animals that lived there foraged and hunted and the wind played through the oak trees and the cabbage palms.

Below the hammock where the river was born, bald cypress obscured the midday sun, their ancient knees rising out of black water flecked with gold and green. The water was alive with light, dimpled with the feet of spiders and water bugs, patterned by the wakes of otters and cottonmouths, studded with the knobbed eyes of alligators and churned by their kills. There, when night fell, the moon reigned over darkness as old as God.

Somewhere in the telling, his terrors put to rest, Lucas Walker had fallen asleep. But Raymond had stayed awake a long time afterwards, pondering the island Ben had described. It seemed to him larger and more real than the one he'd actually seen, and capable of holding a man's whole life. He saw a house in the hammock, and a woman hanging up clothes, and children playing around her feet. He saw barns and herds and pastures and fields, everything a man might want in this life or the next gathered in that safe and lovely place. Raymond had taken the island to his heart that night as a man might take to his heart a mail order bride, believing on the evidence of a portrait alone that she was all he'd ever dreamed of in a wife.

The story of the island grew with time, stretching and sometimes breaking the limits of all but Lucas's credulity. The animals took on human thought and the trees human form, and the whole place pulsed with a wisdom and justice and peace beyond any those men had ever known, beyond what some of them even wanted. For a long time, though, it remained nameless, until one night, inspired by boredom, perhaps, or derision, Vancey suggested they come up with a name for it. The discussion that followed was spirited and occasionally lewd, and betrayed a certain skepticism among several of Raymond's fellows.

But in Raymond's mind, Ben's stories had infused memory with the scent of myth. He took this naming business seriously, and fumbled for the perfect word with the certainty of a blind man groping among familiar items on a whatnot shelf, frustrated that the very one he wanted was, inexplicably, the only one that was not there. It seemed to tremble on the very edge of his mind, the one name that, when spoken, would say all that the island meant to him.

But Raymond could not find the word he was looking for, and it was Billy who came up with the one they finally chose. Lucas loved it, and the others were tired and wanted to go to sleep, and mostly didn't give a damn, anyhow. From then on, whenever there was trouble and Lucas in his simplicity let loose the fears the rest of them kept hidden, Ben talked them all to sleep by remembering a place known of them had ever really known, a place they called Walker's Island.

Tonight, however, when Lucas's snores finally rumbled gently in the dark, Ben's voice failed to carry Raymond into sleep as it usually did. He gazed up at a little patch of sky directly above him, and wished he were headed to the island that very minute, or at least to Summerlin's ranch. The picture of the little girl was gone from his head, and an ambush by renegades now seemed impossible. Still, he could not sleep, but waited for dawn as hard and fast as he could. Billy sat back down between Dolly and Raymond. His voice was low and quiet when he spoke, but he no longer whispered. Ben's stories of the island had washed his fear away, as well.

"I'm hungry," he said.

"I guess so," Dolly said. "You just puked your supper out in the bushes."

"I couldn't help it," Billy said. He was silent for a moment. "I reckon it's better than pissing myself." He hadn't wet his pants in over a year, but the possibility of it happening again troubled him quite a bit.

"It's considerably better," Dolly said. "Now go to sleep."

"I can't," Billy said. "I've got too much on my mind. Dolly?"

"What?"

"One thing I want real bad is a puppy out of one of Hiram's dogs. He's sure got some good dogs."

"You're right about that," Dolly said. "We'll get you a puppy from the next litter."

"I want a glass of buttermilk, too. And I want to sit in a chair to drink it. Sit right up to a table. Don't that sound good?"

"It surely does."

"Dolly?"

"One more question," Dolly said. "Then if you open your mouth again, I'm going to stuff it full of moss and tie it shut."

"I ain't never wanted anything in my whole life as much as I want to go home."

"We'll be there before you know it, Bill," Dolly said. "Now go to sleep." Billy sighed, but didn't say anything else. After a while, his breathing slowed and deepened into sleep. Raymond was still awake, though, when the moon rose, shiny as a brand new silver dollar beyond the trees. Low voices rumbled in the silvered darkness of the clearing, followed by silence. Moments later, a hand touched Raymond on the shoulder.

"Vancey's still watching," Hebron said. "He says he ain't tired. You want to play some cards?"

"Yes," Raymond said. He moved to wake Dolly, but he was already up and had put his blanket over Billy. The three of them crossed the moonlit clearing. Lucas was sprawled out on his back, his arm flung over Ben's chest. Everett and Wallace slept side by side, Everett with his hands clasped on his chest, his spectacles on the ground near his head, Wallace curled into a ball, the little wooden woman in his arms. Raymond couldn't see Vancey anywhere.

"Vancey?" he whispered.

Hebron rapped him sharply on the back in warning. If Lucas woke up in the middle of the night, not even Ben would be able to get him back to sleep.

On the far side of the clearing was an ancient hickory tree, blown over in some long-ago storm. Huge and fully canopied, its roots still deep within the earth, it lay on its side, shrouded in fox grape vines and cat claw briars. Raymond and Hebron climbed over it, tendrils and hooked thorns plucking at their skin and clothes. Dolly stood for a moment looking back at the clearing.

"Where do you reckon Vancey is?" he asked.

"He's out there," Hebron said. "Waiting for morning, just like the rest of us. Now sit yourself down so I can take your money."

He fished a pack of cards out of his pocket and untied the string that held them. There, propped against the trunk of the hickory tree, the three men played as fiercely for acorns as they ever had for money, winning meaning something for its own sake now in a way it never had before. The night grew old and the moon fell toward the west.

"Count me out," Dolly said. He slipped into the curve of a branch and closed his eyes. Hebron fell asleep sitting straight up, and Raymond gathered the cards that fell from his hands. A pair of deuces, he thought. May as well go to sleep. He added them to the three tens in his own hand, then gathered up Hebron's acorns and a few more besides, and put them in his pocket. He tied the string around the cards again and put them in his pocket with the acorns. An owl hooted and something shrieked. The hair prickled on the back of Raymond's neck. He listened, straining to hear.

"Vancey?" he whispered. "Is that you?"

No one answered. Dolly and Hebron were hidden in shadow. Raymond could hear them breathing. He yawned. It was best to stay awake, at least until he knew where Vancey was. After all, somebody had to take the next watch. Just for a moment, though, he rested his head on the ground, and that was long enough to fall asleep.

Hooves thudded into Raymond's dreams and gunfire jerked him out of one nightmare into another. He was scrabbling under the hickory tree before the first scream ripped the dawn. The present came apart: the snort of horses, the shouts of men, Everett nattering about his sticks, the sweaty stink of fear rising from Dolly beside him, Hebron's breath whistling so loudly that Raymond kept waiting for the uproar in the clearing to stop while everyone, attackers and attacked alike, looked for its source. The dew in his hair, the thorn under his nail, the sharp, medicinal odor of prickly ash, the bright red of a ladybug raising its wings on his knuckle, the bile in his throat, the trembling of his head on his neck, all of these things existed with no relation to each other or himself. His hands operated independently of the rest of him, tearing at the undergrowth with thorn-ripped flesh whose pain was isolated, while elbows dragged his body through the dirt to the other side of the hickory tree. He squinted through a gray-green latticework of vines at Vancey Adams in the act of getting on a horse. With his left foot in the stirrup, Vancey hopped one-legged after a chestnut gelding that circled a Union officer standing at its head. And all the while, the two of them were yelling at each other about horses.

"Where are the horses?" the officer screamed. "Why aren't there any horses?"

"I don't know," Vancey yelled. "Leave me alone! Let me go! I don't know!"

The picture was odd, even in the midst of chaos. Everett yelled something about his sticks again, and fumbled at the buckles on his pack, until the officer pulled out a revolver and shot him in the chest. Everett grunted and slumped across his pack. Then Vancey was in the saddle, gathering up the reins and leaning forward, kicking the horse that lunged and stopped, lunged and stopped, pummeled by Vancey, snatched back by the officer who tried to drag Vancey to the ground.

"Get off my horse, you lying…"

Vancey kicked him in the face and lashed at the horse with the reins. The soldier fell and the chestnut bolted across the clearing, then gathered itself and jumped the fallen hickory tree in a long, black, sweat-slick streak of belly and thighs and blood-gorged veins. Then the horse and Vancey were gone and Billy was running across the clearing, his hair messy with leaves where he'd rolled off his blanket in his sleep. He went by the officer as though he didn't see him. The officer let him pass, then shot him in the back.

The bullet added so to Billy's momentum that he almost made it to the hickory tree. He reached out with both arms, his blue eyes eager, his wide mouth bright with blood. He must have seen Dolly, the way he grinned and called his name. It took everything Raymond had to shove Dolly's face down in the dirt so he couldn't answer. Then there was a second shot, and it took Raymond and Hebron both to hold him down while Billy died.

Chapter Three

Four soldiers sat on their horses at the edge of the clearing. One of them, a private, dismounted and started pawing the bodies. He held up Wallace's woman. "Look at this, Captain," he said.

The officer left off staring after Vancey's vanished form, and glanced at the carving. He grimaced with distaste. "Leave it alone," he said. His voice had an absent-minded quality to it, as if he didn't mean what he said. The private grinned and stuck the woman under his arm, then put his hand in Wallace's pants pocket. The captain turned slowly in the clearing, gazing out through the trees at something Raymond couldn't see.

"Looking for something special, Cap?" one of the mounted men said.

"He said there were eight altogether," the captain answered. "And a horse for each, plus provisions and loot. Seems to be a lot missing."

"Maybe they hid it, and them that ran off are planning to come back later," the private said. He grabbed Everett's pack, spilled it on the ground, and kicked at the sticks. "I can tell you one thing, these here are so damn poor it didn't hardly pay to shoot them."

Another soldier on a black horse rode into the clearing and over to the hickory tree. The horse perked its ears at Raymond, who held his breath. It blew a long, rattling sigh and relaxed, cocking a hind foot. Raymond breathed again, feeling sick

"Five men are dead," the soldier on the black horse said. "What more do you want?"

"The truth," the captain said. He walked up to the black horse and laid a hand on its neck. "I hate being lied to."

"Well, that feller got you this time, Cap," the private said. "Lied to you, and stole your horse, too. He got you good." He stood up, hands filled with loot, and started walking toward his horse.

The captain swung himself up on the black horse, behind the man in the saddle, and nodded at the bodies in the clearing. "He got these here even better," he said.

"Yessir, he did," the private said.

"Just like I'm going to get you if you don't drop all that right now."

"Aw, Cap. It's just some souvenirs."

The captain trained his revolver on his subordinate. "Let me tell you something," he said. "I pride myself on my ability to judge men. Last night I made a mistake. Now my horse is gone and so are a number of the criminals I came after, providing they were ever here. But I don't think I've misjudged you, and it would give me satisfaction to leave you here among those you so closely resemble, in the same mortal condition as they."

The private frowned at the man in the saddle, who cleared his throat. "He means you're no better than a raider," he said. "And he's going to kill you if you don't put those things down."

The private opened his hands, and dropped a pocketknife, a watch, a powder horn, and the wooden woman on the ground. "Why couldn't he just say so?" he asked. Then he got on his horse, and followed the others out of the clearing.

Except for Everett and Billy, the bodies lay as if in sleep, all of them oddly foreshortened in Raymond's field of vision and so utterly still they seemed unreal. Underneath the hickory tree, things were noisier. Hebron's breath continued to whistle, and Dolly's voice droned in Raymond's ear, chiding him and Billy for their stupidity and peppering them with questions that Billy couldn't hear and Raymond couldn't answer. He didn't know why Billy had run like that, or why he hadn't stayed where he was, and pretended he was dead. Nor did he know why he, Raymond, had stopped Dolly from going to Billy when he fell, though he, Raymond, did agree that if he'd let Dolly go, they'd all be dead now, instead of laying up under a tree with nothing but dead men for company. Every now and then, Dolly would stop and quietly damn Vancey to hell for all eternity, after which he'd start back in on Billy and Raymond.

Raymond gave up listening after a while. He shaded his eyes against the glare that lit the scene before him, as weighed down by the enormity of Vancey's actions as if the hickory tree had rolled on top of him. He might have stayed beneath the tree for days, had it not been for the flies. They were bluebottle flies, the biggest Raymond had ever seen, and they were swarming all over Billy. A greasy sweat broke out on Raymond's forehead, and he crawled out from under the tree. He heard a rustling sound, and turned to find Hebron behind him.

"I'm tired of Dolly's noise," Hebron said.

"I don't know what to do with him," Raymond said.

Hebron squatted down in front of Dolly "Quit that moaning," he said. "Get out here and help me and Raymond with this mess. You hear me, Dolly?"

"Go to hell, Hebron," Dolly said, and went back to his harangue.

Hebron sat down. "It's no good, Ray. You think of something."

"Dolly," Raymond said. "Billy's pissed his pants and Hebron's out here laughing at him."

It worked. Dolly quit cursing and put his face back in the dirt, his wide shoulders shaking so hard they looked to Raymond like they might break in half. He waited for the crying to stop. Hebron started complaining again. But it was the fat blue flies, not Hebron, that finally pushed Raymond to action. He got to his feet, and with Hebron's help, dragged Dolly out from under the hickory tree. Bumbling around like drunks, they set about burying the dead.

The camp shovel was still in Ben's pack. It was short-handled in the first place, and broke off near the blade before the grave was finished. They took turns kneeling in the hole, hacking and scraping with the blade between their hands. It was better that way, maybe, the strain on backs and thighs and shoulders easing the one on their hearts.

The hole was hard work, but the dead were harder. Lucas was particularly difficult to carry, so heavy and every whichaway that Dolly got mad and insisted on separating him from Ben. They put him on the bottom between Everett and Wallace, each wrapped in his own blanket, then covered them with moss and leaves and put Ben and Billy on top.

Their treasures went in there with them: Ben's watch, Everett's spectacles and sticks, Wallace's pocketknife and woman, Billy's powder horn. Only Lucas had nothing dear to hold, so Raymond put his hand in Ben's. He didn't think Ben would mind.

It was hard to leave Billy there. Dolly straightened his brother's legs again, tucking them well into the blanket. He tried to close the eyelids with his thumb, only they kept coming open again. Finally, he covered them with moss, and stepped back so Raymond could fill the hole.

Every decision after that seemed to depend on Vancey.

"I think he'll go on to Summerlin's," Dolly said. "Providing he thinks we're all dead."

"No reason for him to think otherwise," Hebron said.

"He didn't stick around to count heads," Dolly said. "It's got to be bothering him some."

"So where would he go, if he's not sure?" Hebron asked.

"Some place that feels safe to him," Dolly said. "Some place he can hide." He paused. "Like Walker's Island."

Hebron hooted. "Come on, Dolly," he said. "That weren't no more than a fairy tale, critters talking like men, and God walking amongst the trees, and all such as that. This mess has addled your brain. Tell him, Ray. Tell him he's crazy."

But Raymond just studied the thicket beyond the hickory tree where the chestnut horse had broken the bushes down as it landed. He was shocked by Dolly's statement. It had never occurred to him that others might feel about the island as he did, and he needed to hide his face while he took the knowledge in. It went down hard, and he had to swallow twice before he could answer.

"All that about the animals and God was made up," he said. "But the rest of it wasn't. We were there, we saw it. Could be Vancey would go to ground there, if he thought any of us made it. Or even if he didn't. It's fine country. One thing's for sure. He'll go south. Vancey's never been one for cold weather." He shrugged his pack on. "Wherever he is, we'll find him."

"What then?" Dolly asked.

"I don't know," Raymond said. "Ask me when we find him."

They got shot at the first farm they came to. Nobody answered the door when they knocked, so they made their way across the yard and over a pole fence to a field green with sweet potato vines. They were pulling up sweet potatoes when the shots rang out. It scared Raymond so bad he threw a sweet potato on the ground like he'd never touched it, then got hot in the face and grabbed it up again as he ran for the woods.

Their reception was better at the next farm, where an ancient farmer allowed them to work all day for a bowl of mustard greens and a slice of fried pone. A fortnight later they came on a Union dispatch rider who stopped long enough to tell them that the war had ended three weeks before. The news made Raymond lurch, as if a wall he'd been leaning against had just collapsed. Afterwards, he felt sick and tired inside with something he couldn't put a name to, but that had something to do with living and dying at the same time.

Hebron left them a week later at the railroad tracks, about ten miles south of a burned-out farm they'd seen earlier in the day. They'd stood outside the gate, eyes fixed on the charred house, sniffing a foulness, more than burnt wood, that drifted by on the stale wind. Hebron was spooked by the stench and emptiness of the farm. He talked nonstop about his people in Gulf Hammock, and by the time they reached the railroad tracks, had made up his mind to go home.

"That was bad back there," he said. "Real bad. I got to make sure my folks are all right before I do anything else." He shook Dolly's hand. "I'll be in Gulf Hammock when you're ready to go after Vancey."

"I'm ready now," Dolly said.

"Well, I ain't," Hebron said. "And you can't go without me, else I'll have to do to you what you're aiming to do to him." He slapped Raymond on the shoulder. "Don't let Miss Dolly go off half-cocked."

"I'll keep an eye on him," Raymond said.

Hebron shouldered his musket and headed west along the tracks. Raymond and Dolly watched until he was out of sight, then turned east toward the little town of Debussy.

Three years before, Raymond, Dolly, and Billy had helped load three hundred head of steers onto the stock cars that ran the Florida Railroad Company's narrow gauge line from Fernandina to the Cedar Keys, then decided to go along for the ride. They'd whooped and hollered across the state, enjoying the hot, bone-jarring ride as only the young can do. Midway on the trip, the train had jerked to a halt, and they'd off-loaded the steers for watering at the Debussy stockyards.

Debussy had never been much of a town, even in the best of times. It sat a little west of midway on the line and earned its living from railroad crews and cattle drovers. That was enough to support a stationmaster, a small hotel with a blacksmith shop and whiskey still in back, a general mercantile store, and one small church, which the boys only saw from the outside.

They'd barely had time to wolf down a slice of pie at the hotel and run to the mercantile store for candy when the whistle blew, and almost missed the train because Billy stopped to court a girl watching them from the store window. He swept his hat off and bowed to her, then fell to the ground when Dolly hit him in the back. Billy came up mad, and Raymond had to pull the brothers apart. Then the three of them ran to the train, the girl forgotten in the heat of the race. In the Cedar Keys, they'd bought horses, equipment, and supplies with Jacob Summerlin's money, and ridden down the west coast to the ranch. Soon after their trip, the Yankees had shelled the railhead at the Cedar Keys, so Raymond and Dolly didn't expect to get another train ride. But they weren't coming this close to Debussy without seeing how it had fared. For as Dolly said, if he and Raymond could grow into men in three years - Dolly with a beer barrel voice and Raymond with a beard - then Debussy could grow into a full-fledged town.

They left the rusted rails a mile out of Debussy, skirting a dense hammock that lay on the edge of a pasture full of cow pats and brambles. A three-quarter moon gave the illusion of light, and they stumbled over gopher holes and fallen tree limbs, Dolly cursing his boots. He had tied the uppers to what remained of the soles with vines, and sometimes the flap would catch on things and trip him. On the east side of the hammock was a hedge with a house beyond it. Between the house and the hedge was a barn and a smaller outbuilding.

"Think we can make it to that barn?" Raymond asked.

"If I can get there without killing myself," Dolly said. He bent down and tightened the string around his boots, then straightened up and slapped Raymond gently on the arm. "Let's go."

The smaller building was a hen house with a fenced yard. Dolly wanted to slip in and grab some eggs, but Raymond stopped him. There wouldn't be any eggs until morning, he said, and besides, there wasn't any way to cook them. They had milk, instead, bribing the cow with shelled corn from the feed room while they milked her into a rusted lard can they found in a corner of the barn. When they were full, they climbed up in the loft and bedded down in the hay. They could hear rats down below, cleaning up the corn they'd dropped.

"Come first light," Dolly said, "we can slip down there and get some more breakfast. And I bet if we took some of them chickens to town, we could trade them for a pair of boots."

But Raymond didn't want to talk about tomorrow, anymore than he wanted to think about yesterday. Right now, full and warm and comfortable, was all he cared about. The moonlight slipped through a crack in the floor of the loft, running a white stripe between the mounds of hay where he and Dolly had put their bedrolls. The hay was softer than Raymond had remembered a bed could be, and the play of light and shadow in the eaves was restful.

"Ray?"

"Hmmm?"

"I wish I'd listened to Billy that last night, and left like he wanted to. Or just let him talk, instead of shushing him. And I wish you'd let me go to him, there at the end."

Raymond waited for the moonlight to shimmer in his eyes, but no tears came. He didn't know what to say. The events of that night - the deaths of Billy and Ben and the others, Vancey's mysterious behavior, his own unthinking act of self-preservation - all these were questions he could not answer. Maybe there was no understanding what had happened. Some lived. Some died. Maybe that's all the reason there was.

"Ray?"

"What?"

"Are you sorry you didn't let me go to Billy?"

"No," Raymond said.

Dolly started crying. Raymond waited. After a while, he started snoring. Only then did Raymond close his eyes, grateful for a full belly, a soft bed, and moonlight to keep the darkness at bay.

Chapter Four

Raymond woke to sunlight glancing through the same crack the moon had used, the clank of a milk pail, and the sound of a girl's voice in the barn beneath him. The voice was soothing, though he couldn't make out the words. He heard the board fall in the stanchion, and the ring of the pail as the milk went in. His stomach rumbled. He'd meant to get up early enough to drink breakfast before anybody got to the barn.

Something jabbed him in the ribs. Raymond looked at Dolly, who was sitting beside him with a finger over his lips and a stick in his hand. He pointed with the stick at the floor of the loft. Raymond leaned over and looked down through a knothole into the barn. The cow stood below him, its head in the stanchion. A girl about his age was sitting beside the cow on a milking stool. She had brown hair in a braid down her back and wore a blue dress with white flowers all over it. Her head was resting on the cow's flank. The steady, even rhythm of the milk hitting the bucket almost put Raymond to sleep again.

When she was finished, the girl turned the cow out to pasture and left the barn. Raymond and Dolly watched her through a space between the siding as she headed for the chicken pen. She lifted the latch and stepped into the pen, calling "chick, chick, chick." They could see her better now, slender and not very tall, flushed with the heat of the morning. Just a pretty girl with a pleasant voice talking to her chickens while the day rose fine and warm around her.

"That's nice," Dolly said.

Raymond looked at him, thinking he was being smart, but he wasn't. It was just nice, was all Dolly meant, nice to see a pretty girl doing homey things. It made life seem sane.

"It sure is," he said.

"She likes them chickens, don't she?" Dolly said.

Raymond suddenly remembered a canning jar with yellow flowers in it falling to the ground, and his mother weeping as she picked up the broken pieces. The memory filled him with sadness. "Womenfolk have peculiar affections, sometimes," he said.

"You know a lot about 'em, of course," Dolly said. Raymond turned red. Dolly rolled over on his back. "It's a shame to steal from somebody like that," he said. "Makes me feel like a scoundrel."

"You are a scoundrel," Raymond said. "We both are. Scoundrels, thieves, and murderers." He hated hiding, and spying on the girl below, hated that he had stolen from her, and planned to steal again. Hated that he wasn't clean and working and able to stand up in front of her and tell her his name and ask for hers. He put his hand over the space in the boards. "I wish she'd leave off talking to them chickens," he said. "Maybe she's dimwitted."

"There ain't nothing wrong with that gal," Dolly said. "And I ain't a thief nor a murderer. It's not like I do this kind of thing for a living, you know. Besides, I never killed anybody but a Yankee, and that was a fair fight. Shoot, the whole country was at it." He glared at Raymond. "I ought to blow your head off for saying that."

"You talk big," Raymond said.

"I ain't just talking," Dolly said. "I ought to kill you for calling me names. Scoundrel. Thief. Murderer. Take 'em for yourself or take 'em back, but leave 'em off of me. Or else..." He pointed a finger at Raymond and whispered, "Pow."

Raymond tucked an imaginary rifle into his shoulder. "Ker blam!" he whispered back. "You're dead." He put his arm down. "Put your pop gun away. You've been shot by a real man."

Dolly flopped back down in the hay, pretending to be dead. Raymond turned back over on his stomach. He looked through the knothole again. The girl was gone. He missed her.

"Well?" Dolly asked.

"She's gone," Raymond said.

"Then what are we waiting for?" Dolly said.

Raymond followed him down the ladder, and the two of them headed cautiously for the chicken pen.

An hour later, the two men followed the railroad tracks into Debussy. Dolly carried a croaker sack over his shoulder. In it were three chickens and a calico dress he'd taken from the clothesline as they made off across the yard.

Raymond hadn't wanted to take the dress. "I ain't about to go stealing the girl's clothes," he'd said.

But Dolly had pulled it off the line and stuffed it in on top of the hens. "Once you slip a little bit," he'd said, "it ain't all that hard to slip a little more."

Beyond the stockyards the road turned south between the mercantile store and the hotel. Passing the hotel - it looked deserted, and besides, they had no money - the two men opened the front door of the Winters Mercantile Store, stepped inside, and stopped.

A stoop-shouldered man with an intent expression was bent over a counter top writing in a book of some kind. He looked up and raised his hand in greeting, but didn't speak. Raymond tipped his hat in response, equally silent. He wasn't sure what to say. He'd never seen a store like this one before. It was hot, for one thing, the air heavy with the odors of leather and metal and grain. Except for the counter, which was polished to a deep luster, the contents of the store were covered in mustard-colored oak bloom that had drifted through the broken window. Underneath the dust was the wildest disorder Raymond had ever seen. There were boxes and bins and sacks piled up and leaning against one another, broken crockery and tool handles, spilled flour and corn meal mixed with leaves and twigs, scraps of paper, broken glass, scattered nails, and acorns. Raymond looked at Dolly. His hard face had softened, and he shook his head as if in answer to an unspoken question of his own.

"You fellers need some help?" the man at the counter asked. Even standing up straight he wasn't very tall, and his shoulders bent forward protectively, as if anticipating a blow. He took his spectacles off and squinted at them from clouded gray eyes as though he'd seen them before, but couldn't remember where or when.

"I'm looking for boots," Dolly said. "The ones I got is wore out."

The clerk put his spectacles back on. His eyes got big behind them, making him look like an underfed owl. "Well, now," he said.

"We've got a pair of boots. Secondhand, I'm afraid, and maybe not your size, but we've sure got them."

He closed the ledger with care and came around the end of the counter, all the time gazing distractedly around the store. "I know we have them. Not sure exactly where, right this minute."

He turned back toward the counter. "Jessie?" he called, apparently at the wall. "Jessie, you there? Where'd you put the boots?" No one answered.

The clerk picked up a box, balanced it precariously on an upturned barrel near the counter, then shoved the barrel over where the box had been. "I know they're in here somewhere," he repeated, beginning to sound a little anxious.

Grinning, Dolly took a mildewed wad of chewing tobacco out of a box on the counter and sliced a plug off with a broken pocketknife he picked up off the floor. Never taking his eyes off the clerk, he tucked the plug in his cheek, folded the broken knife blade back into the case, and stuck it, along with the rest of the tobacco, in his pocket. "We got no money," he said.

The clerk stopped turning boxes over and looked at him. "No money," he said. His shoulders slumped even more, and his gray eyes turned fretful.

"We came to trade," Raymond said, stepping up beside Dolly. "Got some things right here."

The clerk brightened. "We do a sight of trading these days," he said. "Times being what they are. Not a lot of Federal money floating around." He sniffed. "Come up here and show me what you got." He returned to his side of the counter.

Dolly took the croaker sack from Raymond and dropped it in front of him. "A dress and three chickens," he said.

The clerk reached into the bag and pulled the dress out. He fingered it, then sighed. "Mind my asking how you came by the dress?" he asked.

Dolly gave Raymond a look and Raymond gave it right back to him, with raised eyebrows. Dolly cleared his throat. "I made it," he said.

"You made it." The clerk didn't seem surprised or disbelieving, just repeated what Dolly had said as though he was making sure he got it right.

"Yessir. Learned to sew from my mama. She always wanted a girl." Dolly's face was placid and sincere.

The clerk peered at him, the gray eyes speculative. "You must have been quite a disappointment to her," he remarked.

"Well, it helped some that she finally went blind."

"Yes. I imagine it did." The clerk picked up the dress and turned it inside out, looking closely at the seams. "It looks well made, though I am no expert on dressmaking. My daughter sews, however. In fact, I think she has a dress very much like this one."

"It's a popular pattern," Dolly said. He smiled at the older man. "You know, I learned something from my mama's troubles. Sometimes, what a person don't see does more good than harm. It allows things to go by that can't be helped, smoothes the rough spots some, if you take my meaning."

"I don't think I do," the clerk replied.

"Well, take this situation, for instance," Dolly said. "I real bad need a pair of boots. And you just happen to have what I need, while here I am wandering around with a dress I've outgrown, plus..." Dolly leaned heavily on the word 'plus,' "There's three little birds in the bag to go with it, and you look like a man who could put some fresh eggs away in a hurry. Now, I'll bet you haven't had an offer like that in a while."

"I don't believe I've ever had one like it," the clerk said.

"Well, all right then!" Dolly crowed. He slapped his palms on the counter. "Sounds like we got us a deal!"

The clerk smiled at Dolly. Turning to Raymond, he looked at him over the top of his spectacles. "What about you?" he asked. "Do you need a pair of boots, too? We've only got the one pair."

"No, sir," Raymond said. "I've got boots."

The clerk leaned over the counter and inspected Raymond's boots. He seemed to agree they were presentable. "Nearly new, are they?"

"Hand-me-downs," Raymond said. He didn't want to tell the man about the dead Yankee.

"You must need something," the clerk said.

Raymond looked at the list he kept in his head of everything he needed, and started at the top. "A horse," he said.

"We don't carry horses," the clerk said. "Besides, you'd need more chickens. What else?"

"A gun."

"The guns have been gone for a long time. Try again."

Raymond thought hard - work, a home, a wife, a family, a chance to make something of himself - none of them things to be gotten in a store, particularly this store. "Nothing," he said.

But the clerk wouldn't accept that, either. He smiled, a kind of slyness about him now. "Everybody needs something," he said. "And what they don't need, they want." He disappeared behind the counter, and came back up holding a candy jar with three sticks of licorice in it, dusty black with age. He pulled a stick out of the jar and waved it at Raymond "How about a piece of licorice?" he asked.

Raymond took a deep breath, his mouth watering at the sight of the candy. "You're right," he said. "I surely would like to have that."

"You want a licorice stick."

"I do."

The man nodded. "All right," he said. "Show me what you've got to trade for it."

Raymond scratched his head, uncomfortable with whatever game the man was playing, then spread his hands out. "I don't have anything to trade," he said.

The clerk smiled, all trace of slyness gone. "Then you'll just have to take it as a gift," he said, and handed the licorice stick to Raymond.

Raymond was embarrassed, but accepted the candy anyhow. He stuck one end of it in his mouth, the thick molasses taste of it washing over his tongue. He sucked on the licorice very slowly, taking care not to bite it.

"Look at that," Dolly said. "The boy's eyes is rolled back in his head with pure pleasure. You're a fine man, Mr....,"

"Winters," the clerk said.

"Mr. Winters." Dolly stuffed the dress back in the sack and handed the sack to Raymond. "You hang on to these while I help Mr. Winters find those boots," he said. He turned away, talking to the older man as they walked to the back of the store. "You sure got a mess here, Mr. Winters. It's a wonder you know what you got and what you ain't got."

"It is difficult," Mr. Winters said. He kept picking things up and putting them somewhere else, not looking at them so much as simply moving them around. "My wife is gone," he said. "She was an orderly person. But she didn't like the weather, so she died."

"Hell of a way to take on about the weather," Dolly said. "If you'll pardon my saying so."

"She was a woman of strong convictions," Mr. Winters replied.

His voice faded as the two of them worked their way further and further from where Raymond stood at the counter, their heads coming closer together as the search for the missing boots intensified, which is how Raymond came to be standing by himself, eating free candy and holding a sack full of stolen goods, when the girl they'd seen in the barn that morning walked into the store from the back door. She came around behind the counter as though she owned it, and looked at Raymond as if daring him to hit her.

"Can I help you?" she asked. Raymond stared at her, jerked the sack off the counter and stuck it behind his back, then pulled the licorice stick out of his mouth,

"No, ma'am," he said. "I don't think you can help me at all."

She was just as pretty up close as she'd been from a distance, though younger than he'd first thought - maybe fifteen, if that - and thin. Her eyes were nice, mostly gray with some green and blue flecks, and her hair was just right, brown, and curly around her temples. She had a wide mouth turned down at the corners with disapproval or unhappiness. The brightest thing about her was the dress she wore, the same one she'd had on that morning, blue, with little white flowers on it. Raymond hoped she hadn't gone looking for the one in the sack before she came in to the store. The girl leaned a little forward, and he started counting the freckles on her nose. He 'd gotten to eight when she pulled back.

"What's in the sack?" she asked.

Raymond looked at her for a long moment and tried to think of something to say. His mouth was full of spit and licorice, though, and the only words that came to mind were ones he didn't think she'd want to hear. He swallowed. "Sack?" he asked.

"That one." She pointed. "In your hand, behind your back."

Raymond turned around and looked at the sack, then looked back at her. "I don't know," he said. "It ain't mine." He pointed with the licorice stick. "It's that fella's over there. The one next to the old man."

She studied the two men moving boxes at the back of the store. "That's my father," she said. "He's had a hard time. The war unsettled him some." She looked at Raymond again, her hands clasped tightly together. "You just passing through?"

"Yes, ma'am," Raymond said. He wanted to tell her how he'd gotten there, and where he was going, and why, but the whole subject was simply too much. He jerked his head toward the back of the room. "We just stopped because he needed some boots."

"Is he a friend of yours?" she asked.

Raymond mentally winked at Dolly, one man to another. "Not exactly," he said. "We were in the same unit together, is how we met. Us two is all that's left." He looked at her to see how she took that information. The mouth softened some at the corners. Raymond considered that a good sign. A drop of sweat ran the spiral of one short curl beside her ear to dangle on the very end. He wondered what she'd say if he took it on the tip of his finger. It was hardly any distance at all across the counter. She beat him to it, though, brushing it impatiently away.

"What is it you said you wanted?" she asked.

Raymond gazed around the store, and thought about asking what it was she thought they had to offer. Instead, he held up the shortened licorice stick. "I've got it already," he said. "Your daddy gave it to me." Anger frosted her eyes. Raymond wished he'd cut his tongue out before he'd told her that.

"It doesn't surprise me," she snapped. "We've got next to nothing left, and he can't wait to give that away." The girl watched for a moment as her father poked through trash and confusion, then looked at Raymond again. "You should be glad I came in," she said. "You could have been stuck holding that bag for the rest of the day. Daddy's been that way since Mama died."

Raymond opened his mouth to offer a word of comfort, and listened in horror as his tongue ran off with his brain like a runaway horse. "I sure am glad," he said. "That you're here, I mean. Not about your mama. I'm real sorry to hear about her. Not sorry to hear about her. I mean, I'm sorry she passed on, and the mess and all. About her leaving such a mess. Or it getting to be one. But I'm awful glad you're here. It's good you're here. To find the boots, I mean. You must miss her. Your mama. I'm sorry." In desperation, Raymond stuck the licorice back in his mouth and clamped his teeth on it. The girl looked him straight in the eyes, her gray ones thoughtful. Raymond tried a smile.

The girl smiled back, just barely, then looked immediately away. "I do miss her," she said. "Daddy won't let me clean things up, says he likes it like this. I've had to leave it alone. What did you say the gentleman wants?"

Raymond frowned. "Gentleman?" he asked.

"The man over there with my father," she said. "Whose things you are holding in the bag behind your back." She really smiled then, the wide mouth curving up, the gray eyes warm.

Raymond grinned, and kept the bag firmly behind him. "Oh," he said. "Him. He wants a pair of boots."

"Well, they won't find them there," she said. Coming out from behind the counter, she walked briskly to a stack of crates by the front door, and called to her father. "Those boots are up here, Daddy."

"You moved them, did you?" he asked.

"No," she said. "I wanted to move them, but you said not to. You said they'd be easier to get to up here."

"And so they are," Mr. Winters said. Behind him, Dolly widened his eyes at Raymond. Raymond leaned against the counter and fervently hoped the boots wouldn't fit.

They were too big, but Dolly took them anyway, because, he muttered to Raymond, what could a man expect for three skinny chickens and an old dress? Then he cleared his throat and clapped Raymond on the shoulder. "Well, buddy," he said. "Better finish your candy, 'cause it's time you and me got square with these folks."

The girl moved around behind the counter. Dolly took the sack from Raymond and set it back on the counter. "Them's all yours," he said. Backing up, he grabbed Raymond by the arm. "The boots fit fine, and ole Ray here loved that candy. It's sure been a pleasure trading with you."

Raymond felt like a man with his back turned to a loaded gun all the way to the door. When they hit the sidewalk, Dolly punched him on the shoulder and cut a buck-and-wing down the street. "Tell me I can't make a trade, bubba!" he said. "Now all we got to do is procure a couple of horses and high tail it to Summerlin's."

Raymond had just opened his mouth to ask Dolly where he planned on stealing the horses when something hit him in the back of the head and knocked his hat off. He whirled around to catch another hen in the face and a third one in the chest. He tucked the limp bodies under his arm while he groped for his hat, too busy to wonder why it seemed so fitting that he should be clobbered with dead chickens when it was Dolly, laughing behind him, who had actually started all this. He found his hat and stuck it on his head, then straightened to face with mingled humiliation and anticipation the approaching hurricane in the blue and white dress.

"Excuse me for saying it, Raymond," Dolly said. "But I think you're in a peck of trouble."

And Raymond, though he couldn't say a word, agreed completely, as a dress smelling of chicken shit settled around his head, and a fist as small and solid as a green grapefruit popped him in the jaw.

Chapter Five

When Jessie Winters was small, she would stand on a wooden box and look out through the store window. Down the road to her right, she could see south all the way to the church. Directly across the road was Mr. and Mrs. Addison's establishment, the Sweet Bay Hotel. To her left, a little north and west of town, where Jessie could have seen had she been able to look through that corner of the store, lay the train station with the stock pens behind it. The railroad tracks crossed the road fifty yards north of the store. She could see them from her window, and hear them, too, when a train went by and the short stretch of iron and wood rumbled briefly into life. The church, the hotel and cafe, the railroad track, and the road itself were Jessie's world, bounded by a sash and frame and separated from her by a piece of real glass with a watery ripple in one corner. Elbows on sill, chin in hand, she watched as life unfolded before her in patterns as mysterious and ordered as the seasons of the moon, the world recreated every seven days.

On Mondays, the train clattered past Debussy carrying cedar logs away east to a place Jessie had never seen, called Fernandina. The gnarled logs swayed and heaved on the backs of the cars, straining against the chains that bound them, while the engine whistled but did not stop, because it never stopped on Mondays. Tuesdays and Wednesdays were uneventful, as Lucy Winters washed clothes on one and cleaned the house and store on the other. Thursdays, however, were the start of something fine, for then the train came back the other way, headed west to the Cedar Keys with a noisy, high-smelling cargo of cattle and their keepers.

Jessie wasn't allowed to go down to the stockyards, but she could see the dust rise when the steers were unloaded for watering, and reveled in the din that shattered quiet Debussy with rowdy life. If local homesteaders were going to ship cattle, Thursday was the day they brought them into town. The steers ran wild-eyed and shaggy past Jessie's window, their horns and hooves snapping like fingers. The drivers followed them with whips and dogs, and by the time they reached the pens, it sounded like a battle going on just around the corner. There was shouting and cursing, and even gunfire. On Thursdays, Debussy trembled with a violent exuberance that fascinated Jessie, and left her feeling restless and uneasy.

By late Thursday afternoon, those who had come with the train got back on it, riding with the cattle to the Gulf and the ships that waited for them there. The rest came to the Sweet Bay Hotel to eat and spend the night. Jessie watched through her window into those of the cafe as Mrs. Addison fed her customers whatever the fields and creeks and woods had provided that week: chicken, soft-shell turtle, gopher tortoise, wild turkey, venison, beef, or pork; field peas, black eye peas, string beans, collards, and sweet potatoes; spoon bread, corn bread, corn pone, and biscuits served with butter, gravy, honey, and cane syrup; pie or cobbler for dessert - peach, pear, dewberry, mulberry, persimmon, or sweet potato - and all of it washed down with endless cups of strong hot coffee. When they finished, the diners pushed back from the table with pained, careful movements, and tipped their hats to the woman who had provoked such gluttony. Mrs. Addison rarely returned their courtesies. Without exception, they would have left food untouched on the table, defeated at last by the sheer volume of it. Mrs. Addison told Jessie's mother she thought it was shameful the way those men wasted food, and fretted that they didn't like her cooking.

Friday and Saturday were like Thursday. Drivers came to the store to buy supplies before they left, and the outlying farmers came to town. The store was busier than it had been all week, and the eight rooms in the hotel filled completely. Those who came too late for a room made camp down by the stockyards, where Mr. Addison sold corn liquor by the pint jar. He wasn't allowed to sell it at the hotel. Mrs. Addison didn't hold with such foolishness, and no one who smelled of the stuff was allowed to spend the night in her establishment. Jessie generally couldn't see the effects of drink since she went to bed early. But she could hear them - the easy laughter and music and fights - and sometimes she thought a little of it might do Mrs. Addison good.

Sunday was the best day of all. Jessie went to church with her parents. Freed from the confines of her window, the world pulsed and shone as Jessie walked down the street. The Winters family squeezed into a narrow, straight-backed pew, where heat and close proximity acted on the mingled odors of the congregants - smoke, sweat, livestock, talcum powder, manure, whiskey, coffee, lye soap, bacon - to create a singular rich scent Jessie associated with worship. Babies cried, children shuffled their feet and pestered one another, men cleared their throats and coughed and sat up straight and stiff, while over, under, and through it all the women whispered, chastised, scolded, comforted, and coerced, and now and then leaned back, exhausted, to fan themselves and sigh amen.

Saints and sinners together petitioned the everlasting arms in prayer and song and sermon, seeking strength and solace in this life and rest from their labors in the next. Jessie loved the singing best, the familiarity of the tunes, and the way the stronger voices held steady to the melody, herding it safely through the verses in spite of those errant few who wandered from key to key like lost sheep. But the preaching was good, too, with Brother Cooper's voice rolling down on her in great waves of wrath and mercy, throwing her down to repentance and lifting her up again to salvation, her chest tight with awe and yearning. By Sunday night she was worn out and ready to go to bed, knowing that Monday would come in the morning, with its train that whistled as it passed, but did not stop.

Jessie turned eleven in 1861, and watched through the window as men mustered outside the hotel, eager to fight the war of northern aggression. Mr. Winters would not go, and neither would Mr. Addison. They had little regard for any government other than their own, though for very different reasons. Mr. Addison refused to be ordered around and had a thriving business, besides. He couldn't stand the interference, and wouldn't spare the time. More gently, but with equal stubbornness, Mr. Winters invoked the golden rule. He would take the path of peace, and that choice would protect all within his care.

The year seemed to prove him right. Traffic was unusually heavy on the sandy road outside Jessie's window. Volunteers headed north to enlist passed army recruiters going south to look for more just like them. Confederate script was more readily available than gold had ever been. Cars were added to the train to haul more cattle, and drivers handled their whips with an added flourish, the mundane raised to greatness by the cause it served. The world spoke to Jessie with the same restless promise of her ripening body, and she inhabited both with the same ignorance, pretense, and certainty with which she'd once played dress-up in her mother's clothes. She looked out the window and down at her chest with equal fascination, and listened to her mother's hazy explanations of feminine functions with the same perplexed concentration with which she overheard discussions of troop movements, confident that something important was going on, but unclear as to exactly what it was, except that it had a great deal to do with males.

Men had always tipped their hats to her just as they did to her mother, a social tribute to her sex, pleasing but impersonal. Boys, on the other hand, though still ugly and stupid and subject to sudden fits of rude noises and flailing limbs, were vastly interesting, and Jessie never tired of observing them. She believed herself invisible behind the window, until one day, three boys, drivers in town with the train, ran out of the store when the whistle blew, and one of them turned around in the street and caught her staring at him. To her astonishment, he swept his hat off and kissed the air at her. One of the other boys shoved him in the back, and he fell down on his hands and knees in the dirt.

Jessie was mortified, and sank beneath the sill to hide while scuffles and hoots of laughter traveled down the street into silence. When she peeked back over the sill, the boys were gone. Three months later, the railhead at the Cedar Keys was shelled. The train never came again, and neither did the boys. Jessie wished with all her heart that she had waved goodbye to the one who kissed the air at her. She wished she had known he would not be coming back again.

A year later, the railroad tracks were rusty and the sandy road was overgrown with grass and dandelions. Mr. Addison took to drinking his surplus product down at the stockyard office with the stationmaster. Mrs. Addison sat on the front porch of the hotel in a rocking chair, where she fanned herself and swatted flies and waited for customers who, for the most part, did not come. Federal blockades prevented most goods from reaching Debussy, and folks had to barter for what little made it through. Salt was particularly hard to come by. Nathan tried to buy a five pound bag of it with a bushel of Confederate script, an offer that so tickled the man who owned it that he had a coughing fit and Lucy had to pound him on the back. When the man recovered, Lucy gave him her gold wedding band, and he gave her the salt. Lucy spent the rest of the afternoon stuffing pincushions with script and jabbing them full of pins. That evening, Nathan stacked the remainder neatly on the outhouse bench.

Union soldiers came to Debussy in July of '63. They loaded their wagons with the Winters' flour, cornmeal, and syrup. Nathan stood by, white-faced and ashamed, but Lucy lost her temper and called them thieves. The captain merely waved her out of his face with the weariness of a man accustomed to calumny, and ordered his grinning troops back down the road.

Debussy was not disturbed again until September of '64, when Confederate soldiers took three Dutch ovens and all five pairs of boots, leaving one pair of their old ones in trade, a hole in one toe, but the soles miraculously intact. They took all the lead bars and bullet forms and would have taken the cow, the mule, and the chickens, except that the first two were hidden in the hammock behind the barn, and Jessie had chased the chickens into the trees. The soldiers got the eggs, though. Lucy lost her temper that time, too, but the sergeant had a temper of his own and turned on Lucy with an expression on his face that silenced her immediately. Nathan stood by wringing his hands. Lucy wept when the soldiers left. When Nathan said he was sorry, she walked out the back door and didn't speak to him for two weeks.

After each interruption, life with its changes settled back down again. Nathan and Lucy Winters spoke to one another now with a careful formality that Jessie had never heard before. It was uncomfortable but not painful and eventually came to feel normal, much like the emptiness outside the store window. Nathan said they were fortunate to have suffered so little, and though Lucy's face grew hard with something like contempt when he said it, Jessie could see his point. For all the boredom and inconvenience caused by the blockade, and the predations of soldiers on both sides, the war had been fairly gentle with Debussy. They were far removed from the conflict and had little to fear as it crept on toward resolution. When months passed and nothing else happened, the little settlement heaved a collective sigh and relaxed, complacent with insignificance. It was ill-prepared when, in the spring of '65, the raiders came.

Jessie was hanging clothes in the back yard when she smelled smoke and burning meat. She looked to the north, where black smoke was roiling up into the cloudless sky. Jessie held to the clothesline with both hands. North was the Bead farm and Mr. Jay Henry's homestead. The smoke could be coming from either place. She ran for the house. By the time she reached the back porch, there were ashes in the air.

"Mama?" she called. No one answered. Jessie let the door slam and ran around the corner of the house, and down the path to the back door of the store. She fumbled with the doorknob - it needed oiling - and almost fell when someone flung the door open from the inside. Nathan stood before her, his face working.

"Go to the barn," he said. "Get the cow and the mule. Take them to the hammock." He shoved a small boy out the door. "Take him with you."

Jessie grabbed the boy by the shoulder. "What is it?" she asked her father.

"Raiders," he said. "They're at the Bead place."

"Are the Beads all right?" Jessie asked.

"Most likely not," Nathan snapped. "Now get to the woods." He went to shut the door, then opened it wide again to look her square in the eyes. He had gray eyes, like hers, but right now they looked as colorless as his face. "You stay there, Jessie, 'til I come for you. No matter what, you stay put. You understand me?"

"Yessir," Jessie said. The door slammed in her face and she ran her fingers down the boy's arm to his hand. It was fever-hot. She pulled him after her. "C'mon," she said. The child followed her without protest or question, almost dreamily, as though he were walking in his sleep.

Jessie turned the chickens loose and took the livestock to the hammock. The Bead child did whatever Jessie told him to - from avoiding the mule's teeth and back feet to gathering deer moss for the cow - but he did nothing on his own, and did not speak at all, unless the little moans he gave every time the wind blew smoke through the hammock could be counted as speech. Jessie, just two months shy of her fifteenth birthday, considered the oldest Bead boy, Jeremiah, potential husband material, so her interest in his welfare was more than neighborly. But his little brother wasn't talking.

"Why don't you say something?" Jessie asked. "Don't you care what's happened to your family?" The boy just looked her. "I bet you don't even know what's happened to them," Jessie continued. "I bet you ran off as soon as you saw trouble coming. And there you sit, not saying a word. I don't understand it. I don't see how you could do that." Bored, she got up to untie the mule, then heard the sound of hoof beats coming down the road to the north.

"I wonder who..." Jessie began, but the child was next to her, his hand clenched so hard on her arm she almost cried out, and would have, but for the terror on his face. The mule pricked its long ears up and opened its mouth to bray. The boy grabbed its upper lip and gave it a vicious twist, distracting the mule as the riders went by. Jessie could see them through the trees, mounted men in slouch hats and black dusters, loping steadily down the road to Debussy.

The boy held onto the mule's lip long after they disappeared. It was another twenty minutes, though, before they heard screams, and Jessie learned, as the Bead child had learned, that it is possible, even wise, to remain very quiet as bad things happen to the people one loves.

At sunrise, the preacher walked into the clearing. His face was purple down one side, the eye swollen shut.

Jessie cried out. "Brother Cooper! What happened to you?"

"Shhh," Cooper said. "Don't wake the boy." The Bead child lay with his head on Jessie's lap, so deep in sleep he looked dead.

Cooper took the boy in his arms. "I'd have come yesterday evening, except your daddy didn't tell me 'til this morning where you were." He laid a hand on the boy's head. "This one here's got nobody left. The raiders shot and burned his family in the house." Cooper gingerly touched the side of his own face. "One of them gave me this on his way out of town. Laid into me with a rifle butt."

"What about Mama and Daddy?" Jessie asked.

Brother Cooper untied the cow as if he hadn't heard her, and started walking toward the barn, the boy over his shoulder.

Jessie followed with the mule. "Brother Cooper?" she asked again. "Did something happen to my mama and daddy?"

"Mr. Addison and George Fender are drunk," Cooper said. "Mr. Jay Henry got in late last night. They torched his shack but didn't find him. He'd slipped down in the cistern and held onto the cracks between the bricks. Said he like to never got out."

"But what about my folks?"

Cooper stopped, took a deep breath, and turned to Jessie. "Your folks are hurt pretty bad," he said.

"How bad?" Jessie asked.

"I don't know, honey," Cooper said. "It don't look good for your mama, and your daddy, well...he don't have any marks you can see, but his mind is affected. You'll see what I mean when we get there."

"Who will take care of this boy?" Jessie asked.

"He's coming home with me," Cooper said. He stroked the child's hair. "A man can't hardly have too many children."

Jessie pictured the Cooper children in the pew at the front of the church. She counted ten heads. One more probably wouldn't be noticed among so many. Her mind shifted again. "Why wouldn't Daddy tell you where I was last night?" she asked.

"He would have, if anybody had asked him proper," Cooper said. "We just kept saying, 'What happened to Jessie? What happened to Jessie?' And he kept saying, 'She's gone. She's gone.' It wasn't until this morning when the wife said, 'Gone where, I wonder?' that Brother Nathan said, 'To the hammock with the cow.' I felt like a fool, I can tell you that."

"Where did you think I'd gone?" Jessie asked.

"We thought the raiders had took you, and we prayed you was dead," Cooper said.

Chill bumps rose up on Jessie's arms. She rubbed them hard to get warm, but stayed cold all the way home, though the sun was good and up by the time they got there.

The store was destroyed. Shelves were torn off the walls, boxes and kegs and crates were hacked to pieces, nails and screws were strewn across the floor and covered with dirt. The glass in Jessie's window lay on the floor in shards. The counter top was deeply scored. Nathan stood behind the counter, staring at the store ledger in his hands. Jessie cleared her throat. Her father did not move or look up. He just kept staring at the ledger. Brother Cooper was standing in the doorway, or Jessie might have turned and run.

"It's all right," Cooper said. "Mrs. Cooper is sitting with your mama in the house. You go on up there soon as you've talked to your daddy." He made as if to leave, then paused, and put his hand on Jessie's head. "Your daddy's a gentle, sweet man, Jessie. Yonder is just his way of carrying more than he was made to bear. Try not to let it trouble you. God understands." He gave her head a pat and left.

Jessie made her way through the mess to the counter. Her father turned a page in the ledger but did not speak to her.

"Daddy..."

"Did you bring the cow home?"

"Yessir. Daddy, I..."

"Good. And the mule?"

"Yessir..."

"Good." He flipped back three pages in the ledger and ran down the lines with his finger to the middle of the page. "Here they are." He made two check marks. "Cow. Mule. Good."

Jessie leaned down and picked up a box.

"What are you doing?" he demanded.

"Just picking up."

"Not right now. You go up to the house and see if your mother needs anything."

"Daddy..."

"Go on, now. I'm so busy here I can't hardly think straight. Tell Lucy I'll be up shortly."

But Jessie couldn't tell her mother anything. Lucy Winters lay open mouthed and unconscious on the bed she shared with Nathan, her face battered beyond recognition. Jessie took one look and vomited into the chamber pot. Glory Cooper rose from Lucy's rocking chair, her kind, thick features heavy with sorrow, and wiped Jessie's face with her apron. Then she gathered her up like a small child and rocked her while she cried. Jessie was still curled up on Sister Glory's wide lap, hiccupping and teary-eyed, when Nathan came into the room. He sat down on the edge of the bed and took his wife's hand in his, weaving their fingers together. Lucy spoke into the silence, the words clear and strong through her swollen purple lips.

"It's too hot in this room," she said, and died before Nathan could answer.

Debussy buried its dead the next day: David and Sally Bead and seven of their children, and Lucy Winters. The oak trees were heavy with bloom in the cemetery. Brother Cooper kept sneezing as he conducted the service. The Bead boy gave himself over to grief, his small body racked with weeping. Nathan was dry-eyed, and remarked to Jessie that he thought ill of her mother for leaving them with a mess to clean up.

The next day, Jessie followed Nathan to the store. He stopped her in the act of picking up the broom, his hand so hard around her wrist it hurt.

"We've got to clean it up," she said.

Nathan looked around as if to make sure they would not be overheard then put his lips to her ear. "We leave it like this," he whispered. "That way, when they come back, they'll figure everything worth taking is gone. You watch."

"What makes you think they'll be back?" she asked, and picked up the broom again.

Nathan jerked it out of her hand. "I said leave it alone!" he cried.

Jessie crossed her arms at her waist and hugged herself for comfort, while Nathan hid the broom behind the counter. That was the day he began the inventory, by counting shards of glass fallen from Jessie's window.

Wagons and high-wheeled ox carts came through Debussy again, drawn by gaunt oxen and led by human scarecrows fleeing the charred earth of Georgia. They seldom stopped. There was no money and nothing to trade. The world was bled dry, and no one was whole.

More frightening even than the very poor were the solitary men. Displaced from hearths and families, they wandered the countryside searching for food and something else they'd lost in the war. It seemed to Jessie that her chickens bore the brunt of their desperation. Once she came on a man squatting in the hen house eating raw eggs, breaking them into his mouth. Screaming for her father, Jessie ran back to the house. But when she returned, dragging Nathan by the elbow, the man was gone, the only signs of his presence the scattered eggshells inside the hen house and a pile of human excrement beside the hen house door.

Another evening, she went to gather eggs and there were none. The next morning an old man brought them to the store to trade for tobacco. He held them carefully in a hat. Sitting on the very top was the brown egg with the white speckles Jessie's bantam hen always laid. Jessie took the eggs, and with them safe in her care, called the old man a worthless thief. To her horror, he collapsed on the floor in a dead faint. Nathan clucked over him like that same bantam hen over a lone chick, and sent Jessie to the house with the eggs with orders to cook them for their customer. She stood by while Nathan fed the eggs to the thief with his own hand. It was then that Jessie realized she was living with someone bereft of everything but kindness and the memory of loss. She found herself seesawed between hope and terror, and nearly worn out with both.

Chapter Six

Jessie saw at first glance a tall, bearded man with enormous hands and wrists that extended a good three inches beyond the sleeves of a dirty brown coat. His lowering silence was as threatening as anything he might have said. Another man stood at the back of the store with her father, whose bare head looked as defenseless as a baby's. It took everything Jessie had to speak calmly to the man in front of her. When he answered, she looked up in surprise, and saw something she'd never seen before.

It wasn't his age, for she could tell now that she really looked at him that he wasn't old at all, and looked even younger with a half-eaten licorice stick wilting in his hand. It wasn't the hollows in his face, either. Most faces were marked like that these days. It wasn't even the sack he'd put behind his back when she walked in, as though he were trying to hide it. It was, quite simply, the way he looked at her.

He stared at her with open-mouthed astonishment, as though he'd never seen a girl before. Jessie, who had never been the object of such wonder, took a moment to study her father's back and collect her wits, then looked again at the man. Generous with pleasure, she was moved to forgive his unkempt appearance and possible feeble-mindedness. She had no idea what she said next to him, but was deeply gratified when it reduced him to idiocy. The confusion she felt was as familiar to her, and yet as foreign, as the shabby, brown-eyed man was both like her, and something else that was completely different.

He would not be questioned or coaxed into revealing the contents of the sack. Jessie wondered what was in it the whole time the other man was trying on the store's one pair of boots. She was still wondering as the two men got ready to leave. The tall stranger gave her one last longing look, and she smiled at him with newfound confidence. His friend took the sack out of his hand and gave it to her. Jessie took it from him in such a state of giddiness that nothing, not even the cold amusement in those hard blue eyes, could have adequately prepared her for what she found inside.

Tangled in her Sunday dress, which was soiled with chicken mess, were three of her hens. They were dead, suffocated by the heat of their own bodies. Jessie sat down on the stool behind the counter with the hens in her lap. Nathan fluttered around, patting her back, thumbing through the ledger for mention of the boots, the hens, the dress, and finding none of them. His fingers trembled on Jessie's arm and she pushed his hand away.

"Did you know what was in here?" she asked.

Nathan's voice was higher than usual when he answered. "Yes," he said. "Yes, I did. A dress and three chickens. They told me that much. I didn't know they were yours, of course. There was no way I could know they were yours."

"They both told you."

"Yes, I'm sure they both said something about it."

"The tall one, the one holding the sack. He knew what was in here?"

"Oh, yes, he knew. I'm sure he knew." Jessie didn't say anything, and Nathan pressed the point further. "He must have known. He said first off they'd brought trade goods in."

He rattled on, eying her with intense concern while he reminded her that men like that were dangerous, that it was better to let well enough alone. Look what had happened to her mother, to the store, to him. When Jessie didn't answer, Nathan stuck his face in hers and said, his voice very loud, that those two men could kill them both just as easily as they had killed her hens, and there was no one to stop them from doing that or worse.

Given the truth of what he was saying and the relentless quality of Nathan's twittering anxiety, Jessie at any other time would have stayed right there on that stool, weepy with rage and too afraid to do anything about it.

But not this time. This time, a man had looked at her with wonder in his eyes then left her with a cheap, mean trick. Well, it was one thing to steal her chickens. It was quite another to betray the glory of that gaze. Blood roared in Jessie's ears as wrath obliterated prudence. She snatched up the hens by their yellow legs, slung the dress over her shoulder, and stormed out the door. She caught up with the stranger at the end of the street, and flung the chickens at him, then the dress. But it was hitting him with her fist that felt really good. In fact, it felt so good Jessie did it again. And she would have done it a third time, except her betrayer got untangled from the dress and caught her hand.

"Wait a minute!" he yelled. "Whoa! Whoa!"

"Maybe she ain't got no whoa," his friend said, laughing. They were both laughing.

Jessie jerked one of the chickens out of the man's arms. "Think it's funny, do you?" she screamed. "Well, here! Laugh at this!" And she flailed him with the carcass as he ducked and covered his head with his hands.

"All right! I'm sorry, I ain't laughing." But he was laughing. He was laughing hard.

Jessie threw the chicken in his face. "You're sorry, all right," she said. "You're as sorry as they come."

He straightened up, his face brilliant red between his beard and the brim of his hat. "Well, now, I don't know about that. I've known some pretty sorry..."

"I don't care what you've known," she said. "You're nothing but a lying, low-down chicken thief. Both of you." They didn't seem to have any argument with that. Jessie pointed at the boots her father had traded to the blue-eyed man. "I want those back."

The man shook his head. "No, ma'am," he said. "The boots are mine. We made an agreement with that old man in there, and you have to abide by it."

"He traded those boots for three chickens and a dress," Jessie said.

"And three chickens and a dress is what he got."

"We didn't know the chickens were dead," the taller man said. "They were alive when we put 'em in the bag."

Jessie gave him a withering look and he fell quiet. "They didn't belong to you," she said. "You got enough learning to know what 'stolen' means?"

The shorter man's face grew very still, but it was the taller one who spoke. "I'll pay for them," he said.

Jessie and his friend both looked at him. "How?" the friend asked.

"You give me room and board and I'll work them off," the tall one said to Jessie. "The boots, everything. And you can keep the chickens and the dress."

"Of course I can keep them!" Jessie snapped. "They're mine!" She paused. "What work would you do?"

The man jerked his head back at the store. "First thing is, I'd clean up that mess in there."

"Daddy won't let you," Jessie said. "He won't let anybody clean it up, not even me."

"He'll let me," the man said. He had pushed his hat back on his head. It made him look young and earnest.

Jessie resisted the temptation to soften. "There's nothing you can do," she said. "Daddy's lost his mind."

"Must be catching," the shorter man said. He shook his friend's arm. "You can't stay here, Raymond. We're going to Summerlin's. There ain't nothing here for you."

"I'll come as soon as I finish this," Raymond told him.

"You ain't a store keeper," the short man said.

"I ain't a thief, neither," Raymond said.

His friend's face darkened and his eyes grew cold. "I sure hope you're not saying that I am," he said. "Because then you'd be saying something you couldn't back off from, and that ain't smart. When we get to Summerlin's, I'll send some money for the boots, and the trade goods, too, if that's what you want. These people will be fine until then. There ain't no call for you to stay."

"I'll stay all the same," Raymond said.

The two men regarded each other with equal belligerence until the shorter one exploded. "I can't believe this," he said. "Everything we've been through and everything we're headed to, and all it takes is some girl a'moaning and a'groaning over some chickens for you to throw it all over and stay here and sweep floors. I just slap can't believe it."

"Leastways he has a conscience," Jessie said, and recoiled when the man turned on her.

"You don't know what he's got and what he ain't got, lady," he said. His voice was low, almost a growl. "You don't know nothing about him. I do, and I'm telling you that this here beat up, wore out, shabby little ole town ain't what Raymond Pennell is looking for."

"Settle down, Dolly," Raymond said. He turned to Jessie. "I ain't going anywhere, ma'am. But it's better if you let me do this by myself."

He half-turned his shoulder to her, and spoke to his friend. "You saw what that place was like, Dolly. I'll have it taken care of in no time, then I'll come on down to Summerlin's. You tell them I'm on my way, and hold me a place." He smiled, and lightly punched Dolly's shoulder with his fist. "I'll be but a month or so behind you. That's no time at all."

"We've got business to take care of," Dolly said. "You ain't forgetting already, are you?"

"I ain't forgetting nothing," Raymond said. "But everything's been tore up around me for so long, and back there is something I can set right. It's just a little thing, but I can do it. It won't take but a little while. And the whole time I'm here, I'll be looking and listening, and you'll be doing the same where you are. Then, when I'm finished, I'll meet you at Summerlin's, and we'll go from there."

Dolly glanced at Jessie, then looked back at Raymond. "What if you get held up here?" he asked.

"I won't. I promise."

"Uh, huh. But just supposing you do, what then?"

"Then you'll come back here and get me."

"And you'll leave, just like that?"

"Just like that," Raymond said.

Dolly chewed his lower lip, and looked back over his shoulder at Debussy. Then he shrugged, as if dismissing it, and nodded. "All right," he said. "That'll have to do." He turned to Jessie. "And just so you know, little missy, I didn't steal anything. You tell that old man back there I'd have sent him the money as soon as I had it. Still will. I ain't stealing these boots. I'm buying them on time. Only thing I got any of right now."

"Maybe you've got more of that than we do," Jessie said sweetly. Too sweetly. Dolly tensed.

Raymond stepped between them, blocking Jessie's view. "You best go on back to the store, ma'am," he said. "I'll be down there shortly."

Jessie stood up straighter, trying to locate the righteous anger she'd felt only moments before. It was hard, though. She felt like an intruder. She was somehow in the wrong, coming between the two of them like she had. And now the one named Raymond was coming back to the store with her, and she didn't know what to do with that, either. "You have a safe trip," she said to Dolly, trying to be polite. He ignored her.

Raymond handed her the dress. "Dolly won't be needing this," he said.

SMITHVILLE PUBLIC LIBRARY

Dolly snorted. "Damn my hide for ever touching it," he said. "Or the chickens, either. Should have run to Summerlin's in my bare feet." Then he fell silent. It took a moment for Jessie to realize they were waiting for her to leave.

Nathan was counting licorice sticks when Jessie got back to the store. There were two of them. The door slammed, and Raymond walked across the room and put his hat on the counter. Nathan looked up. Surprise widened his eyes. He shot a glance at Jessie, then put his hand over the licorice sticks and whispered loudly to Raymond. "You better get out of here," he said. "She knows."

Raymond leaned forward to meet Nathan. "I know she knows," he said. He laid the chickens on the counter. "I told her I'd work them off."

"Doing what?" Nathan asked.

"Helping you around the store," Raymond said.

Nathan looked around, surveying the broken shelves and heaped boxes. "I think everything is fine the way it is. Don't you think so, Jessie?"

Jessie gave Raymond an arch look. "Yes I do," she said. "I think it's just right."

"Where would you start, anyway?" Nathan asked. "Just as a question, where would you start?" He patted his book. "Just so you know, I think the first thing we need is an inventory. That's what I've been working on here."

Jessie's mouth tightened with exasperation, but Raymond merely looked interested. "Can I see it?" he asked.

Nathan looked at him over his spectacles. "I don't guess it could hurt," he said. He handed the book to Raymond.

Raymond paged through it then gave it back. "Looks like it's almost done," he said. "That must have taken you a long time." Nathan look gratified.

Raymond picked up a box and pulled a horse collar out of it. "Looky here. You even got this, and it was way down here in this box."

Nathan nodded in agreement, then frowned. "Well, now wait a minute," he said. "I don't know if I do have it." He peered at page after page, his thin fingers scraping like dry leaves across the paper. He handed the book to Jessie. "Can you see where that collar is entered in here?"

She looked at the pages, line after line filled in with random items, then crossed out, then entered again. "No," she said. "It isn't in here." She handed the book back to Nathan. "But everything else is, I'm sure."

Nathan tucked the book up under his arm. "What did you say your name is?" he asked.

"Raymond Pennell."

"I'm Nathan Winters." The two men shook hands. Nathan turned to Jessie. "Jessie," he said. "This is Raymond Pennell." To Raymond, he said, "This is my daughter Jessie. She is a great help to me."

Raymond nodded to Jessie. "Pleased to meet you, ma'am," he said. "Now, about this collar here, Mr. Winters. You just forgot to enter it, is all. Easy enough to do, considering the size of the store." He laid the collar down in the box then picked it up again. "While I got it here, though, I just as well hang it up. That way it won't get counted twice." With Nathan dogging his heels, Raymond walked to the other side of the room and hung the collar on a nail sticking out of the wall. "How about here?"

Nathan considered its location, his head cocked to one side. "I think that's all right," he said. "What do you think, Jessie?"

"It's as good a place as any," she said ungraciously.

Raymond left it hanging there and came back to the counter. On the way, he stepped on a pile of nails on the floor. He squatted down and started picking them up.

Nathan was immediately beside him. "Now, you don't mess with those," he said. "I've got to count them again. I almost had them down, but was interrupted earlier." He looked angrily at Jessie. "It's not my fault, not my fault at all." The ledger shook in his hands.

"It's aggravating to be bothered when you're trying to get something done, that's for sure," Raymond said, then started in on a long rambling story about the time he was trying to fix a harness while one person after another kept coming by to ask him something, or get him to help them with something, or wanting to know how it was he knew to do what he was doing, or offering to help, until Nathan was listening to him open-mouthed and Jessie was wondering when in the world he would get to the point when she noticed that as Raymond was talking, he was steadily picking the nails up off the floor and sorting them into two boxes. By the time the boxes were filled, the story was ending.

"So what with one thing and then another," he said, "it took me a week to get far enough along on that harness to realize I had to ride into town for some parts before I could even finish it. If I hadn't been so disgusted with the whole thing by then, I might have gone out and got drunk and disorderly, just to aggravate back."

Raymond picked up the two boxes and put them on the counter. Then he tapped Nathan's book. "Now, if you want, we can count and inventory these."

Nathan said nothing, just gazed at the neatly boxed nails in front of him with something like relief. "Tomorrow," he said. "We'll do that tomorrow. I'm too tired right now." He stuck the ledger under the counter along with his apron, and without another word, left the store. Raymond winked at Jessie. Befuddled, she mumbled something about the cow and went after Nathan. Behind her, a hammer thudded against the wall in a hard, steady, two-stroke rhythm that never missed a beat.

Nathan was asleep at the kitchen table, his head resting on his crossed arms. Jessie didn't have the heart to wake him, so went out to the barn to feed the stock. There she discovered that the mule was gone, along with the halter and a bucket. There was a folded piece of paper stuck in the stall door, with "to oner" scrawled on the outside. Inside it read, "i need the mul bad, so i took it. the muny will come. or els ray kin pay for it. good by." Jessie stormed back down to the store, the cow unmilked, the chickens unfed, and threw the note at Raymond. He plucked it out of the air.

"He took the mule," Jessie said.

Raymond looked sympathetic. "He'll pay for it as soon as he can," he said. "Dolly's a man of his word."

"It wasn't for sale," Jessie snapped. "And besides, he says you can pay for it."

Raymond laughed. "That Dolly," he said. "He's a cutter, ain't he?"

"He is not a 'cutter,' whatever that is," Jessie said. "He is a thief and a friend of yours." She could feel the tears coming, and couldn't stop them. "I saved that mule from two armies and a band of murderers," she said. "And it took a scoundrel like your friend to take it from me. That was my mule. Mine." Raymond was staring at her with such a tortured expression that Jessie stopped crying. She swiped her eyes with the heel of her hand.

"What's the matter with you?" she demanded.

"I sure wish you wouldn't cry," Raymond said.

"Don't you worry the least little bit about my crying, mister," Jessie snapped. "I'm crying because I'm mad. You ever see me cry again, you remember that, you hear?" Raymond nodded, apparently mystified.

"Well, did you hear me?"

"Yes, ma'am.," he said. "I heard you." He looked anxious. "Does that mean that every time you get mad, you're going to cry?"

"Maybe, maybe not," Jessie said, furious. "I can't tell ahead of time and it's none of your business, anyhow. Now what about my mule?"

Raymond took his hat off and scratched his head, then put his hat back on. "I'll work until he's paid for, if that's what you want," he said.

"Yes," Jessie said. "That's what I want." She turned to go back to the house, then remembered something else that was bothering her. When she turned back around, Raymond was grinning. "What's so funny?" she demanded.

The grin disappeared. "Not a thing," he said.

"You can sleep in the barn. Come to the back door for your meals." Jessie pointed at his head. "And from now on, kindly take your hat off when you come inside. It's unmannerly to wear a hat indoors."

Raymond took his hat off and held it between his hands. "Yes, ma'am," he said.

There was no more to be said. Jessie left with her head high, and just barely managed to resist looking back.

Chapter Seven

Day after day, Raymond sifted through the whole, the broken, and the scattered, offering each for Nathan's inspection. Nathan then entered the item in his ledger while Raymond gathered and sorted, or mended and dusted whatever it was, then hung it on a wall or gave it to Jessie to place on a newly repaired shelf or cabinet. Nathan calmed as he inventoried what remained of his world, and Jessie settled into a life that came to include them all.

She'd not meant to forgive Raymond for the loss of her chickens and the mule, pay for them as he might with his labor. But she stepped into the store one day at noon carrying dinner for the two men, and caught Raymond as he finished putting up a shelf. He smoothed it with his hand as one might stroke a beloved horse or dog. It was a gesture of favor and of blessing. In that moment, Jessie saw a man who loved order and loved creating it. Raymond met her eyes, and smiled the most wonderful smile she had ever seen, one full of delight with its owner and his accomplishments. Disarmed, she smiled back, and an element of laughter slipped in among them. Jessie took to singing as she worked, hymns and snippets of songs she'd learned over the years, tunes she hummed in the morning that Raymond was whistling by afternoon. Even

Nathan stopped his inventory now and then to tell a joke he'd worked for hours to make up.

One day a shipment of dry goods arrived, hauled in from Fernandina by a teamster driving along the rail line. Nathan opened the box as if it were a treasure, and found inside a wealth of thread and needles ordered and paid for three years before, that had been making its slow way south ever since. The thread glowed on its spools like gems of green and blue and scarlet in the calloused hands of women who had forgotten such beauty existed, if they'd ever known it. Nathan traded the spools one at a time for the least of offers. One spool of brightly colored thread, one packet of shining silver needles to go with it, and he would stand at the door and watch the ox cart roll away, richer himself by an apron full of pine cones, a bundle of fatwood, a basket woven from pine straw and filled with poke greens gathered that very morning. Something in Nathan seemed to leave with the last spool, gone with the shy woman who traded a handful of precious seed corn for the ruby red thread on the shelf behind the register. Every day thereafter found him more diminished. He completed the inventory the first Thursday in August, and died the next morning, the ledger fallen from his hand.

Jessie stood alone beside her father's grave and stared down at the sandy new mound next to Lucy's. The purple flags she had put there were already wilting in the hot sun.

"Jessie?"

She turned around. Raymond stood hat in hand, his dark unruly hair combed back with water, but coming loose in the warm air. She thought how his hair was so unlike the rest of him. It was so disorderly, as though all his playfulness rested in the crown of his head. He looked embarrassed by her attention, and put his hat on.

"I sure am sorry about your daddy," he said. "He was a fine man. I'll miss him."

"That's kind of you," Jessie said. Quick tears burned her eyes, and she tried to blink them away. I'm lost, she wanted to say. I don't know what to do, or where to go. She shaded her eyes, instead, and looked at the sky. "It's close to dinnertime. You hungry?"

"Naw. No call for you to be cooking today, anyhow."

"I won't be. Mrs. Addison and Sister Glory brought food. It's in the kitchen."

"In that case, I reckon I could eat something."

It dawned on Jessie that they were alone in the cemetery. "Where'd everybody go? I thought they'd come back to the house with me."

"They've gone on ahead," Raymond said. "I told them I'd bring you back."

Jessie didn't know which was more frightening, Nathan's death or Raymond's presence. She felt an urge to run. Silence hummed between them like a note from a singing saw, until finally Raymond bent his arm and stuck his elbow out at her as if it were broken. The next move was Jessie's. She set her hand very lightly in the crook of his arm. The two of them walked back to town without speaking, Raymond stiff and awkward, Jessie acutely aware of her palm touching Raymond's sleeve. It was with mingled reluctance and relief when they reached the house and she walked inside. Raymond didn't follow her in, and when questioned, Jessie could not tell Glory why.

Things greatly changed between the two of them after the funeral. Jessie could not get used to her father's absence. It made her feel like a dust mote, light, insubstantial, inconsequential. And Raymond's behavior didn't make her feel any better. He ignored her most of the time, and when he spoke, which was seldom, it was brief, humorless, and to the point. He worked from morning until night on the tasks he had set himself, each one completed more slowly than the one before, as if his inner workings were running down. The heat that had shimmered over Debussy all summer long stretched into the weary green of mid-September, and still Raymond worked, while Jessie waited for the day he would finish, and leave.

It came before the month was out on an overcast day that had threatened rain since morning. Raymond drove the final nail into a shelf, then put the hammer down and looked at Jessie with something like confusion on his face.

"Well," he said. "I guess it's about done." He climbed slowly off the ladder he'd built, and moved it to its place behind the counter. He put the hammer in the toolbox and closed the lid, then sat down on a stool, big hands dangling between his knees. "I'll patch the siding on the house this afternoon, and shore the stalls up in the barn. Then I'll be through." He looked at Jessie, then away, and shrugged. "Unless you got something else for me to do."

Jessie didn't know what to say. She looked around the store. It was greatly changed. No evidence of past destruction remained, no hint of confusion or loss. Her goods, what there were of them, were neatly in place. Bins and barrels and boxes lined the walls, some filled, many empty against the day that trade would pick up again. The oak bloom that had sifted through the broken window earlier in the year had long since been dusted and swept away. Now goldenrod and ragweed pollen crept beneath the shutters and floated in the air.

"No," she said. "There's nothing else I can see to do." She smiled, her face stiff with false cheer. "Your leaving tomorrow will be fine. Or the next day. Either one. It's up to you."

"Tomorrow is good, so long as we're even," Raymond said. "I don't want to leave here owing you anything." His face was hard in a way she'd never seen before, his tone bitter.

"No," she said. "We'll be even." She started to leave, then stopped. "Would it help to know you never really owed me anything?"

Raymond stood up and shoved the stool against the wall with his foot. "No, ma'am, it wouldn't," he said. "I just spent three months of my life working off a debt, and I wouldn't appreciate learning there was never a debt to begin with. I had better have owed you something, and we had better be square."

In the face of Raymond's anger and what she took to be his contempt, Jessie fled to the house. She hid in her parents' room until the growl in her stomach told her it was dinnertime. She hoped that Raymond would come to the back door and knock, just so she could fix him something to eat. But he didn't come. Except for the shrill, monotonous song of the cicadas and the rumble of distant thunder, the place could have been deserted. For a brief, horrible time, Jessie thought Raymond had changed his mind and left without telling her.

Then there was a terrific screech as a board was pulled off the house. Jessie sat down hard on the bed, lightheaded with relief. The noise Raymond made as he worked on the house was as comforting as a lullaby. The wind was picking up outside, and a queer greenish-yellow cast stained the afternoon light. A storm was building. Still grieving, Jessie stretched out on her mother's side of the bed, and fell asleep.

The wind woke her up. It was dark in the bedroom and the shutters were banging against the house. The sky outside was black and the trees were bending before the coming storm. Chilled, Jessie rubbed her arms, then went outside to fight the shutters closed. There was no sign of Raymond. Maybe he was in the store or the barn. Maybe he had already left. The thought terrified her. She felt herself an empty house, an abandoned building for the wind to blow through.

Jessie went back in the house and wandered aimlessly from her parents' room to her own, and from there to the kitchen. She opened the kitchen door and saw a shake fly off the roof of the chicken house, then another. The whole thing was swaying in the wind. Then it collapsed. Above the moan of the wind, she could hear the chickens squawking. Rain spattered her face and arms as she ran to the fallen shed and started tearing at the boards. Water was coming down hard enough to blind her when someone grabbed her shoulders. Jessie turned and saw Raymond. She almost hugged him with relief.

"My chickens!" she yelled. "Help me get the chickens!"

"Damn the chickens!" Raymond yelled back. He pulled at her arm and Jessie slapped at his hands. He grabbed her around the waist and put her over his shoulder, then carried her in an awkward run to the barn while she kicked and hit and slapped and tried to hold her dress down, all at the same time.

Raymond set her down when they reached the barn, and grabbed her wrist when she tried to push past him to the chickens, out there shelterless in the rain and the dark. "Huh, uh," he said. "Not while I'm around, you won't."

"Who do you think you are?" Jessie shrieked, the wind tearing the words out of her mouth. "Coming in here, telling me what to do." She jerked her wrist out of his hand.

"I'm somebody knows chickens ain't worth dying for," Raymond said. He blocked her way with his body and kicked the door shut. "Listen," he said. "Just listen." The wind howled up under the eaves, which rattled with the pressure. A bolt of lightning crackled in the dark and thunder shook the barn.

Jessie started crying. "My chickens," she said. She wrapped her arms around her shoulders, aware for the first time that she was soaking wet and very cold.

Raymond went to the feed room and came back shaking dust and rat droppings out of a handful of croaker sacks. "We can wrap up in these," he said. He pointed up to the loft. "It'll be warmer up there. Come on."

"I don't want nothing on me that's had rat mess in it," she said.

"You worry too much," Raymond said. "If you could see the way you look right now, you wouldn't give rat mess another thought." That silenced her, and she clambered up the ladder behind him, teeth chattering, goose bumps rising on her legs where the wet dress clung to them.

Raymond made a kind of nest in the hay and spread a sack across it. "You sit right there," he ordered. Jessie sat down on the bag. He sat down next to her and covered her shoulders with another sack, then wrapped one around himself. He took a fourth one and put it over their knees. "When it quits raining, you can go in and put on some dry clothes. After that, we'll see about your chickens."

Jessie huddled down in the hay, hugging her knees for warmth. "They'll be dead by then," she muttered.

"Maybe." Raymond shivered beside her. "Damn, it's cold," he said. He put an arm around Jessie, pulling her to his side.

"I don't think you ought to do that," Jessie said.

"If we ever thaw out, you can slap me." Raymond took her chin in his hands and ran his thumb back and forth across her lips. "Your lips are blue," he said. "Can you even feel them?"

"I can feel you," Jessie said. Her hands were shaking with cold and fear and something else, and she grasped them together. Raymond pulled her hands apart and put them on his sides, then pushed her back in the hay and laid down on top of her. Her breath started coming in little sips, like she'd had the wind knocked out of her, and her ankle was cold where the wind blew on it. There was a strong musty odor of old hay and rat, and a sharper, saltier scent that came from Raymond's hair against her cheek. She couldn't stop shaking. Even her knees kept bumping against his legs. There was a funny clicking sound in her ear and she tried to concentrate on it, and not on Raymond's arms around her shoulders or his legs pressed against her thighs.

"What are you doing?" she whispered.

"Freezing," Raymond said. His body trembled on hers. "I think my teeth are going to break." His jaw clenched against hers, and the clicking sound stopped. His teeth had been chattering. "Feel that?" Raymond asked.

"Feel what?" Jessie whispered.

"My back." She became aware of her hands, clenched in fists behind him. She touched his back with one finger. "It's cold."

"Damn straight it's cold. See if you can reach one of those sacks and pull it over me."

Jessie groped to one side and put her hand on a croaker sack. She pulled it over Raymond's back and pushed it as best she could around his shoulders. "Does that help?" she whispered. Then she started crying.

"Some," Raymond said. "Are you crying?"

Jessie nodded, sobs building in gulps and wrenching her worse than the shivers.

"What are you crying about?" Raymond's voice was as sharp as the wind whipping through the loft.

"Because of this," she said, still whispering.

"Because of what?" he demanded. "And what are you whispering for?" Raymond's weight shifted and Jessie found herself looking up at him, propped on one elbow above her. "Just what is it you think I'm doing?" he demanded. His lips were blue at the corners.

Jessie tried to remember when she'd been as miserable. Nothing came to mind. "I don't know," she said.

Raymond pushed himself off her like he'd seen a snake, and sat up, pulling the croaker sack around him like a shawl. He looked angry and disbelieving. "I'm trying to keep warm, is what I'm doing," he said. "Ain't that what you thought?"

"I couldn't tell," Jessie said. She pulled her dress down to her ankles, much colder again.

"You couldn't tell?" Raymond's face was outraged. "You beat all I ever seen, you know that?" He grabbed one of the sacks and threw it at her. "Put that on. It's cold. What's the matter with you, anyhow?"

"Well, what am I supposed to think, with you laying on top of me and all?"

"And all? Laying on top of you and all? All what?"

"All I don't know."

"All you don't know is right. There ain't no 'and all.'" Raymond's dark eyes were angry and hard. "I was trying to keep you warm, and get warm myself, after you ran us both around in a cold rain the likes of which can kill people."

Jessie looked down at her knees, but could feel Raymond's breath on her hair as he leaned over her.

"I've been alone with you for weeks, Jessie," he said, his voice rising steadily. "If I'd wanted you that way I could have had you that way, anytime, in the comfort of a bed with sheets. I didn't have to wait until I was soaked to the skin, and so cold I couldn't keep my teeth from banging together, and laying in a pile of moldy hay covered with a sack full of rat shit!" Raymond picked at the hay on his shirt. "All your fault, anyway, running around in a fall storm. Idiot."

"Don't you call me an idiot!" Jessie said. She felt silly and relieved and hideously disappointed. "You were just going to leave, after all this time. Not 'I'm sorry, wish I could stay," not anything. I couldn't think, couldn't figure out how you could do that. Everything was all tore up, somehow. I don't know. Maybe you're right. Maybe I am an idiot." She looked out through the loft door. The storm was already dying away. It was quiet enough now so that Raymond was louder than the storm.

"When were you all tore up?" he demanded. "I never saw you tore up." He stood up and paced around the loft, one hand holding the ends of the croaker sack at his throat, the other waving in the air. "I was the one tore up, not you. You walked around every day as pretty as any woman that ever lived, looking like sugar wouldn't melt in your mouth and not a word of encouragement or hope or nothing, while I hammered and sawed and toted and cleaned for three solid months because I thought, I thought...hell, I don't know what I thought. That you'd fall in my arms when your daddy died and beg me to take care of you, I guess. But no. The day of the funeral, there at the grave, you put your hand on my arm like it was something nasty and ain't had hardly a word to say to me since. And this afternoon, after everything I've done here, after waiting as patient as any man that's ever lived, I finally say I've got to go, just because I can't see no good reason to stay on, and what do you do? You get all stuffy and mad and stomp off, and then run out in a storm and nearly get us both killed because the hen house falls over!"

At mention of the hen house, Jessie jumped up, reaching for the one thing in her life that still made sense. "The chickens!" she said, and headed for the ladder.

Raymond blocked her way. "To hell with the chickens!" he yelled. "If you mention them one more time, I'm going down there and wring every last scrawny neck that's left alive, do you hear me?"

"Don't you be hollering at me," Jessie screamed, and hit him in the chest with the flat of her hand. "And don't you get in my way, either. I don't care if you are bigger than me!"

Raymond caught her hand and held it for a moment. Then he let her go and stepped aside. "Go on down and check on your hens," he said quietly. "I'll be down in a minute."

Jessie swung onto the ladder and started down. As her eyes came even with the edge of the loft, Raymond spoke to her. She stopped. The tip of his boot was just visible over the opening.

"Jessie?" he asked. He sounded tired.

"What?"

"I want you to marry me."

Jessie felt dizzy. Putting her foot on the ground didn't help any. "I can't talk about such as that right now," she said. "I'm not feeling too good."

She walked out of the barn on legs that felt like the joints had gone soft. Pieces of the hen house were scattered all over the yard, but five of the hens, at least, were alive. They pecked contentedly under a persimmon tree, feathers dripping with water and laying in streaks and clumps against their thin pale skin. Other than that, they seemed none the worse for having been blown out of their coop. Jessie called to them and they clucked down in their throats. She wished she'd thought to bring them some corn. The door to the loft swung out, and she looked up to see Raymond standing in the opening.

"The first time I ever saw you," he said, "I was looking out through a hole in this door while you said good morning to them hens. I'd never seen anything so pretty in all my life, or heard anything so sweet, and nothing had felt that right to me in a long, long time. I lost my heart to you right then, and can never take it back, bad as I may want to. But you need to know something." He leaned out, holding the doorjamb. "There ain't nothing in this world I'm more afraid of than you, not even lightning. So what I'm about to say next won't bother you nearly as much as it bothers me. Which is this: you either agree to marry me right now, or I'm riding Shank's mare out of here just as soon as I can get my bedroll folded. What will it be?"

Jessie opened her mouth to speak and pointed at the hen house, but Raymond stopped her. "I'm telling you, Jessie, I won't be fussed with them chickens right now. Don't push me. What's your answer?"

Jessie felt tears coming and bit her lip to keep from crying. "It's not supposed to be this way," she said.

"I've never known how it was supposed to be," Raymond said. "Maybe it'll suit you better later on. Now, what'll I do? Stay or go, which is it?"

"Stay, I guess. No, I don't guess. I know. I want you to stay. But not that other. I'm scared."

"I'm scared, too," Raymond said. "More scared than you'll ever know. So let's get it over with. I'm ready now. How much time do you need?"

"A month."

"Too long."

"Three weeks."

"All right. Three weeks from today." Raymond grinned at her from the loft, then looked surprised. "That didn't hurt as bad as I thought it would!" He grabbed the loft door, swung out on it as far as it would go then dropped to the ground. "I'll build you a new hen house for a wedding present." He laughed out loud, and kissed her on the cheek. "Your nose is running. I got to talk to the preacher. See you shortly."

Raymond left Jessie standing beside the wrecked chicken pen with tears on her face and a stomachache while the chickens chuckled and clucked and scratched in the dirt beneath the persimmon tree.

Chapter Eight

Raymond and Jessie were married at 5:00 in the afternoon on September 19, 1865. Jessie's dress was the one the chickens had beshat months before, and the Cooper children had stuck her hair full of wildflowers, leaving it wildly disordered. She came up the aisle toward Raymond like a sleepwalker, her eyes so swollen from crying they looked bee stung. The hand she put in his was clammy, and she wouldn't look at him.

Ten long minutes later, Raymond and Jessie were wed before God and His church. Raymond kissed the bride, but she still wouldn't look at him. She didn't look at him during the wedding dinner given by Sister Glory, either, or when Raymond stood and pulled her chair out, and they awkwardly made their goodbyes. She hugged the wedding guests and children and told them all good night, but she didn't say a word to Raymond, and she didn't look at him, and he wondered to himself what it was he'd gotten into, a peck of trouble, as Dolly had warned, and no mistake about it.

Jessie stopped at her own front door like she'd run into a wall. Raymond stepped around her, opened the door, and held it wide.

"You go on in," he said. "Get dressed for bed. I'll be there directly."

His voice was cold and stiff, as if he were talking to a stranger. Jessie felt like a stranger to herself, as if she'd just gotten her body and was trying to break it in, like the new shoes she'd had before the war. Even her own house was strange to her, in particular the bedroom her parents had shared which was now to be hers and Raymond's.

Jessie took her dress off and hung it on the nail beside the bed, then put on her flannel nightgown and climbed into the bed. The evening was pleasant, but she huddled beneath the quilt with her cold hands stuck in her armpits, and first one cold foot, then the other, held against the opposite leg.

She shifted her weight, and the corn shucks in the mattress rustled beneath her. Bats flitted through the deepening twilight outside the window, there, then gone, an occasional squeak accompanying their passing. Jessie watched the glow of the candle on the table by the bed, the side closest to the door. The flame flickered when the door opened, and she turned her head to look out the window again. She heard a quick breath, and the candle went out. The bed sagged as Raymond sat down on it. Jessie heard his boots hit the floor, then the sound of his pants coming off. Her back felt cold when he pulled the quilt back, and the bed sagged again. She resolutely turned away, almost choking her throat was so dry. She heard him sigh, felt him stretch out, felt his feet brush hers. She drew her feet up higher.

"Jessie?" Raymond's voice wasn't stiff now, just quiet.

She wanted to turn to him so badly she could cry, and got sick just thinking about it. "What?" she asked. Her voice felt dry and scratchy, like deer moss.

"Come here," he said.

"I am," she answered.

"No, you're not. Come here. Over here. To me." He spoke to her as one might to a puppy or a child, coaxing and gentle, with an underlying firmness.

"I can't," she whispered.

"Then I'm coming to you," Raymond said. "All right?"

Jessie didn't answer, just waited, eyes closed.

"All right?" he asked again, no louder, but a little clearer.

"Suit yourself," she said. It was neither surrender nor invitation, just an admission that she couldn't stop him from doing as he wished.

Anger flared with her words, and she stared hotly out the window at the twilight. The bed creaked and there he was, against her back, her buttocks, her thighs, her calves, his breath warm on the crown of her head. She crossed her arms tightly against her stomach, and his hand came down between them, searching and insistent, moving them aside and making room, forcing a way past her defenses, until he was holding her across the belly, whereupon he gathered her tightly to himself. She breathed, and felt her belly shift against his arm, and tried to hold her breath.

"Jessie," Raymond said. "Turn over here and talk to me."

"No," she said. Her voice squeaked like a bat's. She cleared her throat, carefully, so as not to pressure his arm lying like some dangerous but inattentive animal across her.

He didn't say anything for a moment, then shifted again and settled around her so that her head rested in the hollow of his throat. He let go of her a moment, and pointed at the window. "Look at the bats," he said. He put his arm around her again, pushing just as stubbornly as before between her arms and body. "You ever seen one up close?"

Jessie shook her head.

"They have the wildest little faces you ever saw. Great big ears, and noses like somebody stepped on them. Squinty eyes. Bony hands so small, one won't hardly go around your little finger."

Jessie didn't move. She knew what he was doing. He was trying to trick her into doing what he wanted like he'd done her father back when they first met.

"And they hang upside down to sleep. That's something, you know? How come they don't let go when they finally go to sleep? You ever thought about that?"

"No," she said. But she was thinking about it now. "How come?"

"I don't know," Raymond said. "That's why I asked you." He fell silent. Jessie stared out the window at the bats.

"Jessie?" Raymond asked.

"What?" She was on guard again, resistant to that voice that was so good with wounded things, seductive in its gentleness.

"Turn over here and look at me."

"No," she said, fear rising in her so suddenly she flushed with it. "No."

His hand came up and smoothed her hair back from her face, tucking it behind her ear, pulling it down her back, touching her spine, returning to her face when she arched away from him as if scalded.

"I'm going to turn you around," he said, and moved away from her. "You can stay right there in that ball, if you want, but I'm going to turn you around so I can talk to you."

She felt his hands on her shoulders, her waist, her hips as he eased her, wooden and cold, little by little, onto her back. She crouched there, knees drawn up and tight together, heels flat on the bed. He rose up on his elbows above her. Jessie turned her face to the window. She felt his fingers on her eyebrows, and closed her eyes. They traveled over her eyelids, her temples, down her cheek, touched her lips, her chin, a thumb lightly down her neck to her shoulder, then to the fabric of her gown over her collarbone. The heel of his hand rested on her breast, and burned so she thought the fabric must catch fire. She flinched when he fumbled at the buttons of her gown, and unbent enough to grab his hand with both of hers, but he took her fingers in his and laid them against his hip as he closed her mouth with his own.

A chuckwill's widow cried out in the darkness, answered by its mate close by. Wind filled the curtains and lifted them, arched and full, across the bed, then let them fall again, spent. And all the while, outside the open window, the little bats squeaked and swooped and darted in the stillness of the night.

Raymond soon discovered that hot blood, sweet feelings, and good intentions could lead a man to places he'd never meant to go and couldn't very easily escape once he was there. Whatever it was he'd felt for Jessie when he was courting was changed beyond recognition by a thousand little choices made through the days and nights that followed. Those choices bound him even closer when Jessie came up pregnant a month after the wedding, and tightened another notch when the baby was born a scant eight months later, too early and too small. Raymond went to bed each night expecting the little thing to die, and woke each morning to a thin wail announcing its claim to one more day. Beau clung to life with a tenacity that moved his father to respect and eventually to affection. Raymond held him in one hand two weeks after his birth, red-faced and wrinkled and mewing like a kitten, and turned him back and forth, eying him thoughtfully.

"I've never seen anything so ugly," he told Jessie, "but darn if the little feller ain't tough."

"He's not ugly, either. He's beautiful."

"He looks like a 'possum."

"Give him here. You don't deserve him."

"That's the truth," Raymond said. "Nothing I've ever done deserves that." He handed the baby back to Jessie, setting the small bundle on her breast. Beau rooted frantically for the nipple and finding it, latched on. He choked when Jessie's milk let down, but held tight, white bubbles frothing out the corners of his mouth.

Raymond looked on in admiration. "Dead serious about his vittles, ain't he?" He picked his hat up off the table and put it on, then bent down to kiss Jessie's forehead. "Guess I better get back to work, so I can keep him in bacon."

He shut the door on the picture of familial bliss and headed to the field to plow, a job Raymond hated with his whole heart. He had to borrow Brother Cooper's horse because Dolly had stolen the mule, and follow it down one furrow after another, day after day, scared by the bony threat of hunger walking off from him and his family one shambling step at a time. Once the field was ready, he rose early in the mornings to plant beans and corn and sweet potatoes before going to the store. A few weeks later, he took to sitting up nights to shoot the deer that came to nibble the news shoots, and then the bears that waddled up and down the rows like carpetbaggers, stripping the new corn from the stalks. And every day except Sunday, when he went to church with Jessie, Raymond put an apron on and minded the store until Beau got bigger and Jessie could mind it, freeing him to clear more of the field behind the house and put it under the plow.

And the whole time, from the moment he got up in the morning until the moment he fell back asleep, he thought about hunting cows, and the feel of a good horse beneath him, and the way the stars filled the night sky when seen from a bedroll on the ground, and how a man could ride for a hundred miles and never hear any voice but his own. Or he thought about the plow, and how it bound him to the very ground he ripped his living from, and how he fought the deer and bears over the crops, scrapping like a dog for the food in his mouth. Or he thought about how he wanted to have something big, to be somebody important, to carve out a destiny that other men would admire and respect and desire. But mostly he felt so trapped and desperate that he was ready to go anywhere in the world, so long as he could get away from that sad little ghost of a town and see the world again with the eyes of a free man.

But before he could run, Jessie would snuggle up against him, or the baby would fix its wandering gaze upon its own small fist until its eyes crossed, and the goodness, the rightness of what Raymond had would tug at him so that he had to stay, not knowing anymore what he felt or wanted, he felt and wanted so many different things.

Sometimes he tried to tell Jessie what was on his heart and mind, but it didn't help much. She pitied him the death of his friends and despised Vancey for his perfidy and even tried to understand his friendship with Dolly, as near as Raymond could come to explaining it. But his distaste for farming made no sense to her, anymore than borrowing from their neighbors brought her shame. And she would not hear - would not even discuss it when he broached the subject - of his going off with Dolly to find Vancey Adams. But it was when he moved on from that to suggest that they leave Debussy to settle Walker's Island that she turned a side to him he'd never seen before, shrewish and mean-spirited. It was their first real fight and Jessie - as slit-eyed and mean as a treed bobcat - proved herself more than equal to any argument Raymond could muster.

Thereafter, Raymond kept his dissatisfaction to himself. He took to missing Dolly, his impatience and vinegary wit, his temper, and his disregard for convention. Raymond recalled the debt to his dead comrades and Vancey, his agreement with Hebron, his promise to Dolly. But mostly he thought of Walker's Island, of its wealth of land and water and cattle, of all that he could be there, and all that he could become. Sometimes he even dreamed about it, and woke smiling and content, only to see the sun rising over the field behind the Winters' house. At those moments, he would think he was dying of homesickness, consumed by a yearning for something he could not name, but that would not let him rest.

Beau was six months old when Raymond decided he'd had enough. He was so fed up with life in Debussy that he could hardly get out of bed in the morning, and so worried that Dolly wasn't coming back that he couldn't sleep at night. For all he knew, Dolly was dead or content to stay wherever he was, and so was Vancey. But Walker's Island was right where it had always been, and Raymond meant to stake his claim to it. He was figuring on a way to tell Jessie when Dolly saved him the trouble.

He rode into town with two other men one late November afternoon in 1866, leading Jessie's mule and a bay mare with a saddle on her back. A yellow cur dog trotted behind the mare, its eyes narrowed against the sweep of her tail. Raymond took one look at the squat, powerful form on the tall gray horse and muttered, "Well, it's about damn time." And when he saw that one of the riders with Dolly was Hebron Wilkes, he knew it was time indeed.

Raymond stood up, draped the harness he'd been mending over the chair, and stepped out into the street to greet them. "I'd about decided you weren't coming," he said.

Dolly gave him a cold blue stare. "If you wouldn't run out on people," he said, "you wouldn't worry about them running out on you."

"I didn't run anywhere," Raymond said, his feelings hurt. "Just hung back a spell."

Hebron and the other man rode up beside Dolly. Hebron leaned down and clapped Raymond on the arm as he wrung his hand. "Dolly said you'd be waiting," he said, "and sure enough, here you are, looking down the street with a lonesome eye. This here's my uncle, Freemont Wilkes. Uncle Free, this is Raymond Pennell."

Groaning, Uncle Freemont got down off his horse and shook Raymond's hand. He was short - not even five feet - with long, greasy hair hanging out from under his hat and a drawn, wrinkled face, leathery and bristling with short gray hairs. A wide gap separated his front teeth when he grinned. "Heard a lot about you," he said. "More than I care to remember, in fact."

"Hope it was good," Raymond said.

"Very little of it," Freemont replied. He stepped up on the porch, shoved the harness to the ground, sat down in Raymond's chair, and addressed himself to Dolly. "You got somewheres else you need to be, Blue Eyes?"

Dolly swung off his horse to the ground. The bay mare snorted and flung her head up. "Put your head down, floozy," He grumbled. "Horse acts like she's got wasps up her nose, way she throws it around." He held out his hand to Raymond. "Did you miss me?"

Raymond shook his hand, letting the relief show in his face. "Not so's I couldn't sleep at night."

The cobalt blue eyes warmed and Dolly laughed. "Liar," he said. He spit a stream of tobacco juice at the dog and it jumped out of the way. "I brung the mule back. Thought you might want something other'n that to ride, though, so brung you that mare and saddle, besides." He cleared his throat. "And I brung a little present to your lady friend."

"You mean my wife," Raymond said.

"Damn Baxter's hide for knowing what the man would do," Hebron complained. He stood up in his stirrups, dug down in his pants pocket, pulled out a silver dollar, and tossed it to Dolly.

Dolly winked at Raymond, put the dollar in his pocket, and flipped open his saddlebag. A yellow puppy stuck its head out, blinking its eyes and yawning. Dolly grabbed it by the scruff of the neck and held it out to Raymond. "It's one of Hiram's," he said. "Like Billy wanted."

That shook Raymond hard. He took the puppy and squatted down to set it on the road, his eyes stinging. A shadow fell across the dirt in front of him, and Hebron's voice rumbled down.

"Dolly tells me that Hiram feller bred this litter special to catch chicken thieves," he said.

Raymond scratched the puppy's ears. "Jessie'd be happy if it just caught Dolly."

"I reckon so," Dolly said. "Seeings as she's caught you already." He nudged Raymond in the back. "Does she know you're leaving?"

"Yes and no," Raymond said, and stood up.

"Yes and no!" Uncle Freemont exclaimed. "Now there speaks a well-married man. Yes. And. No. Uhhhhhh, huhh."

Raymond tried to look more confident than he felt. "Yes, I told her I'd be going off for a spell one of these first days. She got so mad about it I decided to let it rest for the time being. So, no, because she didn't know any more than I did when I'd be leaving."

"Well, I'm no sluggard," Uncle Free said, "but first light tomorrow is soon enough for me."

"A hot meal and a good night's sleep wouldn't bother me none, either," Hebron said. "That is, if your missus don't mind us staying over."

"Oh, she'll mind all right," Dolly said. "She'd rather kiss a rattlesnake on the lips than ever see me again."

Raymond grinned. "We'll throw you in there first; once you're dead, the rest of us will be safe. Y'all come on to the house."

"Let's put the horses in the barn first," Uncle Freemont said, "and work up to that other kinda slow."

"Good idea," Raymond said.

"I'm married, too," Freemont answered. "It's a rough row to hoe. Builds character, though, in them that persevere. I wouldn't be the man I am without it."

Jessie was making butter, the floor shaking with the thunk of the paddle in the churn between her knees. Beau was crawling across the floor, blowing spit bubbles and grasping at sunbeams. He kept sitting down and looking in his palm for the light he thought he'd captured. Jessie watched him closely - he moved quickly, and always toward the door - while she argued with Raymond in her mind. It was a conversation wherein she spoke both parts and always won with words so clear and strong and true that Raymond - though not left speechless since that would spoil the argument - was nevertheless amazed in the face of her gentle wisdom and piercing insight. She was deep into this conversation when a hand touched her shoulder. Startled, she looked up to see Raymond with three men standing behind him. Two of the men were strangers, but the third she recognized immediately. Jessie stopped churning and glared at him. "What're you doing here?" she demanded.

Dolly put his hands in the air. "I've come to turn myself in," he said.

Jessie grimaced and went back to churning. "I guess the others will introduce themselves when they're ready," she said. Beau crawled over to her chair. Jessie kept churning with one hand, and with the other hauled him up on her lap.

"Jessie," Raymond said. "This is Hebron Wilkes. You've heard me talk about him. And this is his Uncle Freemont. I take it you remember Dolly."

"Yes," Jessie said.

"Well, that's fine, then." Raymond pulled a chair out from the table. "Y'all have a seat." Hebron and Freemont sat down.

Dolly, however, moved a chair right next to Jessie and plunked down in it like he owned it. Jessie would have gotten up, but Beau leaned across in front of her and grinned at Dolly. Dolly twiddled his fingers at Beau and winked at Jessie. "I think he likes me," he said.

"He likes everybody," Jessie said coldly. "He's a baby, and doesn't know any better."

"Oh, he knows, all right," Dolly said. "That there is a clear-sighted boy." He offered Beau a finger, who put it in his mouth and gummed it, drool running down his chin.

"He's got some nasty habits, don't he?" Freemont remarked.

Jessie stood up and snatched Beau up on her hip. "I suppose y'all are staying for supper," she said. She didn't want them to stay, but courtesy obliged her to offer. A body would have thought she was falling on their necks in welcome, the way their eyes lit up.

"See there, Dolly?" Freemont said. "Mizz Pennell likes us just fine. And you thought she would be hostile to our presence." He giggled. Jessie shot him a look and he sobered immediately.

"I got something for your mama, buddy," Dolly said to Beau. "Maybe she'll share it with you."

Jessie was immediately curious, and outraged with herself for being so. "I'd settle for the return of the mule," she snapped.

"He's in the barn," Raymond said.

"And three chickens, and my Sunday dress the way it used to be."

"Your mama's got a long memory," Dolly said to Beau. "Come outside and help me with her present. Maybe it'll soften her some."

"I doubt that," Freemont said.

"Beau won't go off with strangers," Jessie said. "He keeps his distance from 'em."

"Is that right?" Dolly asked. "It's a good habit. I'm telling you, he's a smart boy." He crooked a finger at Beau. "Come here, boy."

"You stay here with me, Beau," Jessie said.

Beau held his arms out to Dolly, who picked him up, then pretended to drop him. Beau shrieked with delight.

"We'll be back after a while," Dolly said, and left with Beau on his shoulder.

"Don't you worry, ma'am," Freemont said. "Dolly ain't dropped a baby all day."

"Be quiet, Uncle Free," Hebron said. He smiled gently at Jessie. "It's all right, Mizz Pennell. Dolly loves babies. He told me once he wanted to settle down with six or seven wives and raise babies by the hundredweight. He said when they was grown, he'd have the smartest, toughest, meanest cow crew in Florida. What if they're all girls, I said, and he said girls is what he was talking about." Hebron laughed so hard his eyes watered. "Whooee, that Dolly. He's a cutter, ain't he? A girl cow crew. Ha."

Boots clunked on the porch, the front door opened and shut, and Dolly walked back into the kitchen with Beau in the crook of one arm and a yellow puppy in the other. He set them both down on the floor. The puppy wagged its tail, sniffed at Beau, and barked. Beau grinned.

Jessie couldn't help but smile.

"Cute, ain't he?" Dolly asked.

Jessie stopped smiling. "Cute is as cute does," she said. "I don't want it chewing on things, particularly the baby."

"I'll teach Beau to haul off and slap it," Dolly said. "Then they'll both learn something." The puppy walked off to investigate the kitchen, and Beau crawled right behind it. Dolly caught Jessie's eye. "Do you like your present?" he asked.

Jessie wanted to relent, but something told her it would be foolish. She did it anyway. "Beau likes him," she said. "And we need a dog around here. I thank you for it."

"You're welcome," Dolly said. "I figured you'd want something to keep you company while Ray's gone." Jessie blinked. Dolly coughed. "Of course," he said, "when I decided to bring you the puppy, I didn't know anything about little Beau. He's better company than a dog could ever be, I'm sure."

"What are you talking about?" Jessie demanded. Dolly shrugged. She turned to Raymond. "What is he talking about, Raymond?"

"Maybe we should wash up for supper," Dolly said.

"Good idea," Hebron said, and stood up.

Freemont clapped Raymond on the shoulder. "Call us when the smoke clears," he said.

Dolly picked up the puppy and reached for Beau, but Raymond stopped him. "Best you leave him here."

Dolly tipped his hat to Jessie, stuck the puppy in his coat pocket, and walked with Hebron and Free out the back door.

Jessie turned to Raymond. "What is he talking about?" she asked.

"I made a promise, Jess," Raymond said. "I've got to keep it."

"Why? Just tell me why."

Raymond picked Beau up. "Because I owe Billy and Vancey and Hebron and Dolly," he said. "Most of all, I owe myself. I ain't walking off from any of it." He turned away from her and headed for the back door.

"You mean like you're walking off from me?" Jessie yelled.

Raymond set Beau on his shoulder and looked back at Jessie. "I ain't walking off from you," he said. "I'm going outside to wash up for supper. In the morning, I'm going away for a while to pay a debt. When I've settled it, I'll be back. Then you and me and Beau will go together to wherever it is I decide we'll go, because you're my wife and I need you with me for anything else to make sense. And if you refuse to go, then I'll tie you up and make you go, because I'm not going without you. Meanwhile, I'd appreciate it if you'd cook some supper, because we've got company and I'm hungry and I've got to get to bed so I can get up early and not be tired."

"I'm sorry you ever came here," Jessie said. She turned her back and crossed her arms. The back door slammed. She turned around. Raymond had walked out and taken Beau with him, leaving her alone in the kitchen.

Hebron's hot meal was cooked in haste and served in anger, and the bravest among them did not request a second cup of coffee. Finally,

Uncle Free stood up, stretched, yawned, and scratched his chest, digging between the buttonholes on his shirt.

"Have mercy," he said. "That coffee's strong enough to wake the dead, and we all need to get some sleep. The sooner we take care of Mr. Adams, the sooner we can get home. I left one just as mad as this 'un back at the house." He winked at Jessie, and stuck the tip of his tongue through the space where his two front teeth should have been. It wiggled like a pink maggot.

"Leave Mizz Jessie alone, Uncle Free," Hebron said. "She'll be having nightmares, looking at your ole ugly face." He stood up and bowed awkwardly to Jessie. "He's harmless, ma'am. Just as harmless as he is homely." He took Freemont by the arm and led him toward the back door. "If you don't mind, we'll sleep in the barn."

"I better go with them, Ray," Dolly said.

"That's a good idea," Raymond replied.

"Good night, then," Dolly said. He nodded to Jessie. "Good night, Jessie." Jessie ignored him. Dolly shrugged and left. The back door shut quietly. Dolly's voice drifted back into the kitchen in a gentle falsetto. "Good night, Dolly dear. So good to see you again." Low laughter followed, and one last comment. "Hey, law. Love is grand, I'm telling you." Then silence.

"I hate him," Jessie said.

"I think he knows that," Raymond replied.

They left before dawn. The horses' hooves crunched on the frosty grass, and the breath shot from their nostrils in white plumes of steam. Dolly called the yellow dog to heel behind the gray horse, then tipped his hat to Jessie and turned away, followed by Hebron and Uncle Free.

Raymond stepped off the porch, untied the bay mare from the hitching post, and swung up in the saddle. "You got anything to say to me? Last chance for a while."

Jessie just stood there, arms crossed, lips clamped together. Raymond pushed his hat back on his head, sucked on a tooth, and waited. When she still didn't speak, he pulled his hat back down and reined the mare around. He'd ridden ten steps before Jessie changed her mind.

"Wait," she said. "Wait."

Raymond stopped. Jessie came up beside the horse and held her hands up. Raymond pulled her into his arms and set his mouth hard on hers. The horse shifted uneasily beneath them.

"Come home soon," Jessie said.

"Soon as I can," Raymond said. Then he set her on the ground, and loped off down the road after Dolly.

Chapter Nine

Tension surfaced between Raymond and Dolly their first night out of Debussy, and the further south they traveled, the worse it got. They went from subject to subject looking for disagreements, until finally they were squabbling over where to tie the horses at night. There is nothing peaceful about a manhunt, of course, but this was something else, more like the wrestling matches they'd had when they first became friends, when they were learning each other's strengths and weaknesses, and how to use them to their own advantage. And the closer they came to Walker's Island, the more unfriendly those squabbles became.

It was three weeks since they'd seen a settlement or homestead, or even another human being beside themselves. Deer fled at their approach, bounding past cattle as wild and skittish as themselves. Wolves and panthers hunted at night, and Raymond didn't know which was worse, the howling or the screams. Bears, slick and fat with cool weather and high living, watched their passage with small brown eyes then galloped off, woofing with alarm. Flocks of wood ibises, sandhill cranes, and ducks rose and fell from ponds and lakes where cypresses trailed orchids and Spanish moss. Dove and quail burst from prairies and piney woods, and turkeys ran long-legged through hammocks filled with green light and noisy Carolina parakeets, or took to the air in heavy flight. And the further south they went, the more water there was, and the more abundant the life that accompanied it. Raymond compared the lushness of this country with Debussy, and found Debussy wanting. Everything he saw - beautiful or strange or comic - he wanted Jessie to see with him. He knew that were it not for her and Beau, he would never ride back north again. Now, with the day half spent, familiar landmarks were appearing, and Raymond looked with anticipation for the island to appear.

"That little creek is up here pretty close," Dolly said.

Raymond didn't answer. He didn't remember the creek as being particularly little, and when they broke camp after breakfast had suggested they take the eastern route around the smaller lake at the north end, and come back west over the marsh.

"The other way's closer," Dolly said.

"The creek'll be high," Raymond said. "Wrong time of year to be swimming."

"I can't swim," Freemont said. "Let's go by way of the marsh."

"It won't be that high," Dolly said. "Raymond's just forgotten what it looks like."

"It was February when we were here, and low water. I remember it just fine."

"You don't remember as well as you think you do," Dolly said. "You were off on this lake here. Said it was fifteen miles further east, and here it sits, right where I said it was."

Raymond couldn't argue with that. He'd been surprised when they came on it so soon, as immediately familiar to memory as a noted landmark might be to someone who had once toured a city. Through the cypress, he could see the small north lake, reclaimed from Ben's story, entirely itself again. Wisps of steam rose from its surface in the chilly air, and swirls of water betrayed the presence of feeding bass, the expanding ripples bumping two feet from their path.

"Do you see how high this water is?" Raymond asked.

"The creek won't be that high," Dolly said. Something in his voice dared Raymond to contradict him.

Raymond studied the cobalt blue eyes, and decided to bide his time. "Press on regardless," he said.

Dolly went ahead, followed by Freemont and Hebron, with Raymond last of all. He enjoyed bringing up the rear. It put some distance between him and Dolly.

The creek was high.

Dolly leaned back in the saddle, stretched, then sat up straight and rubbed the back of his neck. "That ain't so bad," he said.

Raymond watched the swift, dark current, and winced. The only other crossing was a half-mile further down, where the water had cut eight-foot bluffs through the hammock on its way south. There was no sense trying to cross there. They could backtrack, and take the route over the marsh. Or they could cross here. "What do you want to do?" he asked.

Hebron didn't say anything but Freemont looked anxiously at Dolly, and repeated his earlier concern. "I can't swim a lick," he said.

"Your horse can," Dolly said.

"Not my horse," Freemont said. "He ain't never learned."

"Then it's time he did," Dolly said. He pulled his rifle from its scabbard and lifted it over his head. "See you fellers on the other side."

He nudged his horse and it stepped into the water, snorting and blowing. The water came over Dolly's boots, his legs, his thighs, and finally covered his saddle, but came no higher. Then the horse was lunging up the opposite bank. It stopped at the top and shook itself. The dog whined up and down the bank, then jumped in. It had to swim hard against the current, and for a moment, Raymond thought it would drown. Then it was up the bank, shaking the water off and rolling in the sand. Raymond looked at Hebron, and lifted his eyebrows.

"Go on, Uncle Free," Hebron said. "There'll be no swimming lessons today. That horse has longer legs than a dog."

"If I drown, I'll kill you," Freemont said.

"Uncle Free, if you drown, I'll kill myself. You have my word on it." Hebron's word must have been good enough, because Freemont rode his horse into the water and came out the other side saying such things as made Raymond's ears turn red. Hebron followed him.

Then it was Raymond's turn. The water was every bit as cold as he'd expected, and his legs were numb by the time the mare came bucking up out of it on the other side. Raymond, his wet britches forgotten, looked past her nervous ears to the wide green expanse of palmetto prairie that fell between the hammock and the little lake they'd just left, east to the marsh and Lake Locknahatchee, south to the distant gray line of cypress.

Raymond tipped his hat to the ghosts who had haunted his dreams with their own. "Well, Lucas," he said softly. "Here it is. Walker's Island. Just like Ben promised." He spurred the bay mare forward to rejoin Dolly, and left the dead to follow on their own.

They knew within the hour the island was inhabited. Bare footprints marked the lake's edge, and north of the hammock was a little hut of palmetto fronds. But finding the owner was more difficult. It took them three days of hide-and-seek before they finally saw, early one morning, a thin, dark stick of a man standing next to a raft pulled up on the lakeshore. He was bent over, hitting something on the ground. Raymond couldn't tell whether he was using a stick or a hatchet, but the sound of blows carried well in that wide space.

"Is that Vancey?" Freemont asked.

"I can't tell," Dolly said. "Let's go ask him."

They had not ridden three yards out from the hammock, however, when the man glanced up and saw them. The next second he was running for the swamp. Hebron, Dolly, and Freemont fanned out toward the southwest end of the cypress, with the dog casting back and forth between them. Raymond headed down to the lake to see what the man had been doing. A huge soft-shelled turtle lay on its back by the water, the headless neck poking around in the mud as if searching for its lost member, while the tough, leathery legs stroked the air. The shell was hacked in two on one side. Raymond searched the ground for the tool or weapon that had made the cut, but whatever it was, the man must have taken it with him. He turned, and headed for the swamp.

Green gold light fell through a hundred feet of cypress limbs before it reached Raymond, revealing a dim path through bald brown knees and black water. Spider webs, still wet with the night's dew, broke against Raymond's stirrups, and water bugs with legs like oars raced across the water in front of him. Off to the west, the dog barked. Something moved in the bushes, and Raymond called out, his voice bouncing against the water.

"Vancey? Vancey, is that you?"

"I can't hear you," Vancey screamed. Water splashed ahead.

Raymond followed it. "Vancey, Dolly's with me. You can't get away."

Shrieking laughter, then, "I can get away. Oh, you bet I can." There was more laughter, and some mumbling, then, "I'm getting right now. You just see me get." There was a tremendous splash, followed by lesser ones. The dog barked again, closer this time, then there was dead silence. The mare picked her way daintily around a fallen cypress tree. Vancey was backed into a kind of dank, black cave formed by the dead roots, brought to bay by the dog. The dog didn't lunge as it would at a cow, but stood snarling and high-shouldered, as if threatening a stranger in its yard.

Vancey didn't look too good. He was skinny and covered with sores. His hair and beard were long and tangled, and dirty with grease and bits of leaves. But the muscles in his arms looked harder than lighter knots, and the green eyes above the flattened bridge of nose were alert. Raymond watched the hatchet in Vancey's right hand with caution. Hebron and Freemont rode up, and with them, Dolly. In one hand, he held a wrinkled brown envelope, in the other, the lead rope of the chestnut gelding, hard-used, scarred, and thin, but the same horse Vancey had ridden out of the clearing.

"You looking for this horse, Vancey?" Dolly said.

"Is it mine?" Vancey asked.

"I don't know," Dolly said. "Is it? I found it tied to a tree back yonder."

"It's mine, then," Vancey said. "Give it here. I need it. Right now. I got to go."

"What's your hurry?" Dolly asked.

Vancey narrowed his eyes with suspicion. "Who wants to know?" he asked.

"Me," Dolly said. "Dolly Baxter." He pointed at Raymond and Hebron. "Raymond Pennell. Hebron Wilkes."

Vancey looked disgusted. "A liar, that's what you are. Them men are dead. Saw it myself." His eyes hunted theirs, then darted off like rabbits, and his tongue kept sneaking out to touch the corners of his mouth, like a lizard's testing the air.

"You never saw us dead," Dolly said. "You left too soon. We came to find you."

"Not dead, huh?" Vancey rubbed his eyes hard with thumb and forefinger. When he quit rubbing, his eyes were red. "You came to find me? Here?"

"We been looking for you since the war ended," Dolly said.

"Is that right? How long is that?" Vancey asked.

"My goodness," Dolly said. "It was...Hebron, how long ago was the war?"

"One year, eleven months, and six days," Hebron said. "Exactly." Vancey scratched a sore on his neck, staring at Hebron as if he'd seen him before, but couldn't remember when or where. Then he frowned hard.

"Hebron? Hebron Wilkes?"

"Hello, Vancey."

"Damn, Hebron. I didn't expect to see you again." Vancey's eyes traveled over Raymond, then Dolly, then back to Raymond. "Raymond? That you?"

"It's me, Vancey."

The quick green eyes darted to Dolly. "Dolly?"

"Hello, Vancey."

Vancey scratched so hard at the sore he made it bleed. He pointed at Freemont. "Who's that? That Everett?"

"Naw," Hebron said. "That's Freemont Wilkes, my daddy's big brother."

Vancey laughed, a high, whinnying sound. "He don't look so big to me," he said.

Freemont grinned at him, then stuck his tongue through the gap in his teeth, and wiggled it at Vancey. Vancey stopped laughing.

"Where's Everett?" he asked. "He with you?"

"No," Dolly said. "He couldn't come."

The horses shifted beneath their riders, and the wind changed direction, coming now from the north.

Vancey shivered. "So y'all come for a visit, is that right? I got a cooter down by the lake. Plenty to eat. Got to finish cleaning it, though." He reached his hand out to Dolly. "I'll just take the horse with me. Save me coming back for him."

Dolly took a wrinkled brown envelope from his coat pocket, bent down, and offered it to Vancey, who took it. "What's this?" he asked.

"Open it," Dolly said.

Vancey pulled a sheet of paper out of the envelope and studied it with the defensive incomprehension of the illiterate. "I lost my glasses," he said. "You tell me what it says."

"It's a list of names," Dolly said. "Five of them. Everybody in our unit, except Raymond, Hebron, me and you. Me and Raymond and Hebron, now, we know why we ain't on there. What we don't know is why you ain't. That's what we come to find out. How come you ain't on that list, Vancey?"

Vancey frowned at the list, then folded it up and stuck it in his pants pocket. The envelope he threw to the ground. "I don't know," he said. "You tell me."

"It ain't on there because you ain't dead," Dolly said.

Vancey snorted. "Well, I could of told you that," he said. He rubbed the back of his neck with one hand.

"Well, now, Vancey," Dolly said patiently. "We know that much. What we don't know is why."

"Why what?" Vancey asked.

"Why you ain't dead," Hebron sang out, as shrill as a bird.

"I ain't dead," Vancey explained, "because I ain't in no way died as yet."

"Why didn't you die?" Raymond demanded. "What happened to you?"

"What do you mean, what happened to me?" Vancey asked. "Nothing happened to me." He sounded confused, but his eyes were bright and green, and didn't look confused at all.

"There were three of us laying up under that hickory tree," Raymond said, counting on his fingers, "and five more on the ground not going anywhere. That made eight. And you would have made nine, only you weren't there. You'd done sailed off over our heads on that chestnut horse, there. How come that Yank gave you a horse, Vancey? None of the rest of us got one."

"The three of you was under that tree?" Vancey asked.

"That's right," Dolly said.

"I'll be damned," Vancey said.

"I wouldn't be surprised," Freemont said.

Vancey ignored him. "Well, as to my leaving," he said. "I can explain that. To begin with, I was taken prisoner, in a manner of speaking."

"Uh, huh," Dolly said. He wrapped one leg around the saddle horn, settling down to listen. Hebron sighed, a deep breath that seemed to hang in the air. Raymond wrapped the reins around his saddle horn, and flexed his hand while he listened to Vancey.

"I'd gone out to see if I could scare up something to eat, you see," Vancey said. "A gopher or a 'possum. Hell, I'd have eat a skunk. Just anything. We were hungry. Remember how hungry we were?"

Dolly nodded his head. "You got that right, Vancey," he said. "We were some kind of hungry. Weren't we, boys?" Raymond and Hebron agreed.

"But it was your watch," Hebron said. "You were supposed to be watching."

"I know, I know," Vancey said. "But I had a deep down, hurting hunger that night. Deep down. And anyway, I was wearing them britches I'd took off that dead Yankee north of Perry. You remember that?"

"Yes," Raymond said. He flexed his toes, feeling again the dead man's boots on his feet.

"I thought you might," Vancey said. "So, anyway, there I was, slipping off from watch just for a minute or two, and wearing a Yankee uniform, and just as I'd decided it weren't no use, and I just as well head on back to camp, I walked slap into them."

"Into who?" Dolly asked, concerned and helpful.

"Them Yankees. A nest of 'em. Just walked right slap dab into the middle of them."

Dolly shook his head again. "Damn, Vancey," he said. "That must have been a bad surprise."

Vancey agreed wholeheartedly. "It was the worst kind of surprise," he said. "The worst kind. Anyways, they put their guns on me."

"They would," Raymond murmured.

Vancey nodded like his head was coming loose on his neck. "And the captain started walking around me, looking at me, and saying, "Well, looky here, we got us a Rebel spy."

'Spy,' I said. 'I ain't no spy. I'm a soldier, fair and square, and I'm surrendering. Yessir, I'm surrendering.'" Vancey banged the hatchet against the tree for emphasis.

"But that captain said, 'Rebel soldier? You ain't no Rebel soldier. They wear gray uniforms, and yours is blue. You're trying to pass for one of us. You're a spy. We hang spies.'

'You got to listen to me, Captain,' I said. 'I ain't no spy, and I ain't never had no gray uniform. They was all gone by the time I joined up. This ain't even my uniform. I took it off a dead man, and I didn't kill him, neither. He just up and died. What am I supposed to do, run around bare-assed? He didn't need 'em no more.'

"Only the captain wouldn't listen. He kept saying I was a spy, and he was going to hang me, and he said it when his men tied my hands behind my back, and when they threw the rope over the tree, and when they hoisted me up on a horse and drawed the rope tight, and I was going to die, I could see that clear, and the captain pulled his sword and drawed it back to hit the horse, and just before he laid it down, I said, 'I ain't no spy. They'll tell you so.'"

Vancey looked at Dolly, his eyes filling with tears. "Now why did I say that, I wonder? I can't figure why I said that. How was that going to work? We walk back into camp, and I shake y'all awake and say, 'Here, you fellers tell the captain here I ain't no spy. Go ahead, tell him, he won't listen to a word I say.' Soon as I'd said it, I knew I'd ought not to have. I'd of cut my own tongue out before I said it, if I'd known that's what I was going to say. But it was too late. That captain had already put his sword down and said, 'Who will tell me so?'

"And there it was. It was said already. So I told him the rest. That you were back there, and there was just eight of you, and not one horse, and no meat or coffee or beans or nothing, just growling bellies and tired minds. And he said, 'Take us to them,' and I said, 'Find 'em yourself,' and he raised his sword again and the horse flinched, and I messed my pants." Vancey was crying now. "I messed my pants like a baby, and I said, 'Please don't hit this horse,' and the captain said, quiet like, 'Take us to them,' so I said, 'All right.' And I did.

Vancey looked up at the men before him, his eyes big and shiny through the hair on his face. "I didn't know he was going to kill you," he said. "I thought he was going to take us all prisoner, give us something to eat. It was all over, anyhow, and we knew it. We'd known it a long time."

"How come he was expecting horses?" Raymond asked.

"What horses?" Vancey asked. "We didn't have none."

"He kept asking you about the horses," Raymond said. "I heard him. And after you left, he was looking around for supplies and loot and all such as that. How come? He should have known we didn't have anything."

Vancey had worried the sore on the back of his neck into a bloody wound. He swiped at the blood trickling down into his beard. "He thought we were raiders," he said.

"He thought what?" Hebron asked.

"Raiders. Like them that done that little girl thataway, the one we found on that farm, when the lieutenant was killed. The ones we was hiding from. That Yankee captain was looking for them raiders. I told him we was them."

Raymond wiped greasy sweat off his face, sick with understanding. "Why?" he whispered. "Why'd you tell him that?"

"'Cause he was going to kill me if I didn't," Vancey said. For the first time, he sounded completely lucid. "He wanted for us to be raiders, so I gave him what he wanted." Then he squinted like his head hurt. "I'm hungry," he said. "Can we go now?"

"What about the horse?" Dolly said. "It looked like he was holding the horse, to let you get on, then changed his mind."

"He said I could have it," Vancey said. "He got the raiders, I got the horse. That was the deal. Son-of-a-bitch tried to cheat me. Hope I broke his jaw."

"What about the rest of us?" Raymond asked. "What was the deal for us?"

"He said he'd arrest you, is all," Vancey said. "No killing. Nothing like that."

"But there was killing," Dolly said. "Those soldiers killed all those sleeping men. Five helpless men shot dead. Five. Billy was one of them. You remember Billy, don't you, Vancey?"

"I remember him," Vancey whispered. "He was a sweet boy, he sure was."

"Good," Dolly said. "I wouldn't want you to forget him. I want you to remember him for as long as you've got breath in your body, him and the others. Billy Baxter, Ben Monroe, Wallace Turner, Everett Asbell, and Lucas Walker. Say those names for me, Vancey."

"Billy Baxter, Ben Monroe, Wallace Turner, Everett Asbell, and Lucas Walker." Vancey giggled. "Lucas Walker. I call this place after him. Walker's Island. Crazy bastard." Then he sobered again, and touched his breast as though it pained him. "I ain't forgot any of them,. Dolly," he said somberly. He winked, and lowered his voice as if he didn't want anybody but Dolly to hear. "But I had to take care of myself," he said. "Same as you did, hiding under that tree. No shame in that, now was there? There weren't no call to come running out when the rest of them got it, was there? That would have been stupid, and none of us is stupid. Nossir, you and me, we're smart. That's why we're alive."

Vancey grinned at whatever he saw in Dolly's face, and started laughing. He laughed so hard he had to lean down to catch his breath, bent over, arms dangling, the hatchet resting on the ground beside his foot. "No, sir," he said, barely able to talk for laughing so hard. "No shame in that. But I'm sorry. So sorry, sorry, sorry." Vancey raised his head, his green eyes squinted with amusement, and Raymond knew he wasn't sorry at all. Then the hatchet was flying through the air to nail Dolly's hat to the tree behind him, and Vancey was running high-legged through the water.

"Uncle Free," Hebron said.

Freemont sighted down his rifle barrel after Vancey. "Dead?" he asked.

"Just down," Hebron said.

The rifle cracked and Vancey screamed. There was the sound of thrashing water. "Your boy won't go far," Freemont said. "He's only got one knee."

Dolly unstuck his hat from the tree and worked the hatchet out of the felt. "Ought to make him buy me a new one," he said. He put his hat on and shoved the hatchet in his saddlebag, then, weaving through the spider webs and cypress knees behind the water bugs, led the chestnut horse to Vancey.

Raymond had to hand it to the man. Traitor and murderer though he was, Vancey was pure grit once he knew it was over. He talked as they went back toward the lake, trussed up like a hog and tied across the back of the chestnut horse.

"That captain told me I could hang or go free," he said. "He said he was going to kill everybody else, but I had a choice. He said he'd even give me his horse. 'Hell,' I said, 'I'll be glad to ride.' The captain thought that was funny." Vancey chuckled. "You hear Everett yammering about them sticks? Right to the end, I'm telling you. Eh, law. And y'all right there under that ole hickory tree the whole time. Damn. Wish I'd known, I surely do. 'Check under that log for snakes, Cap,' I'd a' said. 'You got the little 'uns, now get the big 'uns.' I'm sorry about ole Ben, though. He was a good feller, was Ben. His wife's got her another man by now, I reckon. If anybody'd have her, with all them young 'uns. I offered to let her come here with me, but she wouldn't even give me the time of day. That's 'cause of this nose, here. Guess y'all are sorry about that now, huh? Tell Billy. Tell little piss-in-his-pants Billy Baxter how sorry you are."

With that, Dolly simply stopped. "Now," he said.

Hebron untied a coil of rope from his saddle. "You stay back, Uncle Free," he said. "It's just between us four from now on."

They led Vancey's horse to a massive cypress tree standing fifty feet beyond the edge of the swamp. Raymond untied the rope that bound Vancey to the gelding. Dolly helped set him upright in the saddle, and tied his hands behind his back. Hebron commenced tying a noose in one end of the rope.

Vancey kept right on talking through it all. "Listen here," he said. "I've had enough of this. My knee hurts. I'm hungry. It's all a mistake, anyhow. A man makes a mistake, no call to hang him for it. I was scared, is all. I wasn't even sure they was Union soldiers. Could have been them raiders, for all I knew, dressed up like Yankees, and all fired up to do me like they done that girl. Slip of the tongue, was all it was. This here ain't right."

"Shut your mouth, Vancey," Hebron said. "You sound like Lucas."

"Bastard," Vancey said. "Him and his shrieking. Worse'n a bag of cats. Drives me out of my mind, sometimes. And Everett, with them damn sticks and his snotty looks. I'll wipe 'em right off his face, one of these first days. Only one of the bunch worth saving is Ben. All the rest, hell, let the captain do what he's gonna do. Specially that littlest one. He's the ringleader. Looks young, but he ain't. Little and mean. He done the girl, Captain. She was just his size." Vancey's chin fell on his chest, and bumped up and down with laughter.

Raymond wished Hebron would hurry up. "You want any help with that knot, Hebron?" he asked.

"What are you asking for, Pennell?" Vancey demanded. "You ain't no kind of help to nobody."

"Shut your ugly mouth, Vancey," Dolly said.

"Well, he ain't," Vancey whined. "Always looking out for himself. He didn't help Billy, did he? Bet he held you back, didn't he? Bet you wanted to go to that little ole boy, but Ray here wouldn't let you. Ain't that right?" He leaned sideways as if to fall to the ground, and Raymond caught him in his arms. Their two horses shifted nervously, and Raymond's saddle lurched to one side. He held Vancey tight, the other man's greasy beard rubbing on his own, and struggled to keep his balance.

"Let him die, didn't you, Ray?" Vancey whispered. "That's all right. You were just looking out for yourself. It's what we do, Ray, you and me." He blew in Raymond's face. His breath was rotten. Raymond shoved him upright on the gelding and wiped his face where Vancey had touched him.

Vancey chortled.

"It's the stink of the grave, Raymond," he said. "Get used to it."

"Let's go, Hebron," Dolly said. "Or I'll have to shoot him." Hebron tied the other end of the rope to a low branch, then stepped back from the tree. It took him several tries, but he finally threw the noose over a higher branch. It came swinging down over the gelding. Dolly caught it, and put it around Vancey's neck.

"You ain't set it right, Dolly," Vancey said. "Help him out, Raymond. Set this knot right. I don't want to die slow. It ain't right. Nobody died slow back yonder." Raymond reached for the noose, and Dolly jerked it back.

"No call to make it easy for him," he said.

"I got better things to do than watch somebody strangle," Raymond said, and pulled the noose out of Dolly's hands. He turned it so the knot sat under Vancey's jaw, then tightened it.

Vancey peered at Raymond, his head cocked away from the knot like he had a crick in his neck. A bead of saliva glistened in the corner of his mouth. "I'm scared, boys," he said. "Tell me the story of Walker's Island."

Dolly took the cow whip off his saddle. "Let's get this done," he said.

Raymond backed the mare away from the gelding. Hebron rode up on the other side of Dolly.

"You'll be marked the same as me," Vancey screeched. "You do the same, you're owed the same." His wild green eyes jittered between Dolly and Raymond. "I ain't going to forget this!" he screamed. "You'll see. You can't bury me deep enough to keep me down! I'm coming back for you! I'm coming back!"

Dolly folded his whip in half and raised it high. Hebron did the same. Raymond waited.

"C'mon, Ray," Dolly said. "What are you waiting for?"

Raymond could barely hear him over Vancey's words ringing in his ears. He looked at Dolly. There was something in those blue eyes Raymond had never seen before, a look of calculation, almost of cunning. It flashed, and then was gone, and the Dolly he knew was there again, aggravated and impatient. Raymond took his whip off the saddle, doubled it, and raised it over his head.

"Now!" Dolly yelled. Together, the three men lashed their coiled whips across the gelding's rump. It squealed and jumped forward. There was a crack, and Vancey flailed on the end of the rope. Raymond had set the knot just right.

They buried Vancey beside the hanging tree. Water seeped into the hole as soon as they started digging. This bothered Raymond, though he could not have said why, and he insisted on wrapping the body in his poncho.

Hebron was not the least bit sympathetic. "I don't want to offend your tender sensibilities, Raymond," he said, "but durned if I can see what difference it makes. Vancey don't care if he gets wet. Hell, look at him. A little water might do him some good."

Raymond wrapped Vancey in the poncho anyway, and did not try to explain himself. Thinking about what he'd just done confused him, and he didn't like confusion. Billy and Ben and the others were now avenged, but Raymond couldn't say he felt any better about their deaths. He certainly felt nothing but revulsion about Vancey's. There hadn't been much of a man left in Vancey. It could be that what Raymond had done was closer to putting a sick dog out of its misery. In that case, a blanket to keep his bones dry might satisfy Vancey, might even give him some rest. It'd be a good thing if Vancey could rest. Just the thought of Vancey coming after him made Raymond's flesh crawl. He retreated from the doubts and fears assailing him, and made for the moral high ground. Any stick was good enough to beat the devil with. Vancey had been a bad man, but he had been a man. Honor and obligation had demanded justice, and justice had been served. They now demanded respect, which would be served, as well.

"I just don't like burying him in a mud hole like a dead hog," he said.

Freemont put his hands in his pockets and addressed the horizon over the lake. "It just seems a mite contradictory to kill a man, then wring your hands over how he's buried. That's all I'm saying about it."

Dolly grabbed the shovel from Hebron, stepped into the shallow grave, and stuck it in the ground. He dug hard, pulling up black muck. "Where's a good place to build a house around here, Ray?" he asked. "I like the south end of the hammock." He shoved the blade in again. "What do you think, Ray? Think the south end is a good place to build?"

Raymond heard Dolly's question with a shock of recognition, not because of the house, but because he now knew what they'd been wrestling about all this time. It was the island itself. He pretended to give Dolly's question some thought, though he already knew where he was going to build his house, up near the center of the island. The creek crossings would be hidden, but he'd have a sweeping, front porch view of both lakes, the marsh, and the hanging tree. He'd be able to keep an eye on Vancey."

"I'm partial to higher ground," he said. "I'd say the south end of the hammock is the second best spot."

"At least you've decided this is a good spot for Vancey," Freemont said. "That's what we needed to know right now. Hell, I've got a house already."

"I don't," Dolly said. "You want to dig a while, Ray?"

Raymond took the shovel and stepped into the hole. The mud at the bottom was already halfway up to his ankles. They wouldn't need a cistern, he thought, just a shallow well, twelve, maybe fifteen feet, if that. Now that he'd ridden through the hammock, he could see it all laid out in his mind's eye: the house with porches across the front and back, the well with a wash house nearby, Jessie's chicken pen, the smokehouse, the garden, the outhouse. The barn was south of the house, with a set of cow pens behind it. He'd put six stalls in at first, maybe go to eight later on, depending ...

"Raymond!"

Raymond looked up. Dolly was squatting at the edge of the grave, looking down at him. "What?"

"I said, how deep are you planning to go?"

"Dig it deep enough he can't scratch his way out," Hebron said. The words were joking, but his tone was anxious.

"Bury him face down," Freemont said. "Let him scratch his way to Hell."

Raymond assessed his progress. He measured six feet, three inches in his stocking feet, and the toe of Dolly's boot was at least two inches over his head, so Vancey's grave was just about six and a half feet deep. The water now covered Raymond's ankles. That'd bother him bad, if he were Vancey. Raymond hated being either cold or wet. Both at one time were sheer misery.

Dolly jumped in beside him, sloshing water everywhere. "This is good enough," he said. "Hand him down."

Hebron and Freemont handed the body to them, face up. Raymond took the shoulders, Dolly the feet. Raymond went to set the body on its back, and couldn't. Dolly had turned it the other way, so that Vancey's toes were pointing down.

"What are you doing," Raymond asked.

"Putting him on his face," Dolly said.

"What for?"

"So he can't get out." Dolly gave the body another twist.

Raymond held what he had. "We're putting him on his back," he said. "I don't want his face in the water."

"Why not?" Freemont asked.

Raymond looked up.

Freemont looked like a monkey hanging over the edge of the grave. "You afraid he'll drown or something?" he asked.

"It's a matter of respect," Raymond said. He looked at Dolly. "Put him on his back."

Dolly looked worried. "I'm thinking it's best if we put him on his face, Ray," he said. "Just in case."

"In case what?"

"I wish I knew."

"Well, I do know," Raymond said. "Vancey got what he had coming. It's over. Put him on his back." Raymond set his half of the body down in the water. Dolly stood there for a moment, still twisting the feet. Then he straightened them and put them down.

Raymond watched the water seep over the poncho. "Let's get out of here," he said. Straddling the body, he gave Dolly a leg up, then grabbed the hands that were offered to him and scrambled out of the grave. The four men took turns shoveling the dirt back in, then the other three looked at Raymond.

"What?" he asked.

"You're the one made all the fuss about the hole," Freemont said. "I reckon you should be the one to say something over the grave."

Raymond ignored the hypocrisy he felt, and took his hat off. The others removed theirs, too. Raymond bowed his head, closed his eyes, and took a deep breath. Then he began. "Lord," he said. "Vancey's ending was hard, and..." He paused, thinking. "And we're thankful we have naught to do with him from here on out."

"Vancey probably thanks you, too, Lord," Freemont said.

Raymond opened one eye and looked at him, but both of Freemont's were shut tight. Raymond bowed his head, and continued. "We've done right by Vancey according to our ways, Lord. We ask that you do right by him according to yours." He waited. No one spoke. He watched the grave. It did not move. "Amen," he said.

"Amen," the others echoed. They all put their hats back on.

"I'm glad that's settled," Freemont said. "Now let's make some cooter stew."

They finished cleaning the turtle by the lake, and cooked it at Vancey's camp, a lean-to made of cypress poles and cabbage fronds. Considering Vancey's personal appearance, it was surprisingly clean. Drying racks for curing furs were stacked behind the lean-to, along with ten steel traps thickly coated with rancid grease.

Freemont poked around in the lean-to, and came out with a pot to cook the turtle in. "Either of you boys a trapper?" he asked.

"Not unless Raymond's took that on since we parted last," Dolly said.

"Not me," Raymond said. "You wanting those traps?"

"I could put 'em to good use," Freemont said.

"All right by me," Dolly said. "How about you, Hebron? See anything you want? No point in letting things go to waste."

Hebron stirred the stew. "I'm partial to that chestnut horse," he said, and lifted the spoon to his mouth to taste the gravy.

"Hebron wants the captain's horse," Dolly said. "That all right with you, Raymond?"

"He's got as much right to it as anybody," Raymond said.

"That settles it, then," Dolly said. "The horse is yours, Mr. Wilkes."

Night was falling around them, but Raymond could still see the island in his mind's eye. He followed the line of the creek, trailing it from the hammock to the point it emptied into the cypress. He planned to cut the poles for the barn from that point around to the lake. Grass for grazing cattle would grow in the trees' stead. Then sparks flew up in front of him, interrupting his reverie. Freemont was pulling the pot off the fire. He lifted the lid. The odor of stewed turtle rose in a rich steam. Raymond's mouth watered.

Hebron reached into the pot with his coffee cup, and scooped out a helping. "This sure smells good, Uncle Free," he said. "It sets me to wondering."

"What about, nephew?" Freemont asked.

"About Dolly and Ray," Hebron said. "I've got the horse and you've got the traps. What do you reckon they want?"

"I don't know," Freemont said. "What do they want?"

Dolly poked down in the stew with his pocketknife and speared a piece of meat. "Well, now," he said. "That's a tricky question." He stuck the meat in his mouth, working it around with his tongue while it cooled. "Because if my suspicions are correct, Raymond and I want the same thing."

"We do?" Raymond asked.

"Uh, huh," Dolly said.

"I didn't know that," Raymond said.

"You're a bad liar," Dolly said. "I've always liked that about you. Tell me, Ray. Where do you plan on building your house?" Raymond cut his eyes over at Dolly. The cobalt blue eyes were looking right back at him, friendly, open, and honest.

Raymond smiled. "I already told you," he said. "I like that spot back up under the hammock, there in the middle, facing the lake."

"That's a good spot," Dolly said. "However, by the time you get back here with your wife and son, I'll have a house built there already. Mine."

"Maybe I'll build one before I leave," Raymond said.

"It might burn down while you're gone," Dolly said in a philosophical tone. "Never can tell about these things."

"Hebron, what the hell are they talking about?" Freemont complained.

Hebron laughed. "This here island," he said. "Each of 'em wants the whole thing for himself."

"You think they might kill each other over it?" Freemont asked, his expression hopeful.

"Naw," Hebron said. "Not them two. They got to settle it some way, though."

Freemont swallowed his disappointment, and set himself to thinking. "Y'all could draw cards," he suggested.

"No," Raymond said. "Too much luck involved."

"Arm wrestling," Hebron said.

Freemont compared Raymond's arm to Dolly's and laughed out loud. "May as well give it to Dolly right now," he said. "How about a shooting match?"

"Dolly wouldn't stand a chance," Raymond said.

"A horse race," Dolly said. The others looked at him. He shrugged.

Raymond rolled the idea around in his mind, looking for a problem. He didn't see one.

Hebron sucked a tooth. "That'll work," he said. "Begin on this side of the creek, there where we crossed the other day, go around the hammock on the far side, come back at the south end. First one over the creek wins."

It was a good idea. The more Raymond thought about it, the better he liked it. "That'll do," he said. "What about it, Dolly?"

"Winner takes everything between the marsh and the creek," Dolly said. "Loser takes what's left." He extended his hand. Raymond shook it. The bet was sealed.

They rode to the creek as soon as the sun was up.

"Try not to splash when you cross," Hebron said. "I don't want to get wet. Y'all get ready."

Dolly leaned forward a little and his horse pricked its ears back and forth, restless with his tension. The bay mare was skittish between Raymond's knees, and he felt cold with more than just the thought of the water in front of him. Hebron lifted his pistol in the air, and fired. The mare half-reared, jittering away from the creek bank on her back legs, and came back down just as Dolly's horse slid over the edge, sand churning beneath its hooves. Raymond jabbed the mare with his spurs, and she grunted and lunged into the creek, sending a white sheet of water into the air and eliciting a string of curses from Hebron. She came up the other side a length behind Dolly's horse, but her nose was even with its shoulder as they rounded the corner. By that time, both horses knew it was a race.

Their course was two narrow interweaving game trails that went along the edge of the hammock. The trails sometimes intersected, and other times swung out from one another on their way through the palmettos and cabbage palms that lay between the hammock and a prairie that went much further on the west side of the creek than it did on the east, that moved toward higher, drier ground instead of marsh, and culminated in a ridge of pine scrub dotted with prickly pear and brambles, the loser's portion.

Raymond spurred the bay mare harder. Her breath came hard and loud, as did his, through the swish of the great green fronds and the pounding of hooves on the sandy loam of the hammock's edge, but always, Dolly stayed just a little bit ahead of him, sometimes by a quarter length, sometimes by a neck, while everything inside of Raymond reached out for the island. The mare stretched her neck out, ears flat against her head, and still she could not catch up with Dolly's horse. She stumbled, and Raymond could feel the effort it took for her to regain her stride. He regretted having accepted the gift of her, and suspected Dolly of sabotaging him in just this way, of bringing him a horse that in the end would not have heart enough to win.

Palm fronds whipped him in the face, quail rattled up out of the underbrush like shot, and still the mare stayed just behind Dolly's horse and a little to one side, until they made the sweep around the south end of the hammock. There on the other side of the creek was Freemont's manic form, waving and shouting them on, his shrill voice punctuating the sand-deadened drum of the mare's hooves, the bellows of her lungs, and the dull beat of blood and desire in Raymond's ears.

He came into the final stretch a half-length behind Dolly. Before he could close the gap, Dolly was riding over the edge of the creek, his horse sliding down the bank on its haunches. Then Raymond could see the edge of the bank for himself. He leaned over the mare's shoulders and asked her to jump the creek, though to fail would mean her death and Raymond's, too, and maybe Dolly's as well. As if in answer to his desire, the mare gathered herself, rose, and leaped for the far bank. Raymond looked down at Dolly's face beneath him. The cobalt blue eyes were almost black with disappointment, and a hand raised in salute to one willing to risk everything he loved - life, limb, wife, child, friend - to win his heart's desire. And then the blue eyes were gone, and there was nothing left but wind and sun until the far bank rose to meet him, and the horse beneath him scrabbled at sand and roots, haunches quivering, shoving, lunging to level ground, as Raymond rode the bay mare home to Walker's Island.

Part II

January 1867 - September 1877

Cat Lake

Chapter Ten

Raymond dug the holes for the pilings of his house with a pair of post hole diggers and a shovel. He stood in the last of those black holes - nine feet deep and twice the width of his shoulders - and wondered if the strong-smelling water at the bottom, that turned the skin of his feet dead white inside his boots, had first washed over Vancey's bones, and if so, whether it could taint the foundations of the house with the bitterness of his end. A bucket with a rope tied to the handle sat on the ground between his feet, half-full of dirt. Raymond jerked on the rope and Dolly's head appeared at the edge of the hole.

"Do you think Vancey's grave is leaking into these holes?" Raymond asked.

Dolly frowned. "I can't leave you alone for a second," he said. "Come on out of there."

The other end of the rope was tied to a nearby tree. Raymond held onto the bucket end and crab-walked up the side of the hole, while Dolly pulled from the top. When Raymond's hand came over the rim, each gripped the other's arm above the elbow and pulled. Then Raymond was out, shaky with exertion and something else he couldn't name.

"I was just wondering," he said. "It smells funny down there."

"Probably something you ate," Dolly said. "Let's get this in the ground." He picked up one end of a twelve-foot cypress piling, and the two men walked it upright. Wrapping their arms around it, they picked it up, straddled the hole, and dropped the wide end into the black depths. They took turns leveling the piling while the other tamped the sand in hard around its base with a cypress pole. Finally, the hole was filled, and the piling straight and immovable in the solid earth. Dolly stepped back and looked at it.

"Think it'll hold?" he asked.

"Yep," Raymond said. He pushed on it one more time, just to make sure. It didn't budge. The piling would stay right where he'd put it. "I believe it will."

Afterwards, the pilings set like ribs on the high ground of the hammock, Raymond ripped lumber from cypresses and pines that were old before the Spanish came to Florida, and laid the rough hewn boards across two sawhorses to shape and plane them for walls and ceilings and floors. He hammered the finished boards together with pegs whittled from scrap lumber by the light of fires fed on the rejected branches, and bit by bit, fashioned a house from the substance of the island.

Raymond completed the first room in August of '67. He made Jessie close her eyes while he escorted her up the back steps and into her new kitchen. He closed the door behind her then walked her across the kitchen floor to her front door, where he'd placed her rocking chair. He sat her down in the rocking chair, put a bowl in her lap, set a basket of unshelled peas by her side, and opened the door, swinging it out wide on its leather hinges.

"You can look now," he said.

Jessie held the bowl with both hands and didn't speak. Raymond thought happiness, like a cat, had got her tongue. He stood beside her and gazed out on the land before him. A red-tail hawk swooped across the clearing then fled, pursued by a mockingbird. A cow lowed in the distance. The saw palmettos fell away to the lakes and the marsh, and far beyond them all, the earth met a brilliant blue sky. Dolly was hunting cows on the west side of the Locknahatchee and wouldn't be back until dark. Beau was asleep in the lean-to. In all the world, there was only himself and this woman. Raymond knew how Adam must have felt when the world was new.

"There it is, Jessie," he said. "Walker's Island, viewed from your own front door. How does it look?"

"Empty," Jessie said. Then she stood up, turned the chair around so it faced the back door, sat down, and started shelling peas.

Jessie would never, perhaps, come to care for the island, but by the end of the day, she was in love with that room. Raymond's hands had known every inch of it. From the first piling to the last peg, it was his creation. But he may as well have been living in a boarding house for all the say he had in it once it was finished. Jessie came behind him with her brooms and rags as though to erase the very memory of his touch. He made furniture for her - a kitchen table and four chairs, shelves for the walls, a little corner cupboard - and set every one of them down right where she asked him to. Then she moved them all around again as soon as he left, changing everything so much from day to day that it was worth a man's life to get up in the night to take a piss. For the first time since they'd left Debussy, Jessie sang. Raymond didn't know how much that one little room meant to her, in fact, until the day he told her she'd have to leave it to go with him to Punta Rassa.

"No," she said.

Raymond was sinking a row of pegs across the outside back wall, at Jessie's request. He stopped in the middle of one and looked at her. "What do you mean, no?" he asked.

"I want those pegs all the way across," Jessie said.

"I know that," Raymond said. "I just stopped so I could talk to you."

"You can talk and hammer at the same time."

Raymond hit the peg again and drove it into the wall. "You have to go," he said. "It'll take a month, at least, maybe two. That's too long for you to stay here by yourself."

"I'm used to it," Jessie said. "Just leave me the shotgun and some shells like you usually do. I'll be fine."

"I don't have that many shells, Jessie," Raymond said. Exasperation spoiled his aim and he hit his thumb. "Dammit, woman." He looked at his thumb. A blood blister was already rising. He showed it to Jessie. "Look what you did."

"Don't you be cussing me," she said. "That wasn't my fault."

"It was, too," Raymond said. "How come you got to argue over every little bitty thing in the world? How come you can't just do like somebody wants you to, just once in a while? How come?"

"Because what you want generally makes no sense," Jessie said. "I told you I'd be happy if you built me a house, so you built me a house, and now I'm happy, or as happy as I'm likely to be here in this godforsaken wilderness. That makes sense. Then you come along and want me to leave the very thing that's making me happy. That doesn't make sense, and I'm not going."

"But you like towns and people and all such as that," Raymond said. "And that's where we're going."

"I don't know anybody there, so what good will it do me?"

"I don't know," Raymond said. "But you're going. I'm not leaving you here."

"No, I'm not going," Jessie said. "And you can't make me."

"You hide and watch," Raymond muttered.

"What did you say?"

"I said that's the last peg," Raymond said. "Now, you got anything else you want me to do today?"

"Not right now," Jessie said. "Thank you very much for your help."

"Well, you're sure welcome," Raymond said. "I'd appreciate a little help in return, if you know what I mean."

"How about dinner?" Jessie asked. "It's already cooking."

"It's a start," Raymond said. "But it sure ain't a finish. You can bet this here kitchen on that."

Nothing more was said about Jessie going to Punta Rassa, and she made no preparations whatsoever. Raymond, on the other hand, set about getting ready like a man possessed. The first thing he and Dolly did was catch one of the wild horses that frequented the marsh, and hitch it to the mule. The two animals could graze and drink, but neither one of them could escape the other or cause any real damage. The worst they could do was buck in a clumsy, spastic sort of way, and kick whatever was standing behind them. Raymond watched them for a while - the old mule with its white face and long yellow teeth and the wild horse with its shaggy, dun-colored coat and long, tangled mane - and nodded approvingly.

"I think we've got ourselves a team," he said to Dolly. "What do you think?"

Dolly jerked his head at the house. "If could figure a way to hitch Jessie between 'em, we could leave for Punta Rassa."

"She don't need anything like that," Raymond said. "She's a lot more tractable than that pair."

"I hadn't noticed," Dolly said.

"Well, I'll just show you," Raymond said. He went in the house through the back door. Jessie was making biscuits to put in the Dutch oven for baking. "I'd like a cook stove from Ft. Myers," she said.

"Good idea," Raymond said. "You can pick it out yourself."

"And I want some needles, too, and some gingham."

"All you can carry."

Jessie looked him square in the eye. "I'm not going," she said.

Raymond looked her just as squarely right back. "Oh, yes you are." He opened the back door. Dolly was standing on the ground looking up at him.

"How'd it go?" he asked.

"It ain't over yet," Raymond said.

That night, after supper, Raymond carried Jessie's pots, pans, and dishes out to the wagon, leaving only enough behind to cook and eat breakfast. Jessie, meanwhile, just sat in her rocking chair and sewed on one of Beau's shirts, like she couldn't see what her husband was doing. Next, he took her dresses and undergarments out of the cedar chest, and whatever shawls and bonnets were hanging on the wall, and put them in a carpetbag. By the time he was finished, there was nothing left in the room but the sleeping pallets and Jessie's nightgown. Raymond carried the carpetbag out to the wagon, then came back in the kitchen.

"I didn't know what you'd need so I packed it all," he said.

"I'm not going," Jessie said.

"Put your sewing away and come to bed," Raymond said. "We've got to get an early start."

Jessie got up the next morning at the usual time, and fixed the usual breakfast of venison, gravy, and biscuits. When everyone had finished eating, she washed the dishes and put them on a shelf. Then she sat down in her rocking chair, got Beau's shirt out of her sewing basket, and resumed her mending. Raymond went outside and helped Dolly hitch the team and saddle the horses. Then he came back in the house, packed up the clean dishes, got Jessie's nightgown off its peg, folded it up, put it in the skillet, sat the dishes on top of the nightgown, and carried it all out to the wagon. When he came back in, he stopped in front of the rocker, pushed his hat back on his head, and rolled up his sleeves like a man preparing for a fight.

"Your turn," he said.

"I'm not going," Jessie said.

"Yes by God you are," Raymond said. He took the sewing out of her hands and put it in the basket, then put the basket in her lap. "Now get up and go get in the wagon."

"No."

"Fine." Raymond took his hat off and put it on top of the sewing basket, then squatted down and picked Jessie up, rocker, basket, and all. He carried them down the front steps to the wagon, and set the chair down as close to the bench as possible, then tied it down with rope. When he finished, he offered the lines to Jessie. She looked off in the distance.

"You better drive this team," Raymond said. Jessie folded her arms across her chest. Raymond clenched his jaw and tied the lines to the bench, leaving plenty of slack. Then he got on his horse. "Let's go," he said.

"What about him?" Dolly asked, and pointed at the house. Beau was standing in the open doorway, holding the frame with one small hand. He didn't smile or cry, just watched his father with somber gray eyes.

"Damn," Raymond said. "I forgot about him." He got down off his horse and picked Beau up, took a step, stopped, took another step, stopped.

"What's the matter?" Dolly asked.

"I don't know what to do with him," Raymond said. "It's not safe in that wagon."

Dolly took the rolled poncho off the back of his saddle and tied it across the cantle. Raymond handed Beau up, and Dolly sat him down on the poncho.

Beau smiled.

Raymond felt a rising frustration. "We can't haul him around like that for the whole trip," he said. "We've got cattle to work."

"It's just for now," Dolly said. "Best we take care of that over yonder before we worry about aught else."

Raymond pondered the wagon and its contents for a moment, then nodded in agreement. "Good point," he said. He led the team and wagon out to the front yard, and pointed it north. "You're going that way, Jessie. Over the north crossing, then south again, around Black Hammock, and along the west side of the river. We're going across the marsh and around the east side of the big lake. We'll meet you at the first crossing on the river."

Jessie didn't answer.

"You can change your mind, if you want. Pick up those lines. Take Beau with you. Drive the team. It sure would make things easier."

Jessie didn't say a word.

Raymond sighed. "All right, woman. We'll do it the hard way." He took his hat off and slapped the dun horse in the rear. "Hyah!" he yelled. "Giddup!"

The dun horse tried to move off, but the mule only stuttered forward a few steps, then stopped. Dolly rode up behind them, unwinding the whip from his saddle. He flung it out behind him then brought it forward. The popper raised a little puff of dust right over the base of the mule's tail when it cracked. The mule took off, dragging the horse with it. When the horse caught up, it dragged the mule. The two of them went off through the palmettos that way, bucking and farting, the wagon lurching behind them. The palmettos crashed and the axles screamed. Jessie grabbed both arms of the rocker, but didn't utter a sound. Not one that Raymond could hear, anyway.

"I hope she makes it to the crossing," Dolly said.

Raymond grunted.

Beau pummeled Dolly's horse with his fists. "Giddup!" he demanded. "Go!"

Dolly gathered up the reins. "This trip could take a while," he said.

"So be it," Raymond said. Then he got on his horse, and headed with Dolly and Beau to the marsh.

It took five weeks to the day for that sunburned, fly-bitten, travel-weary crew of two men, two dogs, a woman, and a boy to deliver their 157 head of scrub steers to the docks at Punta Rassa. They arrived the following night in Ft. Myers with eighteen hundred dollars in Spanish gold in a leather bag under Jessie's feet.

They got to the hotel too tired to do anything but eat and go to bed. The next morning, though, Raymond, Beau, and Dolly left early in the morning to eat breakfast, then look at some mules.

Left completely alone for the first time in three years, Jessie enjoyed pleasures she'd only dreamed of. She stayed in bed until she got tired of it, then took a bath in water nobody else had used, before stepping into one of the dresses, wrinkled but clean, that Raymond had packed back at the island, and that she'd saved the whole trip for such an occasion. Then she went down to the lobby and out the front door to the street with nothing in the world to do but enjoy herself. She almost didn't know where to start.

It was warm and busy outside, the sunlight on the sidewalk patterned by storefronts, the sound of wind and birds drowned in the clamor of wheels and boots, whistles and bullwhips. Jessie walked up one side of the street and down the other, ate breakfast in a small cafe, then stepped into a general store two blocks from the hotel. She marveled at all the merchandise, touching it with fingertips acutely sensitive to texture and shape. Entranced by shawls and bonnets and pretty dresses, she took a long time to answer the man who had walked up beside her.

"Excuse me, madam," he said. "Madam?"

Jessie stroked a paisley shawl, wincing when her fingers caught on its fine threads.

"Madam," the man said. His voice was loud and nasal, and seemed to Jessie to have a quality of disapproval about it. She jerked her hand away from the shawl like a guilty child and tried to compose herself.

"Are you talking to me?" she asked.

"Yes, I am," the man said. He was small and slender and neat, and smelled like jasmine. "I said, it's a hot day, isn't it?" He'd tucked his hands into the pocket of a spotless white apron, and seemed to expect a special answer from Jessie. She tried to oblige.

"I hadn't noticed," she said.

"Well, I have," he said. "I'm from New York City. It's cooler there this time of year."

"Well, I swan," Jessie said. "You're a far piece from home."

The man smiled as if she amused him. "You must be from around here."

Jessie looked around 'here.' There were dresses and nail barrels, notions and hammers, washtubs and hip tubs, and a row of derby hats down one wall. Through the windows at the front of the store, she could see people passing by. Long ago, she'd come from a place much like it, a place with all kinds of people - women and children and men, folks busy about their lives, alone and together - and a place to eat - like the one she'd eaten breakfast in, only cleaner, with better food - and a store full of things that people could use - like boot buttons and logging chains and fly swatters, though it had never had anything so fine as a paisley shawl - where people got drunk and loved and fought and sang on Saturday nights, then sang again on Sunday mornings when they were almost sober, while the preacher courted their souls with threats and promises and exhortations, and readied them for Monday morning, when life together began anew, and nobody had to be alone if they didn't want to be. But she didn't come from a place like that now. Not anymore.

"I'm from Walker's Island," she said.

"Never heard of it," the clerk said. "Whereabouts is it?" He patted his face with a white handkerchief held in the cleanest hands Jessie had ever seen.

She looked at her own hands - calloused, rough, the fingertips dark with dirt-stained whorls and lines - and clasped them together. The island was just about everywhere, she guessed: in the skin of her hands, in her dreams and nightmares, in the distance between her and this stranger. Her father had said once that a man was known by his enemies. Well, Jessie reckoned a woman was known the same way. She was known by Walker's Island, defined by its loneliness and bound by its isolation, as wild and shy as any creature there. She would open her mouth one day and out would come, not words, but screeches and trills and clacks and bellows, the language of the island.

"It's north of here a'ways," she said.

"Like New York City," the clerk said. He laughed, tickled with his own humor.

Jessie smiled back, not sure what the joke was. "That's right," she said. Feeling safer, she dared to touch the paisley shawl again. The fringe on it was a foot long. Jessie had never seen anything so fine.

"Do you like it?" the clerk asked.

"I surely do," she said.

"Try it on," he said. He pulled the shawl off its hanger and held it out. "Turn around. I'll help you."

Flustered and wooden, Jessie turned around and let him drape the shawl around her shoulders. She lifted the fringe, softer than dandelion down, to her face, and drew it across her cheek.

"What brings you to Ft. Myers?" the clerk asked.

Jessie dropped the fringe, undone by the question. Raymond Pennell had brought her there, hauled like a sack of onions behind an unevenly yoked team while her only child - a miniature version of his father - sat beside her and complained because he had no horse to ride and was not allowed to drive cattle of questionable ownership along an unmarked road through hell that ended, by some miracle, in Ft. Myers, which she found as strange and wonderful as the Debussy of her childhood, and which she had to leave tomorrow, thanks, once again, to the aforementioned Raymond Pennell.

"My husband brought me," she said.

"Good for him," the clerk said. "I bet he's been selling cattle in Punta Rassa. Well, he's got money to burn now. Make him buy you this shawl. You'll be the envy of all the other ladies back home."

Jessie pulled the shawl closer as the clerk extolled the virtues of its workmanship. There were no ladies back home, she wanted to say, but had there been, she'd have wanted their friendship, not their envy. Jessie could see them very clearly. They were just like her mother - small and bossy and full of unsolicited advice - or like Glory Cooper, with her wide lap and big face, gentle, frumpy, and kind - or else they were a combination of the two, like Mrs. Addison. They sat with her across kitchen tables and quilting frames, sharing their wisdom and strength, making light of hard work and hard times. Jessie could see those women clearly, as through a window, and then they were gone, and there was no one left but the chatty, sweet-smelling man beside her. Silk rippled down Jessie's arm in a rivulet of crimson, blue, and gold as she pulled the shawl off her shoulders and handed it back to the clerk, interrupting what she had not heard.

"There's no call for such as this where I live," she said, and realized as she spoke that she was tired of talking. She was getting to be like Raymond. A few more months in his company, and all she'd be able to do was grunt.

The clerk chatted on about the profitability of cattle as Jessie bought and paid for three packets of needles, two pairs of factory-made cotton drawers, and a cook stove. He referred again to the weather in New York City as he followed her to the front of the store, and exclaimed over the heat outside as he opened the door for her upon the crowded sidewalk, where his voice and the noise of the street were drowned by the bell over the door, which tinkled like island bird song as she left.

Chapter Eleven

The Pennells returned to Walker's Island laden with the evidence of new wealth: a fine pair of mules, a new wagon, Jessie's cook stove, and bundles and boxes of tools, hardware, house goods, and foodstuffs. There were even four windowpanes, wrapped up with burlap and string and set carefully on their sides between two bolts of cloth. The one room of their house was packed so tight there was scarcely room to move, and Jessie was full of plans for expansion, beginning with the installation of the stove. Raymond was deep into that chore a week after their homecoming when Dolly came by, hands in his pockets and a grin on his face, to give Jessie what he called a surprise.

Jessie lifted the broom like a shield when Dolly made his announcement, then set it to the floor and gave it a push as though to sweep him off the back steps. "I don't have time for your foolishness," she said. "I've got cleaning to do, and Raymond's busy, too."

"He'll stop for this," Dolly said. He squeezed around her into the room, and picked his way around the lengths of stovepipe to Raymond's side. Raymond nodded to him but kept on working, aware of Jessie's displeasure. It was his eagerness to set work aside for more entertaining pursuits that she was sure would make of Dolly Baxter a poor man and a needy neighbor. Raymond didn't worry about that eventuality, but had noticed disinclination on Dolly's part to start a job, or to stay with one once he had. Jessie called him a grasshopper.

Dolly grinned at Raymond now with the delight of a child. "Hey, Ray," he said. "Come on outside for a minute. I've got something to show you."

Raymond set the hammer down and followed Dolly to the front door and down the steps to the yard, Beau hard on their heels. Jessie came last, clearly irritated but too curious to remain inside. She stood in the doorway and looked off toward the lake.

"I don't see anything," she said.

"That's because you don't know where to look," Dolly said. He walked around to the edge of the house and pointed off to the northwest, squinting against the afternoon sun. "See that?"

"Why don't you just go ahead and tell us what it is so we can have some peace," Jessie said. "There's things still to do around here today."

"It's the smoke from a campfire," Dolly said.

Jessie caught the broom handle to her breast. "Where?" she asked. Then she ran down the steps and across the yard to stand beside Raymond. A thin gray wisp rose over Dry Hammock, six miles away. "Who is it?"

"It's a man and his wife and two boys," Dolly said. "I met them yesterday evening. They intend to settle hereabouts."

"Neighbors!" Jessie said. "Raymond, we've got neighbors!" The two men exchanged a rueful glance that she chose to ignore. Dolly was Raymond's neighbor, not hers. She patted her hair and straightened her apron, nearly beside herself with anticipation. "I'll have to take them a little something tomorrow," she said. "A house-warming gift. Molasses cookies, baked in the new stove."

"A bar of that lye soap like you gave me might stand 'em in better stead," Dolly said. "Specially them young 'uns."

"What are them young 'uns' names?" Beau asked.

Dolly took a brick of chewing tobacco out of his pocket, cut a sliver off, and handed it to Beau. "Uglier and Ugliest," he said.

"Well, that's nice," Jessie snapped. "Makes me wonder what you call Beau behind our backs."

"Just plain Ugly," Dolly said. He cut a chew off for himself, and stuck the rest in his back pocket. Then he tucked the plug in his cheek, and winked at Beau. Beau put his sliver in his cheek, and winked back.

Dolly hooked his thumbs in his overalls. Beau hooked his thumbs in his overalls. Dolly spit. Beau spit. Jessie wanted to smack them both.

"Did you happen to get their real names?" she asked.

"I don't know about the boys," Dolly said. "But the man's name is Rainey. Tate Rainey. His wife's name is Red."

"Red?" Jessie asked. "Are you sure they said 'Red'?"

"I'm sure," Dolly said.

"Peculiar name for a woman," Raymond said.

"Might be because of her hair," Dolly said. "It's sort of reddish colored."

It was the hot, brilliant red of a pitch pine fire, shot through with gleaming copper lights and piled on top of her head in a heap of curls and tendrils and waves that were barely contained by three large tortoiseshell combs. Its weight seemed to bear down on the woman beneath it, who supported herself with an elbow on a rough cypress table, head in hand. Unnoticed, Jessie picked her way past a ragged canvas tent, skirting a campfire littered with tin cans and broken glass, and watching in consternation as the woman drank from a brown jug in her other hand. Two little boys sat on the tabletop, legs dangling over the edge, and scratched the sores on one bare foot with the dirty toenails on the other.

"Why don't you two get out of here?" the woman said. "There must be some other sick animal you can torment, besides me."

"I'm hungry, Mam," one of the boys whined.

Jessie, ashamed for bringing cookies when this family needed so much more, accidentally kicked a can in her path. One of the children looked up, its expression unpleasantly feral. He had thin arms and legs and a round, too-big belly. That one would be Ugliest, Jessie thought. The child poked his brother, who swung his head in her direction. She'd gotten it wrong. No one could be uglier than the child who now looked at her.

His hazel eyes were pink-rimmed, his skin the color of rawhide – yellow and gray and brown all at once - and like his brother, his belly was too big for the rest of him. But the worst part was his teeth. They were broken and dark, and his tongue flicked over them with the restless intensity of a 'coon fingering little black snails along the lakeshore.

"Mam," he said. "Looky behind you."

"Look behind yourself, Bob," the woman said. "There's a stink following you around."

Jessie cleared her throat. "Pardon me," she said.

The woman slowly turned, revealing a tarnished silver candlestick with five arms coming out from it, a candleholder at the end of each arm. In each holder, a two-inch stump of candle burned. There was a raised pattern of some sort on the base. Wax had dripped down the candles and arms, and built castles on the table. Jessie didn't where to stare first: at the five-armed candlestick with its bright-burning candles, or at the woman herself.

She had skin the color of new milk and blue eyes so pale they were almost white. She wore a man's pants and a white cotton shirt open at the neck. The cloth of the shirt was thin, and Jessie could see the woman's naked body beneath it, with its high, round breasts and slender waist. Even sitting down, she looked tall. And that hair, that blazing, impossible hair, escaping like tongues of flame from the combs. Jessie had never seen such a woman, beautiful and strange and terribly wrong, somehow, freakishly wrong, and not just because of the pale, pale blue of her eyes.

"What the hell are you gaping at?" the woman demanded. Her voice was husky, low, and surly.

Jessie's face grew hot. "I am not gaping," she said.

"Another goddamn liar," the woman said. "World's full of them." She pointed to the other side of the table. "There's a chair over there."

"I don't think..." Jessie began.

"Sit down," the woman said.

Jessie edged past the children to the chair. It lurched when she sat in it, almost flinging her to the ground. No one seemed to notice.

"You're late," the woman said. "That feller yesterday said you'd be along first thing this morning."

"I couldn't get here any sooner," Jessie said. "I was making cookies."

The woman took another swallow from the jug, her pale eyes fixed on Jessie. "What's you're name?"

"Jessie Pennell," Jessie said. "My husband's name is Raymond."

"I don't care what his name is," the woman said. She took another drink from the jug. "I'm Red."

Jessie held the basket up. "The cookies..."

The woman held her hand up and turned her head away.

"She don't like 'em," the ugliest child said. "But me and my brother do." He reached for the basket. Jessie folded the napkin back, and the rich odor of molasses mingled with others less pleasant. A drop of saliva gleamed on the boy's lip, and his tongue flicked out to catch it. He grabbed a cookie out of the basket and stuffed it in his mouth, chewing and swallowing with a desperation Jessie had not seen since the war. She gave one to the other boy - she couldn't help thinking of him as Uglier - who scootched down the table away from his brother to eat, watching Jessie through a thin hank of blond hair as he chewed. Ugliest reached for the basket, and Jessie looked to Red for permission to give it to him.

"Hell, I don't care," she said. "Feed 'em all you want to. It keeps 'em quiet. That one closest to you is Bob. You got to watch him. He'll snatch the food right out of Clyde's mouth. Little bastard."

Jessie gave Bob another cookie. "How old are they?" she asked.

"Five, come April," Red said. "Should have drowned them when they were born. Too late now, I guess." She took another drink from the jug. "You don't live far from here." It was a statement, not a question.

"About six miles," Jessie said.

"We're neighbors," Red said.

"Yes," Jessie said. Her excitement was gone. All she felt now was dull amazement. "Neighbors."

"Bet that pleases you no end," Red said.

Jessie opened her mouth.

"I hate a liar," Red said.

Jessie closed her mouth.

Red grunted, then spit on her thumb and rubbed the tarnished silver in front of her. When the silence grew overlong, Jessie tried to fill it.

"That's a beautiful candlestick," she said. "I've never seen one like it before."

"It's a candelabra," Red said. "Belongs to my grandmother up in Tallahassee. She thinks I stole it, but I didn't. Just borrowed it, when I ran off with Tate." She snorted. "Five candles to light my way to this. Ha. Blow 'em out. I've seen all I can stand." She huffed at the candles. The candles burned on. Red took another drink, and offered the jug to Jessie.

"No, thank you," Jessie said.

"It's good," Red said. "Made it myself. Whiskey and horses. Two things in the world I know something about." She caught and held Jessie's eyes with her own. "I guess I'm not what you expected."

"Not exactly," Jessie said.

Red turned loose of the jug, and rested her head in both hands.

"Red...," Jessie began.

"I hate that name," Red said. "Call me Clemency. Clemency Margaret O'Donahey Rainey."

"Clemency...," Jessie said

"Clemency!" Red cried. "Ha!" She leaned across the table, breasts taut against the weave of her shirt, and glared at Jessie. A chill December breeze licked the flames of her hair around the slender column of her white neck. Her voice fell to a rough whisper. "Do you know what 'clemency' means?"

Jessie shook her head.

"It means 'mercy,'" Red growled. "Mercy. Ha." She swung her arm wide around her, encompassing the littered campsite, the ragged tent, the rough cypress table with the blackened candelabra in the center, and the two ill-favored children perched on the edge. "Does this look merciful to you?" she yelled. "Does it?"

"No," Jessie said. "No, it doesn't."

But Red didn't hear her. Borne down to the table as if by grief and the weight of her hair, she was crying, her sobs mingled with mumbled words Jessie couldn't understand, but which sounded like curses and prayers together. She looked at the boys and raised her eyebrows in mute question. Bob pointed at his mother with a molasses cookie.

"She does that there sometimes," he said. "You know what she's saying?"

"No," Jessie said.

The child looked glum. "Us neither," he said. "Don't none of us like it. We want her to stop."

Jessie wanted her to stop, too. She stood up and walked around the table to the weeping woman and laid her hand on her shoulder. "Clemency," she said. "Clemency. Please."

"Her name's Red."

Jessie looked up, startled. A man stood at the end of the table. He was almost as tall as Raymond, and slender, with long, tense hands. He wore a spotless white shirt with a patch on the pocket seam and carried a black duster over one shoulder. He had just bathed, for his hair was wet and combed back in waves, and his face was freshly shaven, a trace of soap still on his jaw. He must have had a beard very recently, Jessie thought, because his chin and cheeks were startling white against the tan on his nose and around his eyes. He smelled clean. Not flowery like the clerk in Ft. Myers, but sharp, like liniment. He was the handsomest man Jessie had ever seen, except for his eyes. They were lifeless. The hair rose on the back of Jessie's neck and her mouth opened of its own accord, spilling excuses and explanations.

"I'm your neighbor, Jessie Pennell," she said. "I came to visit. Your wife was expecting me. And I brought some cookies." She picked up the cookie basket. It was empty. "The boys ate them all. They were hungry."

The man said nothing. Jessie glanced at the woman lying across the table. Her neck was eggshell white beneath the small loose curls at the nape, and fragile-looking. "I can help get her to bed, if you need me to," she said. "Or cook supper for the boys." She looked around the filthy campsite. "Or clean."

"We don't need your help," Tate said. His voice was very soft. For no reason that she could have named, Jessie's stomach soured with fear.

"I best be going then," she said. The man just looked at her. Jessie untied the mule, climbed onto the seat, and gathered the lines. She pulled hard, and the mule backed away from the table, then turned and headed for home, one slow step at a time. She looked back once. The man was watching her. She didn't look back again.

Chapter Twelve

The Raineys did in that one meeting what Raymond had failed to accomplish in a year, which was turn Walker's Island into Jessie's sanctuary. Like the raiders at the end of the war, Tate and Red had embraced passions Jessie would not permit herself even to imagine. The consequent despair and cruelty backed her into the first moral corner of her adult life. Compassion struggled with revulsion, and surrendered in the name of decency. Jessie retreated to the island, vowing never to set foot on Rainey property again.

So the Raineys came to the island, instead. Once or twice a month Red rode one of her green broke colts from her place to Jessie's, the twins - as tough and stringy and mean as cur dogs - trotting on foot behind her, but well out of kicking range of the horse. She wore men's trousers and a slouch hat and carried a medicine bottle full of whiskey in her hip pocket, and never wiped her feet when she came in the house. Jessie went around behind her with a broom and a dishrag, while Red sat at the table, drinking and telling stories. She talked about everything - the privileged life she'd led before her elopement, the fights she'd had with Tate, her hatred of children - as though the twins were not squatting in the corner, crouched over a plate of food and listening to every word she said.

When she wasn't visiting, drinking, or recovering from a drunk, Red worked with Tate to catch, break, and train wild horses. Raymond and Dolly soon became customers, thereby providing the only excuse Tate ever used to visit Walker's Island. He'd come into the house at Raymond's invitation - never Jessie's - but stonily refuse even a glass of water. While Red drank whiskey and the boys ate, Tate devoured the Pennells' possessions with his eyes: the house itself, always in some stage of construction; the completed kitchen with its glass-paned windows; the starched and ironed curtains; the bright rag rugs; the well-crafted table and chairs; the stove; the back porch; the big garden; the smokehouse full of meat. After every visit, so Red confided to Dolly, Tate would go back to his own house and try to duplicate something he'd seen on the island, and when it failed or fell short, would drink himself into a cold fury and beat his wife and children.

In June of '68, another family moved into the area. The Gibbses were farmers, and while not so fraught with drama as the Raineys, were still trying in their own way. Able was morose, sour, and opinionated, the kind of man who Raymond said gave Yankees a bad name. Myrtle was afflicted with delicate sensibilities - her words - and easily flustered by references, however carefully phrased, to such things as bodily functions, animal appetites, and childbirth. Lila was their only child. She was an awkward, unattractive girl, and so shy as to be almost invisible. Given her profound distaste for the earthier aspects of womanhood, then, Myrtle was a poor choice for a midwife. But when Jessie discovered she was pregnant in the fall of that same year, she all but begged Myrtle's assistance at the birth. Myrtle, who knew that Jessie's only other option was Red Rainey, agreed.

The first pain woke Jessie long before dawn in mid-July. It ran down between her legs from deep inside, a long, sharp knife that stabbed once and then was gone. She got out of bed and dressed, then woke Raymond, who made the fire in the stove, milked the cow, and went down to the barn to saddle his horse. Jessie prepared and served breakfast in a state of deep preoccupation, standing by the stove with her hand on the small of her back while Beau gulped his food and ran outside, and Raymond ate biscuits and sausage gravy as though Jessie had nothing more pressing to do than wait on him. He was still chewing the last bite when Jessie relieved him of his coffee cup, handed him his hat, and shooed him to the back porch steps where he'd left his horse. Beau was sitting in the saddle with a determined look on his face.

"Where do you think you're going?" Raymond asked.

"With you," Beau said.

"I don't recall inviting you," Raymond said.

"Well, I'm going," Beau said. "Dolly said I could."

"He did, huh?" Raymond said. "Well, we wouldn't want to argue with Dolly." He untied the reins, and stepped off the porch into the saddle behind Beau. "Tell your mama goodbye." Beau raised one hand in solemn farewell, but didn't speak.

"Don't dawdle," Jessie said.

"We'll be back before you know it," Raymond said. He reined the horse around, and headed down the path to Dolly's house.

Jessie watched them leave without the slightest misgiving. The plan was for Raymond to go get Dolly, who would go get Myrtle Gibbs, while Raymond came back to the house and waited with Jessie for Myrtle to get there. It was a simple plan, and easy to carry out. Not even Dolly could mess it up. Jessie put her hand on her belly. It was as hard as wood. She turned to go back inside the house and another pain came, a stunning cut that took her breath away and then subsided, more slowly this time, a leisurely departure that was more threat than relief. When it was gone, Jessie went inside and started dusting, picking up, moving things from one place to another, counting the minutes like a Catholic counting beads.

The dogs started barking when Raymond and Beau crossed Deep Creek to Dolly's homestead, and Dolly came out in the yard to meet them.

"It's time, Dolly," Beau yelled.

"I'm ready," Dolly said. He walked with them to the barn, where he saddled a horse and pulled himself up on its back. "Go home and put the coffee on, Ray. I'll be right back."

"No, you won't, either," Raymond said. "It's a good fifteen miles to the Gibbs's."

"Then I better go to Red's," Dolly said. He winked at Beau, and lowered his voice to a conspiratorial growl. "She's probably had more experience, anyhow."

Beau nodded in agreement, but Raymond just laughed. "You do that, Baxter," he said dryly. "Jessie'll love you for it."

By the time Raymond and Beau got back to the house, Jessie was pacing the floor.

"Dolly's gone to Mizz Rainey's," Beau said.

Jessie, whose back ached so bad she wanted to scream. She flung her head up and glared at Raymond. "He better not have," she said.

Raymond grinned. “Naw,” he said. “That was a joke. He’s gone for Myrtle.”

Beau looked stubborn. “He said he was going to Red’s,” he said.

“Come with me, Beau,” Raymond said, and took him outside to feed the chickens.

But Jessie didn’t even hear the door close behind them. Her body was her whole world. Knees buckled almost to a squat, legs spread, hips softening, bones and joints pulled apart, the channel running past her bowels widened until water poured down her legs and spread across the floor. When Raymond came back in, she was sitting straddle-legged in a chair, her skirt pulled up around her waist, her hands gripping her thighs.

“Dolly better hurry,” she said. Raymond got her into the bedroom and helped her up on the bed.

“Raymond,” she said. “Do something.”

“Whatever you need, Jess,” he said.

But everything he did was wrong. Jessie didn’t want to be touched, didn’t want a damp cloth on her head, didn’t want him to stay, didn’t want him to leave. Suddenly, all she could feel was her dress; it was crawling over her skin like ants. She screamed again at Raymond, whose face was too close to hers, so concerned and anxious and helpless it made him look stupid.

“What do you want me to do?” he asked.

“Get this dress off me,” she yelled.

“You mean, so you’re naked?” Raymond asked.

“Get it off,” she hissed.

Raymond worked her out of the dress, then rummaged around in the bureau until he found her nightgown. “Here, honey,” he said, and tried to stuff her arm down a sleeve.

“Get away from me,” she shrieked.

“But you got no clothes on, Jessie,” he said.

“I don’t care. Leave me alone. Do something.” But all he could do was look helplessly at her, like a big dog.

“Where’s Myrtle?” Jessie screamed.

“She’ll be here any time, Jess,” he said. “There, she’s right there at the door.”

But it was only Beau, eyes huge in his white face, come to stare his mother’s naked, big-bellied form twisting on the bed, her knees bent and spread. He hunkered down with his hands over his ears every time she screamed.

“It’s coming!” Jessie yelled. “I think it’s coming. Is it coming?”

Raymond bobbed down between her thighs to report. The baby's butt was appearing, he said, but then kept disappearing. Jessie groaned and the butt appeared again. Raymond got a tweezer's grip on one of the tiny cheeks, his fingers trembling as hard as her legs.

"Hang on, Jessie," he said. "I think I've got it."

Then something hit him so hard he almost fell. He caught hold of Jessie's knee and turned around. Red Rainy was looking him dead in the eye - all six feet of her. He stared back, transfixed by the sight of the flaming red hair and peculiar eyes, like those of a glass-eyed dog. The stink of whiskey was rank on her breath. Rumor had it she fought Tate like a man - with fists and feet - and won more often than she lost. Raymond didn't doubt it for a second.

"You better leave that thing alone, boy," she said. "You've caused enough trouble already, playing around with it."

Raymond flushed as hot as Red's hair, and he opened his mouth to protest.

"Just get the hell out of here," Red said. She jerked her thumb back over her shoulder at Beau. "And take Pie Eyes over there with you. He's already seen more than he knows what to do with."

She shoved Raymond out of the room with a hand between his shoulder blades. He grabbed Beau on the way out, and the door slammed behind them.

Raymond was there one minute and gone the next, replaced by the lunatic face of Red Rainey. Jessie took one look and screamed with all her might.

"Oh God! Oh God! Oh God!"

"What good do you think he'll do you?' Red replied. Her strong fingers probed between Jessie's legs.

"Don't touch me," Jessie shrieked.

"Hush your noise," Red said. "The baby's breech." She bent down and came back up with the sheet Jessie had thrown to the floor.

"Don't put that thing on me," Jessie yelled. "I don't want anything on me."

There was the sound of tearing cloth then Red was bending over the bed, trying white strips to the headboard and wrapping the ends around Jessie's hands.

Jessie groaned. "No, please, not winding sheets."

"Not yet," Red said. "Hold these. Like this. Quit your squalling and listen. When I tell you to push, then you push for all you're worth.

No hollering, and no letting up. But not until I tell you." She disappeared, and came back with a stoppered jar and a straight razor. She snapped open the razor, then uncorked the bottle and poured its contents over the razor. The sharp, strong odor of corn whiskey burned Jessie's nose.

"This is going to sting," Red said.

Jessie felt something cold, then a sting like a sawgrass cut. Her bowels moved and her buttocks pressed into the mattress as she pushed with all her strength.

"I told you to wait," Red yelled. "You're tearing."

But Jessie didn't care because the baby was coming out in a quick, slick rush, and then it was done and she could lay still.

Red held the baby upside down, oblivious to its thin cries. "It's a boy," she said. "Nothing I can do about that."

"I like boys," Jessie said.

"Good for you," Red said. "I'll be back in a minute."

The bedroom door slammed shut, and Jessie was alone. The bedroom smelled like a still. Jessie wanted her baby, and wondered where Red had gone with it, and what she'd done with the razor.

Thrown like a trespasser out of his own bedroom, Raymond stumbled to the kitchen where a mud-spattered Dolly was drinking whiskey straight from the jug. Raymond followed the dark print of his boots across Jessie's spotless floor and sat down at the table. "I thought you were going for Myrtle Gibbs," he said.

"Uh, uh," Dolly said. "She don't like me. 'Sides, Red told me one time she's done this before. She's even got a little kit she carries with her."

"A kit?" Raymond asked.

"Yep," Dolly said. "A birthing kit. She keeps it in the kitchen, ready to go."

"I never heard of a birthing kit," Raymond said.

"Me neither," Dolly said. "But I reckon somebody that's got one must know what she's doing."

"Can't argue with that," Raymond said. He nodded at the jug. "Where'd you get the whiskey?"

Dolly shoved the jug across the table to him. "Red brung it with her. Have a pull."

Raymond hooked his right forefinger through the handle on the neck and lifted the jug, its weight resting on his elbow, to his mouth. He took a long drink, then set it down and closed his watery eyes. He didn't dare try to talk, for fear he'd blow fire out his mouth. After a moment, he wiped his eyes and blinked them open. His voice was hoarse when he spoke. "Lord have mercy, that's fine. Did she mind coming with you?"

Dolly shook his head. "Naw," he said. "They don't come any finer than Red. She just talks rough. Anyhow, she's too drunk right now to mind much of anything."

"What about Tate?"

"He was passed out when I got there. I reckon the boys'll tell him when he wakes up."

Jessie screamed, then screamed again.

"I hope her and that baby are all right," Raymond said. He took another drink. Another scream issued from the bedroom, followed by a weak, quavery cry. It was joined by a third wail in the kitchen.

"What in the world?" Dolly asked.

Beau was howling, his face, wet with tears, turned imploringly toward the ceiling. Dolly's deep blue eyes grew large, perfectly round and slightly protuberant. He jerked his thumb toward the hallway. "You might ought to put one of them back," he said. "Both of them together make too much noise."

Raymond squinted at his friend through the whiskey in his head and gave the matter some serious thought. Red appeared in the doorway. She was holding the new baby by the feet. It dangled upside down in her hand, shaking with screams. It was the reddest baby Raymond had ever seen.

"It's a boy," Red said. She had to yell to make herself heard over the crying. "Could be your wife wanted a girl. I know I wanted me one. Got them two boys, instead. Sorry little bastards."

Raymond took another pull at the jug. "We just wanted a live one, is all," he said. "One that works."

Red held the baby up higher and squinted at it. "Well, this one's alive, all right, and liable to stay that way. The poorly ones don't generally make such a racket. I don't know if it'll work, though. Too early to tell."

Jessie called from the bedroom. "Raymond? Is the baby all right?"

"Durned if I know," Raymond yelled back.

Red held the baby out to Raymond. "Here," she said. "You hold it while I tend to her in there."

"What's wrong with her?" Raymond asked.

"She tore pretty bad," Red said.

"Tore what?" Raymond asked.

"What do you think?" Red demanded.

Raymond cut his eyes over at Dolly and winced.

Dolly looked pained. "Damn," he said. "I'm sorry to hear that." He took another drink from the jug, then jerked his chin at Red. "You best take hold of that baby, Ray. She's fixing to fling it at you."

Raymond belched fumes out of his mouth and stood up, pinwheels of brightly colored lights spinning behind his eyes. He lifted the baby out of Red's hand and turned him upright, which quieted him some. Holding the baby in one hand and Beau's shoulder in the other, he followed Red to the bedroom door. She wouldn't let him in."

"I got to sew that hole up in there," she said.

Raymond clutched her arm. "There's supposed to be a hole there," he said

"Not like that one," Red said. "Looks like the swinging doors to a saloon. You stay in the kitchen and take care of them boys." She shook Raymond's hand off and slammed the door in his face.

Jessie watched warily as Red approached the bed. The red hair was a roiling mass around her head, except where sweat had stuck it, like thin lines of blood, to the sides of her face.

"I guess you know you're slap naked," Red said.

"I couldn't stand anything touching me," Jessie said. "I can put a nightgown on now."

"Later," Red said. "We've got some things to do first. Where are the sheets?"

"In that trunk over there," Jessie said. Seconds later, a coarse cotton sheet fell on Jessie's skin, bearing the odors of hammock and sun in its folds. Jessie felt tears welling up from deep inside. "Where's my baby?" she asked.

"In the kitchen," Red said.

Jessie closed her eyes. Something hit the bed beside her and she opened them again. A dirty carpetbag was sitting next to her leg and Red - flask in one hand, razor in the other - was watching her. Jessie closed her eyes again, tight this time, and waited to die.

"What's the matter with you?" Red asked.

Unable to speak, Jessie shook her head. Tears oozed from the corners of her eyes and trickled down the sides of her face into her ears.

"Quit your sniveling," Red said. "What color thread do you want?"

Jessie opened her eyes. "What?" she asked.

"I said what color thread do you want?" Red held up a little leather pouch for Jessie to see. "I've got purple, red, green, blue, and pink. No white." She took a swig from the flask and eyed the area between Jessie's legs. Jessie put her knees together. Red pulled up a chair, and spread them apart again. "Since you can't make up your mind, we'll use purple. It's my favorite." She threaded a needle and squinted at Jessie's bottom. "Hold still, now. You might feel this."

Jessie did indeed feel it. She shuddered every time the needle went in, and got chill bumps when the thread dragged through her flesh. "Do you really have to do that?" she snapped once, jerking away.

"You'll thank me later," Red said. "Otherwise, ole Raymond will be sticking in and flopping right back out again."

"Never," Jessie said loyally.

"Hah," Red said, and kept sewing. After a while, she went digging in the bag again, and pulled out a stoppered glass bottle that she held up for Jessie's inspection. The liquid inside was deep purple. "Tincture of violet. If it'll heal saddle sores, it'll heal this here."

"Where's the baby?" Jessie asked again.

"I told you, it's in the kitchen," Red said. "What are you thinking? That I cut its throat?" She put the bottle back in the carpetbag and picked up Jessie's nightgown off the floor.

Jessie watched her but said nothing.

Red snorted. "I saved his goddamn life," she said. "And yours, too. You think Myrtle Gibbs could have done that?"

"I don't know," Jessie said.

"Well, I do," Red said. "Ole Sour Puss wouldn't have had the first idea what to do." Red helped Jessie into the nightgown, her touch firm and sure. When she spoke again, the rough, raw plea in her voice struck Jessie like a blow. "So, who're you going to send Ole Baldy for the next time you need a midwife? Me or Myrtle Gibbs?"

Jessie looked at Red – she of the fiery, disordered hair and pale blue eyes, who stank of whiskey and held a straight razor and hated liars - and gave her what she said she wanted: the truth. "Myrtle Gibbs," she said.

Red flinched. "Fine," she said. "But if you ever need any help, any kind of help, you call me, and I'll come."

"I won't need your help," Jessie said.

Red nodded. Her chin went up and her expression hardened. "Fine," she said again. Then she picked up the carpetbag and walked to the door.

Shut out of the bedroom again, Raymond had gone back to the kitchen where Beau continued to cry, a loud, monotonous "wah, wah, wah," that grated on Raymond's nerves.

"Beau," he said, and stopped. He wanted to say something deep to his son, something about life and fatherhood and community and maybe even God, something the boy would remember forever. He waited for a minute, but nothing specific came to mind. "Beau," he said again. "Son. You got to quit that." Beau choked back his tears. Raymond felt for a chair with the back of his legs."

"Looky there, Beau," Dolly said. "Your little brother was born naked. Shame on him. Feel of his butt, see if it's cold."

Raymond felt the baby's backside. It was softer than the finest buckskin and cool to the touch. "Grab me a dishtowel, Beau," he said. Beau did as he was told, then climbed up on Raymond's lap, his breath still shuddering with sobs. Raymond wrapped the baby in the towel and tucked it in the crook of his arm, anxious because its face was all screwed up like it was fixing to sound off again. Raymond didn't think he could stand that. He closed his eyes. What everybody needed around here, he thought, was a nap.

"Hey, Pennell," Red bellowed. "Bring the baby here."

Raymond sighed. "You got to get down, Beau," he said.

"C'mere, buddy," Dolly said. Beau slid to the floor and went to him without a word of protest. Raymond went on to the bedroom with the baby. Red stood in the open doorway. She wiped a strand of that fiery hair out of her eyes, and jerked a thumb back at the bed. Jessie was sunk in the mattress, her face the same pale shade of ivory as the cotton sheet.

"Show it to her," Red said. "She thinks I killed it."

Raymond walked past her and laid the baby in Jessie's arms. She pulled the dishtowel away to look him over.

"Is he all right?" she asked.

"Far as I can tell," Raymond said. "He cries good."

"He's right enough for now," Red said, her voice rough. "Give him something to eat and go to sleep."

"You look like you could use some sleep yourself," Raymond said. "We can put you up here for the night."

"I'm leaving," Red said.

"I sure appreciate your coming," Raymond said. "Don't know what we'd have done without you. Come again, real soon." Red snorted and walked out. Raymond turned to Jessie. "What's wrong with her?" he asked.

"Nothing," Jessie said. She put the baby to her breast and laid her finger in its tiny palm. The minute fingers closed around hers. She smiled up at Raymond. "I want to call him Jack."

"After who?" Raymond asked. He had wanted to call the baby Jasper after his own father.

"After himself," Jessie said. "Where's Beau?"

"Dolly's got him," Raymond said. Jessie grimaced, and pulled the sheet up over the baby, hiding him from view.

"This one's mine," she said, and closed her eyes.

The next thing Raymond knew, his wife was snoring, the small lump over her breast rising and falling with each breath.

Chapter Thirteen

Three months after Jack's birth, the Dempsey family settled on the southwest side of Cat Lake, some four miles from Raymond and Jessie's house. The Dempseys were followed by John and Lucinda Ellis in February of '70. Thereafter, family followed family until there were almost fifty homesteads within a thirty-mile radius of Walker's Island. Most of these folks were too far away to visit regularly, had Jessie been inclined that way. But she felt no need. Carefully at first, and then with endless satisfaction, she entered into friendship with the Dempseys and Ellises.

The Dempseys were Jessie's favorites. Even Raymond liked them. Dolly did, too, but he liked Red Rainey, as well, and Jessie took no account of his opinion. George Dempsey was as tall as Raymond and as wide as Dolly, a big, slow-talking, slow-moving man with a gravelly voice and a deep, rumbling laugh. His wife Ann was thin but strong-boned, with a good-humored, easy-going manner. She reminded Jessie of Glory Cooper, except she was prettier. The Dempseys had five sons, two of them - Seth and Jacob - close to Beau's age. George made it clear from the outset that he was in serious competition for cattle. That didn't bother Raymond any. He just got up sooner, rode further, worked harder, and branded more cattle than George or Dolly either one. And every year, he took one half of his profits from the sale of the cattle and rode to Gainesville with it, where he took title of as many acres of Walker's Island as it would buy. Dolly and George poked fun at Raymond for putting so much money into property when open range was available to them all. Homesteading, they said, was all a man needed to do. Raymond just smiled, and kept on buying land.

Meanwhile, John Ellis was buying up land on the west shore of Cat Lake. He'd sold his hardware business in Delaware for a large profit, and come south to open another store. But when he reached Florida, with its hundreds of square miles of cheap land, he decided he'd been thinking too small. He proposed, instead, to build an entire town and name it after himself. By the time Jessie and Raymond got to know him, he'd already platted six sections and was advertising lots in newspapers up north. Raymond found Ellis's endless energy and nonstop conversation wearing, but Jessie admired him no end, and his wife, Lucinda, too, who was even shorter than her husband but just as round and equally shrewd.

Hours spent quilting with Ann and Lucinda were pure heaven for Jessie, and the best of all were those when Myrtle Gibbs was absent. No one even suggested that they invite Red Rainey. Stories about the Raineys were fast becoming the stuff of local legend. Jessie, who was not a gossip, did not add hers to the mix until 1871, when she got pregnant again and desired to impress on her friends the depth of her antipathy towards Red. It was Ann Dempsey, an experienced midwife, who attended Jessie when her last two children were born. The births, Bekah's late in '71 and Jonelle's in '73, were blessedly unremarkable. Raymond's girls, as Jessie called them, were strong, healthy, pretty, and of sound mind, qualities which she attributed as much to Ann's character as to her skill. Jessie was convinced that, had Ann Dempsey been present in July of '69, Jack would not be the way he was.

Because Jack was different. It wasn't his odor, which was grassy and sweet like cured hay, or his hair, which was fine and thin and floated on his head like dandelion silk. It wasn't even his peckish appetite or small, skinny, fragile-looking frame. The problem, at least in the beginning, was Jack's speech. He made odd sounds. Jack trilled, hooted, squeaked, and twittered. He hiccupped, snorted, sneezed, coughed, and popped his lips like a feeding bream. He twitched, too, tapping and fluttering fingers as thin as chicken bones. And he watched things as he tweeted and twitched - bugs and dust motes, sunlight reflecting off a pot, Jessie's hands on the biscuit dough - with an absorption that went beyond concentration.

The boy just wasn't right, and Jessie, good Christian woman though she was, had a hard time forgiving the persons she held responsible. It was her opinion that Raymond had been criminally careless with the wellbeing of his own child. Red Rainey - whom Jessie always referred to as Clemency - was a drunken, violent woman, a danger to herself and others. And as for that rascal across the creek, well, Raymond would do well to show Mr. Dolly Baxter his back, as Jessie had done with Clemency. They were kindred spirits, those two: pitiable, irresponsible, wayward souls who brought nothing but trouble on their neighbors. Jessie had a damaged child to prove it.

Jack said his first word when he was almost three. Riding Jessie's hip as she walked through the garden, he touched her face with his hand and said, "Moon."

"Mama," Jessie answered, correcting him even as her heart turned over in her chest.

"Moon," Jack said again.

"Oh, Jack, I'm not moon. I'm Mama. Please say Mama." Jessie hugged her boy close, rocking him back and forth between two cornrows to stifle a grief she had not known she carried, that now threatened to overwhelm her. "Dear God," she said. "Make him say Mama."

"Moon," Jack said again.

"Oh, Jacky," Jessie said. She whirled around to run to the house with her poor child. There, hanging in the morning sky, was a pale new moon. Jessie stopped as if she'd run into a wall. "The moon!" she cried. She held Jack away from her, looked closely at him, then pointed to the sky. "Moon," she said.

Jack nodded his head. "Moon," he replied. Then he put his head on her shoulder, and went to sleep.

From that day on, words tumbled out of Jack's mouth like prison escapees. He stopped making odd noises and named things, instead, saying phrases like, 'fork 'n knife,' 'over yonder,' and 'heah, dog, heah,' over and over again with various emphases, pitches, and tones. He started singing when he was four, and could repeat a hymn after one hearing, the words and tune exactly as he'd heard them, in a voice so high and pure it gave Jessie the shivers. Even Raymond had to allow that Jack's voice was special. But it would break and deepen as he grew older, he added, and the sooner the better, since maybe then the boy would leave off warbling and learn to work.

Work was a problem for Jack. The least little chore found him sidetracked by a tune or a rhythm halfway through its completion. Forgotten chicken eggs rotted in the nest boxes; rats gnawed a bridle dropped on the tack room floor; hogs got in through an unlatched garden gate and rooted up three rows of sweet potatoes; Beau stepped on a hatchet left on the ground by the kindling pile and cut his foot. If a task could be done poorly or not at all, that's how Jack did it. Time and again, he would begin his chores only to wander off again, or worse yet, stop right where he was and start singing.

Jessie coaxed and gently scolded him. Raymond yelled at him, beat him with a belt, and sent him to bed without his supper. Beau knocked him down, picked him up, shoved him around, and set him straight, over and over again. None of it did any good. Raymond finally gave up, convinced that Jack, like Jessie's father, was soft in the heart and weak in the head. Beau assumed an air of martyrdom, and Dolly marveled and joked. But Jessie only loved Jack all the more, and covered for his mistakes whenever and wherever she could.

Which didn't leave her much time for Beau. Fortunately, he didn't seem to care. He'd been running away from his mother since he could walk, charging after Raymond and Dolly as they went to work, livid with rage at being left behind. She'd chased him down and brought him back, time after time. After Jack was born, however, she became an accessory to his escape.

Beau had taken Nathan Winters' ill-tempered old mule on as a challenge while Jessie was pregnant, naming him Balaam and teaching him to bray back when Beau hee-hawed at him. The two of them made so much commotion that Jessie went down to the barn one morning and threw a bucket of water on them both. By then, Balaam had formed a belligerent attachment to Beau that consisted primarily of sudden nudges and slobbery, loose-lipped attentions to his hair. Beau was nearly five when he started going fishing by himself, and one day, when Balaam tried to follow him, decided he would rather ride than walk.

Jessie, worn out with nursing Jack and chasing Beau, held Balaam's halter while her firstborn climbed up on his back. When she let go, the mule bucked Beau off. The three of them repeated this process several times, until Beau told her he could do it alone. She watched the two of them ride away, Balaam periodically bucking Beau off, Beau climbing back on, until they disappeared down the path to Deep Creek. It was almost suppertime when the two of them returned, Beau holding a stringer full of bass and mastery of the mule.

There was no stopping him after that. He rode the island with complete freedom, privy to a solitude all his own, and so hard put, sometimes, to express himself that he was almost mute, as though the same sorrow, curiosity, and joy that filled Jack's head with music had no other outlet in Beau than his moody gray eyes and taut, explosive temper, and the peculiar affinity he shared with horses. With them, his awkwardness and melancholy disappeared, and his face relaxed until it was almost peaceful. Even then, perhaps particularly then, he was too much like Raymond for Jessie's comfort. She felt sorry for Beau's wife, whoever she might be, and hoped she wouldn't break herself against that wall of privacy before she learned to let it be.

For his part, Beau had never wanted a brother and regarded the arrival of one with a lackluster eye. He did not remember the details of Jack's birth, but that which followed stayed with him for years. To begin with, he wasn't allowed to hardly touch the baby. His hands were always too dirty or too clumsy. And he was in the way. His mother shooed him off with the same distracted irritation she showed to houseflies, and the doors she'd closed prior to Jack's birth she now opened wide, sending Beau on his way with a whack on the seat of the very same pants she'd clutched mere weeks before. For the first time in his life, Beau was left to his own resources: a cranky, silver-muzzled mule and a head full of stories at whose heart lay the legend of Walker's Island.

He knew the stories as if he'd been in them, his elders' memories weaving so intricately through his that their histories had become his own, remembered in the kitchen through long, rain-washed winter days, and the fire lit hours of the night. He could describe sweet-natured Billy Baxter, and mimic Lucas Walker's scream, and tell Ben Monroe's stories of the island. He could recount details of cattle drives made thirty years before, and argue the location of skirmishes during the war. He knew the names and habits of long dead cowhunters and soldiers, and those of their horses and dogs. He comforted his mother as she wept over her own, and heard the raiders riding through his dreams. But Beau's favorite story of all was the hanging of Vancey Adams, and he could hardly wait for Jack to grow up so he could tell him all about it. He didn't know how much of it his little brother would understand - Dolly had already explained to him that Jack was feeble-minded - but Beau was determined to share the information with him anyway.

Jack was four-years-old and Beau seven before their mother would allow the two of them to travel freely together, and the first thing Beau did was lead his small follower to the hanging tree. He pulled the frog fruit and dollar weed from around the roots, baring the ground beneath them.

"You see that spot?" he asked.

Jack nodded.

"Don't ever touch it."

Jack promptly put his hand on it, his thin fingers kneading the dirt.

"There's a dead man buried under there," Beau said.

Jack snatched his hand away and wiped it on his britches. "Where'd he come from?" he asked.

"Daddy and Dolly put him there," Beau said.

"Whose is he?" Jack asked.

"Ours," Beau said. "Daddy and Dolly both hanged him, but he's buried here on Walker's Island. That makes him ours."

"What did they hang him on?"

Beau pointed to the branch above them. "That there. He deserved it, though. He'd done wrong."

Jack took a deep breath that swelled his belly out beyond his skinny ribs, then let it go. "What'd he do wrong?" he asked.

Beau patted the ground beside the grave. "Sit down here," he said. "I'll tell you all about it." He proceeded to tell Jack everything he knew about Vancey Adams, and finished on the satisfactory note of the hanging. Jack looked unhappy.

"What're you looking so peaked about?" Beau demanded. "He got what he had coming."

"I can hear him," Jack said.

"You can not," Beau said. "He's dead. Dead people don't make any sound."

"He's scratching, trying to get out."

"He is not." Beau listened hard. He could hear the wind in the cypress needles, but not scratching sounds. It was getting on to late afternoon, though. The sun would be going down before long. "We ought to be getting home," he said.

"He smells bad, too," Jack said.

Beau sniffed, but couldn't smell anything but earth. "What's he smell like?" he asked.

"Dead men's fingers," Jack said.

Beau looked around for the little cone-shaped toadstools of that name, with their wrinkled white skin and dank, nasty odor of a spit-soaked thumb. There weren't any. The hair rose up on the back of his neck.

"You can't smell him," he said. "He's buried deep."

"He stinks," Jack insisted.

Beau grabbed Jack by the hair and dragged him to his feet. "Get up," he said. "You're stupid and ignorant. I shouldn't have brought you here, no more sense than you've got." But it was too late for good sense. Jack had already poisoned Beau's imaginings with his own. Beau avoided the grave after that, terrified of scratchings and stinks he could neither hear nor smell, while Jack invoked Vancey's name every time he got crosswise with Beau. To escape the fear, Beau finally quit believing in Vancey at all.

But there was no escaping Jack himself, who soon became Beau's chief responsibility. It was a miserable job. Jack didn't have good sense, and he carried a past. Folks remembered his babyhood quirks - what Dolly called 'Jack's erstwhile peculiarities' - and even now, he wasn't right. Singing was for church, sitting on the porch after supper, or bedtime, maybe now and then for cows, if a man was alone and pretty sure nobody was around to hear him. But Jack did it all the time, and sounded like a girl. It was deeply embarrassing. Their mother complained about town being so far away, but Beau was glad. Otherwise, Jack would be warbling on a street corner with a tin cup tied around his neck. That's what their father threatened to do with him if Jack didn't start earning his keep around the island. If that happened, Beau intended to run away from home. Anything was better than walking away with his arm around Jack's shoulders while people as stupid and butt-ugly as Bob Rainey made faces and called him names. Beau hated Bob Rainey. He hated Clyde, too, just on principle. And their mother was crazy. She was the craziest human being Beau had ever seen or heard tell of, bar none, not even Jack. Her and her blue-white eyes and white, white skin. Loud, too. And that hair. The first time Beau had ever seen Red, he'd thought her head was on fire. He'd thought that was why she was yelling so loud.

But he admired Tate Rainey no end. He stood on the front porch, sometimes, and watched the Raineys catch the wild horses. Sometimes they trapped them, and other times chased them in relays until one fell behind and Tate could rope and halter it. Then he'd drag it, rearing and pawing, back to their place to buck it out. Red rode the wild horses the same as Tate, and according to Dolly, better. Dolly said Red Rainey was the best rider he'd ever seen, even better than Tate. He said she was savvy about horses in a way Tate wasn't, that she could get inside their heads and walk around in there. Beau found that hard to believe, seeing she was a woman and all. However, Dolly had said it, so it must be true. Still, Beau just wanted to watch Tate ride. Dolly said not to worry about it, that he'd handle it. All Beau had to do was wait.

Chapter Fourteen

Tate threw a saddle on the sorrel colt and cinched the girth. He worked fast, sweat glistening on his face and hands. The other riders were dirty from hitting the ground, but Tate's white shirt was still clean, barring the sweat marks under the arms. He didn't get bucked off very often. Raymond hadn't seen it happen yet, and he'd been there all morning.

Tate dropped the stirrup leather, slapping the colt in the side. The colt, snubbed to a post, flinched and tried to jerk away, but the movement twisted its neck, halting resistance. Tate grasped the halter rope and a handful of mane with his left hand, the cantle with his right, set his left foot in the stirrup, and swung up into the saddle. He set his right foot in the other stirrup and took up the slack in the rope.

"Let him go," he said. A man started to climb down off the fence.

"Let Bob do it," Tate said.

The man stopped, and looked at Bob Rainey. So did everybody else. At twelve, he wasn't much bigger than Jack, who was almost six. Beau was two inches taller and ten pounds heavier, though he was only nine. Bob's face was never a pretty sight even on the best days, but now, greasy white with fear, it was downright unpleasant, and his small, pink-rimmed blue eyes stared so hard at his father they almost bulged. Tate gazed impassively back at his son. "I'm waiting," he said.

Bob climbed halfway down the side of the pen. He held onto a board with one hand. With the other, he reached out and grabbed one of the two halters the colt was wearing.

"Not that one," Tate said.

Bob released the halter as if it had burned him. The movement unbalanced him, and he clutched the fence with both hands. He hung there for a moment then turned loose again, this time with the other hand, which he laid on the horse's head. His fingers groped their way to the buckle on the outside halter, and fumbled with it.

"Use both hands," Tate said.

Bob's shoulders sagged. He climbed down into the pen, and stood between the post and the fence. The post was set right in the corner of the pen, only a foot from the boards, enough room for a man to squeeze through, but too small for a horse. Bob hardly took up any room at all. Beau was surprised at the other boy's fear. What Bob lacked in size, he usually made up for in meanness. Right now, though, he was almost whimpering. Bob Rainey was bad scared of that horse.

He had to stand on tiptoe to unbuckle the halter, and his fingers skittered around the horse's head like fiddler crabs. When the two ends of the halter finally came away in his hands, the colt jerked its head away and spun around. Untouched, Bob squealed and fell against the fence, then scuttled back up and over the other side.

The colt bucked hard, coming up with all four hooves in the air, and hitting the ground with a solid thud. Tate rode with one hand in the air, pulling the colt's head with the halter rope, shortening its stride. He made it look easy.

Raymond smiled at Beau, who was sitting on the top rail of the fence. "What do you think, son?" he asked.

Beau didn't take his eyes off Tate. "I could do that," he said.

"I bet," Raymond said. He studied Beau's profile, noting the stubbornness there. It wasn't enough that Beau was actually here, at the Rainey's, as he'd been begging for weeks. Now he wanted to ride, too. Sometimes Raymond regretted ever listening to Dolly. He leaned forward to catch Baxter's eye, but was unsuccessful. The man was too busy talking. Making or taking a bet, most likely. Dolly was free with his money. Raymond enjoyed a friendly wager as much as the next man, but he wasn't careless about it. A dollar a bet, five dollars a day, was his limit. Once that five dollars was played, win or lose, Raymond was through for the day. Dolly called him stingy, but Raymond didn't care. His money had been hard to come by, and he wouldn't risk it lightly. Plus there was Jessie to think about. Let her find out that Raymond had brought Beau to this place, and she wouldn't talk to him for a year. Let her find out he'd been gambling, and she'd leave him.

"What's Dolly doing over there?" Beau asked.

"Acting foolish," Raymond said. He nodded at Tate. "What do you think he's going to do? I've got a dollar says he's going to ride that colt to a standstill."

"Nossir," Beau said. "He's going to step off. He's tired of him."

"What do you mean, tired of him?" Raymond said. "He looks pretty worked up to me."

"That horse is slowing down," Beau said. "It's not hard to stay on him anymore. Tate'll get off. I'd get off, if was me."

"You would, huh?"

"Sure I would."

Raymond found his son's confidence annoying at times. He recalled being more humble when he himself was nine. That was Dolly's doing, making Beau all big-headed. It didn't help any that Tate was, indeed, getting off the horse, as casually as stepping off a slow-moving train onto a railroad siding, right leg swinging over the cantle, one foot on the ground and then the other, and Tate just walking away with never a stumble or break in his stride. The colt came to a stop once Tate was off. It stood there, spraddle-legged and trembly. Tate flipped the halter rope at the horse as if he were throwing trash at it.

"Y'all come get the saddle off this thing," he said. "Get me a real horse in here."

"Told you," Beau said. He stuck his hand out.

Raymond looked at the boy's palm. "What's that for?" he asked.

"Your dollar," Beau said.

"Where was your dollar?" Raymond demanded. "The bet's no good if you didn't have the money to back it."

Beau dug down in his overalls and pulled out a silver dollar. "Right here it is," he said. "Dolly gave it to me." He stuck the dollar back in his pocket and held his hand out again. Raymond fished a dollar out of his own pocket and handed it to his son.

"You're picking up some bad habits, boy," he said. "If your mama finds out you've been gambling, you're as good as dead."

"Dolly says if she finds out about this here" - Beau flung his arm out in a gesture that included the entire Rainey homestead - "we're all dead."

"He's got that right," Raymond said. He put one foot on the bottom rail. "Let's make sure she don't find out."

"She won't hear about it from me," Beau said.

Raymond looked again at his son--the curly dark hair, the gray eyes, the childish mouth, the slender face--and felt a twinge of unease. Beau looked back at him, and grinned. Comforted, Raymond slapped him on the back in a comradely fashion, and turned his attention again to the pen. The sorrel colt was gone. A black filly was snubbed to the post, her tail twitching like a cat's.

"She looks a mite irritable," Raymond said.

"Reminds me of Mama," Beau said.

A stout boy, the son of a local farmer, dragged a saddle out to the post and fumbled it up on the filly. She sidled around, crowding him into the fence as he tried to cinch the girth.

"Somebody help me down here," he yelled.

Beau wiggled and Raymond grabbed his suspender. "No you don't," he said.

"Aw, Daddy," Beau said.

"No," Raymond said. "That was the agreement. You'd watch and nothing else. Just watch."

Beau slumped down, sulking. "I'm tired of watching," he said. "And my butt's sore, too, from sitting on this board."

"Then we'll go home."

"I don't want to go home."

"Then sit. But you're not getting down there with those horses."

"It ain't fair."

"What ain't fair?"

"Bob and Clyde," Beau said. "They hate horses. Scared to death of 'em. And their daddy rides them for a living, has them all over the place. While as for me, I ain't a bit scared of a horse. Dolly says I ride like the wind..."

"You do something like wind," Raymond said. "I don't know that it's riding."

"I ride like the wind," Beau continued. "But my daddy just hunts cows, and won't ride a horse unless it's already broke. What's worse, he buys broke horses from Tate Rainey when he could pay me to break them. It ain't fair."

"I buy horses that Red Rainey has trained," Raymond said. "There's a difference."

The plowboy had been joined by one of his buddies, and the two of them were trying to saddle the filly. The effect was comical. Tate just leaned against the inside of the pen, a boot heel hooked into the bottom rail, thumbs in his belt, and watched them. He didn't help the paying riders. He just took their money and let them make fools of themselves. If they chickened out, or got bucked off, or got kicked in the head, or broke an arm or a leg, or lost some teeth - all of which had happened at one time or another - the money was still his. Once it touched his hand, it was gone. The filly wasn't helping any, either. They hadn't snubbed her tight enough, and she had too much room to move her head. She was doing everything but hold those boys by their collars and slap their faces.

"Good luck, fellers," Raymond murmured.

The plowboy was cussing the filly to a fare-thee-well. Around the fence, the comments of the onlookers were growing louder and less polite. Down the side of the pen, Dolly was counting out money to another man. It wasn't exactly a church-going crowd, but there was no real harm in it. Raymond had only been coming for a year or so, and then only once or twice a month, just dropping in with Dolly to see what was going on, and to put a little money on some of the riders. He'd heard it could get ugly, especially when Tate and Red got to fighting. But that only happened at night, when they'd been drinking all day. It was a safe bet that nothing would happen this early in the day, and it was good to see Beau so content. Lord knew, he'd wanted to come bad enough. He'd started in on Raymond more than a month ago about bringing him, saying he wanted to ride one of Tate Rainey's horses so bad it made his teeth ache.

"They'd ache sure enough if you got on one of 'em," Raymond had told him. "You wait a few years. Twelve is old enough to ride bucking horses."

"How many years is that?" Beau asked.

"If you'd pay more attention to your schooling, you'd know," Raymond said. One of the first things Lucinda Ellis had done in her new town was open a school, and Beau was in her first class of pupils. Jessie stayed on Beau about his studies, but Raymond couldn't tell that it was doing much good.

"Three," Dolly had said. That kind of interference from Dolly made Jessie hopping mad; sometimes Raymond could see her point.

"Three years!" Beau had said. "That's too long!"

"Way too long," Dolly said. "Let's you and me take him over there, Ray. All he wants to do is watch the riding. That can't hurt him any."

Raymond had said no at the time, and meant it. He'd said it and meant it every day for weeks. But little by little, Dolly had convinced him that there was nothing at the Raineys' to hurt a living soul.

"I'm telling you, Ray," Dolly kept saying. "All he'll see is them horses. He wouldn't notice anything else even if it was there, which it probably won't be. C'mon, Ray. Trust me."

And now, here they were, and Beau was not only tired of watching, and wanting to ride, but he was taking bets, as well. Next thing Raymond knew, he'd be drinking hard whiskey. Raymond wished the boy would learn arithmetic this fast, and mentally kicked himself for ever bringing him. Back on the island, the danger had seemed so distant. He'd forgotten until now just how loud it got as the morning wore on, and the way men stood around gambling and drinking and cussing. The longer he stood there, the less he liked the view, and the more disgruntled he got with Dolly for talking him into it. Another ride or two and he'd take Beau home, and that would be the end of it.

"Want to bet on that rider?" Beau asked.

"No," Raymond said.

"Double or nothing. You could win your dollar back, and mine, too."

"I said no."

"Too bad. Look at that."

Raymond tore his attention from Beau and looked with asperity at the horse and its rider. The plowboy was lying on his back in the middle of the pen while the filly trotted around the inside of the fence looking for a way out, cowkicking every now and then as the stirrups hit her sides.

"When did that happen?" Raymond asked.

"About two seconds after he got on," Beau said. "I'm telling you..."

"Yeah, I know," Raymond said. "You could do it better."

"Lookit that," Dolly said. He'd come up between them, slapping Beau on the back and Raymond on the shoulder. "I just won ten dollars off that boy. I'd buy him a drink if he weren't so young."

"Who did you know was stupid enough to bet on him?" Raymond asked. "A feller that can't saddle a horse more'n likely can't ride one either."

"His daddy bet on him," Dolly said. "You'd bet on ole Beau, here, if it was him out there, wouldn't you?"

"Daddy won't let me ride," Beau said. His tone was sullen. Raymond cocked an eyebrow at him, but Beau just scowled and hunched his shoulders up around his ears, hiding his face.

"He's just looking out for you, Beau," Dolly said. "Ain't that right, Ray?"

"I'm not so sure," Raymond said. "As a matter of fact, I think we ought to be heading home. I'd like to find at least one cow between here and the island." He'd told Jessie that him and Dolly and Beau were going cow hunting today, and he'd just as soon do that before he saw her again. Miss Jessie had a sharp nose for a lie.

Beau's response came in a blink. "I'm sorry, Daddy," he said. "I won't say another word, I promise. Just let's stay a while longer."

"Hush, Beau," Dolly said. "Sometimes I wonder if you've lost all the sense you ever had. Your daddy's ready to go. Where's your respect?" Raymond looked sharply at Dolly, but the cobalt blue eyes were guileless. "I'm ready when you are, Ray. And so's Beau. He just don't know it yet."

"Looky there," Beau said. "Tate's going to ride that filly."

"You don't say." Dolly climbed up on the fence and sat down next to Beau as if the subject of leaving had never come up.

Raymond tapped Beau on the back. "C'mon, son," he said. "We're going now."

"Wait just a second, Daddy, please. I just want to see Tate ride one more time."

"Now, Beau."

"Aw, Daddy."

"C'mon, Daddy," another voice mocked.

Raymond turned around. Red Rainey was standing behind him, a smile as friendly as a cottonmouth's on her face. "Morning, Red," he said.

"So how come you're leaving so soon?" she asked.

"I just think it's time to go," Raymond said.

"Well, let me tell you what I think," Red said.

Raymond reached up and grabbed Beau around the waist. He wasn't about to bandy words with Red Rainey. Tall and slim, with her weird, blue-white eyes and white skin and fiery hair, she'd be a beautiful woman, albeit a strange-looking one, if it weren't for that mouth. She didn't care what she said, or whom she said it to. Whatever was coming, he didn't want his son to hear it. Ignoring Beau's pleas, Raymond dragged him off the fence and set him on the ground.

"Say hello to Miz Rainey," Raymond said.

Beau shoved his hands down in his pockets and bobbed his head. "'Lo, Miz Rainey," he muttered.

"Well, ain't we got fine manners," she said. "Good morning to you, little mister." She nodded her head at the pen. "You like seeing Tate ride?"

"Yes, ma'am," Beau said. "I could watch him all day long."

"Is that so?" She squatted down in front of Beau. He regarded her with alarm. Raymond didn't blame him. It wasn't just her skin and hair and eyes, but her clothes. She was the only woman Raymond or Beau, either one, had ever seen wearing trousers. Tucked into their small waistband was the tail of a thin, blue, man's shirt with – clearly - nothing underneath it except Red herself. On her head, covering most of her hair and shading her face, was a wide-brimmed hat with a scarf over it that came down on either side of the crown, through the brim, and tied under her chin. And she was wearing gloves. It was quite a get-up. But then, Red Rainey was quite a woman.

"Have you ever seen me ride a bucking horse," she asked.

Beau shook his head. "No, ma'am," he said. "But Dolly has."

"And...?"

"He says you ride better'n Tate." Beau's doubts were evident in his voice.

Red stood up and pointed through the rails at the horse in the pen. "Did you see that last ride?" she asked.

"Yes, ma'am," Beau said.

"What do you think of the filly?"

"I think she's tricky," Beau said.

Red looked at him again, speculatively this time. "Tricky," she said. "In what way?"

"She ducked," Beau said. "She didn't buck so much as she slipped out from underneath him. It's like she was thinking."

"A thinking gal," Red said. "The very worst kind. I wonder how her and Tate'll get along." She moved up close to the fence, and as she did so, reached out with a gloved hand and squeezed Dolly's leg behind the knee. Beau's eyes got big.

"Hey, Baxter," Red said. "I heard you say you was leaving."

"I'm going to watch Tate ride this horse," Dolly said. "Then I'm leaving." He called down to Raymond without turning around. "That all right with you, Ray?"

"That's fine," Raymond said. He put a hand on Beau's shoulder. "We're leaving now."

"Please, Daddy," Beau said. "Please. It won't take long. Please."

"C'mon, Pennell," Red said. "One more ride. What can it hurt?" She turned around, hooked both elbows on the rail behind her, and smiled at him. "Got a dollar left, Moneybags?"

Raymond's face got hot. It was one thing for Dolly to think him cheap, quite another for the whole world to think so. "One," he said, feeling defensive.

"Good," Red said. "I'll bet you a dollar that filly puts Tate on the ground."

Raymond pshawed. "There ain't nothing to that little horse," he said.

"Put your money on Tate, then," Red said. "And I'll put mine on the filly. Is it a bet?" She stuck her hand out. Raymond shook it. The glove was soft but the grip within it was as strong as a man's.

"It's a bet," he said.

Red turned back around and climbed up on the fence. She didn't sit on the top rail, but hung on it, cocking one leg up so that her trousered rear end stuck out. Raymond couldn't help but notice what a fine rear end it was, its shape spoiled only a little bit by the outline of a flask in her right hip pocket.

"Daddy?"

Raymond looked at Beau. The gray eyes were uncertain. Raymond cleared his throat, and nodded at the pen. "We'll watch this one ride, then we'll go," he said.

Beau grinned, then climbed back up on the fence and sat down next to Dolly. Raymond leaned against a post and looked through the rails. The black filly was snubbed so tight to the pole that her nose was bleeding, and Tate was in the saddle.

"Bob!" he called. "Bob!" There were a lot of men on the fence, but no Bob.

"He's over in the hen house with the rest of the chickens!"

Tate turned in the saddle, searching the crowd. Red waved her hand, and his black eyes stopped and rested on her. Tension shimmered in the air between them, a kind of heat. Raymond found he was holding his breath. Tate was a proud man, and a violent one, maybe even a little crazy. Goading him was neither smart nor funny. It sure was interesting, though, and Raymond, like the rest of the men around the fence, wanted to see what would happen.

Apparently nothing. Tate turned his back on Red, and said something to one of the men on the fence. The man got down in the pen and walked over to the post. The filly snorted and leaned back on the halter. Tate jabbed her in the sides with his spurs and she jumped forward, relieving the pressure on the halter long enough for the man to unbuckle it. The halter fell off her head.

What followed happened so fast that Raymond almost missed it. The filly took a step backward, then ducked down as if going under a tree limb, switching her back end around at the same time. It was quick, neat, deliberate, and effective. One second Tate was in the saddle, the next he was on the ground. There was a moment of silence, then one great guffawing laugh from Red Rainey. Tate got up and dusted himself off. There was a big smudge on the back of his shirt where he'd hit the ground on his shoulder. He didn't try to get it off. Raymond didn't think he knew it was there. Tate picked up his hat and started walking to the fence.

"Hey, Tate," Red yelled. "Your shirt's dirty."

Tate stopped. Then he started walking again. When he reached the fence, he put a hand on the rail and took a step up.

"Hey, Tate," Red yelled again. "She threw your ass, didn't she? I told that plowboy she would."

Tate stopped. Then he stepped back down off the fence, turned around, and started walking across the pen toward Red.

She got up on the fence and straddled it like she would a horse. "I told that boy, here, take this twenty-dollar gold piece and give it to Tate to ride that horse, watch her throw him on the ground. I thought it would make little Bob feel better. Wasn't that thoughtful of me? Wasn't it kind?" She laughed again, a hard, raucous laugh that fractured the silence.

Tate kept walking toward her. His boots made little puffs of dust in the sandy dirt. One leg of his dungarees was dirty, and there was a streak of dirt on his cheek. Raymond couldn't recall when he'd ever seen Tate with dirt on him.

"I'm just sorry Bob missed it," Red said. Her voice was lower now, as if recognizing the closing distance between her and Tate. "I'll give you a hundred dollars to do it again. Get on that filly and let her give you a whirl, Tate, so Bob can see you in the dirt. It'll do his sorry little heart good."

Tate reached the fence and stopped. He took his hat off and held it in his hands as if he had come begging. His voice was soft when he spoke, almost caressing. "You think you can do any better?" he asked.

Red leaned out over the fence toward him and spat out her answer. "You know it," she said.

"Be my guest," Tate said, and gestured with his hat toward the horse.

Red reached into her back pocket and pulled out the flask. She unstoppered it, took a long swallow, put the stopper back in the neck, and offered it to Tate. "What will you pay me to ride her?" she asked.

Tate reached up and took the flask. He put it in his pocket without drinking from it. "What do you want?" he asked.

Red leaned way out and smacked her lips, loud and slow, three times. "A kiss," she said.

This was too much for some. Laughter broke out in the crowd. "Cheap at twice the price, if you ask me," a man said.

"I sure hope Tate don't start charging the same," another said. "I'll have rode my last horse if he does."

Tate held up his hand, and the raillery stopped. "Special rates for special people," he said quietly. "Come and get it, sweetheart."

There was scattered applause as Red climbed down into the pen and stood, hands on her hips, in front of the post Raymond was leaning on, and even more applause when she spoke. "Ready when you are," she said.

Tate stepped up, put his hand on her waist, and drew her close. Then he bent the brim of her hat back and put his mouth on hers. It was deathly quiet. Raymond, holding his breath, saw Red's body relax and sway toward Tate, and let his breath out real slow. It was a long kiss and Raymond was feeling the heat of it when he saw Red flinch. Perhaps, because he was so close to her, he was the only one who saw it, that and the way her hands hit Tate's shoulders and stayed there, pressing with the heels, and the way Tate's right hand tightened on her waist as the left one moved from the brim of her hat to the back of her head, fingers gripping her hair as she struggled to break away from him. What Raymond didn't see until she broke away was the blood on Red's mouth where Tate had bitten her bottom lip, and the way her lip trembled before she sucked it in between her teeth and held it, so that she looked to be grinning when she held up her joined hands in a victory sign.

Shaken, Raymond watched Red walk across the pen as if nothing had happened. The men around the fence - and the number had grown considerably since the kiss began - cheered and whistled and catcalled. Only Tate, Red, and Beau were silent. Two men had jumped off the fence as soon as the kiss started, and had the filly caught and tied to the post by the time Red got there. She tightened the girth and shortened the stirrups, then took the halter rope from one of the men and got in the saddle. She looked real good there. Dolly peered down at Raymond from the top rail, his face flushed.

"Which way you betting, Ray?" he asked.

"I've used up my money," Raymond said.

"If you had any, how would you bet?"

"What's Tate doing?" Raymond asked.

Dolly turned back around, facing the pens. Raymond climbed up on the rail where Red had stood. Tate was halfway across the pen, his stride long and even and purposeful.

"Where's he going?" Beau asked.

"Maybe he's going to help Red," Dolly said.

"I don't think so," Raymond said.

Tate reached the post, spoke to the two men, then reached up to the filly's halter. One of the men said something, but backed up when Tate answered him. Red leaned down across the filly's neck and swatted at Tate's hands, but all it did was spook the horse. The filly crouched on her haunches, jerking on the rope and grunting. Red sat back down in the saddle and pulled on the halter rope. It came away in her hands, the halter dangling at the end of it.

"He's taken the bucking halter off," Dolly said.

"Daddy,..." Beau began.

Raymond put his hand on Beau's knee, and the boy fell quiet. A murmur was growing in the crowd that erupted into a full-fledged roar when Tate took the snub halter off and turned the filly loose with Red on her back.

The horse moved like a wounded snake, writhing and twisting and jerking. There was no rhythm, no predictability, no sense or plan to it. And Red wasn't riding her. She was clinging to the saddle, thrown backwards and forwards and sideways like a popper on the end of a whip. The scarf came loose under her chin, the ends flying across her face. She went over the side, her body jolting back and forth, and the hat came off as she bounced upright again, thrown back into the saddle by the filly's convulsions. The horse heaved and ducked and spun, and Red's hair came loose, its curls and waves rising in flames around her head as she came down, and falling as she rose, shrouding her face in fire as the rag doll body with its scarecrow angles and lines slowly turned into something they'd never seen before, something balanced and light and yielding that bent and swayed in unison with the horse beneath it, legs free of the stirrups, bound by the muscles and tendons in thighs and knees and feet to the body of the horse between them, hips thrusting back and forth beneath the supple waist, hands pulling the gloves from long, white fingers that found and loosed the buttons of the thin, blue shirt until it opened, revealing a milk white body of hollows and hillocks veined in lavender and tipped with coral, breasts rising and falling beneath the wild hair as Red whipped the filly with the shirt around and around the pen, bucking and kicking, breathing hard and pounding like the blood in the bodies of the men who watched hers as it arched and bowed over the horse until the bucking became a lope that lifted and dropped the hair blazing over her shoulders and back and breasts and belly until the horse gave out, and fell into a trot, and then into a walk, and finally stopped, and Red dropped her arm and the shirt and pushed the hair out of her face and drew her right leg slowly over the cantle of the saddle to meet the left before sliding down the sweat slick side of the filly to the ground not ten feet from where she'd started, where Tate still stood as if he'd been waiting for her all this time.

Red swayed there for a moment, then walked up to him, white breasts peeking through the tangle of hair, and stopped so close to him her nipples grazed the front of his shirt. She put her hand on Tate's shoulder, then slid it down his back to his buttocks and into his hip pocket from which she drew the flask she'd given him earlier. Turning slightly away, she pulled the stopper out and lifted the bottle to her mouth. Some of the whiskey she swallowed, but the rest ran down her naked front and soaked into the waist of her dungarees. When it was empty, Red tossed the flask against the fence.

"That," she said, "is the way to ride a tricky filly." She licked the cut on her lip. "Maybe you'd like to try it sometime."

"Get to the house," Tate said. His voice was so soft Raymond could barely hear it.

"What do you think I am?" Red snarled. "Your dog?"

Tate's black eyes traveled over his wife, from the red, red hair to the naked breasts to the dark spot where the whiskey had wet the front of her britches. A muscle twitched in his cheek. Then he hit her so hard on the side of the head that it knocked her to the ground. Red was still trying to get up when Raymond left, one hand gripping Beau's, the other holding the dollar he owed her.

Chapter Fifteen

Jessie Pennell suffered righteous indignation in the small of her back. It was a chronic condition, and had never been more painful than this morning, when she was on her way to a fifth Sunday church service sitting next to a man she no longer trusted. Raymond had lied, cheated, gambled, and exposed her son to depravity. In a way, Jessie had lost her husband. She'd kissed him goodbye in the morning, and eaten supper with an impostor that evening. Only she hadn't eaten, anymore than she'd slept. She'd risen from the table with no more love or affection in her heart than a stone could hold, and walked back and forth between the front porch and the back all night long, alternately beseeching God for the grace to forgive and calling down His wrath on Raymond, Dolly, Tate, Red, and - if he ever showed the first sign between now and the day he died of behaving like those other four - Beau.

Jessie couldn't even look at Raymond. He was sitting beside her on the wagon seat, but that made no difference. She could not look at him, and she would not speak. She had not spoken since supper last night, and didn't know when she would again. Certainly not until she recovered from the sight of Beau leaning over his plate and sobbing as if somebody had died.

"What in the world is the matter with you, child?" she'd asked. He hadn't been able to speak, so she'd gotten up, put her hand on his forehead to see if he was feverish, checked the color of his gums and eyelids, probed his throat and neck and armpits for lumps and soreness. But he just cried all the harder, shaking his head back and forth in such a state of misery that she'd been almost crazy with worry. Well, she just hadn't known how much she had to worry about until she'd turned to Raymond to ask him if he knew what was wrong with Beau and saw that he didn't look one whit better. In fact, he looked worse. Guilt would do that to a body.

And Raymond was guilty of such things as Jessie could scarcely bear to think about. Watching Clemency Rainey as she...well...Jessie just wouldn't think about it. She squirmed at the thought of ever undressing again, even to bathe. Modesty was a woman's crowning glory and now she, Jessie Pennell, would have to bear a double weight of it if she were ever to drive from Raymond's mind the memory of what he'd seen.

Jessie shuddered with revulsion and bone-deep offense, and clasped her shawl more closely about her. The wagon rattled on. Even the children were quiet. As they came up the road to the Rainey place, Jessie turned her head away from what had happened there, and her eyes fell on something by the side of the road. She almost didn't recognize what it was she was seeing. When she did, indignation deserted her, leaving her weak with dread. She put her hand out blindly, seeking Raymond, and touched his shoulder.

"Stop," she said.

The horse pulled up.

"Jessie, please," Raymond said. "Not here, not again. I said I was sorry."

"It's Bob. Bob Rainey."

"Oh, Lord," Raymond said. The wagon swayed and creaked, and he came around to her side of the wagon. Bob was crouched down in the grass, arms wrapped around his shins. He didn't look up when Raymond spoke to him. "Hey, Bob."

Bob didn't answer.

"Where's Clyde?" Raymond asked. "Where's your mama and daddy?"

Bob still didn't answer.

Goose pimples rose on Jessie's arms. She looked at Raymond for the first time in twelve hours, and saw her fear reflected in his face. Something was terribly wrong.

"We better give ole Bob a ride home," Raymond said. He picked the boy up and set him down in the back of the wagon. Then he climbed back up beside Jessie. "You might miss church today," he said.

"Raymond..." she began.

"Let's just wait and see," he said. "Could be nothing."

Jessie didn't believe that for a second, but folded her hands in her lap, willing to wait forever. Behind them, someone gagged.

"Bob, you smell like a dead hog," Beau said.

"Beau," Raymond said.

"Yessir?"

"That's enough."

"Yessir."

Jessie turned around. Her four were crowded together against the seat, united against the wretched lump next to the tailgate. Bob caught her looking at him, and stuck his face between his knees. Jessie faced the oncoming road again. The Rainey house was just visible on the other side of a cabbage hammock in the curve of the road. It was more of a shack, really, than a house. Tate had refused help with raising it. The barn was a stone's throw away, with a stout set of pens behind it, where yesterday, Red had...Jessie's mind darted away, and she looked elsewhere. Horses grazed in the adjoining pasture. She could hear them grazing in the Sunday stillness, ripping the grass from the ground. One of them was black, and Jessie wondered if it was the one Clemency had ridden. Everything was so quiet. She took a deep breath - of grass, dirt, leaves, hay - the hot, sweet odors of August. Nothing more. Her hands were shaking. She clasped them together in her lap and squeezed hard.

Raymond stopped the wagon in front of the house and got out, wrapping the lines around the brake. "You wait here," he said. His steps fell like blows on the empty porch, and Jessie winced when he knocked on the door. "Tate? Red? Y'all home? I've got Bob out here in the wagon. He's not feeling too good."

No one answered.

"Tate? It's me, Raymond Pennell. I'm alone, unarmed. Just stepping inside. Nothing to worry about." Raymond opened the front door of the Rainey house, went inside, and shut the door behind him. Jessie closed her eyes. There was a silence that seemed to go on forever, then Raymond came back out. He shut the door very quietly, then stepped off the porch and walked back to the wagon.

"My four climb out of there," he said. "I need your help." He lifted Bekah and Jonelle out of the wagon bed, while Beau and Jack clambered over the side and jumped to the ground. Raymond squatted down in front of the three youngest ones, and turning on the balls of his feet, pointed to the barn, the pens, the field behind them, and the cabbage hammock they'd passed on the way in.

"I want you three to go find Clyde," he said. "Look in the barn, the pens, the pasture. Look in the hammock, and as far as the road, but no further. If you find him, come get me. Stand right there by the wagon and holler for me. I'll come to the door." He pulled them close to him, and held their eyes with his. "You hear me? If you find Clyde, stand by the wagon and holler. I'll come to the door. Don't you come in the house. Not for any reason. You understand?"

"Is something wrong with the Raineys, Daddy?" Beau asked.

"Yes, there is, son," Raymond said. "Mizz Rainey's dead. Tate's in there with her. He says Clyde's run off, like Bob. He's hid somewhere."

"Like a baby rabbit," Jack said.

Raymond gave him a sharp look, but Jack wasn't being cute. He was just being Jack. "That's right. Like a baby rabbit. He's hiding under a bush, maybe, or down a hole, or behind something big, like a stump. But he's out there, and I want you and your sisters to find him."

He stood up, using Beau's shoulder for support. "Beau, you get a bridle out of the barn. Unhitch one of our mules. Ride to the church. Tell the preacher what I told you, that Red's dead and the family's in a bad way. He'll know what to do. Interrupt the sermon if you have to."

Beau pointed at Bob. "What about him?"

"Never mind him," Raymond said. "You just do what I tell you."

Jessie watched her children running to the barn and wished she could go with them. She felt a hand on her knee.

"I need you," Raymond said. He helped her down out of the wagon, and gripped her upper arm as they walked to the porch. Jessie didn't know if he was holding her to comfort her, support her, or prevent her from running away. She stopped when she reached the porch steps, and saw the blood.

"I can't do this alone," Raymond said. His hand on her arm compelled her up the steps and across the porch. He opened the door and led her beside a trail of blood across the front room to the kitchen, past Tate sitting at the kitchen table with a jug at his elbow and a glass in his hand, to the windowless room beyond, where guttering candles in the silver candelabra threw a wan light on Clemency Rainey's naked body and the fiery red hair that spilled with her blood to the floor.

Later, when Jessie got back to the island, she burned the clothes and shoes she'd worn that day, right down to her petticoats and drawers, and washed every inch of her body with scalding water and lye soap. It took weeks to rid herself of the smell of blood, and years to distance herself from the memory. But on that day, the day Clemency Rainey died, no amount of washing could make things clean. Blood, and the smell of blood, was everywhere.

Even her own children had blood on them. Clyde jumped out of a palmetto patch and bit Jack on the ankle when Jack stepped on his hand, which is how they discovered his hiding place. Raymond heard Jack screaming and went to rescue him, leaving Jessie alone in the house with Tate to wash Clemency's body and hair, clothe her - in a nightgown and a shawl, because there was no dress in the house and Jessie refused to put her in long pants - and comb the tangles out of her hair. Tate sat in the kitchen the whole time and never offered to speak or help. He didn't get up from the table until Clemency was in the coffin and the lid nailed shut, and he only did it then because the sheriff threatened to arrest him if he didn't.

Beau, directed by his father to fetch the preacher immediately, rode first to Dolly's and then back to the church, where his news caused the most satisfying ruckus it was reasonable to hope for in this life. By the time he returned with the preacher and the sheriff, his father had already made a coffin from siding off the barn. The sheriff inspected Red's body - Jessie forbade Beau to watch, to his bitter disappointment - then Raymond nailed the lid down, and with the sheriff's help - and Beau's, too, now that there was nothing interesting to see - carried the coffin out to the pasture where Dolly and Jack had dug a grave.

Beau stood next to Bob at the burying. The older boy stank of sweat and privy dirt, and kept wiping his nose on his shirttail. When Jessie told Bob to use her handkerchief instead, he started bawling. His two front teeth, pointy and black as charcoal, protruded beyond his top lip. With his mouth stretched open and his eyes squinched shut, he looked just like a shrunken head Dolly had brought back from Tampa some years before, only bigger. Jack seemed particularly fascinated with the sight, and kept peering around Jessie to stare. After the funeral, Beau's mother and Mrs. Dempsey let the Rainey twins eat all the collard greens and pone. Beau never got the first bite. He wondered if Red had died on purpose, on account of her boys being so ugly, mean, and greedy. He wouldn't have blamed her if she had.

On the way home that evening, rocked by the steady rhythm of horse and wagon, the horror of the day finally caught up with Beau. He was nestled with his brother and sisters up under the driver's bench, deep in coats and blankets, Jack's breath coming even and sour-sweet from his open mouth.

"Daddy?" he called. He said it soft, though there was no need. The three beside him would not have awakened had he poured water on them. He knew, because he'd done it before.

"What is it, son?"

"How did Red die?"

"Tate says a horse kicked her in the head."

"Do you believe him?"

"The sheriff says he believes him."

"But do *you* believe him?"

"No, son," his father said. "I believe Tate killed her."

Beau waited a moment, then asked the question that was troubling him the most. "Daddy, are you going to kill Mama?"

"No, baby. I would never do anything like that."

His father had not called Beau 'baby' in years. Ordinarily he'd have been profoundly offended, but tonight it gave him comfort. And because he was exhausted from the events and emotions of the day, and because he trusted his father, Beau went to sleep, leaving his elders in peace, or what passed for it on a night like this.

Part III

September – November 1881

The Pennell Barn

Chapter Sixteen

The house seemed part of the island itself, gray-green and brown, and rough to the touch like the cypress and pine from which it was built. It turned silver in dry seasons and droughts, shimmering in the heat like a mirage, then darkened in the rains, the lichen that pitted its sides gleaming coral and jade. The house was most visible in a storm, when the trees around it bent and swayed, because it didn't move. A stubborn permanence set it apart, as though the cypress pilings that bound it to the earth went deeper than the roots of trees and held with greater tenacity to the island.

A wide front porch supported by the tall trunks of cabbage palms faced Lake Locknahatchee. It caught the rising sun beneath its eaves each morning, stopping it a foot from the front door. It was always shady in that spot, a favorite place for the cats to sleep in the summertime. They lay as if boneless in that endless shadow, quick, shallow breaths patting their dusty sides in the heat. In cold weather, they took their morning naps on the sunny top step. A rocker, some ladderback chairs, and a wooden swing looked out on a sandy yard littered with sandspurs and the broken tips of palm fronds. The yard was flanked by a wagon track that ran north along the edge of the hammock, curving west on the far end to the crossing at Deep Creek.

Going south, the track followed the hammock until it reached the barnyard, and dead-ended at the back gate of the barn, which opened onto a horse pasture. The cypress tree that marked Vancey's grave was most clearly visible from the barn. It could also be seen from the house, but only from the front porch.

The rear of the house looked into the hammock. Early on, it had been part of it, backed up under the overhanging oaks and cabbage palms. But little by little, the trees on the sides and back had been cleared to make way for a bigger garden, a cane field, and a number of outbuildings. Another porch, not as deep as the one across the front of the house, ran the length of the kitchen and butted against the north wall of the pantry. It had a cluttered, busy look - clothesline, hand pump, buckets, washtubs, shelves with empty canning jars and gardening tools, dirty boots, scrub brushes, a broken bridle and broom - and a back door into the kitchen that creaked open and banged shut all day long.

The cats slept on the back porch on chilly afternoons, draped across the warm, silvered boards, drenched in sunlight stolen from the hammock. On this fine September morning, though, they were begging at the top of the back porch steps for a bowl of milk. They'd trotted after Raymond as he left the barn, tails straight up in the air and stiff as cordwood. A young dog crawled out from under the house when Raymond got to the porch. Resting his muzzle on the bottom step, he followed the bucket of milk with despondent eyes. He would come no further on the porch than that step, neither would he threaten the cats. Jessie had disabused him of such notions by the time he was weaned. The cats arched their back and purred and wove themselves between the porch railings, scarred faces turned imploringly toward Raymond. But they didn't rub his ankles. Like the dog, they had learned their limits.

Raymond opened the back door. Bekah was already standing there, a pitcher of hot water in her hand.

"Trade you," she said.

Raymond eyed the steaming pitcher with dislike. "Don't I get a cup of coffee first?"

Bekah called back over her shoulder to her mother. "Daddy says he wants a cup of coffee."

Jessie's voice came back clear and determined. "Tell him I'll bring him a cup directly."

Bekah offered him the pitcher of water again. Raymond took the pitcher and gave Bekah the bucket of milk. The cats ignored him now.

They turned their attention to the door, instead, batting at it with tentative paws.

"Good luck," Raymond muttered.

A table was built into the corner of the porch where it met the pantry. Above it, a spotted mirror hung on the wall between two nails. From one of the nails dangled a thin towel, from the other, a leather strap. The table held a porcelain bowl, a soap mug with a shaving brush in it, and a leather case. Raymond set the pitcher down next to the bowl, yawned, and scratched his chest. The young dog sighed, its head still resting on the porch step. Raymond grunted in commiseration. The back door opened, and Jessie set a bowl of milk out for the cats. She disappeared for a moment then stepped out on the porch with a cup of coffee that she carried to the table and set down next to the pitcher.

"Breakfast'll be ready by the time you're through," she said.

Raymond looked out across the yard to the line of the hammock. The trees there were still ragged with mist, but the yard was almost clear. It must have been close on to seven o'clock, and his stomach was growling. He picked the cup up, and took a careful sip. The coffee was scorching hot. "This is good," he said. He studied Jessie's face across the rim of the cup - the calm gray eyes with their specks of blue and green, the brown hair curling at the temples - and added, "It'd go better with grits and bacon."

Jessie appeared unmoved by the reproach in his voice. "It won't be long," she said. "You're not ready yet, anyhow." With a sudden, startled movement, she rose up on tiptoe and kissed him on the cheek.

Spontaneous gestures of affection were rare for Jessie and always took Raymond by surprise. Their unexpected sweetness left him feeling as awkward and found-out as the youth he'd been sixteen years before. As clearly as if it'd been just yesterday, he could see her standing small and prim behind the counter of her father's store. He tasted again the licorice in his mouth, and felt the weight of the chickens he'd stolen in the burlap bag slung behind his back. Jessie smiled at him like she knew what he was thinking. Raymond turned away to set the coffee down on the table, and stuck his finger in the pitcher. "This water's nearly cold," he said.

Again, Jessie ignored him, her mind full of her own concerns. "Don't hurry," she said. "You always cut yourself when you hurry."

"Try scraping your face with a razor and see if it don't bleed," Raymond complained. He was waiting for her answer when the back door slammed, and he realized she'd gone back in the house. A moment later, the smell of frying bacon came through the window.

Raymond poured half the water from the pitcher into the bowl, soaked the towel in it then held it to his beard to soften the whiskers. He could see the cats in the mirror. Replete with milk, they sat on the edge of the porch and cleaned their faces. "It's a sad day in a man's life when the cats eat breakfast before he does," Raymond said.

The cats ignored him. They were like Jessie in that way. She was mainly responsible for the interruptions in his life. Some of them - elections, hangings, county commission and bank director meetings - were necessary and unavoidable. But Jessie's reasons didn't have to be important. She dragged the family off to weddings, christenings, funerals, and barn-raisings whether Raymond cared for the people involved or not. And at least six times a year - the Fourth of July; every fifth Sunday for the Lord's Supper; the annual Sunday School picnic in May; and today, the Dempsey's cane grinding - Jessie rose before the sun to disrupt Raymond's life. She made him perform unaccustomed chores, insisted he shave before his face was awake, and cooked his breakfast so late it may as well have been dinner. She knocked his whole day out of kilter in her haste to leave Walker's Island, its rhythms and habits in tatters around her like the discarded remnants of a cocoon.

Raymond opened the leather case that had belonged to Jessie's father. A straight razor lay inside on a faded velvet lining. He picked it up, tested the sharpness of the blade on his thumb, then stropped it on a leather strap hanging beside the mirror. The sound woke the young dog. It stretched its legs and toes, then laid its head back down and groaned. In the kitchen, there were sounds of a scuffle followed by a sharp slap.

"Get out of that bacon, young man!" Jessie cried. High, delighted laughter followed her reprimand. There was another slap. Footsteps thudded across the kitchen floor and faded away.

"How much did he get?" Jessie demanded.

"A handful," Bekah said.

"Rascal," Jessie said. The word was honey in her mouth.

Raymond dipped the razor in the washbowl and started on his cheekbone. Nothing had changed as far as Jack was concerned. Twelve years old and still as peculiar and lazy as ever. He'd started playing the fiddle soon after Red Rainey died and now was worse off than he'd ever been. The noise he'd made with that thing had been awful at first, like cats breeding. But soon he was not only playing tunes even Raymond could recognize, but was making up his own. Pretty things, Jessie called them, that made her want to dance. Raymond scowled at himself in the mirror. Pretty things, indeed. Why, if it weren't for Beau, he'd have despaired of the island's future.

Raymond rinsed the razor again then twisted his mouth to one side, pulling the side of his face tight. He scraped the razor carefully through his beard, then stopped, peering at his reflection. Change the brown eyes to gray, knock off three inches and eighteen years, and it was Beau looking back at him. It seemed to Raymond that some kind of understanding ought to come with that resemblance, some meeting of the minds behind the faces. But when Raymond looked at Beau, he saw a stranger. A dull, familiar heartache accompanied that thought, compounded of anger and a sense of loss.

Raymond stropped the razor again and resumed shaving. There was a resistance in Beau that didn't used to be there. If Raymond pushed him to do something, Beau pushed back: not hard, not ugly, but with an unmistakable opposing pressure. If Raymond said to do something one way, Beau did it another. Sometimes he argued up front. Other times he pretended to listen, then went about things his own way, or worse yet, said he'd learned it another way - a different, faster, smarter, stronger way - from Dolly. Somehow, Raymond had lost to Dolly - not Beau's respect; he knew his son respected him - but his affection. He mentioned something about it once to Jessie. She said he sounded jealous.

Raymond flicked lather into the bowl with a jerk of his wrist, and started on the other side of his face. Jealous. Now that was a hell of a thing to say. He wasn't jealous, he was concerned. Dolly went to trouble like a witching wand to water. Beau would fall into it right along with him if he dogged the man's heels too closely.

Raymond rinsed the razor one more time, then dried it on the towel. Boys were hard to raise, he thought. A sensible man would stick to girls. Bekah and Jonelle were as pretty as Jessie, with her neat, homey ways, and equally unknowable. He ate the biscuits the two of them made, hard and gray with much handling, and dipped them in honey he said was no sweeter than they were. He admired their new dresses and the hats they made for their dolls. He dandled them on his knee and kissed their hurts and sometimes even thought to bring them flowers. But he suspected they found him wanting, just as Jessie did, and as, in a way, he found them. Daughters were too simple, their love too easily won. There was no need to pursue them, and he could not conquer what was surrendered to him at the first sign of his approval. Boys were harder, no doubt about it. More unpredictable, too. He stuck the razor back in the case.

The young dog scrambled to its feet, growling. It bayed once, then trotted down the path that wound its way among the outbuildings, through the hammock and across the creek to Dolly's house. Raymond emptied the washbowl over the porch rail and filled it again from the pitcher. The water was completely cool now. He rinsed the towel in it anyway, and wiped the remaining lather from his face while he watched the dog. The scent of biscuits baking drifted across the back porch. Jessie was convinced that odor went all the way to Dolly's window and drew him to the Pennell's in time for meals. Raymond hung the towel back on its nail and buckled shut the leather case. Well, that wouldn't be happening so often anymore, because Dolly had gone off to Tampa and come back with a wife. Dolly loved surprising people, but this time he'd outdone himself.

Raymond stood at the top of the steps and followed the path with his eyes until it disappeared into the hammock. He'd taken it the day before to see if Dolly was back yet, hoping to share a cup of coffee. Dolly had started going to Tampa five or six years ago, making the trip alone and without warning two or three times a year. He always left the same note. It said, "Gone to Tampa," and lay on the kitchen table beside an empty whiskey bottle and a worn Bible opened to the Song of Songs. When Raymond saw him again - always exactly three weeks later - the table would be empty. In all these years, neither one of them had ever mentioned the note, the bottle, the Bible, or the Song.

"Your trip to Tampa turn out like you wanted?" Raymond would ask.

"Right as rain," Dolly would say - or "fine as frog hair" or "couldn't beat it with a stick" - and that would be that. The next topic of conversation would be hunting or dogs or cattle. It almost drove Jessie crazy.

"What does he do down there?" she asked.

"None of my business," Raymond always answered. He'd trained himself, back when the trips first started, not to speculate. The possibilities that came to mind were too troublesome. Raymond didn't worry about Dolly. He just waited for him to return.

Yesterday had been three weeks to the day since the last departure, and so, creature of habit that he was, Raymond had ridden unsuspecting into Dolly's front yard. The dogs had announced his arrival as always, crawling out from under the house with their hackles raised, and baying. Then they'd sniffed at this horse and whined, tails wagging back and forth in lukewarm greeting.

"Hey, Dolly," Raymond hollered. Nobody answered. He rode up to the porch and had just gotten off his horse when the front door swung open. A woman stood in the doorway. Raymond thought for a moment he'd come to the wrong house.

Long, disheveled black hair hung loose around her face, and her eyes had a sleepy look, as if she'd just awakened. The patina of sweat on her honey-brown skin, however, and the full lips, red and swollen-looking, suggested otherwise. She had on a thin cotton shift, and nothing else. Raymond didn't know where to put his eyes, and finally trained his gaze on her left eyebrow.

"Morning," he said. "My name's Raymond Pennell, from across the creek there. I just came to see if maybe Dolly was back from Tampa yet." He sounded stupid to himself, but the woman didn't seem to notice.

"He's here," she said. "I'll get him." She went back inside. In a moment, Dolly stepped out on the porch with his hat under his arm, fumbling with the buttons on his long underwear.

"Morning, Ray," he said. He stopped buttoning to swipe a hand over his bald, red, sweat-streaked head, then put his hat on and went back to work on his buttons. "You ain't going to believe what's happened."

"I sure didn't mean to interrupt anything," Raymond said. He bit the amusement off his lower lip, but couldn't keep it out of his eyes. "If I'd known you had company..."

Dolly looked up with a sly smile. "She ain't company," he said. "You are."

Raymond's amusement at Dolly's discomfort faded, and Dolly's smile broadened to a grin. "Hey, Lupe," he called. "Come on out here."

The woman came to the door again, a shawl wrapped around her shoulders. Dolly put his arm around her waist. "Lupe, this is the feller I've been telling you about, Raymond Pennell. Ray, this is Lupe Baxter, my wife."

"Your wife?" Raymond asked. He felt poleaxed, then realized he was staring. Gathering up the remnants of his manners, Raymond took his hat off and stepped up on the porch to shake her hand. "A pleasure to meet you, ma'am," he said.

Lupe acknowledged his greeting with the faintest pressure of her smooth, cool hand, then withdrew it. "Thank you," she said. "I've heard a lot about you."

Raymond put his hat back on and addressed her with a certain peevishness. "Well, I ain't heard a thing about you," he said. "I didn't even know you two was courting."

The woman - Raymond would give her that, though she couldn't have been much older than Beau - opened her mouth as though to reply, but Dolly interrupted her.

"I guess I ain't got to tell you everything I know," he said. He sounded grumpy, and Raymond wanted to ask him what the hell he was so irritable about, but didn't know how to do it in front of his wife. Dolly's wife. The phrase was an obstacle in Raymond's mind, like a tree fallen across a much-traveled road. He wished he'd stayed home.

"You ain't got to tell nothing at all, if you don't want to," Raymond said. He touched the brim of his hat to the new Mrs. Baxter. "It's a pleasure to have you here, ma'am," he lied. "Congratulations, Dolly. I'll let Jessie know she has company in the neighborhood."

It was Dolly's turn to act hurt. "You ain't' got to leave so soon," he said. "Lupe can make a pot of coffee, maybe cook some eggs or something. Time we were getting up, anyhow."

Raymond felt the high ground under his feet and decided to stand on it. "I can't stay," he said. "Jessie's expecting me back." He stepped off the porch, got back on his horse, and turned to leave.

"Hey, Raymond," Dolly said.

Raymond pulled up. "What?"

"You sure you didn't have something on your mind?"

Raymond heard the note of wistfulness in Dolly's voice. It was something - not much - but something. He unbent a little. "Well," he said. "The cane grinding at the Dempsey's is tomorrow. I came to remind you. But I don't reckon you'll be going now."

"Why not?" Dolly demanded. "It'd give Lupe a chance to meet everybody."

Raymond looked at the half-dressed girl, her face tight and watchful. Then he looked at Dolly, standing in his misbuttoned underwear beside his young wife. She was taller than he by a good two inches.

"Is that what you want?" Raymond asked. "For her to meet everybody?"

Dolly grinned and pushed his hat back on his head. "You bet," he said. "Ain't nobody going to believe it. No more than I do myself."

Raymond thought that was probably true. He wondered what Lupe wanted, but she didn't offer an opinion. Dolly was looking at him like an orphan. Raymond relented.

"Y'all come to the island in the morning," he said. "Then you can go with us to the grinding."

Dolly hugged Lupe to his side. "We'll be there," he said. "It'll be a durn wedding parade. And Ray..."

"Yeah?"

"Don't tell Jessie about me and Lupe. I want her to be surprised."

Raymond glanced again at the woman in Dolly's arm. The shawl had fallen off one shoulder, and he could see the thin material of the shift hugging one round breast. He looked away again.

"Oh, she'll be surprised, all right," he said. "You can count on that." He touched the brim of his hat to Lupe. "Ma'am."

Lupe lifted her hand in a brief gesture of farewell.

"Nice meeting you," she said. There was no conviction in her words, nor were they followed by an invitation to return. It gave Raymond a hollow feeling in the pit of his stomach. He reined his horse around and started back down the path. At the edge of the hammock, Raymond looked back over his shoulder. Dolly was standing alone at the bottom of the steps, waving goodbye. He was still there when the tall fronds of the palmettos hid him from Raymond's view.

Raymond sat down on the bottom step. The morning sun had burned all the mists away and dulled the dew-bright green of the cabbage palms. The young dog returned from the hammock and dropped its head in Raymond's lap. He rubbed its ears. A cool wind came off the lake, filling the hammock with whispers. Suddenly the everydayness of things looked different to Raymond, as though the world had just made some imperceptible but significant shift. Everything had moved a hairbreadth, down to the very foundations of his house, and now stood in precarious imbalance. A chill ran down Raymond's spine, prickling the hairs on his neck. He pushed the dog off his lap and stood up.

"This happens to a man's mind when he don't get his breakfast on time," he explained, and rubbed his face as though making its acquaintance. The back door swung open.

"Daddy?" Bekah said. "You done yet? We're about to starve in here."

"Yes," Raymond said. "I'm done." He held the door open, and she ducked under his arm to go inside. Behind him, the whispers of the hammock died, drowned by the clatter of pots and pans, and Jessie's voice calling him to breakfast.

Chapter Seventeen

Beau stared at his plate. The yolks of two fried eggs stared back. Elbows on table, chin in hand, he stabbed them with his fork, covered the oozing remains with grits, and put the fork down on the table. He looked up to find his mother watching him.

"Something the matter with your breakfast?" she asked.

Beau shook his head. "No, ma'am," he said. "I guess I'm just not hungry."

She persisted. "Are you sick? I don't think you should go today, if you're sick."

"I'm not sick," Beau said. "I'm just not hungry, is all."

"Eat your breakfast, son," Raymond said. "You've got a long day ahead of you." His expression brooked no discussion.

Beau smeared butter on a piece of cornbread, picked it up, and put it back down. He couldn't put it in his mouth. He wasn't sick, but he sure had a bad case of the sours. That was Dolly's word for the way he felt right now - like a catch dog on a chain - twitchy, unpredictable, and mean. When it got bad, it affected his appetite. When it got real bad, he wanted to hurt somebody. He stood up. "I'm sorry, Mama," he said. "But I can't eat. I'll puke if I do."

No one spoke.

Beau pushed his chair under the table. "I'm going down to the barn, now, and hitch the mules," he said.

No one had anything to say about that, either, so he walked around the table to the door and took his hat off the nail next to the jamb. But he didn't put it on until he got outside, and didn't take a good deep breath until he was all the way down the porch steps. There were murmurs in the kitchen behind him, and his father's voice rose in anger. The back door slammed. Seconds later, Jack was trotting down the path beside him.

"You don't eat," he said, "and I get yelled at. Do you think that's fair?"

Beau lengthened his stride, forcing Jack to take two steps to his one. "You must have said something to make it worse," he said. "He wasn't yelling when I left."

"I asked to be excused, is all, just as sweet as the preacher's daughter," Jack said. "And he tells me to get my butt to the barn and help hitch." He tripped on a root, and Beau grabbed his shirt. Jack rubbed his throat, and looked uncertainly grateful for the help.

"You don't have to jerk so hard," he said.

"And you don't have to follow me around," Beau said.

Jack stopped so suddenly in the middle of the path that Beau ran into him. "Hitch 'em by yourself, then," he said. "I hope it takes you all day."

Beau pushed his way around him. "That would suit me fine," he said. He walked on by himself, relieved to be alone, then got irritated all over again when he discovered Jack was coming anyway, preceded by a clear, tuneful whistle whose lilting joy only added to Beau's discontent.

He couldn't remember exactly when this misery had begun, several months before, he thought, sometime around his fifteenth birthday. He just woke up one morning with his teeth on edge, pain in every joint, and so tired he could hardly put his feet on the floor. He'd lain there in the bed, feeling for fever with one hand and prodding his legs with the other, hunting the source of the bone-deep ache that afflicted him. His condition worsened over several days. When it got so bad he thought he must be dying, he'd gone to Dolly with a list of symptoms.

"You've got the sours," Dolly said. He was sitting on an upended bucket in the pens behind the barn, peeling an orange and washing the sections in the water trough before he ate them, like a 'coon. Beau had been so relieved to hear his condition had a name that his legs got weak.

He sat down on the edge of the trough and took his hat off, spinning it around a forefinger to give his hands something to do.

"What are the sours?" he asked.

"What you've got," Dolly said.

Beau tried another direction. "Well, what do I do about them?"

Dolly an orange section back in his cheek with his tongue the way he would a tobacco plug, and grinned at Beau. "You need a little sweetening, and a lot of sleep."

For a cure, it didn't sound too bad. Beau came to his feet, dropping his hat. "What kind of sweetening?" he asked.

Dolly picked Beau's hat up off the ground and stuck it on his head. "If you've got to ask, you ain't ready for it. Just crawl up under that tree over yonder and take a nap. Maybe you'll feel better when you wake up."

"What if I don't?" Beau asked, as miserable and ignorant as he'd been before the conversation started.

Dolly shrugged. "You'll still be mean and ugly. I'm here to tell you, ain't nobody ever died of it."

But on days like today, Beau was not so sure of that. This particular morning had started out just fine. He'd awakened well before dawn and tiptoed out of the sleeping house in his bare feet. He hadn't even put his boots on until he got to the barn, when the wet chill of the dew and the stiff breeze that swept the bats through the loft like charred paper reminded him that his feet were cold. He'd skirted the wagons in front of the barn--one empty, the other piled high with ribbon cane--and felt his way along the gate into the alley, rapping on boards along the way to scare the rats out of the feed room.

The barn smelled of horse sweat, leather, manure, rat mess, and dust. Dirt dauber nests clung to the eaves. Every now and then, a horse would kick the side of a stall, or bump it with hip or shoulder, and a nest would break and fall, sprinkling the horse and the brown dirt floor with dried mud and fine gray dust. Cobwebs heavy with flies and chaff and pollen cluttered the beams and drooped between the uprights, beaded with black droplets of dew that would sparkle when the sun rose.

Beau had gotten a bucket of shelled corn from the feed room, and put a lard can full in each stall, then unlatched the back gate and stood in the opening to call the horses and mules from the night's pasture. His high-pitched "colt, colt, colt," had brought them through the breaking dawn at a dead run. They'd churned up dirt and tempers at the back gate until he flung it open, then fought their way past him up the dark alleyway to the stalls. A dew-dampened haunch slammed his hip, a rippled shoulder glanced against his back, a mouth opened in a squeal and trailed the hot, sweet scents of horse breath and grass across his face. And then the horses were in their stalls, attacking the corn in the feed boxes with the same fierce vigor with which they'd stormed the barn. He could have stayed there all day, perfectly at peace, had anybody seen fit to leave him alone. But he'd been called to breakfast despite his lack of appetite, and now, stomach churning and the night's peace destroyed, Beau felt as though the day had been stolen from him.

The horses perked their ears as he entered the barn, then gazed past him at the one-man parade bringing up the rear. Beau got two lead ropes out of the saddle room, and turned around to give one to Jack. The younger boy was swinging back and forth on the front gate, a practice that irritated Beau even more than the whistling. Hanging on a gate that way broke the hinges down. Even on the best of days, Beau couldn't stand to see a thing misused.

"Get off the gate," he said.

Jack stopped whistling. "Make me," he said. Beau took a step toward him. Jack jumped off the gate, shoving it closed between them. "Look out, now," he said. "I don't want to have to hurt you."

Beau almost laughed, the idea was so ludicrous. "Uh, huh," he said. "You and who else?"

Jack gave the question some thought, then cocked a thumb back over his shoulder. "Vancey Adams," he said.

Beau glanced past Jack at the cypress tree a quarter mile away that marked the old grave. "He's no good to you anymore," he said. "I'm too old to believe in ghosts." He turned away, headed for Jezebel's stall.

"Vancey don't need you to believe in him," Jack called. "He does fine all on his own."

Ignoring the high, indignant voice at his back, Beau stepped into Jezebel's stall and tied the lead rope to her halter.

"He's dazed," he muttered into her long ear.

The mule raised her head and regarded Beau with a thick-lashed brown eye. He led her out into the alleyway, and snubbed her head to a post, then got the harness out of the saddle room and threw it over her back. Behind him, he could hear Jack fussing around in the saddle room, and in a minute, the soft clomp of Rahab's hooves in the alleyway. Before too long, Beau knew, Jack would have the harness tied up in knots. But he'd have to ask for help. Beau wouldn't volunteer it. It was some small revenge on Beau's part, a payback for Jack's brotherly deficiencies. Beau pulled the hames into place on the collar, and ran his hand down Jezebel's back, slipping the harness over her haunches and pulling her tail through the crupper.

"Hey, Beau," Jack said. "Could you help me with this here? I think there's some pieces missing."

Beau ducked under Jezebel's neck to check his brother's progress. Jack had gotten no further than the collar on Rahab's neck, and that was crooked. The rest of the harness was in a pile on the ground. Rahab, long ears backed, neck craning, was flubbing her lips at a grass stem Jack was trying to stick up her nose. He drew the seed head across her lower lip, and Rahab snatched it away from him.

"She thinks I'm special," Jack said.

"About as special as a horsefly," Beau said. He picked up the harness off the ground - hames, back pad, and breeching - and threw it over Rahab's back, then set about untangling the mess Jack had made of it. When he'd finished, Beau patted the mule's rump.

"That's got it," he said. "Try to get her to the wagon without tearing anything up."

He handed Rahab's lines to Jack, then untied Jezebel and led her out of the barn. With Jack hindering more than he helped, Beau hitched Jezebel to the cane wagon, and Rahab to the empty one. Jack climbed into the latter, and Beau handed him the whip.

"You go on to the house," he said. "I'll come with the cane as soon as I get the horses saddled." He walked back into the barn before Jack could argue, and listened as the clatter of the wagon muffled, and finally extinguished, that clear whistle.

Twenty minutes later, Beau drove up in the front yard, his father's bay mare and a dun gelding Beau was training for George Dempsey tied to the tailgate. Rahab dozed in the front yard, the wagon behind her piled with an assortment of baskets, pillows, boxes, quilts, and bags over and around which climbed Jack, Bekah, and Jonelle, their efforts directed by Jessie, who was standing on the front porch.

"Put that box up under the front seat," she called. "It's got a pie in it."

"There's no more room under there," Bekah shouted.

"Then take something else out," Jessie said. "Or move it around a little bit."

Beau tied the lines to the brake and jumped to the ground. With his mother standing right there, he was careful to knock the dirt off his boots before stepping onto the porch.

"But everything that's under there is what you said to put under there," Bekah said. "So how do I know what to take out?"

"Use your head," Beau called. "Else you may as well be ass at both ends." He laughed at his own wit, and Jessie smacked him on the arm.

"Mind your tongue, mister," she said. Beau pulled away from her in mock alarm, but she didn't smile. "What took you so long?"

"I didn't know it had," he said.

Jessie looked back at the activity on the wagon. "Stack it careful," she said. "I don't want it falling out before we get there." She pushed a strand of hair behind her ear and tsked her tongue. "I may as well do it myself, for all the help I get around here. Tuck your shirt in, Beau. You look a mess."

Beau studied his mother's face. Her hair was escaping the bun she'd put it in that morning, curling light and dry-looking around her temples. It wasn't a pretty face, Beau thought, not anymore. It was too worn and thin, with fine wrinkles around the eyes and two lines that ran from the freckled nose to the corners of the firm mouth. But it was a good, strong face, and every now and then his mother could still burst into laughter that if you weren't looking at her, sounded like a girl's. She wasn't laughing now, though. She looked irritable, like a cat with its fur rubbed the wrong way. Beau eyed her cautiously and tucked his shirt in his pants.

"Dolly here yet?" he asked. He was thinking of penknives, peacock feathers, and coconut masks carved into monkey faces; a scrimshaw needle case and a tiger's tooth on a gold chain; a book no bigger than Bekah's thumbnail with the Lord's prayer printed inside and a magnifying glass to read it with; a glass paperweight with a real rose inside, an ant encased in amber, and best of all, the marvelous shrunken head from Borneo, wherever that was, with all its teeth intact, just a few of the surprises that Dolly had brought back with him from Tampa. There was never any telling what he'd have with him, and expectation lifted Beau's heart like a feather on a breeze.

"Your father's looking for you," Jessie said.

Beau's heart plummeted again. "Where is he?" he asked.

"Out back, waiting on Dolly. That's a good place for him, too. The man's not fit to talk to."

A fight broke out on the wagon between Bekah and Jonelle. Jonelle hollered and fell backward into the bed. "I'm hurt!" she screamed.

"If you've broken Myrtle Gibbs's custard cups, you'll be hurting sure enough," Jessie called. She pushed past Beau to the porch steps and was halfway across the yard before what she'd said registered with Beau.

"What are you doing with Myrtle Gibbs's custard cups?" he asked.

"Those were her custards we had this Sunday past. I told you then that Lila gave them to me at church to give to you. I think you need your ears checked."

Beau felt a little panicked. "Don't tell her I ate one."

Jessie laughed out loud. "I'm going to tell her you ate every one, because you did."

"I'll never eat another," Beau said. "I'll die of starvation first."

Jessie waved him off as she would a gnat. "She's a good girl. I like her," she said. "And you could do worse. Now don't be fussing me, I've got things to do."

Beau didn't know how his name had gotten stuck to Lila Gibbs's, but he sure hadn't done it. She was a very ordinary girl, plain-faced and quiet, with nothing special about her at all, unless the way she followed him around like a lost puppy could be called special. He was fascinated by her bosom, but he felt that way about all bosoms. They didn't even need heads on them. What mattered most about girls was the part between their necks and their ankles. If it was covered up, it had to be interesting. He had danced with Lila before and had a gentleman's idea of her shape. She was solid. Not solid like firm. Solid like a sack of feed on wheels. It took an effort to get her started, another to get her stopped, and quick feet to keep from getting run over in between. And her cooking was nothing to get excited about, either. They had been very ordinary custards, not one whit better than the ones his mother made. Oh, no. Lila Gibbs was not the girl for him, he didn't care how much his mother liked her. He'd not ask her to dance again. And he wasn't eating anything else she cooked, either.

The thought of food made his stomach growl, and he went through the house to the kitchen. A plate full of biscuits was sitting in the warmer. Beau ate nine, and washed them down with black coffee. Further investigation proved fruitless. His mother had packed every leftover, pie, and pickle in the house to take to the cane grinding. She'd trade around with other women and come back home with just as much tomorrow night, but all of it different, and some of it much better than the rest. Beau didn't know how some people survived, considering what they ate.

He got the can of bacon grease out of the pie safe and the plate with the last biscuit on it, and carried them to the table, along with his coffee cup. He sat down and split the biscuit, poured bacon grease all over it, then leaned back in the chair with the plate in his hand and lifted the bottom half of the grease-soaked biscuit to his mouth. He'd no sooner closed his teeth on it than the back door opened and his father walked in.

A familiar dissatisfaction came over Raymond's face when he saw Beau. "I thought you were down at the barn," he said. "What are you doing here?"

Beau put the chair legs on the floor and set the rest of the biscuit back on the plate. The bite marks in it looked huge. He pushed the plate away from him in a vain attempt to disown it.

"Go ahead and eat," Raymond said. "Don't let me stop you." He got a cup off a shelf and poured himself some coffee, then leaned against the cold stove to drink it, the brown eyes fixed on Beau over the rim.

"That's all I want," Beau said. It was a bald-faced lie. He could have eaten another ten biscuits, a few fried eggs, and some grits, besides, but he wasn't about to admit it to the man standing by the stove.

"Where are the horses?" Raymond asked.

"Out front."

Raymond nodded and looked almost satisfied. Relieved, Beau pulled the plate back to him and took another bite. Raymond took a swallow of coffee. "Now that you're done with the Dempsey horse," he said, "I told Baker Howell you'd break his filly. He's bringing her to the grinding. You can take her from there."

The biscuit turned to clay in Beau's mouth. "I can't, Daddy," he said. "I've already got something else lined up.

The brown eyes studying him over the rim of the cup didn't change their expression.

"What is it?" Raymond asked.

"I'm contracted to Tate Rainey."

"How'd that happen?"

"Dolly put me on to it."

"When?"

"A few weeks back, before he left for Tampa. Said it was a sure money-maker."

Raymond took a swallow of coffee. "First I've heard of it," he said.

"I must have forgot," Beau said, who had not forgotten for a second.

"So tell me about this job," Raymond said.

Beau tried to keep the eagerness out of his voice. "Tate's been needing help with the wild horses, so he can take them down to Ft. Myers and sell them. He's got a buyer lined up already, some feller that uses them for livery. Dolly said I ought to talk to Tate about it, so I did, and Tate's agreed to hire me. He's giving me ten dollars a head to ride them out, plus a percentage of anything he sells."

"What percentage?" Raymond asked.

Beau blinked. "Uh, I don't recall him saying." He brightened. "But it'll be fair, I know. Tate strikes me as fair."

"I see," Raymond said. "What if he don't sell any?"

Here Beau was more confident. "Oh, he will. Dolly says it's a sure-fire deal."

"Well," Raymond said, his voice dry. "I'm sure Dolly would know."

"Amen to that," Beau said. He finished the rest of the biscuit and thought about licking the plate, but refrained. Then, uncomfortable with the silence, he tried to move the conversation in a more pleasant direction. "Mama said Dolly's got a surprise," he said.

"That's right."

"She says he's been shopping in Tampa again."

"Something like that," Raymond said. As he spoke, a horse pounded out of the hammock, across the back yard, and around the side of the house, a pack of dogs baying in its wake. Shrill screams erupted from the front yard.

"What in the world..." Beau said.

"Dolly's surprise," Raymond said. He put his cup on the table and walked out of the kitchen, headed for the front door, Beau close on his heels.

Out in the yard, what looked like twenty dogs were embroiled in the worst dog fight Beau had ever seen. At its center, like the eye of a hurricane, danced a tall gray horse upon which sat Dolly Baxter and a woman. Dogs ran out of the fray, bloodied and yelping, then leaped into it again, crawling back and forth under the porch, twisting and rolling in masses of yellow and black and tan that writhed under the wagons and in the bushes and in between the horse's legs while Dolly drove them on to an even greater frenzy, whooping and yelling, and the girls screamed.

Beau tore a branch off the orange tree by the porch and pummeled the snarling dogs with green oranges. Jack beat them with a length of ribbon cane, clearing a path for Jessie, who ran through the fight and up the front steps, grabbed a broom and waded back into the free-for-all like a windmill. A strange dog jumped at her, lips peeled so far back it looked like it didn't have any, and caught the end of the upraised broom in its mouth. It hung there, eyes closed, growling. Unable to shake it off the broom, Jessie flailed the other dogs with its body.

A sound like a rifle shot smacked the air, and the dogs fell apart, yelping and groveling. Another crack, and the Pennell dogs wiggled back under the house, while the others dropped to the ground around the horse and lay there, panting and licking their wounds. Another one, and the dog on the end of Jessie's broom dropped off like a bloated tick and started crawling away on its belly. One more crack, hurtful to Beau's ears, and the dog moaned, rolled over on its back, and pissed on itself.

Raymond stood beside the bay mare, a cow whip crawling to him through the dirt as he coiled it up, then tied it back on his saddle. A dog lifted its head and watched intently as a horsefly circled in front of it. White teeth snicked, and the horsefly was gone.

"Well, Dolly," Raymond said. "Glad you could make it."

Dolly swayed in the saddle. The strong odor of sour mash whiskey wafted across the yard. "Damn dogs," he said, to no one in particular. "Can't fight worth a damn. Raymond. Want you to meet Lupe. Lupe...Oh, that's right. Y'all already met. Well, up there on the porch is his wife, Jessie. Also Beau, his first boy, there with the oranges. And Jack. Where's Jacky? Yep. That's Jack, all right. Over there by that wagon. He's the second boy. And in that other wagon - durn, there's a lot of wagons around here - is Miss Bekah and pretty little baby Jonelle. That's all the Pennells. Pennells, this here is Mrs. Lupe Baxter. My wife." Then he smiled, and paused, as if giving them an opportunity to speak.

Beau didn't have anything to say. He was too busy staring at Mrs. Baxter's leg. It was, from knee to foot, completely bare. Beau touched the brim of his hat and looked at Jack. He was staring at the leg, too, and smiling like somebody had just given him a thousand dollars. Then the woman spoke.

"It's a pleasure to meet you," she said.

Beau had never heard a voice like that, so low and throaty and personal. It made the ordinary words she'd spoken sound like they'd never been said before. Beau had never seen a grown woman's leg all the way to the knee before, either, and had managed to disconnect it from its owner in his fascination with it. The voice, however, laid claim to its own, and Beau, his face uncomfortably warm, was forced to look up at the woman on the horse. She returned his gaze with a boredom that completely belied her voice. It was confusing, but Beau didn't care. She could have barked at him, and it wouldn't have mattered. She was beautiful: bare leg, boredom, and all.

Everything about her seemed full and round with an earthy richness. Blue black hair rippled down her long straight back almost to her waist, and might have fallen below her waist had it not been caught at the neck with a ribbon that may once have been as red as the faded skirt she wore. Her bare forearm rested along her thigh, the palm and fingers nestling in the hollow of Dolly's hip. And the skin of her face and arm and hand, and that of her knee and leg and long bare foot, was smooth and warm-looking and golden brown, like palmetto honey. The gray horse shifted back and forth, fretful, while Beau pondered the eighth wonder of the world that was Lupe Baxter.

"The pleasure is ours, I'm sure," Jessie said. "Raymond didn't tell me Dolly had married."

"It was Dolly's idea," Raymond said.

"I see," Jessie said. Beau could have packed fish in her mouth and kept them fresh for a week.

"Met her in Tampa this last trip," Dolly said. "We ain't been home but three days. When Raymond came to tell me about the grinding, I swore him to silence. Wanted it to be a surprise."

"Well, it certainly is that," Jessie said. She gave Lupe a critical look that Beau knew only too well. "Do you own any shoes?" she asked.

Lupe opened her mouth to say something, but Dolly stepped in first. "They're right here," he said. He fumbled with a pair of high-topped boots dangling from the cantle.

Jessie took them from him and started untying the laces. "You get down from there, Lupe," she said, "and come put your boots on. Then you can ride with me in the wagon to the Dempseys'."

Lupe went to slip a leg over the horse, but Dolly caught hold of it, his fingers half-hidden by the edge of the skirt. Beau wished he'd move his fingers, and hoped he'd keep them there. Dolly backed the horse away from Jessie.

"You can take the shoes with you," Dolly said. "But not her. She stays with me."

Jessie threw the shoes in the back of the wagon, the corners of her mouth pinched and white. "Have it your own way," she said. Without another word, she climbed in beside Jonelle on the wagon seat, untied the lines from the brake, and slapped Rahab on the butt. "Giddup," she said.

The mule headed out of the yard at a good trot, Jonelle bouncing around on the wagon seat like a cloth-covered ball, while Bekah waved goodbye atop her perch on the baggage.

Raymond untied the horses from the tailgate of the cane wagon, handed Beau the reins to the dun horse, and pulled himself up on the bay. "Jack," he said. "You drive this wagon."

"Yessir," Jack said. He scrambled up on the seat and untied the lines. "Giddup, Jezebel!" he hollered. He gave Lupe an abashed look as the wagon rolled forward. "That's what we call the mule," he explained.

Lupe laughed. She had a wide mouth and strong, even, white teeth. "I never heard a mule called that before," she said.

Jack beamed. "It was Dolly's idea," he said. "The other one's named Rahab. They was both lewd women, way back in Bible times."

Lupe laughed again. Jack grinned back at her, delighted at her response. Beau could see his mind working, and knew he'd say something worse directly. Raymond rode up beside him.

"Just drive the wagon, Jack," he said.

"Yessir," Jack said. He tipped his hat to Lupe and she favored him with a wink. Beau, speechless and sick with envy, rode around to the other side of the gray horse. Mrs. Baxter's other leg was bare, as well. Beau had it to himself until his father called him. "Yessir?" he said. Lately, he'd avoided calling his father 'sir,' but for the moment, all of creation had his utmost respect.

"Go ahead with your brother."

"Yessir." Beau, disappointed but not dismayed, loped up beside Jack, who was leaning against the back of the wagon seat with his eyes closed and a smile spread across his face like jam.

"I have seen heaven," Jack said. "I'm going to write a fiddle tune about her. It'll be sweeter than 'Soldier's Joy' and wilder than 'Rose of the Mountain.' It'll make your blood run hot just to hear it. Pieces of it are playing in my head right this second."

There was no music playing in Beau's head, that was for sure, just an intensifying of the dark confusion already there. He turned to look when Lupe crossed the river, and turned away again at the reproach in his father's face. The image of her thigh beneath the red skirt burned in his mind for several miles, however, and he looked again when they passed the Rainey place. Raymond was talking to Dolly, Lupe's head bent forward as though she were listening. As though his eyes had tapped her on the shoulder, Lupe raised her head and looked back. She returned Beau's stare, unsmiling, until he turned around again. That's when he saw the Rainey twins.

They came tearing down the road the way they went everywhere, yelling, and at breakneck speed. They passed the entire Pennell party, clods of dirty flying from beneath their horses' hooves, then hauled their mounts around and trotted back, grinning like fools.

"They are plumb nasty," Jack said. He could not stand the Rainey twins, and claimed they were the only two people he'd never liked. They didn't like him, either, but that didn't mean anything. Bob and Clyde Rainey didn't like anybody.

The twins had not improved with age, and were still identical - with dirty blonde hair, pale blue, red-rimmed eyes, and thin, tough bodies - except for their teeth. Clyde's front teeth were bucked and gray, and Bob's were gone. The two of them grinned constantly, Clyde because he couldn't help it, and Bob for reasons of his own. Perhaps, as Dolly said, he didn't want to be confused with Clyde, who was the more obviously stupid of the two. Beau regarded them with profound distaste, and wished they'd keep their mouths shut. He wasn't interested in telling them apart.

Their manners weren't any better than their appearance. The two of them rode back past Jessie and the girls as though they weren't there, hats firmly on their heads. They stopped when they came to Beau and Jack, however, sandwiching the wagon and the dun horse between them. Bob sidled close to Beau, crowding him against the wagon. The rims of his eyes were so red they made Beau's itch.

"Getting kind of a late start, ain't you?" Bob asked. "Hell, it's almost dinnertime. Most folks are there by now."

"Can't but one family grind at a time," Beau said. "So there's no point in hurrying. Your folks going?" Tate had gone to Southport for a wife after Red's death, a wan, timid woman named Sylla who had as much sayso over the twins as she did over the weather. She'd given Tate four more children, none of them equal to the twins, according to Tate.

"Yep," Clyde said. "Ma's already gone, took the cane with her. Daddy'll be along if he sobers up enough to find the road." He jerked his head at the road. "Where'd Dolly get the woman?"

Beau wasn't about to discuss Dolly's wife with the likes of Clyde Rainey. "What woman?" he asked.

Clyde looked puzzled. "That one back there," he said. He turned in the saddle and looked behind him as if to make sure of what he was talking about. "Yeah. That one."

"Shut your mouth, Clyde," Bob said. He rode out in front of the wagon and stopped. Clyde joined his brother, the two of them blocking the road. Jack pulled back on the lines and Jezebel ambled to a halt. Ahead of them, the supply wagon rolled another twenty feet, then it stopped, too. The riders pulled up behind the second wagon. The bay mare ducked her head and shook herself, flapping the saddle leathers.

"Hold on a minute, everybody," Bob said. "Like ole Beau here says, there ain't no sense in hurrying." He winked at Lupe, and let his eyes slide down her leg. She wiped her knee with her skirt.

"Morning, Bob," Dolly said. "Clyde." He wasn't weaving in the saddle now, but sat straight up, hands relaxed over the cantle.

"Morning, Dolly. How do, Raymond." Bob kicked his horse alongside Dolly's, then stuck his boot under Lupe's bare foot and jiggled it up and down. "You sure are pretty," he said. "You got a name?"

"She does," Dolly said. In a motion as smooth as water, he pulled his rifle out of the scabbard and stuck the muzzle in Bob's mouth. "It's Mrs. Baxter. Mrs. Baxter, this is Bob Rainey." Lupe inclined her head. "Bob, this is Mrs. Baxter. Say hello." Bob grunted and Dolly stuck the barrel a fraction further into his mouth. "I said, say hello. It don't have to come out just right. Mrs. Baxter will understand."

"Eh-oh, Ih-ih Ah-uh," Bob said. Saliva drooled down his lower lip.

"That's good," Dolly said. "Now, Clyde, you say hello to Mrs. Baxter."

"I ain't telling her nothing," Clyde said.

"If you don't tell Mrs. Baxter hello, Clyde, I'm going to blow the rest of your brother's teeth out the back of his head."

"Go ahead," Clyde said.

Bob slurped and choked, filling the air with gargled, strangulated noises. Dolly cocked the trigger. Raymond watched Dolly, his face expressionless. Beau waited for the explosion. Bob whimpered and squeezed his eyes shut. A tear oozed out between his lids and trickled past his nose into his thin beard.

"You titty baby," Clyde said. He nudged his horse forward a step and said in a loud voice, "Hello, Mrs. Baxter." He looked with great scorn on his brother. "Are you satisfied?"

Bob nodded as well as he could with a rifle barrel down his throat. It made him gag, so he stopped.

Dolly took the gun out of Bob's mouth and aimed it at Clyde. "Now," he said. "When you two get home, which will be just as soon as you leave here, you can tell your daddy that you just met Dolly Baxter's wife and you have a whole new respect for womanhood. Ain't that right?"

Bob nodded and swallowed, then sat there kneading the inside of his mouth with his tongue. Clyde looked off in the distance, like he was thinking. Then he looked back at Dolly.

"After the grinding," he said.

Bob quit massaging the roof of his mouth. "We'll go tell him right now, Dolly," he said. "C'mon, Clyde."

Reluctantly, Clyde followed his brother. A hundred yards down the road, he turned and whistled at Lupe. Beau wouldn't have believed that a flutey sound like that coming out of a mouth could sound so nasty.

"That wormy little son-of-a-bitch," Dolly said. He laid the stock of the rifle against his cheek. Raymond grabbed the gray's bridle and jerked its head around. The next thing Beau knew, his father was looking down the long, black barrel of Dolly's rifle. The brown eyes never blinked, but gazed steadily into the cobalt blue eyes at the other end.

"What will happen to Lupe when they hang you?" Raymond asked.

Dolly frowned. "I hadn't thought of that," he said.

"Maybe you should," Raymond said.

The rifle remained steady on Raymond's forehead while Dolly thought. A drop of greasy sweat rolled off Beau's chin and plopped on his saddle. It made a small, round, dark spot on the cantle, like a bullet hole. A mockingbird in a pine tree was singing, running through its songs one by one, over and over again. It flew off so suddenly that Beau jumped.

"Well, Mr. Baxter," Jessie said. "Look what you've done," She'd pushed her way between Beau and the wagon, and now stood in front of the gray horse, hands on hips, voice shrill with anger. She pointed after the Rainey boys. "They're going ahead of us to tell everyone what they've seen, which is more of your wife's body than you ought to see yourself. I hope you're ashamed of yourself. Now you put that girl down here right this minute and let her come with me, or we're turning around this minute and going back to the island. I refuse to watch how people are going to treat her if you insist on going like this."

"What about the cane?" Beau asked, visions of a winter with no syrup darkening his imagination.

"The cane can rot. And put that rifle away, Dolly Baxter. What do you think you're doing with it, anyway? Who do you think you're going to shoot? Raymond? Were you aiming at Raymond?" Jessie's voice rose on her husband's name, squeaky with outrage.

Dolly squinted his eyes like his ears hurt, and put the rifle back in the scabbard. "I was just holding it," he said. "No harm in that."

Lupe slid off the back of the horse. "I better go with Mrs. Pennell," she said.

Dolly didn't try to stop her, but he seemed to shrink with her departure. When they reached the cutoff to the Dempsey homestead, the supply wagon stopped. Jessie turned and motioned to Beau. He rode up to see what she wanted.

"You boys go with your daddy to the Dempseys, and take Mr. Addlepate with you," she said. "Mrs. Baxter and the girls are going with me to town. We'll see you in the morning. Better get you some victuals out of the back." Beau got down off his horse and took a basket of food and two blankets out of the wagon.

"Take Jack's fiddle, too," Jessie said.

Beau stuck the fiddle case under his arm. "I don't think Dolly is going to like this," he said.

"Tell him I said to mind his own business," Jessie said.

Beau stepped back and his mother drove on, right past the road into the Dempsey homestead toward town. Beau watched them leave, the wonder of the day diminishing with Lupe's receding form. Dolly and his father rode up behind him.

"Where's she taking Lupe?" Dolly demanded.

"To town," Beau said. "Mama says they're going to spend the night there."

"The hell she says."

"That's what I told her you'd say."

"What'd she say to that?"

"She said for you to mind your own business."

Jessie's comment had the same effect on Dolly it'd had on Beau, which was momentarily to deprive him of speech.

There was curiosity when they arrived at the Dempseys' without Jessie, and hilarity when Dolly said she'd run off to town with his new wife. No one believed either that Dolly had gotten married or that Jessie wasn't coming, until the four men got the basket of cold food out of the wagon and sat down on the tailgate to eat it. Only then were they invited to pull up beside a campfire and have a hot meal. But Dolly was surly and the Pennells uncommunicative, so people finally left them alone with nothing to say to one another and nothing to do but go to sleep.

Beau lay on a blanket with his hands under his head, his thoughts circling like a deerfly on a string, full of noise and movement and going nowhere. Next to him, Jack stood up and went to the wagon, where he reached under the seat for his fiddle. Without speaking, he tucked it up under his arm and walked off. Beau watched him leave, his mind confused with images: Bob Rainey's grinning mouth; Dolly's finger on the trigger; his father's impassive face; the curve of Lupe's arm and breast and thigh. Beyond the fire, Jack's fiddle started up, tentative notes looking for connections to one another and not finding them. It stopped and started, wandered around and came back again, until Beau found he was holding his breath, waiting for the tune to take form.

"Is that who I think it is?" Dolly asked.

"Yes," Beau said. "He's working on a tune."

"He needs to work on it somewhere else," Dolly said. "I can't sleep."

"It won't take long," Beau said. "It's in his head already."

Dolly grunted. "Well, somebody needs to tell him to hurry up, and quit bothering people."

But the fiddle played on, starting and stopping, then starting again somewhere else, until it abandoned its singular nature and became another night sound, an owl, a mouse, a whippoorwill, a fox for the dogs to chase, whimpering and paddling, through their dreams.

Chapter Eighteen

Jessie may have suffered from strong opinions and a quick temper, but she was not a busybody, so no one was more surprised than she herself when she commandeered Mrs. Baxter's person. In fact, Jessie's reaction to that young woman - more reflex than choice - troubled her a great deal. She wanted nothing more than a quiet moment to be still and ponder its meaning, but was denied any such opportunity by her traveling companions, all three of whom were possessed by an alarming impropriety.

To begin with, Jonelle and Bekah couldn't keep their hands off Mrs. Baxter. The wagon wheels had no sooner started turning than the two of them were crab-walking their way up behind the bench, where they perched on piles of baskets and blankets to touch Lupe's arms, her shoulders, and her hair. Most especially that hair. Despite Jessie's remonstrances and rebukes, Lupe gave them permission to let it down. The girls loosed it from its bedraggled ribbon, and by the time they'd left the men behind at the Dempseys', had divided it between them like loot, strewing its blue-black luxuriance in their laps. Had it not been attached at the other end to Lupe's head, Jessie thought with exasperation, they'd have laid it down in the wagon bed and wallowed in it.

"You don't have to let them do that," she told Lupe. "They know better than to fuss with company that way."

The younger woman was leaning against the back of the seat with her eyes closed, her honey brown throat taut as the girls tugged at her hair with a brush and comb they'd taken out of Jessie's bag. "I like it," she said. "It soothes me."

She yawned, showing her teeth. Jessie couldn't help but notice how white and strong-looking they were. She was unprepared for the suddenness with which Lupe opened her eyes. They were large and thick-lashed, so dark they were almost black, with an oddly deliberate expression of sleepiness, and fixed directly on Jessie's. Just when Jessie thought she'd have to look away, the dark eyes left hers, perused her hair, instead, traveled over her dress and boots, and returned to her hair, where they narrowed with a critical consideration that Jessie found unnerving.

"I can do something about that hair, if you want," Lupe said. "It probably ain't as far gone as it looks."

Jessie stiffened right down to her toes. "No thank you," she said.

Lupe shrugged and closed her eyes again, then jerked a shoulder at the back. "I'll do theirs, then. Something fancy."

"Oh, yes!" Bekah cried. "I ain't never had fancy hair."

"You have never had fancy hair," Jessie corrected. "Nor will you. Plain hair is good enough for us." It was as though she had not spoken.

"Have you ever looked fancy?" Bekah asked Lupe. "I mean, more than now?"

"Go on with you, girl," Lupe said. She spread her arms wide as if offering herself for view, straining the thin red dress across her breasts until Lupe feared they would burst through. "I ain't fancy now, no, ma'am. I left Tampa in just what I've got on. But you can bet I was fancy down there. Had me some high heels and silk stockings and a red satin petticoat with matching garters. Wish I still had 'em. I sure liked them garters." Lupe pulled her skirt up past her knees and studied her exposed thighs as if waiting for her missing garters to appear. Bekah and Jonelle studied her limbs, as well, her hair momentarily forgotten. Jessie reached over and jerked Lupe's skirt back down her legs. Lupe flicked at her hand, but left the skirt where Jessie had put it.

"Satin garters," Bekah said. Her voice was hushed, as if she were talking in church.

Jessie'd had enough of those garters. "So what does your father do, Lupe?" she asked.

"I don't know," Lupe said.

"Where does he live?" Jessie asked.

"I don't know that, either," Lupe said. "I ain't never met him. Don't even know his name."

For a moment, no one said anything.

"I never met anybody without a daddy before," Bekah said.

"That's because you never met anybody like me before," Lupe said.

"That is so true," Jonelle said fervently. "Never, ever in my whole life have I met anybody like you. You are...you are..."

"Full of splendor!" Bekah cried. It was a phrase from the sampler she was presently embroidering, a teaching on the blinding majesty of the Almighty.

"I hardly think..." Jessie began.

"Yes," Jonelle interrupted, her voice hushed with reverence. "You are full of splendor." Her voice took on a note of regret. "I bet your mama is too."

Jessie took umbrage at her daughter's tone. It seemed to suggest that she, Jessie Winters Pennell, had been tried and found wanting merely for lack of a pair of satin garters. "Handsome is as handsome..."

"I don't know if she was or wasn't," Lupe said, riding over Jessie as if she were not there. "I never met her, either. My grandma raised me, near as I was raised."

"Where is she?" Bekah asked.

"Who?"

"Your grandma."

"Dead," Lupe said. "Yellow fever. New Orleans."

"I'm very sorry," Bekah said.

"Not me, " Lupe said. "She was a mean woman. Good riddance, if you ask me."

"Well, what do you think of Harris County?" Jessie asked. Her own voice sounded strange to her, high and warbly with false cheer.

"There's not much to it, far as I can tell," Lupe said. "And that house of Dolly's ain't much better than a shack."

"I'm sure all it needs is a woman's touch," Jessie said.

"Is that where you're from, New Orleans?" Bekah asked.

"I stayed there until I was fourteen," Lupe said.

"Curtains, a few throw rugs, some pictures on the walls, and that house will be pretty in no time."

"It must have been exciting to live there," Jonelle said.

"It was real exciting when we had money," Lupe said. "Me and Granny would strut down Bourbon Streets like peacocks. Other times, it was just hard."

"Of course a garden softens a house on the outside," Jessie said. "And inside you've got canning on the shelves and the smells of cooking and cleaning. All that's part of making a home."

"What happened when you were fourteen?" Bekah asked.

"Granny died, and I left."

"But it's certainly no shack," Jessie said. "Raymond did most of the work on it himself - pardon my saying so, but Dolly's not all that handy with wood and tools and such - and it's as solid as a rock."

"By yourself?" Bekah asked.

"No," Lupe said. "With a man."

There was a moment of silence. Then Jessie took a deep breath.

"You could start right off with some plants around the porch," she said. "I've got a Cherokee rose. You can take some cuttings off of it."

"What man?" Jonelle asked.

There was another silence.

"My Uncle Charlie," Lupe said. She sat up straight and pulled her hair away from the girls. With quick, practiced movements she pulled it into seven strands and braided it, then tied the end with the ribbon. That done, she leaned forward a little bit, elbows on her knees, and seemed to draw into herself.

"That must have been a blessing," Jessie said. "To have family to turn to."

Lupe studied Jessie's face for a moment, a speculative expression in the black eyes. Then she looked away. "More blessing than I knew what to do with," she said.

"Did your Uncle Charlie take you to Tampa?" Jonelle asked.

Lupe didn't answer.

Jessie shook her head at the girls. "I think we've worn Miz Lupe out with all our chatter," she said. "Let's be quiet now, so she can rest." And so I can think, she might have added, for the conversation just ended had wearied and worried her, and left her feeling protective of the young woman beside her, though Jessie could not have said why.

They rode into town forty-five minutes later. The street was empty, the cafe as quiet as the saloon. The town looked empty and closed-up. Most everybody was at the Dempseys'.

"So this is Elliston," Lupe said.

"Yes," Jessie said."

"What am I looking at?"

Jessie pointed down the road ahead of them. "At the very end of the main street is the livery stable where we'll leave the wagon. Next to it is the hotel. We'll stay there because we don't have any choice. Then there's the barber and dentist shop, two lawyers, the bank, and the First Methodist Church." She pointed east. "That way is the courthouse - the jail is one block over, behind the courthouse, the doctor, the mercantile store - -the post office and the telegraph office are inside the store - and the First Baptist Church. The street ends at Cat Lake. And that's our town."

"Must seem like a pretty big town to the likes of you," Lupe said.

Jessie looked at her. "What do you mean by that?" she asked.

"Dolly told me you come from some little place up in north Florida. Says it wasn't no bigger than a broom closet."

"It was big enough," Jessie said. "I had no complaints."

"Do you miss it?" Lupe asked.

"Not anymore," Jessie said. "That was a long time ago, and I've stayed busy."

Lupe laughed. "I hear busy is what you do best," she said.

"It keeps me out of trouble," Jessie said. "Which is more than I can say for some people."

Lupe's beautiful face turned sullen and not very attractive, and she went into a sulk from which she didn't seem likely to recover. Except for brief exchanges at the stable regarding various bags and baskets, she refused to speak at all. Lupe's silence didn't bother Jessie in the least. In fact, she preferred it. Once the oddments were sorted out, she left Mrs. Baxter and the girls to carry them, took her skirts in hand, and headed next door to the Tropical Palms Hotel.

Jessie opened the front door of the hotel and banged it shut behind her, causing a little puff of dust to start up from the rug beneath her feet. Behind the desk sat Mr. Horace Greene, the proprietor, and as sorry a hotel manager as Jessie could imagine. She shook her head at the dust settling back down on her shoes. Dirt was an abiding issue between Jessie and Mr. Greene.

"Well, Mr. Greene," she said. "I've come to spend the night once again in your hotel. I see it is no cleaner than it was the last time I was here."

"If I'd known you was coming, Miz Pennell, I'd have scrubbed the floors until my hands bled. As it is..." Mr. Greene shrugged, his meaty hands raised in regret. "I wasn't expecting anybody today, what with the cane grinding. Haven't run off and left your old man, now, have you?"

Mr. Greene leered at Jessie. She was not impressed. Aside from being a sloven, Mr. Greene was quite fat. He also liked to stick things in his ears. He did it now, twirling the sharp end of a letter opener in his right ear. He seemed oblivious to the effect this had on other people, or the potential for damage to his own person. Next to his poor housekeeping, Jessie considered this to be Mr. Greene's most objectionable habit - she'd seen him use pen knives, nut picks, and mustache scissors, to name a few - and thought it a shame he had no wife to break him of it.

"No, Mr. Greene, I haven't left him. I've come to do a little shopping, and..."

The front door slammed open and the girls staggered in with the bags, followed by Lupe, who was eating a molasses cookie taken from the food basket over her arm. Mr. Greene paused - the letter opener's revolutions slowing to a stop in his ear - and stared at Lupe. Her feet were finally booted, but the laces dragged across the floor behind her and her arms were still bare. Jessie had given her a shawl to wear, but instead of draping it decently over her shoulders, as intended, she'd tied it around her waist, positioning the knot to one side. The knot bobbed when Lupe cocked her hip, as impudent as a wink. Mr. Greene resumed twirling the letter opener in his ear, and turned to Jessie.

"Who's that?" he asked.

"That's Mrs. Dolly Baxter," Jessie said.

"I'll be durned," Mr. Greene said. He considered Lupe again. "Are there anymore like you where you come from?" he asked.

Lupe picked a piece of cookie out of her teeth and sucked it off the end of her finger. "More'n likely," she said. "What's that in your ear?"

Mr. Greene turned deep red, and withdrew the letter opener. "Nothing," he said. "Can I show you to your room?"

Lupe surveyed the lobby: four square walls and an unpainted, uncarpeted stair rising beside the desk. "I can find my way," she said. "Just tell me which one it is and save yourself the trouble."

Mr. Greene hesitated, torn between his desire to be of assistance to Lupe and his distaste for climbing stairs. Jessie made up his mind for him.

"We'll have the room in the northeast corner, if no one's in it," she said. "The one with the double bed. I thank you for carrying our bags."

The twinkle in Mr. Greene's little blue eyes gave way to misery, which Jessie ignored. Lupe Baxter was a married woman, for all she neither looked nor acted like one, and Horace Greene could keep his eyes to himself. Jessie regretted her decision on the way to the room, though. The man huffed and puffed so that she expected him to fall down dead on the stairs. She was glad when he made it back down to the clerk's desk alive.

Mrs. Baxter sauntered around the room after Mr. Greene left, scrutinizing the accommodations. "Not bad," she said. She took her boots off and slung them one at a time across the room. "Maybe that'll scare the roaches into hiding." Jessie grimaced with distaste. Lupe laughed and plopped down on the bed, yawning. "I've been in places a lot worse than this," she said.

"I'm sure," Jessie said. She raised the window and opened the shutters. "Bring me the coverlet, please, Bekah."

Lupe got off the bed so Bekah could get the quilt. She took it to Jessie, who hung it out the window and gave it a good shake, then dragged it back in.

"Where do we eat around here?" Lupe asked.

"At the cafe," Bekah said.

Jessie held the quilt up, checking it for bugs, and caught a glimpse of Lupe's bare shoulder through a hole in the upper right hand corner. Mrs. Farnsworth, the cook at the cafe, would find enough skin there to talk about for weeks. She nodded at the basket on the floor. "We'll eat right here," she said. "Breakfast, too. Then I'll do my errands, and we'll go back to the Dempseys'."

She spread the quilt on the bed and carefully smoothed the top, then stepped back to make sure the corners were even. Lupe sat back down, swung her long legs up on the bed, and stretched out. The soles of her feet were dirty.

"I generally wash my feet before I get into bed," Jessie said.

"I generally don't," Lupe answered. She flung an arm over her face and crossed her ankles. "Wake me up when it's time to eat," she said. "All the excitement has plumb wore me out." In less than a minute, she was sound asleep, her body slack with cat-like abandon. Bekah and Jonelle crept up carefully on the bed, quiet lest they wake the exotic creature sleeping there. Jonelle, her hands clasped tightly together as if to keep from touching Lupe, smiled up at Jessie.

"Can you believe it, Mama?" she asked.

"Just barely," Jessie said.

"Do you like her, Mama?" Bekah asked.

"I only met her today," Jessie said. "It's too soon to know."

"Well, it's not too soon for me," Jonelle said. "I think she's wonderful."

"You can be hasty at times," Jessie said. "Now wash your face and hands before we eat. Bekah, after you have washed, wake Mrs. Baxter for supper." Thus rewarding Bekah's prudent silence and rebuking Jonelle's lack of it, Jessie pushed the blanket chest against the wall, and set out for supper.

Lupe had a hearty appetite, and ate with one haunch perched on the windowsill, chewing and talking at the same time. "Your little town looks deserted," she said.

Jessie, who'd been sitting at the wash table, stood up and joined her at the window. The darkening street was empty. "It's suppertime," she said. "Besides which, most folks have gone to the cane-grinding."

Lupe bit into a wedge of sweet potato pie. "I guess grinding cane is pretty big in these parts," she said. "It don't seem too exciting to me, but then, I've never been to one. Maybe there's more to it than it sounds."

"It's a chance for neighbors to get together," Jessie said. "I enjoy it."

"I don't care for neighbors," Lupe said. "They're nosy. Dolly went on about it so, is the only reason I'm going. I'd just as soon have stayed at the house."

"It's good to get to know your neighbors, though," Jessie said. "Some day you may need them."

"I don't need anybody," Lupe said.

Jessie regarded her in the dying light, but didn't answer.

"What are you staring at?" Lupe demanded.

"You remind me of someone I used to know," Jessie said.

Lupe made a rude sound. "I bet you didn't know her long," she said.

"No," Jessie said. "Not very long. And not very well, either." Suddenly exhausted, though the sun had not yet set, she went to the bed and pulled back the quilt. "We've got a big day tomorrow," she said. "Let's get some rest."

It was all Jessie could do to keep from screaming as she herded her charges into bed: Lupe - who refused to sleep between the girls - against the wall; then Jonelle, who won the coveted position next to Lupe by producing the deepest, most pathetic sobs Jessie had ever heard; then Bekah, bitterly resentful for losing the crying contest, a victim of grave injustice who might very possibly remain angry for the rest of her life; and finally Jessie, right on the very edge of the bed. Even then, it wasn't quiet. Lupe flopped from her back to her side to her back again, and complained about the earliness of the hour. Jonelle kept pushing the covers off herself and everyone else, too. Bekah fidgeted and sighed, the heavy breaths accompanied by little clicks of her tongue.

"It's hot in here," she said. "I wish it'd cool off some."

"People in Hell wish they had ice water," Jonelle piped.

"Be quiet, both of you, and go to sleep," Jessie said. She heaved a sigh of her own. It was meant as a warning and sufficed as such. Neither Bekah nor Jonelle said another word. Jessie closed her eyes. A drop of sweat meandered through her hair, tickling her scalp. She rubbed it away and crossed her arms over her chest, ready to grab somebody if she started to fall. She was almost asleep when Lupe spoke.

"I've drunk ice water," she said.

"I saw ice one time," Jonelle said. "It froze in the water bucket."

"It was like a pot lid on the water," Bekah said. "We broke it and ate some. It didn't taste like anything."

"I've drunk ice water from a silver goblet in mid-July," Lupe said.

The three of them were silent for a moment.

"What's a silver goblet?" Jonelle asked.

"It's a cup on a stem, made of pure silver," Lupe said. "It had a chunk of ice in it as big as my fist, and little beads of water on the outside. That silver was so cold it burned my lips when I drank from it."

The air in the room was thick with heat gathered throughout the day and stored in walls and ceiling and shutters and bedclothes. Jessie licked her lips, dry-mouthed with thirst. There was water in the pitcher on the dresser. She'd had a drink from it earlier that evening. The water was as warm as her tongue, and tasted like brass.

"Where'd that ice come from?" Bekah asked.

"It came from way up north on a train to Jacksonville," Lupe said. "Blocks of it packed in sawdust. The man I was with bought a whole box of it. Every time I asked him to, he'd chop a piece off with a gold knife and give it to me in the goblet. I held a piece up to the sun. It was silver and blue and sparkled like diamonds. And so cold."

"Was the man your uncle?" Bekah asked.

"That's right," Lupe said. "Uncle George."

"You said his name was Uncle Charlie," Bekah said.

Lupe didn't answer.

"Y'all go to sleep," Jessie said.

"But..." Jonelle began.

"It was Uncle Charlie George," Lupe said. "He had two names and I used both of 'em. I'm going to sleep now. Don't be bothering me again."

The bed shook and jounced as Lupe made herself comfortable. Jessie gripped the bedpost until it grew still, then lay staring at the dark. A roach crawled across the floor, a slow, dry, scratchy sound. Lupe snored, and Jonelle echoed her.

Bekah touched her arm. "Mama?" she whispered.

"What?"

"Who is it Lupe..."

"Mrs. Baxter."

"Who is it Mrs. Baxter reminds you of?"

"I forget," Jessie said. She turned her back to her daughter and pretended to go to sleep, forestalling further questions. She lay on the edge, crowded and uncomfortable, angry with the woman on the other side of the bed who had watched the morning's violence without dismay, as though she did not know herself the cause of it, or did not care, and who now could sleep so easily, her rest unmarred by the day's events, and angry all over again with another like her, to whom, after all these years, Jessie still owed a neighbor's debt.

Jessie squirmed, as wide awake as if she'd drunk a pot of coffee, then stuck her feet over the edge of the bed and sat up. Groping across the beside table, she found the matches and lit the lamp, turning the wick down low. She shone it along the floor, looking for roaches. Seeing none, she got out of bed and made her way across the gritty floor to the rocking chair in the corner of the room. She sat down and put the lamp on the floor beside her, then set to rocking, and thinking of Clemency Rainey.

That's how Jessie thought of her now - Clemency - though in all the years they'd known each other, Jessie had never again called her anything but Red. Neither had the wild-haired woman ever alluded to her given name again. The shadow of Tate Rainey had lain across that name, full of menace and foreboding, lending excuse to Jessie's failure to befriend the woman who bore it.

But the truth cut deeper than that. Jessie had gone to that campsite all those years ago looking for solace, for security, for someone to talk to who would listen and understand, even, perhaps, for someone to hold her, as a mother might hold her child. What she'd found there was a woman in rebellion against everything Jessie believed in.

Jessie pressed her head against the back of the rocker, then consciously relaxed. She'd been so young. Younger than Clemency in years, and infinitely younger in experience. What she'd seen at that first meeting had terrified her, and rightly so. She'd made the wise choice, running with all her might, flinging herself into the arms of propriety, binding to herself the doctrine of decency that Clemency had rejected: that rules exist to save us from our base inclinations, and the chaos that attends their indulgence. Forced to choose between what was right and what was kind, Jessie had chosen what was right. She had never regretted that choice, only that she had not been able to help Clemency, in some way, find something better for herself than public humiliation and violent death. For the first time since it happened, Jessie allowed herself to imagine, not only the way Clemency died, but that which led up to it, that shameless ride on the black filly and the blow from her husband that knocked her to the ground. Jessie made herself look at those pictures in as much detail as she could muster, and knew, also for the first time, neither condemnation nor disgust, but searing pity for the woman who had all but begged for Jessie's friendship, and been denied. And, for the first time since washing the blood from her lifeless face, Jessie wept for Clemency Rainey, until she fell asleep.

The sun woke her, shining in her eyes. Bone tired and stiff-jointed, Jessie shivered in the morning chill and glanced at the bed. Lupe had twined the quilt in her legs, pulling it off Bekah and Jonelle. The girls were huddled together, their arms bumpy with cold. Jessie untangled the quilt and pulled it over the three of them, leaning across the bed to tuck one edge between Lupe and the wall, and the other beneath the mattress on Bekah's side. She smoothed the wrinkles from the quilt, her hands brusque with remembered sorrow.

Clemency Rainey lived seven years in Harris County, and earned herself quite a reputation: Red Rainey, the horse woman; Red Rainey, the moonshine woman; Red Rainey, the fighting woman. Finally, she was Red Rainey, the dead whore. Five people came to mark her passing, besides her children and the Pennells: the preacher, the sheriff, George and Ann Dempsey, and Dolly. It was, in Jessie's opinion, a pitiful showing for any life, no matter how dissolute or lost. Even after last night, after finally forgiving her, Jessie still ached for the passionate, lonely, fiery-headed woman who had made such a spectacle and outcast of herself, and for her own younger self, so helpless in the face of it.

"I wonder how she died," Beau had said on the way home from the funeral.

"Tate says it was an accident," Raymond replied. "Says a horse kicked her in the head. He carried her in the house. He got drunk. She died. The boys ran off. Yesterday evening, he said."

"A horse kicked her," Dolly said.

The words hung in the air, rank with doubt. It was impossible, then and now, to believe that Clemency Rainey had been killed by a horse. She bossed them around so, with the same affectionate contempt for their tempers and tricks that Beau had, the same respect for their strength and peculiar intelligence.

"What'd the sheriff say?" Jessie had asked.

Raymond had rubbed his neck as though it pained him. His voice, when he spoke, had sounded old. "He said he couldn't find any evidence to the contrary. The dent in that candlestick matched the wound, but a horse's hoof could have marked her just the same."

"Candelabra," Jessie had said.

"What?" Raymond had asked.

"It's called a candelabra," she'd repeated. "Not a candlestick."

"I can't see that it matters," Raymond had said.

Jessie had seen again Red trying to clean the tarnished silver with her thumbnail. "Well, it does," she'd said back then. "It matters a whole lot."

"And it still matters," she said now, addressing Lupe's bare foot which had poked out from under the quilt. "It matters what you think of yourself, and what other people think of you. It matters how you behave, and how people behave toward you. Modesty matters. Decency matters. Rules matter." She covered the foot, pushing the edge of the quilt far underneath the mattress so Lupe couldn't kick it off again. "So don't you be thinking otherwise, Mrs. Lupe Baxter."

And then, Lupe and the girls securely covered and firmly confined, Jessie changed her dressed and washed her face and brushed her hair, determined this time to hold her neighbor to accountability. She moved quietly and quickly, so as not to wake the three still sleeping in the bed, and took care to lock the door behind her when she left.

Jessie backed in the front door of the hotel an hour later with an armful of packages, and walked past Horace Greene with the same cheerful indifference she'd shown him earlier on her way to the mercantile store.

"Please don't bother, Mr. Greene," she said. "These don't weigh a thing. It's kind of you, but no need to get up."

Horace sank back down on his stool, hands fidgeting with the letter opener in frustrated curiosity, while Jessie smiled over her bundles and felt her way up the stairs with her feet. When she got to the door of the room, she wedged the packages against the wall, fumbled the key into the lock, and knocked on the door with her elbow.

"Who is it?" a sullen voice asked.

"It's me," she said. "Open the door before I drop everything."

The door flung open. Jessie pushed her way in and dropped her purchases on the bed. She batted her hands together, dusting them off, and put them on her hips to survey her project. Lupe had insisted on sleeping in her dress, and now looked even worse than she had the day before. Her hair had fallen out of the ribbon and was half-covering one eye. The look she gave Jessie out of the clear one wasn't friendly.

"I guess you know you locked me in here," she said.

Jessie's smile didn't touch her eyes. "I'm so sorry," she said. "I didn't think you'd mind, what with it being a strange town and all."

"You're the one who's strange," Lupe said. "I ain't your prisoner, you know."

Jessie fingered the room key in her pocket, and mentally begged to differ. "Of course not," she said. "But you are my guest and I felt responsible for you. You weren't dressed, and neither were the girls. It seemed safer to lock the door."

Lupe's expression didn't soften. Jessie picked up one of the packages while Bekah and Jonelle watched with anticipation from the bed. Shaking a brown gingham dress out of the wrapping paper, Jessie nodded at the empty basket on the floor by the foot of the bed, and smiled at her daughters.

"Did you get enough to eat?"

"The buttermilk's warm," Jonelle said. "But the biscuits and ham were fine. I ate mine in the bed. Lupe says that's where real ladies eat breakfast."

"Draws roaches," Jessie said. She held the dress up and turned around to show it to Lupe.

"What do you think?" she asked.

Lupe shrugged one shoulder, the full mouth still pouty. "Looks all right," she said. "But what you have on looks all right, too."

Jessie held the shoulders of the dress against Lupe's. "But this isn't for me," she said. "It's for you."

Lupe took the dress and held it against herself, smoothing it down her body. She eyed Jessie suspiciously. "I ain't got no money," she said.

"You don't need any," Jessie said. "It's a wedding present. And these, too." She unwrapped another package and draped the contents over Lupe's arm: a pair of cotton drawers with a corded drawstring; a cotton chemise with mother-of-pearl buttons; a cotton petticoat with lace around the hem. Lupe hung the dress over her shoulder and ran a forefinger over the lace on the petticoat.

"It's all real nice," she said. "Only wedding presents I've got." She pulled the dress off her shoulder and laid it over the undergarments, smoothing the wrinkles out. "What is it you want?"

"Beg pardon?" Jessie asked.

"I asked you what it is you want." Lupe said. She held the clothes up, her brown eyes almost black and onyx-hard. "A woman like you don't do this sort of thing for a woman like me, unless she wants something."

Jessie unwrapped the last package, and held up a corset. "I want you to wear this," she said.

Lupe took one look, threw her head back, and laughed so hard somebody in the next room pounded on the wall and yelled, "Hush that noise in there!"

"Hush your own self," Lupe hollered back. She stopped laughing, and walked past Jessie to toss the clothes on the bed. "I ain't about to get strapped into that thing," she said. "So you can just have the...wedding presents...back."

Jessie went to the door, locked it, and put the key back in her pocket. "We're not leaving here until you put that corset on," she said.

"Mama!" Bekah said. "I don't think you can do this."

"You hush," Jessie said. She walked across the room and pulled the rocking chair in front of the window, then sat down with her back to Lupe and the girls. Folding her hands in her lap, she sat there without speaking, rocking back and forth.

"You can't make me put it on," Lupe said.

"I can refuse to move until you do. We can sit here all day. I don't care."

"Mama," Jonelle wailed.

"Be quiet." Jessie pulled the shade up. A cow browsed on the grass growing up between the boards of the sidewalk. A dust devil twirled down the middle of the street, kicking up sand. Other than that, it was deserted. Jessie could feel Lupe's eyes on her back. The silence felt dangerous, like playing chicken with someone who might actually shoot.

"I could break you like a stick," Lupe said. She snapped her fingers. "Just that easy."

The cow finished the grass and moved on down the street. Jessie could see the tuft of its tail flicking back and forth in the frame of the window. "Like Raymond," she said.

"What?"

"Like Raymond. The man you nearly killed yesterday. My husband."

Lupe snorted. "That wasn't me. That was Dolly and them two boys."

"It happened because of you. You weren't decent."

"I was, too."

"You were not. Your legs and arms were naked, your hair all loose and every whichaway. Dolly out of his mind, ready to fight, to kill, even. Ashamed of you, I expect."

"He was not ashamed of me!" Lupe cried.

Jessie knew she'd drawn blood, and pressed her attack. "Of course he was. And well he should have been."

"He was not!" Lupe shouted. There was another thump on the wall, louder this time. Lupe lowered her voice to a furious whisper. "He was not ashamed of me!"

"Mama," Bekah said.

"Bekah," Jessie said. "If either you or Jonelle interrupt again, I will send you both downstairs to sit with Mr. Greene. Do you understand me?"

"Yes, ma'am," Bekah said.

Jessie leaned back in the rocker and closed her eyes. "I don't know anything about you, Lupe," she said. "Who you are. Where you come from. What it is you think you're doing. But I can tell you this. If you dress like a loose woman, and behave like a loose woman, people have every right to treat you like a loose woman, and when that happens, Dolly is going to get angry and somebody is going to get killed. I don't want it to be my husband."

Silence fell again. The rocker developed a squeak. The heat through the window was giving Jessie a headache.

"Are all of the woman around here like you?" Lupe asked.

"Some are worse," Jessie said. She rocked and looked out the window. The cow was completely gone. The room was already hot, and it wasn't even ten o'clock. There was the sound of bedsprings and footsteps, then Lupe's voice right behind her.

"Take back what you said, about Dolly being ashamed."

"I take it back."

"I am not a loose woman."

"I never said you were. I said you acted like one."

"You think that corset will make me a lady?"

"It'll make you look like one. The rest is up to you." There was a long silence, broken only by the creak of the rocker. Finally, Lupe took a deep breath.

"All right," she said. "We'll try it your way." There was quiet for a moment, a rustle, and then oooohs from the bed.

Jessie rose from the rocker, turned, and gasped. Lupe was standing stark naked in the middle of the room, Bekah and Jonelle taking her in just as quick as their eyes would let them.

"Where are your drawers?" Jessie demanded.

Lupe looked irritated. "Dolly said there wasn't time to put them on."

"Do you mean to tell me that you haven't had them on at all?"

"So what?"

Jessie was outraged. "I cannot believe that you have been without your drawers since you came to my house yesterday. I don't care where you were raised, or by whom, or how soon you have to get somewhere, you do not go around like, like… You do not go around butt-naked. Ever." She whirled around and shook her finger at Bekah and Jonelle. "And if I ever catch either one of you leaving the house in such a condition, I'll whip you so hard you won't sit down for a week!"

The girls shook their heads, their mouths wide open. "And for pity's sake," Jessie said. "Close your mouths. You look like the Rainey twins." They closed their mouths. Jessie handed Lupe the new drawers. "Put these on first."

Lupe put them on, one hand on the bed post for balance.

"Now this."

Lupe took her time with the mother-of-pearl buttons on the chemise. It was a close fit. When it was done, Jessie picked up the corset.

"Now," she said. "Let's do something about the rest of you." Lupe held her arms out as though preparing to fly. Jessie wrapped the corset around her "Get a good grip," she said. Lupe grasped the bed post with both hands and held on, while Jessie, one small foot planted firmly on Lupe's backside, pulled the laces tight.

Twenty minutes later, an outwardly transfigured Mrs. Baxter stood for inspection before her roommates. "Well?" she asked. "What do you think?"

"Turn around," Jessie said.

Lupe made one slow circle and stopped. "Well?" she demanded.

"I think that'll do it," Jessie said. She poked Jonelle in the ribs. "What do you think?"

"She's still more beautiful than anybody," Jonelle said. "You can't take that away from her."

"I wasn't trying to," Jessie snapped. She nodded at Lupe. "How does it feel?"

"Fine, so long as I don't try to breathe," Lupe said. She giggled. "Dolly won't even know who I am."

"He'll figure it out," Jessie said. She handed the parcels around so that everyone was carrying something, and glanced one more time around the room to make sure they had everything. Then she put on her bonnet, and followed her charges down the stairs.

Chapter Nineteen

Raymond was waiting his turn at the grinder when Jessie drove up. He left Jezebel dozing in the sun, and made his way with Dolly at his elbow to the newly arrived wagon with the two women in the seat. Jessie smiled at him as happily as if she'd planned everything just this way. But even up close, Raymond almost didn't recognize the woman beside her as Lupe Baxter.

She sat perfectly straight, not with the easy balance of the day before, but rigidly, as though the long neck of the dress she now wore had pushed her chin up, and the long sleeves that covered her arms had forced her hands down and held them, prim and captive, in her lap. The long black hair was pulled tightly back in a bun at the nape of her neck, taking some of the fullness out of her face, widening her eyes and emphasizing the high cheekbones. It took Raymond a moment, though, to put a name to what was really different about her. Properly dressed, with shoes on and her hair pulled back, young Mrs. Baxter looked scared. Dolly stepped past him and laid a hand on Rahab's bridle. He seemed stunned by Lupe's appearance.

"How are you?" he asked, as if what he really meant to ask was, who are you?"

"I'm all right, I guess," Lupe said. She cleared her throat and touched her hair. "But maybe not so's you can tell."

Tentatively, as if afraid of hurting her, Dolly reached up and put his hands on her waist. "Come on down here and let me look at you," he said.

Lupe put her hands on his shoulders and he swung her off the seat to the ground. Frowning in concentration, he probed her middle with his thick fingers as though she were a horse whose soundness he found suspect. Lupe bent her head and whispered in his ear. His face cleared, then clouded again, his expressions as fitful as summer weather. She whispered something again, and batted his hands away. For the first time, Dolly seemed aware of an audience. He put his arm around Lupe's waist and hugged her to his side. "She's here, just like I promised," he said. "Mrs. Dolly Baxter, my wife."

"Looks like your luck is turning, Baxter," somebody called. There were cheers and catcalls and scattered applause. Raymond walked around the other side of the wagon to help Jessie down, while Dolly made introductions, grinning and waving his arm and shaking hands.

"Look at him," Jessie said. "Acts like he's showing a horse."

"Go easy on him, Jess," Raymond said. "He's so proud of her he's about to bust." He eyed with appreciation the lines of Lupe's new dress. "She sure cleans up good, don't she?"

Jessie harrumphed. "Good enough," she said. "I wish I'd something a little older that fit her, though. Folks will think it's foolish, her wearing a brand new dress to a cane grinding. Can't be helped, though." She smiled at Lupe and the girls. "Well, ladies, are we ready to go?"

Lupe let go of Dolly's hand. "I guess so," she said.

Dolly caught her hand again, and looked pleadingly at Jessie. "She can stay here with me if she wants to," he said. "There's no call for you to bother anymore."

Jessie took a firm hold on Lupe's arm. "It's no bother at all," she said. "Bekah, Jonelle. Come with me."

Dolly watched Jessie abscond a second time with his wife, then turned to Raymond, clearly bewildered. Raymond slapped him on the back. "Looky there," he said. "She's gone again. And here all you thought you had to worry about was these ole ugly men."

"It ain't funny, Ray," Dolly said.

"Maybe not to you," Raymond said. He tied Rahab to a tree and went to get Jezebel and the load of cane. George Dempsey had stopped the Gibbs's mule and was unhitching it from the pole. It was the Pennell's turn to grind.

The cane press was bolted onto four sixteen-foot pilings sunk into the ground, and powered by a mule that walked in a sandy circle around it. Raymond drove the wagon up beside the grinder, then unhitched Jezebel and led her into the circle of sand. Dolly caught hold of the narrow end of a thirty-foot cypress pole that stuck out for most of its length from the gears, and walked it around to Raymond, who hooked it through the singletree on the mule's harness. Dolly then brought a line - tied on the other end to a short lead pole attached to the butt end of the sweep - around in front of the mule and tied it to her halter. Then he stepped back and smacked Jezebel on the hip.

"Giddup, Jezzie-belle," he said.

The mule leaned into the harness and pulled the sweep forward. As she did, the butt end of the sweep pulled on the lead pole, which pulled the line on the mule's halter and led her forward. Gears powered by the sweep engaged three crushing rollers, massive iron cylinders set upright at varying distances from one another into which the cane was fed, four to five stalks at a time. The clear green juice ran out through an iron pipe into heavy oak barrels, used the rest of the year to catch rainwater. The slow, tedious work, normally accompanied by ruminative silences broken by sporadic conversation, was now lively with wisecracks and observations on Dolly's newly acquired status as a married man. Sometimes a joke betrayed the bitter satisfaction of misery welcoming company; other times, it resonated with honest pleasure. Either way, Dolly held himself aloof, unresponsive and uncommunicative, until Able Gibbs stepped in.

"Are there anymore like her where she comes from?" he asked.

It was an innocent enough question. Still, Raymond thought it best to be cautious after yesterday's run-in with the Rainey twins. He stood up, ready to follow Dolly into a fight if he took offense at Able's words or tone.

But Dolly didn't take offense at all. The question seemed to inspire him. He studied the ribbon cane stacked on the wagon, the stalks Raymond was feeding into the rollers, the mule walking the sandy circle, all with a far-look in his eyes as though he could see something in these common articles the others could not. Then, with the finality of utter conviction, he said, "There's nobody else like her in the whole world."

Able glanced around, his raised eyebrow an invitation to scorn that one man accepted with a stifled laugh, another with a smile. But Raymond remembered a girl in a blue and white dress he'd glimpsed through a crack in a board one bright spring morning, and knew what Dolly meant, how one female could step out from among all the others, and become the only woman in the world. It gave a man a single eye and narrowed his thinking. It was a stricture Raymond believed to be necessary, however painful. Any man who thought he could figure out more than one woman at a time was either a genius or a fool. Unsure whether to rejoice with Dolly or mourn for him, Raymond kept silent, and fed cane into the crushing rollers until the sweet green juice ran out the other side.

With one hand on Lupe's elbow and the other on the small of her back, Jessie guided her new neighbor through the crowd of admiring, hat-tipping men. Their introductions and congratulations buzzed like smoked bees, low-pitched, slow, and incessant. Subtle messages of admiration, invitation, or sly conjecture elicited merely downcast eyes and a frigid shoulder. Jessie watched with satisfaction as expectation faded into disappointment and finally disinterest, and the men turned their attentions back to the grinding and the familiar and undemanding comfort of their own company

The two women made their way toward the shed, avoiding with care the dogs and small children that, intent and unpredictable and oblivious to any purpose but their own, obstructed their way. And all the while, Jessie kept one hand on Lupe's back, the confining security of whalebone beneath her fingertips. She knew that introducing a woman into the established society of her own kind was more challenging than walking her through a crowd of strange men. For the most part, Jessie had a real affection for the women of her community, and generally found their company a solace and a joy. But not all of them were generous of heart, and even those who were had mean streaks. It was their refusal to indulge them that made those women generous. Jessie's hens were affectionate and trusting, and the sounds they made as they went about their business was pleasurable. But wound one of them, or weaken it in some way, and the others would peck it to death. It was simply in them to do that, just as it was in them to call their chicks out of danger and hide them beneath their own wings until the danger passed, even at the cost of their own lives. Jessie hoped for the best in this encounter, but expected the worst. That way, she wouldn't be disappointed, and might even be pleasantly surprised.

Under the shed was a brick boiler, inside of which sat a huge iron vat. An oven sat on the same side of the boiler as the flue, so that the heat had to circle the entire bottom of the vat before it could escape. The air around the oven shimmered with it. Women stood around the boiler, not only to talk and work, but to shield the children from it so they would not get burned. They paused in their conversations to watch Jessie and Lupe approach, and when they spoke among themselves again, Jessie knew what they were talking about. A small thin woman poked at the coals in the oven with a rake, then straightened and smiled.

"We'd begun to think Dolly had lost his mind," she said. She leaned the rake against an upright and wiped her hands on her apron before holding one out to Lupe. "I'm Arimantha Sanders. You must be Lupe Baxter."

Lupe pasted on another smile and shook the other woman's hand. "I am very pleased to meet you," she said. Jessie nodded approval, and some of the tension left Lupe's face.

The introductions were slower here than among the men, as each woman named not only herself, but her husband, as well, going to the edge of the shed to point him out and make sure Lupe knew which one was hers. That clarified, she would vaguely motion toward any number of the many children, rattling off one to ten names. The schoolteacher, Esther Maybree, gave Lupe a brisk tap on the shoulder. "We're giving you an examination on all these names here in a minute," she said. "So you pay attention."

"I wasn't too good in school," Lupe said. "Sit me down at a desk, and my brain shrivels up like a pea."

"Is that so?" Esther asked. "Whereabouts did you go to school?" Lupe looked at her blank-faced. The women exchanged glances.

Jessie cleared her throat. "Tampa," she said. "Lupe went to school in Tampa until she took sick and had to quit."

Esther looked Lupe over. "You don't look like you've ever been sick a day in your life," she said.

"I don't stay down long," Lupe said. "And I ain't afraid of work." She unbuttoned her sleeve and started rolling it up. "What can I do to help?"

"That's what I like to hear," Esther said. She lifted the lid on a barrel near the boiler, ladled cane juice out of it, and strained it through a muslin bag held over the vat. Other women laid cordwood in the oven over the coals, and waved palmetto fans at it until it caught, and the smell of burning wood filled the shed. When the vat was almost full, Esther hung the ladle back on the barrel and closed the lid, then hung the bag over the lid. Women stood like homespun witches around the boiler, poking the fire and stirring the juice until it boiled and a dark brown foam began to form on the surface.

"Lila, honey," Esther said. "Hand me that skimmer, will you?"

A stocky, plain-faced girl took a long hickory handle with a flat piece of perforated tin on one end off a nail near the roof of the shed, and handed it to Esther.

"This is Lila Gibbs," Esther said. "She's got her sights set on your near neighbor, Beau Pennell."

Lila blushed deep red, and Jessie hugged her shoulders while the other women laughed. They teased Lila all the time about boys, but especially about Beau. Nobody took it seriously, least of all Jessie.

"Now, Lupe," Esther said. "You just got here, so you're fresher than the rest of us. Skim that foam off of there and put it in this bucket. When it's full, I'll get you another one. You do that until the syrup boils clear."

Lupe dipped the skimmer under the foam and held it over the vat until the syrup ran through the holes. Then she poured the foam in the bucket. "What are you saving this for?" she asked.

Myrtle Gibbs tittered. "Well," she said. "Some people feed it to their hogs. Others - your husband, for instance - make liquor out of it. Maybe now he's married, he'll quit that foolishness."

Jessie shot Lupe a warning glance, but needn't have bothered. The dark eyes were as soft as a doe's when she smiled at Myrtle. "Maybe," she said. And let it go.

Children darted into the shed with sticks, which the women dipped into the hot syrup, then held them up to cool before the children stuck them in their mouths. Jessie made a sucker for Lupe and another for herself, then tossed the empty stick on the fire and took over its care, adding more wood or raking it out, as needed, to keep the heat beneath the vat steady. When the syrup was thick enough, the women ladled it into small buckets, covered them with tin lids, and set them aside in groups, according to whose cane it had come from.

Dolly brought the first barrel of Pennell juice to be cooked, and the women badgered him about his new wife, his drinking habits, his bald head, and his blue, blue eyes, until they drove him away again, reduced to stutters by their teasing. Lupe skimmed until she nearly fainted. Then Jessie made her sit down on a bench and took over the skimmer herself, the heat of the fire competing with her for air.

The women went at it all day long - tending the fire, stirring the juice, skimming the syrup, ladling it into buckets to cool - and all the while they talked - about their men and their children, and their quirks, illnesses, and accidents, about recipes, sickness, death, love, marriage, sewing, cooking, birth - the colors and textures and tastes of life itself. Jessie marked the moment when they let Lupe in - there was a change in the air as clear and certain as a south wind rising after a freeze - and she almost sat right down in the dirt with relief. She sighed, instead, one that went right down to her toes. When it was done, she heard a low laugh. Lupe was smiling at her, the light of victory in her eyes, though her lips were pale, and there were dark circles under her eyes.

Beau left to go 'coon hunting with Lester Mason as soon as his mother and Lupe got to the Dempsey's, and watched his dogs get beat all afternoon. It wasn't a fair contest. Lester used his uncle's dogs that had come all the way from North Carolina. They had glossy black saddles and tan heads and legs and insistent, single-minded noses that sorted through the mingled odors of swamp and hammock for the scent of 'coon, then followed it with unswerving commitment through water, over sand, under palmettos and around windfalls to its snarling, black-masked source up a tree. There they'd stand, fore feet on the trunk, sad eyes closed, heads thrown back and mouths wide open, bawling in ecstasy, until somebody climbed the tree and shook the 'coon out for them to kill. Bloody-mouthed and pleased beyond all measure, the hounds jumped big-footed and slobbery on the boys, then loped off to do it all over again.

Meanwhile, Beau's dogs ran foxes, rabbits, 'possums, 'coons, and deer with equal enthusiasm though uneven success. They treed once, but it didn't count, since there was a bobcat on the branch above the 'coon, and the sorry pack had already run so much trash there was no proving they'd treed the 'coon and not the cat. Beau even had to stop on the way into camp and pull them off a gopher turtle. They were trying to dig it out of its hole, scratching and sniffing then scratching again, with manic, concentrated energy. He cuffed them away from the hole while Lester guffawed. They yelped and dodged his hand, then fled into a palmetto thicket, bob tails wagging like admonishing fingers as they disappeared. Beau retreated in disgrace to the cane grinder, where he fed cane into the rollers and watched Lupe over in the syrup shed until Jack squatted down beside him.

"You better quit staring at her," he said.

Beau's face got hot, and he jabbed another stalk of cane into the rollers. "Mind your own business," he said.

"Can't," Jack said. "There's something I want you to see." He stood up. "Hey, Dolly. Come here and feed this cane, will you? Me and Beau got to see a man about a dog."

Dolly made his way to them and took the end of the stalk from Beau. "You boys always take care of that sort of thing together?" he asked.

"Every chance we get," Jack said. He grabbed Beau's shirtsleeve. "Hurry up."

Beau jerked his arm away. "I'm coming," he said. But Jack just struck up a trot that turned into a dead run as he motioned Beau to follow. When they got to the barn, Jack pointed down the road.

"Looky there," he said. Beau followed his finger and felt sick at his stomach. The Rainey twins were sitting at the turn off, arguing, but moving slowly and surely toward the Dempsey's road.

"Dolly'll kill 'em," Jack said.

Beau took a deep breath. "No, he won't." He pointed south toward the main road into town. "Head off that way, quick as you can, and see if you can get them to follow you back the other way. Lead them down that hammock on the other side of the road."

Jack looked doubtful. "There's two of them," he said. "And you're supposed to ride for Tate next week. He won't like it if you mix it up with his boys."

"I won't need to," Beau said. "They're nothing but wind."

"I don't know," Jack said. "I bet they're pretty mad about yesterday." His face was pinched with worry. It made him look like a little old man. Beau clapped him on the shoulder.

"Well, so what? You're worth two of them and a panther, too. And don't you worry about Tate. He needs me."

Jack grinned and whistled through his teeth, then took off running. The twins didn't wait for Jack to call them. They followed his running form like dogs after a rabbit, and had him backed up against an oak tree by the time Beau could get to them.

"Look here, Clyde," Bob crowed. "We've done caught us a fiddle player. C'mon, boy, play something for us."

Jack held his hands up. "Good as I am, I can't play without a fiddle. Lemme go get it, and I'll play as long as you want." He took a step forward and Bob kicked him in the stomach, setting him down on the ground with a woof.

"You ain't talking your way out of this one, Pennell," Bob said. "How come you're out here by yourself? Seems kind of dangerous for a little boy such as yourself."

"He ain't by himself," Beau said. He had a stitch in his side from running, and trying to talk without acting winded just made it worse.

Bob moved his horse between Beau and Jack. "Well, if it ain't Dolly Baxter's pet, the horse boy." His tone took on an added belligerence. "We've come anyhow."

"Dolly won't like it," Beau said.

Bob grinned, exposing scarlet gums. "Dolly won't like it," he mocked. "Don't make no difference to me what he likes."

"That's not what you said yesterday." Beau spoke mildly enough, but it set Bob off.

"Don't you be throwing that up at me," he threatened. "I ain't got to take nothing off of you." He leaned over his horse's shoulder and motioned Beau closer. Beau took a step forward. Clyde left Jack alone and rode up behind Beau to listen.

"We're going to the Dempseys'," Bob said. "When we get there, we're going to tell everybody that ole Dolly Baxter's married himself a whore, and we're claiming her when she tires him out." He reached into his pocket and pulled out a twenty dollar gold piece. "Daddy give us that. Ten dollars each for as long as she can take it." He giggled.

Beau smiled. Then he almost killed the Rainey twins. Afterwards, he couldn't remember what happened between pulling Bob off his horse by one skinny leg, and Jacky slapping him in the face, yelling at him to let go of Clyde. He only remembered a shifting vision of Lupe publicly shamed beside the cane press, and Dolly shooting his way through a mass of men, trying to get to Beau who could not stop himself from putting his hand on his neighbor's wife, right where Dolly's had been. His hand burned like he was holding a hot coal, then his mother's screams turned into Jack's, and the flesh he held turned out to be Clyde's face pulped beneath his fist. He returned to himself just as Jack put his foot on his shoulder and shoved him backwards into the dirt.

"Good God, Beau!" he shouted. "What's the matter with you?" Then he burst into tears.

Beau couldn't remember when he'd last seen Jack cry. He looked at his brother's hands. They were fine, unlike his own which were swelling into bear paws, thick and fat-fingered. He patted Jack's boot with one of them, and the crying sniffled to a stop. Beau sat up and leaned against the tree, motioning clumsily at Clyde's unconscious form. "Is he alive?"

Jack put his ear down to Clyde's face. "He's breathing." Bob groaned nearby. "So's Bob."

"That's fine," Beau said. He gazed up into the leaves of the tree. "I'm not doing too good, Jacky."

"I can tell," Jack said. He picked up a twig and tossed it at Clyde. It hit him on the cheekbone, and his eyelid twitched. Jack stood up and dusted his pants off. Something glittered in the dirt by Beau's foot and he picked it up. It was the gold piece. Jack polished it against his shirt, and dropped it on Bob's chest. "Get yourself some teeth," he suggested. Then he scratched the back of his neck and gave Beau a considering look. "You ready to go back?"

"Yeah," Beau said. "Yeah, I guess so." He looked at the twins, and felt a twinge of regret. "I don't suppose I'll be riding for Tate next week."

"I reckon not," Jack said. He grabbed Beau by an elbow and hauled him to his feet. "Your hands hurt?"

"Like they've been through those cane rollers," Beau said. He tried to grin. "Next time, I better use a stick."

Jack didn't laugh. "Next time, you better use a gun."

It was dusk when they got back to the barn. The Pennell cane was ground, their buckets of syrup loaded and ready to go home. Beau hooked his thumbs in his hip pockets so no one would notice his hands, and took the verbal lashing he was given for his absence with one shoulder up to hide the weak grin behind it. It was solid dark and the stars were out by the time supper was finished. Jack wandered off, fiddle in hand, and the men stood around the dying fire in the shed, finishing last year's cane whiskey, and talking about cattle and the drive to Punta Rassa the end of the month.

Achy and out-of-sorts, Beau went to the house, hoping to see Lupe. She was on the porch with his mother and Lila Gibbs. He wanted to speak to her, and would have, had she not turned away as if he smelled bad. He stood there, anyway, hopeful and mute, shifting from one foot to the other, until he realized they were talking about childbirth. Embarrassed, he went on in the house.

The young people were gathered in the kitchen for a taffy pull, closely supervised by mothers anxious to see their children successfully paired and married off, with grandchildren on the way nine months later and not one second sooner. It was crowded and noisy, and Beau didn't want any part of it. He decided to return to the boiler shed, where there was every possibility he could sneak some liquor behind his father's back.

He was negotiating a passage between two matrons when someone caught his sleeve.

"Don't leave," Lila said. She held up a bowl for his inspection. "Taffy. You can help me pull."

"I guess not," Beau said. He didn't want to be seen pulling taffy with Lila Gibbs, for one thing; for another, the idea of pulling taffy in his present condition made his eyes water. He held up his swollen hands. "I'm not much help tonight."

Lila's eyes widened. "What in the world happened to your hands?"

"Me and the Rainey twins mixed it up this evening."

"Should have used your feet."

Beau grinned. "I guess so. Anyhow, I can't pull taffy."

"Maybe if you just held it between your wrists," Lila said wistfully. "I could pull it. You wouldn't have to do much." She looked so sad Beau couldn't stand it.

"All right," he said. "But you better not laugh if I cry."

Lila's smile was almost enough to make her pretty. "You go wash up," she said. "I'll find us a spot at the table."

It was not easy to hold a warm, oozing ball of syrup between one's buttered wrists. But with a considerable amount of fumbling, Beau held it tight enough for Lila to pull it out. Then she rolled it up again and put it back between his wrists, batting his hands and fingers with light, buttery touches. Ordinarily, Beau would have been intrigued just touching a girl's skin, even if she was only Lila Gibbs, but not tonight. Every time Lila touched him, he saw the long, slim-fingered hands of Lupe Baxter, and the familiarity with which they'd rested on Dolly's thighs as she sat bare-legged on the back of the gray horse. That memory stirred feelings below his belt that had nothing to do with Lila, no matter how she tugged and pulled at the candy, and smiled, and touched his fingers with hers.

Outside, the laughter of the men ebbed and flowed, then the sound of the fiddle started, and Beau sighed. Why Jack thought anybody would want to dance at this hour of the night was more than he knew. The music rollicked into the room, joyful and warm and inviting. Lila continued to work the taffy, even though it was getting hard to pull. The growing pressure hurt Beau's hands, and something in the music gave him a gnawing pain deep in his gut. He wanted to go home. He wanted everything to be the way it had been, before Dolly brought Lupe to Walker's Island. The music swirled past him again, gentle now, and yearning. Mrs. Dempsey stood up and looked out the door.

"Would you look at that," she said.

Beau, grateful for the opportunity to escape, released the taffy to Lila with a wink and a smile, and got up from the table to look outside. The kitchen door, though, was too crowded. He walked out the back door, instead, and came around the edge of the porch. Jack stood beside the silent men, back lit by the embers that glowed in the syrup oven. He was playing a tune Beau had never heard before. The light from the lanterns in the shed and the house spilled out towards each other across the yard, and Dolly danced with Lupe where they joined.

Lupe's hair hung down past her waist, and she moved in Dolly's arms with the easy grace of yesterday. The women lined the porch, watching and listening, their faces as unreadable as those of the men across the lighted yard, disguised or hidden by distance and the vagaries of light and shadow. Beau felt a kind of desperation, an impulse to strike out, to force the music into silence, the dance into stillness, the mystery from the night, with its beauty and fierce desire. But he stood as silent as everyone else while the music played, and Dolly and Lupe danced.

The wild, sweet music whirled them through the lantern light, turning and parting and coming together again, spinning around and around, until it couldn't hold them anymore, and they spun free into the surrounding night, and Jack stood in the light alone, playing the wild, sweet tune for no one, and them all.

Chapter Twenty

Lupe's presence in Beau's life afforded all the painful pleasure of an erupting wisdom tooth. She was an unpredictable presence at best, walking or riding to the Pennells' to visit with Jessie one day, keeping to her house across the creek like some kind of hermit the next. Her moods were as changeable as her visits. She either ignored Beau, which left him stricken, or showered him with the same careless attention she bestowed on Bekah and Jonelle, which made him so self-conscious that what little grace he possessed forsook him completely. Only with Jack was she consistently affectionate, coddling him the same way Jessie did. Sometimes it made Beau almost crazy with jealousy; other times, it just made him wistful, like a hound eying a pan of gravy through the kitchen window. Lupe's absences were easier to bear, really, than her visits, for then he was free simply to think about her. And think about her he did, to the exclusion of almost everything else.

He thought about the way her eyes looked sleepy when she was bored or put out; the way she laughed when she got tickled, right out loud and big, with her head thrown back and her mouth wide open; her sudden temper tantrums, when she threw anything there was to hand, regardless of ownership - buckets, dishtowels, rakes, butter molds, plates - only to laugh again, or leave in high-headed disdain, when met with

Jessie's disapproval; the casual way she treated her own body - sitting on the porch steps with her knees spread apart beneath her skirt; hiking her blouse out of her waistband to scratch the bare skin of her back; leaning against a fence rail to talk and coming away with the outline of her breasts defined by dust - as though knees and backs and breasts were no more remarkable than skirts, or blouses, or dust. Everything about her was unexpected, wonderful, and amazing. Everything, that is, except her husband, who had become a problem Beau could not resolve.

Dolly Baxter had always been there, closer to Beau than his own father, a short, thick man with a bantering way of speaking, a bald, white head, and eyes of an arresting cobalt blue. Dolly loved all the Pennell children, but had always spent extra time with Beau. Dolly was his friend, and his teacher. Dolly had taught him to ride a horse, to shoot a gun, to skin a deer. Dolly had taught him how to drag a rabbit from its burrow by twisting its fur in a forked stick, and how to call a doe deer out of a thicket - black nose twitching for the wounded fawn she could hear, but neither smell nor see - by blowing on a blade of grass held taut between his thumbs. Dolly had made Beau his first cow whip, and made him practice with it over and over again, his arm quivering with fatigue, his mouth trembling with frustration and pain, until it came to him, suddenly, without thought or will, the perfect, fluid motion of shoulder, arm, elbow, wrist, and fingers, and the long whip snaked out and licked a dragonfly off a fence post, freckling the air with amber and crimson. Dolly had slapped him on the shoulder so hard it almost knocked him down, reminding Beau again of the power in him, the strength that was so much a part of his love. He had wondered more than once what Dolly's hatred would feel like, when his love was sometimes so hard to bear.

Now Beau wanted Dolly's wife - wanted her so bad it made him ache inside and out - and he hurt, not only with confusion and desire, but with rank fear of the man with the cobalt blue eyes, and what he would do to Beau if he could read his mind.

And if all that weren't bad enough, Tate Rainey had yet to come back at him for the beatings he'd given Bob and Clyde. It wasn't natural. The man should have done something by now, dropped a word, at least, of anger, complaint, or threat somewhere - mercantile store, saloon, barbershop, jail - to let Beau know what he could expect in return. But there was nothing. The silence made Beau nervous. He'd about decided to ride to the Raineys and force a confrontation, regardless of the consequences, when there came a knock at the front door one evening, and Beau opened it to find Bob Rainey standing on the porch.

Bob didn't look too good. His thin blonde hair hung over a knot on his forehead the size and shape of a green persimmon, and the rings around his watery blue eyes were a dirty yellow. His upper lip, lopsided with swelling, drooped halfway over the lower. It gave him an air of disapproval. Beau expected an attitude to match the injuries, and kept a good grip on the door so he could slam it if attacked.

Bob, however, kept his distance. "We're going after them horses in the morning," he said. "Pa sent me to remind you."

"What about that other?" Beau asked.

Bob frowned at him, scanty eyebrows raised in question. "What other?"

Beau jerked his chin at Bob's lip. "That there. What I did at the cane grinding."

Bob shrugged. "Pa says it was a misunderstanding."

"What do you say?" Beau asked.

"I don't argue with Pa." Bob scowled, as though irritated of a sudden. "So, are you coming tomorrow or not?"

Beau searched his face, looking for signs of duplicity, but all he saw was dirt and bruises. He nodded, tentatively at first, and then with confidence. "Yeah," he said. "I'll be there."

"I'll tell Pa." Bob turned to leave.

"Hey, Bob. I'm sorry about what happened. Guess I got carried away, Dolly being a good friend and...."

Bob raised one hand in the air, cutting Beau off. "See you in the morning. We'll meet you at the pens on the marsh at daybreak." He started down the steps. Beau shut the door and went back in the kitchen.

"Who was that?" Raymond asked.

"Bob Rainey. He came to remind me about tomorrow."

"You should have asked him in," Jessie said.

Beau shook his head. "He wouldn't have come in. He didn't have much to say."

Neither did Tate, who abruptly interrupted Beau's stammered apology the next morning. "A misunderstanding," he said. "We got work to do."

For the first time since the fight, Beau really believed that he and the Raineys had no business together but the capture and breaking of the wild horses that still roamed up and down the river and grazed on the marsh east of Walker's Island. Like unclaimed scrub cattle, they belonged to anyone who could catch and brand them. Few people, though, had the will to hunt them, given their speed and cunning and the treachery of the country they inhabited. The marsh was filled with bogs and saw grass ponds, and pocked with 'gator holes. It was worth a man's life to treat it carelessly.

But Beau welcomed the danger, riding headlong and heedless after the herd to form a wide, hat-waving, whip-popping half-circle with Tate and the twins that drove the horses into a barbed wire crevice that narrowed at the other end into a set of stout cypress pens. There the Raineys cut out the two-year-olds and sent them one at a time down a chute into another pen, where Beau roped, saddled, and bucked them out. Day after day, Beau's loop sailed through the air, past flattened ears, flared nostrils, a gaping mouth, to settle around a shaggy neck that had never known the touch of a human hand. Then he'd dally the other end around a post sunk in the middle of the pen, wrap the end around his hips, and sit back on it like a sling, waiting for the slack to run out. When that moment came, the horse jerked backward, flailing like a tarpon on a line, then crashed back down to earth in a green black shower of grass and dirt, grunting with effort, terror, and rage.

Beau met that fury with his own. From the first rope around its neck to the saddle on its back, he fought each horse to a quivering halt, finding in every struggle and eventual surrender a bleak joy matched only by the relief he felt at his own exhaustion. Life was the heaving bodies of horses and enormous quantities of food he barely tasted, and sleep so deep and dreamless even Lupe couldn't find him in it. He might have purged himself of her completely, had it not been for the gray colt.

He'd noticed early on that it was different from the others, more watchful, snorty with fear, but not panicked. When Beau finally got to him - number fifteen out of twenty - the colt fought with everything he had, and bucked hard enough to loosen one of Beau's teeth. Smarter than most, though, the gray horse had come to a standstill long before any of the others - ears pricked forward, legs trembling as though with cold - and waited to see what would happen next. He was quick, smart, bold, and handsome - barring a thick Roman nose - and Beau wanted him.

Two weeks after the job had begun, and three days before he was to leave on the drive to Punta Rassa, Beau slipped his bridle off the last half-broke horse, and hung it on a fence post. "That's got it," he said. "Twenty horses, broke to ride."

Tate counted the contract price into Beau's hand: ten ten-dollar gold pieces. "You're quite a rider, Pennell," he said.

Beau put the money in his pocket and shrugged, uncomfortable with the praise. "Beats working for a living," he said. "If you pick up anything between here and Ft. Myers, I'll break 'em for you when I get there."

"We'll see. I'd like to find something for you a little more challenging. These here were pretty good, but there's worse." Tate smiled. "You deserve worse."

It was an odd thing to say, and sent a prickle up Beau's spine. He laughed, nervous for the first time since the horse hunt had begun. "Don't go out of your way for me," he said.

"Oh, I don't mind," Tate said. He picked a grass stem, and stuck it in his mouth. "See you in Ft. Myers." He started to walk away, and Beau stopped him.

"Hey, Tate," he said. "How much you want for that gray colt over yonder?"

Tate rolled the grass stem back and forth in his mouth, and studied the colt for a moment before replying. "That's a pretty good horse," he said finally. "Best one of the bunch. Thought about keeping him myself."

Tate's reluctance undermined Beau's caution. "Aw, c'mon," he said. "You're horse poor already. Let me have the ole sorry thing. He ain't that broke, anyhow."

"I hate to hear that," Tate said. "I hired a feller to break him. Guess he didn't get the job done." He spit the grass stem out as though it tasted bad. "One hundred dollars."

Beau grinned. Tate was playing with him, he knew. "Twenty-five, and that's too high."

A muscle twitched in Tate's jaw. "One hundred ten," he said.

Still incredulous, Beau laughed. "But you just said a hundred. You can't raise the price."

"I just did," Tate said softly.

"But nobody does that."

"One hundred and twe..."

"All right, all right," Beau said. "A hundred and ten." He shoved his hand down in the pockets of his overalls, and rolled the gold pieces around. There were still only ten of them. He'd have to borrow the extra ten dollars from his father or Dolly against his pay for the drive to Punta Rassa. The thought made Beau squirm. "I don't guess you've got another horse to break."

"Nope," Tate said. He held out his hand. Beau put the gold pieces in it. Tate closed his fingers over them, and put them in his pocket. "I'll need the rest by tomorrow. Day after, me and my boys are taking these horses to Ft. Myers." He walked off before Beau could think of anything to say.

So Beau had to borrow ten dollars from his father, who gave him a hard time about it, just as Beau expected. Then Raymond turned around and told Dolly about it, who thought it was just about the funniest thing he'd ever heard, until he saw the gray colt.

"Well, now," he said. "You didn't get took as bad as I thought. Excepting his nose, that's a darn good-looking horse."

Beau was pleased at the compliment, and disposed to be friendly. "Glad you like him," he said. "He's as smart as he is handsome. And he'll watch a cow, too, even if he don't know what to do with her yet."

Dolly laid a hand on the colt's rump, which visibly tightened. "Yessir," he said. "Not a bad deal at all." He looked up at Beau. "How much you want for him?"

For all the scorn and expense it had cost him, Beau hadn't thought of selling the colt. "I don't know," he said. "I guess I'd take what I paid for him."

Dolly grinned. "I guess you would. Only you paid too much. I'll give you twenty dollars for him, just as he stands. It's a fair price. You can pay your daddy back and still have some jingle in your pocket. It'll hurt, I know, but you'll have learned a good lesson, and a cheap one, too, as lessons go."

There was some truth in that, and squaring with his father now would make the trip to come a whole lot easier. Nevertheless, Beau hesitated, torn between pride of ownership and the burning desire to put a hasty decision behind him. He scratched behind the colt's ears. "What do you want with a green broke colt, anyhow?" he asked.

"Oh, I don't know," Dolly said. "Guess I just like pretty girls and gray horses."

That did it for Beau. The memory of Lupe on the back of Dolly's gray horse with her hand on the older man's thigh came back as real as ever. It was bad enough that Dolly had Lupe. That he should have the colt, as well, and at Beau's expense, was too much. Beau would pay in blood for the horse before he'd sell him to Dolly. "I guess I'll hang onto him," he said.

Dolly's hand slipped off the colt's rump. "Let me know if you change your mind," he said. "I'll stand by my offer."

Three days later, Beau was packing for the fall drive. He tied his gear - cow whip, poncho, bedroll, rope, rifle, saddlebags - onto his saddle. In his pockets he carried a pocketknife, chewing tobacco, and three rawhide poppers to plait on the end of his whip as the old one wore out. He filled one bag with corn for his horse, and left the other empty until he reached the house, when he'd stuff it with sweet potatoes, cold biscuits, cured beef, salt pork, and coffee. His father, Jack, and Dolly would do the same. That plus the game they shot would last them until they met up with the chuck wagon at Hog Hammock, some two weeks away.

When he got back to the house, the others were in the kitchen drinking coffee with the lugubrious person of Fess Peck. Fess was tall and emaciated and wore undertaker's suits that were too big for him. His sole vanity was the well-tended mustache that completely covered both lips. He lived in a shack on the east side of Cat Lake, where he kept bees and supported himself through most of the year selling honey and honey cakes, with a little trapping on the side. But twice a year - the drive to Punta Rassa in the fall, and marking and branding in the spring - he drove the chuck wagon for Raymond and Dolly, trips he'd been making since Beau was five.

Fess loved to cook, but couldn't eat much, due to ulcers aggravated by his drinking. He was seldom drunk, but never quite sober, and enjoyed singing sad songs - in a nasal whine and slightly off-key - about picking cotton. When pressed, Fess would admit that he'd never actually picked any cotton, but still considered it just about the saddest thing a man could do with his life, and a fit expression for the sorrows all men endured. Dolly disagreed. He said the saddest thing a man could endure was Fess's singing, and claimed he only tolerated the noise for the beans. He thought Fess's beans were the best he'd ever eaten. Beau was partial to his sweet potatoes, which he seasoned with cloves and wildflower honey.

When breakfast was over, Beau followed Fess as he escorted Bekah and Jonelle to the front yard where the chuck wagon was parked. The cook leaned against the porch, sipping from a Mason jar full of hot, syrup-sweetened coffee laced with whiskey, and watched as the girls explored the wagon. Every now and then he'd hunch his narrow shoulders inside the baggy black coat as though chilled, and nibble on a honey-soaked biscuit, the same one he'd been trying to eat since he sat down at the kitchen table an hour before. The girls giggled and whispered in the wagon. Beau knew how they felt. It was a magical place.

Shelves lined the sides, and boxes marked with penciled sketches of skillets and Dutch ovens, plates, forks, spoons, and cups were stacked neatly on and beneath them. The remaining space was packed with enough food for five men for two months, as well as feed for the mules and ten horses. It was plentiful and simple: barrels of flour and cornmeal, bags of sweet potatoes, coffee beans, pinto beans, and shelled corn; lard for frying and baking; jugs of syrup and honey for sweetening; and salt, cloves, sage, and cayenne pepper for flavoring. That was it. Along the way, they'd cut cabbage palms for swamp cabbage, and kill deer, hogs, or a steer for fresh meat. But mostly, they'd just eat what was in the wagon. Various knives and a cleaver dangled on nails that jutted out of the ribs above the wagon sides, and from the top of the rib arching over the bed of the wagon hung five empty meat hooks.

Fess tossed back his coffee and fed the biscuit to the mules, then went with Beau to the smokehouse, trailed by the girls and an assortment of hopeful dogs. They returned carrying two sides of a steer. The carcass, bereft of head and hooves, was thickly covered with cayenne pepper and black with smoke. Another trip provided a smoked ham and two sides of bacon. All the meat was hung on the hooks, where it swayed gently back and forth, watched by the same dogs with the same undying hope.

When the wagon was loaded, Fess pulled himself up on the seat and gathered the lines. The mules pricked their ears and stirred, setting cocked hooves firmly on the ground.

Raymond got on his horse and sidled it up to the front porch where Jessie stood with her hands in her apron pockets. "I'll bring you back something special," he said.

"You just bring yourself and those boys back safe," she said. "That's all the special I need." She got up on tiptoe to kiss him goodbye. Jack rode up, jostling Raymond's horse, and stepped off onto the porch to give his mother a hug.

"Stay out of trouble," she said.

"You don't have to worry about me," he said.

"You're the only one I ever worry about," Jessie said. "Don't upset your daddy."

"Never," Jack said, and kissed her on the cheek. Laughing, Jessie shooed him away with her apron. It was Beau's turn, but he sat his fractious horse ten feet away, rigidly unapproachable.

"Beau," Jessie called. "You be careful."

He made a dismissive gesture that startled the colt. It blew air out its distended nostrils and looked wildly around, finding danger in every shadow and swirl of dust, and relieving Beau of further conversation with his mother. One of the mules brayed, a brassy, ear-splitting sound that destroyed the morning's quiet.

"Guess that about says it," Dolly remarked. "Let's go."

Raymond reined his horse around, and Dolly fell in beside him, followed by Jack. Beau nodded at Fess, and the older man slapped the lines on the mules' backs.

"Giddup," he said. The mules leaned into their collars, hooves digging into the sandy ground. "Giddup, now," Fess said again, his voice sharp. The wagon creaked, rocked, rolled forward down the road. Beau followed it, the gray colt walking across the yard as if the dirt were studded with broken glass.

They crossed Deep Creek together, and parted company on the other side: the riders north to hunt cattle, Fess south to set up camp at Hog Hammock, some fifteen away.

"See you in two weeks," Raymond said. "Have the coffee hot."

"That's fourteen days, exactly," Fess said. "Don't be late. I don't hold supper for laggards." The mules brayed a mournful farewell as the wagon rolled away, the two sides of the steer carcass swaying forward and back on their hooks like some weird black rocking horse severely off its stride.

Chapter Twenty-One

The riders made camp together the first few days and worked steadily northeast. Evening was a pleasant time, and ordinarily, the four of them would sit with their backs against some tree or fallen log, eating bacon, biscuits, and sweet potatoes while they regaled one another with the day's events. Afterwards, coffee cups in hand, they'd reminisce or listen to Jack play his fiddle before rolling up in their blankets and falling asleep beneath the stars.

But not this trip. The chuck wagon was no sooner out of sight than Dolly started in about the colt, rubbing Beau's sore spot raw. Beau did not turn red, as he used to do when teased, or join in the laughter at himself. He got angry. Within days, the teasing had become all out war. Dolly stuck sandspurs under the colt's tail to make him buck, or pulled the bridle off as he rode by. Beau threw hot coals in Dolly's lap, and filled his boots with water. But no matter how hard Beau tried, he couldn't match Dolly's verbal ingenuity or boldness; anger made him stupid, and discretion killed his nerve.

Dolly suffered no such handicaps. He made endless observations on Beau's youth and inexperience in horsemanship, horse trading, cattle lore, and love. He belittled the colt. He compared Beau unfavorably to the Rainey twins. And all along, as Beau fumed and sulked, or lashed out in bitter, vengeful jest, there was a kind of hurt puzzlement in Dolly's eyes that belied the roughness of his jokes, and a growing tension in him that nothing - neither Raymond's peacemaking nor Jack's music - could ease.

The fifth night after leaving Walker's Island, Beau dreamed that Lupe's arms were holding him underwater until he drowned, and floated to the surface again, light and flaccid, emptied of desire and bereft of something infinitely precious that had no name. He woke suddenly, cold and frantically aware that he really was drowning. Dolly was standing over him with a bucket, pouring water in a thin, steady stream directly in his face.

"Now your head's as wet as your britches, Romeo," he said.

Beau would rather have been lying in a muddy bull wallow being gored to death by a razorback hog than be where he was right then. It must have shown on his face, because Dolly squatted down beside him, and assumed a commiserating expression.

"Tell me," he said in a stage whisper. "Was she pretty?"

Beau wiped water off his face with his shirtsleeve. "I hope you die soon and slow," he said.

Dolly laughed and stood up. "Don't worry about it none, Beau," he said. "They're all pretty enough for what you want."

Beau lay there in the mud - dirty, wet, and humiliated - and hated Dolly from somewhere deep inside. At the same time, he longed for the way things used to be. He'd not realized misery could come so purely to a person. Two hundred proof, as Fess would say.

The next morning dawned cool and overcast, and Beau left camp early, before the coffee was ready. He returned late, unsaddled the colt, and went to fill a feedbag. When he got back, Dolly was scratching the colt's nose. The sight took Beau's appetite away. Not so the colt's. It shoved its nose at Dolly's shirt, twitching its upper lip at his pockets.

"Smell that chewing tobacco, don't you buddy?" Dolly said. "Try some, see if you like it." He spit a stream of tobacco juice on the horse's nose. It blew hard, then stuck out a long pink tongue to catch the molasses running into its mouth.

Beau just about lost his mind. He wiped Dolly's spit off the colt's face with vicious slaps of his hand while the terrified horse flung its head up and down and backed away from him until it hit a tree and stopped, haunches bunched and quivering. Beau threw his hat down and whirled around to face Dolly.

The older man was leaning against the wagon, the blue eyes unreadable. "Temper, temper, little mister," he said. It was a term he hadn't used with Beau in years.

"Spit on your own damn horse," Beau said. "And stay away from me and everything that belongs to me. And don't call me 'little mister.'"

Dolly sucked his tooth, the corners of his eyes crinkling with amusement. "Having big boy dreams has puffed you up something fierce," he said. "You keep your head straight and your mouth shut, you may live long enough to make them dreams come true." He put his hands in his pockets and sauntered over to where Beau stood, fists bunched by his side, and put one hand on the tree beside Beau's head. "In the meantime, here's a deal. I'll spit on your horse any time I feel like it, and you stop me any time you're able. How about that?" He winked at Beau and added, "Here's how my part works." He turned to the horse and spit on its upper lip. The colt jerked, then stuck its tongue out again, and gave its nose a tentative lick. When it smacked its lips, Beau punched Dolly in the mouth.

The next thing he knew, he was pinned to the tree with Dolly's hand around his throat and his feet dancing on air. The evening was blackening in front of him and stars were bursting in his eyes before he was dropped. Beau turned, hugging the tree and sucking the wind back inside his lungs. Behind him, Raymond and Dolly were yelling at each other, Jack was shouting and wringing his hands, and Fess was banging pots and pans as if by sheer volume of noise he could drown the rest of them into silence.

"Stop it," Beau croaked. No one listened. He closed his eyes, took a deep breath, and yelled. 'Stop it! Everybody! Stop it!"

Fess quit banging the pans. Dolly walked off. Raymond put his fists down. Jack kept sniffling. Beau picked up his saddle and threw it on the colt.

"What are you doing?" Raymond demanded.

"Leaving." Beau nodded toward the west. "I'll swing around and work the other side of Elliston and Walker's Island, and meet you at Hog Hammock with whatever I pick up." He pulled himself into the saddle before looking at Raymond. Beau had never seen his father helpless before. It made him sick at his stomach.

"What the hell is going on around here, anyway?" Raymond asked.

"Ask Dolly," Beau said. "He knows everything." He touched the colt with his spurs, and rode into the woods, taking the long way around the wagon so he wouldn't have to pass Dolly.

"At least wait 'til morning," Jack called. Beau ignored him and rode on. No one else tried to stop him, and no one followed him except his dogs.

Three days later, Beau was nearly back to Elliston. The gray colt moved down the cattle trail on the last day of September with a smooth running walk, the Roman nose bobbing in time with its own quick steps. The colt had settled down since that morning, when it had greeted Beau's presence on its back with three bone-jarring bucks that drove one end of Beau's spine into his tailbone and the other end into his skull. It moved out of camp afterwards with the tight, nervous gait of a green-broke horse - half-trot, half-crowhop - that told Beau he was ready to fly into a million pieces with the slightest excuse, an attitude that mirrored Beau's own. And while thirteen miles of hard riding had steadied the colt, the boy still felt fly-bit, jumpy, and mean.

Beau skirted Elliston in mid-afternoon, continuing west to a small hammock behind the Gibbs homestead, about three miles south of town. He could see Able Gibbs in the distance, following a harrow and a pair of oxen across a stubbled field, as deliberate in motion as the pied team he was so proud of. The sight of someone working in a field always filled Beau with alarm. As a chore, he found it repugnant; as a way of life, unthinkable. He studied the hundreds of ordered rows and shook his head, marveling anew at the brutal labor that had cleared the way for them. "I can't figure what drives a man to do such as that," he'd said once to his father. "Bet he's walked from here to California and back again, and ain't never left his homestead."

"Dirt farmer," Raymond said. Those words held everything - pity, contempt, disregard, amusement, distrust - except explanation. Even Able couldn't explain it, though he tried one time, responding to a careless comment Beau made once at a barnraising regarding dirt farmers and their preoccupation with clearing land best left as it was. Able had grasped Beau's shoulder in his massive hand, leaned toward him in rough, unwelcome intimacy, and shared with embarrassing sincerity what it meant to him to lay the frail seed in the ground and wait - through heat and cold and drought and flood, pestilence and plague, high wind and hail - for it to sprout and grow and ripen to maturity, providing it ever did. Able's grip on Beau's shoulder had tightened, and his voice had risen with evangelical fervor

"You mind my words, boy," Able had said. "There's heartaches a plenty in bringing a crop to harvest. But there's nothing finer, either, when it happens. The bounty of the earth given up for the world's sustenance, filled with the goodness of the dirt itself, made palatable for humankind." There was something almost hungry in Able's expression as he searched Beau's face, and his thick fingers kneaded Beau's shoulder as though to work a response out of him. Beau, his understanding limited by prejudice and a certain failure of imagination, did his best to cooperate.

"Maybe you should try hunting cattle," he'd suggested. "It's less work, and you get to see a fair piece of the country."

Able had dropped his hand, a disgusted look on his face. "You're a Pennell through and through," he'd said. He'd pointed past Beau's nose at the prairie stretching out behind the barn. "You see all that? Someday, that will be cleared, and the marshes behind it drained, and all of it fenced and planted in grass and grain and produce to the horizon. When that day comes, you'll drive your cattle no further than Elliston and ship them out by rail, and go back home. None of this rambling around the countryside like you own it all, the way you do now. That's going to end one of these first days, as sure as you live and breathe."

Beau, who recognized no set boundaries but houses, barns, high water, and the sea, hadn't believed Able for a second. But he hadn't argued with him, either. Able Gibbs's stubbornness was a community joke, as was his determination to see land cleared and fenced that had been open grazing land forever, and always would be. Beau had just smiled, and said a patient 'yessir,' and let Able's heated words rise on past his face like smoke into the thick, sweet, summer air. Able hadn't called him 'son' since. Beau still found talking to him difficult. The fact that today he had no choice was nothing short of painful. He waved to Able, who drove the team to the end of the row, then stopped, the two oxen and the man standing silent, stolid and unmoving, until Beau reached them. He dismounted and shook Able's hand.

"Come with us to Punta Rassa," Beau said. "That plow will be there when you get back."

"Probably so," Able said. "It's yet to move on its own." He dropped Beau's hand as though glad to be rid of it, and eyed him suspiciously. "Picked up any of my stock?"

"About thirty head, so far," Beau said. "Daddy said to tell you we'll be glad to take 'em with us, same as usual, if that's what you want. We'll cut the steers out at Hog Hammock, and turn the cows and heifers back."

"That's fine," Able said.

"That's what we'll do, then," Beau said. Further speech seemed obligatory, but impossible. Then a howl quavered at the edge of the field, and an old dog appeared, walking wobbly-legged down a furrow, and growling. Beau grinned, relieved to find an easy topic for conversation so close to hand. "Soon's a scrapper right on, ain't she?"

"Yep," Able said. "She'll light right into your help, there, if you don't watch out." Soon - so named because she'd as soon catch something as look at it - was a long-eared, tricolored hound with a nasty attitude. She'd maintained a fearsome reputation in the county for many years and aspired to it still, though white-faced, now, and nearly toothless with age. Beau's dogs cocked their ears, whining in anticipation of a fight. He raised his hand and they dropped to their bellies. Able's old dog couldn't hurt anybody anymore, but she was willing to die trying. Given the opportunity, the Pennell dogs would oblige her.

The back door slammed and Lila walked out on the porch. She waved, and started down the steps. Beau, eager to be gone, all but pawed the ground in irritation. Able waited silently with folded arms for his daughter to cover the distance between house and field.

"Hey, Beau," she said. "You staying for supper?"

This abrupt invitation seemed to surprise Able as much as it did Beau, and he frowned with obvious displeasure. "His daddy ain't sent him all this way to dawdle at the dinner table," Able said. "He's probably running late already, with all his chitter-chattering." Beau was neither lazy nor chatty, and his face burned with embarrassment at being so accused. Nevertheless, he took the out that was offered him, and declined Lila's invitation. Able sent her back to the house, and dismissed Beau with a raised hand and curt goodbye, as though impatient to return to his work.

Beau continued southwest after leaving the Gibbs's. The dogs ranged far ahead of him, while the hooves of the gray colt beat a constant rhythm over sand and grass. He skirted the Rainey place on the west side and came back east again toward Deep Creek. A red-tail hawk caught a mouse and lit in a pine tree to eat it; one of the dogs barked in the tall grass, scaring up a rabbit; a rattler whirred beneath a dead palmetto frond laying beside the trail. Other than these, and the occasional crack of the whip in the dust, there was nothing but the sun, the sky, and the ground beneath the colt's hooves. Beau closed his eyes against the sun, and gave himself up to thoughts of Lupe Baxter.

The dogs barked sharply, and the frantic bawling of a calf erupted in the brush ahead of him. Beau spurred the colt forward into a clearing to find the dogs with a yearling steer at bay, its nose dripping blood. The cow got there about the same time Beau did, high-headed and looking to hurt somebody. The dogs left the calf and jumped the cow. She whirled around in a circle, one dog on her ear, the other swinging on the end of her tail. Like most scrub cows, she was small - less than four hundred pounds - and like many in the area, bore the Pennell mark and brand. Beau called the dogs off and they backed away, still barking. Beau gave a sharp whistle, expecting the cow to turn south. Instead, she charged the colt, bawling with rage. Beau slapped her in the face with his hat.

"Git on out of here, now," he said. "And take your baby with you. Go on, git!" The calf moved alongside its mother. She whipped around as if she were going to hook it, then sniffed it carefully. Satisfied it belonged to her, the cow threw her head up and made off to the northwest with such determination that the dogs couldn't turn her.

"Damned ole outlaw," Beau muttered. He sighed, and reined the colt around. "C'mon, you," he said. "We got to go get her." The cow could not have moved more directly toward Able's farm if Beau drawn her a map, and he was less than a mile from the house when he finally convinced her to move south. That was far enough away that he could not be seen through the trees, but close enough for his dogs to trade insults with Soon.

"Why don't you two tell the world we're here?" he grumped. The rumble in Beau's belly prompted him to accept Lila's earlier invitation, in spite of the misunderstanding such a decision might create. On the other hand, her daddy hadn't acted the least bit friendly, so maybe it'd be better to keep a safe distance. He chose the path of discretion, and reined the colt east to Cat Lake.

Beau made camp at dusk on the west shore of the lake where the Sunday school held its semi-annual picnics. By nightfall, he had finished eating and heaped the embers with dried cowpats to make smudge against the mosquitoes. He stretched out on his bedroll, and threw bits of meat and biscuits to the dogs. They snapped their supper out of the air until it was gone, then flopped down by the fire, eyebrows furrowed in concentration, to hunt fleas along their bellies and sandspurs between their toes. Then they stretched out on their sides, and sighed, and went to sleep.

Beau adjusted the saddle beneath his head, and closed his eyes against the sting of the smoke. Come morning, he'd head south again to hunt Walker's Island and Black Hammock west of the creek. That's where the Baxter place was. Maybe, if he got there early enough, he'd see Lupe. Maybe she'd still be wearing her nightgown. According to his scandalized mother, Lupe never dressed before nine o'clock. Beau felt a stirring below the belt and swallowed hard. Broken images of Lupe flashed against his eyelids, jagged around the edges like pages torn from a picture book. He thought about her voice, low and throaty and personal, and tried to think of something clever to say to her, but as always happened, his throat went dry and his mind went blank. He shoved that difficulty aside and coaxed her image back. It came to him, sleepy-eyed with desire. He let that look wash over him, then pictured Lupe as he'd first seen her, astride the tall gray horse, Dolly's hand resting on her bare knee, his fingers hidden beneath the hem of her dress. The image quivered, a watery reflection shattered by a stone, then came back together again, only this time, Lupe was sitting on the back of the gray colt behind Beau, her arms around his waist, her breasts pressed against his back, her thighs laying alongside his. He put his own hand on her round bare knee, lifted the edge of her skirt with the tips of his fingers, and moved his hand slowly up her leg, his body aching with pleasure.

The dogs growled. Beau's eyes popped open. He snatched his hand off his own leg and ran it down the saddle cantle to the scabbard, easing the rifle out, pulling the stock into his belly with his finger on the trigger. He sat up and shoved the fire with his foot. Flames shot up from the embers, and he screamed.

Soon stood in the firelight, wrinkled, liver-spotted lips pulled up over her remaining yellow tooth, upraised hackles as stiff and sparse as hog bristles. Little tongues of light played over the silvered death's head of her face. There was a chain around her neck. Holding the other end of the chain was Lila Gibbs.

"What the hell are you sneaking up on me like that for?" Beau yelled. He poked the rifle at the scabbard, shaking with fury and relief, and sick with shame for having screamed like some stupid girl, never mind if the dog did look like a haunt. "Damn me for not shooting that sorry animal," he raged. "It would teach you, Miss Lila Gibbs, to come creeping up on a sleeping man in the middle of the night."

"I wasn't sneaking..."

"I almost shot you! What do you think of that? I almost shot you! You and that sorry ole dog, both! Well, what do you think of that?"

"I'm sorry..."

"You're sorry! What good is sorry when you're laying dead in the dirt, you tell me that. Go on, tell me. What good is it? Well?"

Lila's face puckered and she started crying. Beau was disgusted. "What're you crying for? I'm the one ought to be crying, scared out of my full growth and right mind. You and your damned ole ugly dog. That's the ugliest dog I ever saw. I wouldn't have a dog looked thataway. Shut up!"

This last was directed at the dogs. Soon, impervious to Beau's opinion of her, had not stopped growling at his dogs since she arrived in camp, nor they at her. And the three of them ignored Beau now. But when he wrenched the cow whip off the saddle, they sank to the ground and lapsed into silence, even Soon. Lila, however, only cried the harder. Beau threw the whip back down, feeling stupid. He clambered to his feet and patted Lila on the shoulder. "I was talking to the dogs," he said.

Lila was crying too hard to talk, but that didn't stop her from trying. "I, munh, sunh, sunh, sunh, ah, re, ree," she sobbed. "I, unh, unh..."

"Don't do that," Beau said. He'd never seen anybody cry so hard before, or heard anybody sound so awful. He couldn't imagine what had brought it on, and did not know what to do about it. Lila bent over, face in her hands, shoulders heaving so violently Beau thought she might come apart. For want of a better solution, he put his arms around her.

He'd always thought of Lila Gibbs as a big girl, but found he could hold her and still touch his elbows with his hands. He could feel the dampness of her dress against his skin, and the strength of her body, racked by sobs, straining against his arms. He held her harder, determined to force the crying to a stop, though he couldn't help but laugh at the funny way she talked, and told her so. It made a difference. Little by little, Lila quieted. After awhile, her hands fell away from her face and slipped around Beau's waist with light, butterfly touches, to hold him in return. It was Beau who shuddered now. Lila sighed, a deep, quivering sigh, warm against his neck, that upon its release, brought her body against his. And when the crying was stilled, and he could have let her go, Beau held her still, his body trembling. She pulled away from him and looked up in his face, a question in her eyes he didn't know how to answer. He looked away from her eyes to her lips, swollen with crying and soft-looking, almost as red and full as Lupe's. He bent down and touched them with his own.

He could be holding Lupe if he closed his eyes, the day dreams and the night dreams come together in this place, where there was not a soul to see or hear except the silent dogs with their glittering eyes. He had not known a woman's body would feel like this, warm and cool, soft and firm, all at once, its mounds and hollows quenching the fire in his mind only to ignite another in his body more urgent than he'd ever known. He laid his face on her hair and stroked her back with one trembling hand, stopping at the swell where back turned into buttock to pull her hard against himself. And all the while, he talked to her - assuring, cajoling, pleading - needing Lila's willingness, wanting to believe what his body insisted must be true, that she could be taken in this way without consequence, though her flesh burned his like a brand.

Chapter Twenty-Two

Lila Gibbs was not a pretty girl. She was tall, sturdy, awkward, with straight, thick hair, a wide face, and small hazel eyes surrounded by thin, almost invisible lashes. Her mother tried her best not to care.

"No matter," Myrtle Gibbs would say. "It's what's inside that counts. Better to be good than beautiful."

But Lila would gladly have traded what little goodness she possessed for whatever beauty it would buy. She kept that particular to herself, however. Lila's mother, whose brittle prettiness was exceeded only by her icy virtue, would have looked at her with horror, and said, "The very idea!"

Three such small words to hold, as they could, so much scorn. Myrtle Gibbs used them, with varying degrees of intensity, for everything and everyone she disapproved of, even, on occasion, her daughter. Myrtle had never laid a hand on Lila. She reduced her, instead, to abject shame with her tongue, and the lowest tone of voice imaginable. She didn't have to do it often, either. Lila was a good child, respectful and eager to please. Myrtle thanked her lucky stars for her sweet daughter, and desired for her the best that life could offer. If she had qualms about Lila's marriage prospects, she kept them to herself.

Able Gibbs was less grateful for Lila, but more certain of her future. He had wanted sons: big, strapping boys to help him with the farm, and into whose grateful and well-trained hands he could entrust it at his death. He got one daughter. He provided that daughter with food, shelter, clothing, moral guidance, and as much deliberate kindness as it was in him to bestow, whenever it crossed his mind to bestow it. He asked for very little in return: that she be quiet and obedient and stay out from under his feet. In time, he found Lila satisfied him as much as any daughter could, and he bore her no ill-will for what she was not. It was life, circumstances, fate - or possibly his wife - that had failed him, but not Lila. And when her girl's body began to change, and take on the forms and ways of womanhood, Able's hopes blossomed again, as fresh and green and sweet as they had ever been. He came to see his daughter as a precious possession - a honey tree, a white roe deer, a pearl of great price - by which he might beget a son to himself through the gift of her hand in marriage, and he guarded her with the fierce care of a man who must risk all he has on one chance to win his heart's desire.

Able - his mind as narrow, rigid, and straightforward as a plow blade - never dreamed that Lila might have intentions of her own, just as Lila, who was more like her father than she knew, never suspected her father of having any other. Which was why Able's gruff rebuke, delivered at the supper table hard on the blessing's heels, surprised her so.

"It's not fitting for a girl to ask a boy to supper that way," he said. He forked a sweet potato out of a bowl and split it on his plate to butter it. "Word gets out quick when a girl is forward. You hadn't asked me the first thing about it, and don't think he couldn't tell."

"Your father's absolutely right," Myrtle said. "A girl should never let a young man know she's interested in him before he declares himself."

"She ain't interested in the Pennell boy, for Pete's sake," Able said. "I'm talking in general."

"But..." Lila began, then stopped. Myrtle had very deliberately turned the gravy boat over on its side.

"Oh, my," she said. "I've spilled the gravy." She smiled at Lila, her eyes wide with innocent dismay. "Fetch me a dishtowel from the kitchen, honey. I can't believe I was so clumsy."

Lila got a dishtowel from the kitchen, then was sent back to rinse it out, then was sent back again to refill the gravy boat, while Able ate and shared with his wife his plans for Lila's future.

"This place needs another man," he said. "A man that knows the land, cares about it, wants to see it prosper. I've had my eye on a couple. Terrence Wilson, Judd Wilson's second oldest boy, has got some sense to him, and so has that young 'un of Harry Beaumont's. But there's no hurry. Lila ain't but fifteen. Judd and Henry both know I'm going to take my time deciding. We'll see."

Myrtle cleared her throat and patted a drop of gravy off the table. "Of course, Lila may have her eye on someone else."

Able stopped chewing to look at his wife. "And who might that be?" he demanded.

"No one in particular," Myrtle said. "I just meant that, as a general principle, Lila might want to have some say in who she marries."

"You ought to say what you mean, then," Able said. He resumed chewing. "Lila will marry who I tell her to. She's my daughter, and I know what's best for her."

Lila stood in the doorway, the gravy boat in her hands, and turned cold. Her mother was smiling at her with her brightest expression, the one that accompanied doses of castor oil and frosty mornings when Able needed help in the fields.

"She's a fine girl," Myrtle agreed. "I'm sure we'll have no problems with her."

Soon raised a racket outside, and Able went out on the porch. He came back and sat down heavily in his chair. "I reckon we're having company after all," he said. "Pennell's dogs are out yonder. Cow must have got away from him." He broke a piece of cornbread in half before, drowned it in syrup, and put it in his mouth. "That wouldn't happen if they'd quit treating the whole blasted country like their own back yard."

Lila waited until the gravy congealed on her plate, but company didn't come, and after a while, the dogs quit barking.

"Thought better of it," Able said. "Good. Shows he's got some sense, anyway. At least he knows when he's not wanted. He'll make camp over at Cat Lake, and even that's too close for my comfort. Soon'll be moaning all night long, wanting to go over there and have it out with his dogs." He pushed away from the table. "That was mighty good eating, ladies."

Lila didn't answer him. He'd said the same thing after every meal since she could remember. It didn't mean anything to her anymore.

She went to bed as soon as the dishes were done, pleading fatigue, and lay down on the bed in her shift. Not two miles away, Beau Pennell was probably already asleep, worn out enough with his day to find the ground as welcoming as a mattress. Soon bayed in the back yard, her ancient voice quavering with threat. From the east, another dog answered. Lila smiled. On the other hand, maybe Mr. Pennell wasn't asleep, after all. Maybe the dogs were keeping him awake. Maybe he was lying there next to his fire, brown eyes wide beneath the stars, as restless on this night as she. Lila flushed, the wash of blood jittering across her skin, making it sensitive and irritable, itchy, as if with prickly heat. She twisted in the bed, uncomfortable and vaguely angry.

There were footsteps in the hall. Low voices. The back door banged. Her father shouted at the dog. Soon fell quiet. The back door banged again. Footsteps. The door across the hall opened and closed. The bed creaked beneath her father's weight. Silence. Then Soon howled again, complaining of strangers nearby. Her father got up twice more to yell at the dog, but it did no good. After the second time, he didn't go out again. When she heard her father snoring, Lila rose from her bed and opened the shutter. Goose fleshed in the night air, which her mother believed carried fevers, Lila sat on the sill to watch the stars, a dull resentment the only cloud between their bright cold beauty and her.

She felt her father's desire for sons to be evidence of a kind of stinginess. If he needed more help in the fields than she could give, let him hire it, a thought she'd shared once with her mother, only to find that Myrtle's thrift was as great as her husband's, if not greater. Lila had known, too, of her father's resentment toward the local cattlemen, whose scrawny, unfenced cattle, unlike the well-behaved bovines of Ohio, were as much a menace to his crops as deer. But she'd never realized his prejudice extended as far as the Pennells, and she'd certainly no idea he meant to marry her off to a son of one of his cronies.

Lila's neck grew hot with humiliation. She would not be bred, like a dog or a horse, at the bidding and direction of her father. She knew she was expected to marry, had to marry. It was a woman's duty and purpose. But she'd assumed she'd have some say in whom she wed, given the chance, at least, to use what power she had to make the match of her heart, if that power were no more than the sheer depth and intensity of her desire, which for the last two years had been focused like sunlight through a magnifying glass on Beau Pennell.

He hadn't said fifty words to her since she set her sights on him, and she remembered every one of them. She'd danced with him exactly three times, her feet awkward with the need for grace, her hand and waist burning where his hands touched her, though they'd done so too carefully to provide direction. Lila took every word, every smile, every attention he paid, and bathed it in the light of possibility. But it was not until his mother had started teasing her that Lila really believed she had a chance. She'd caught Beau's glance after the cane grinding, when the fiddle was playing, and hoped it was seeking her. She'd almost gone to him and asked him to dance, but the music had ended before she could muster the courage. And now Beau slept beside Cat Lake, close enough to talk to, perhaps to touch, even, if she dared. Lila's heart thudded in her throat, and she smiled. Perhaps her mother was right, and the night air did carry fevers. Maybe her father was right, as well, when he said the only people who ever got anywhere in this world were those who knew what they wanted, and what it cost, and paid the price to have it.

Lila slipped her dress on over her shift, and tucked her shoes under her arm before venturing out into the hall. Myrtle's snores countered Able's in depth and volume, and neither diminished when Lila went by their bedroom door. She let herself out on the back porch. Soon thumped her tail on the ground, mumbling and woofing in mingled greeting and reproach. Lila unhooked her chain from the stake and led her in a wide circle around the yard to the road, then slacked up on the chain.

"Go find him, gal," she whispered. "Go find him." Soon's tail wagged back and forth, but she didn't move. Lila gave the chain more slack. "Whoop, catch him!" she said, her voice high and sharp. With that, Soon growled and wobbled off, nose to the ground, toward Cat Lake.

The moment she saw Beau's hand moving languorously up his own thigh, Lila knew she'd made a terrible mistake. It was almost a comfort when he started yelling at her; at least the focus was then on her shame, and not on his. She was grateful for the darkness that hid her burning face, and equally so for the chain that occupied her hands. She wouldn't have known what to do with them, otherwise, stuck like they were on the ends of her arms and needing more comfort than they could find in one another. Finally, even that would not suffice, and she dissolved into tears.

Lila didn't cry often. She bottled her tears for weeks, sometimes months, storing them way down inside herself where she couldn't feel or see them, until the place she kept them was full, and they overflowed. But she'd never cried before like she cried now, great tearing sobs from deep in her belly that shook her like a tree in a gale as they wrenched their way out. Strong arms went around her, and held her, and it was as though she'd never been held before, and the tears came even harder as she tried again to tell him why she'd come, things about desperation and longing and wonder and dreams and desire came stumbling out of her, jerked out between the sobs that tore at her until she thought she couldn't stand it any more, and all she could think of to say was, "I'm sorry." But she had trouble getting it out, not least because Beau kept shushing her. "Shhh," he said. "Shhhh."

"I-unh-unh-unh-unh-c-c-c-c-ca-a-nt't shhh," Lila said.

Unbelievably, Beau laughed.

"Wha-a-a-what's so-o-o fuh-funny?"

"Nothing," he said.

But she could hear the amusement in his voice. Ashamed, she tried to pull away from him. Beau wouldn't let her go.

"Please don't," he said. "You just sound funny, is all, crying and talking at the same time. "I'm sorry. Don't go." He held her closer. For the first time, her head on his shoulder, she was aware of the fabric of his shirt against her cheek. She took a shuddering breath, and yawned.

"That's better," Beau said. He trembled against her, like a horse fluttering its skin to get the flies off. She pulled away to look at him, to ask him what was wrong, and he kissed her.

Lila's first kiss was an unpleasant mental shock, something like static electricity. Had Beau not been holding her so tight, she'd have stepped away. But he was holding her, scrunching her arms against her breasts, her hands caught up by her face. She was aware of them now, and acutely uncomfortable. She pulled them down to her sides, and he held her closer. Timidly, not knowing what Beau wanted, Lila slipped her arms - stiff and sore from being held so hard - around his waist. He shivered against her as though he were cold, and snugged her close.

Lila closed her eyes, trying to think of a way to tell him what this was like for her, she who had never been held so closely in her life that she could remember, who was so hungry for recognition and attention she would stand there and take it forever. "Beau," she said. He kissed her again. This time was better, but still not as good as the holding. He put his hand on her breast. She jerked away, more surprised than offended.

"I'm sorry," he said. "I'm sorry. Come here. I won't do it again." His lips were harder on hers, almost hurting. He pulled her closer, a thigh pressed insistently against hers. "Lila. Sweet Lila."

Very suddenly, something in Lila stepped back from these proceedings, and took a look around. It was as though there were two of her - an outside her, that shuddered and felt hot and achy and did as Beau asked - and an inside her, that grew colder and more remote the more aware of the other she became. This part of herself knew quite clearly that she was no longer being comforted, and did not enjoy any longer being held. On the other hand, if Beau were telling the truth, then no one had ever needed or wanted her like he did now, and there was power in that, of a sort, that she had never known. Such happiness had never been hers to give before. It gave her an importance she'd never possessed until now. It made her really matter. When he put his hand on her breast a second time, she did not pull away.

"Does that hurt?" he asked.

"No," she said.

"Do you want me to stop?"

It wasn't an easy question to answer. Beau's mouth and hands on her flesh and her body's response, her confusion and fear, her own desires, everything distracted her, made it difficult to think, to decide. She wavered, wanting to stop, wanting to please, unwilling to lose him, or whatever she had of him.

"Now's the time," Beau said. "I don't know, later, if I'll be able to."

Lila had been raised around farm animals. She knew what 'later' ultimately involved. She thought about Terrence Wilson, about her father, about the forceful hunger of Beau's body, hard against her thigh, about his need, his terrible need, and her power to fulfill it. She made her choice. "Don't stop," she said.

He didn't.

What was done was done on the ground, the bedroll twisted beneath her back and lumpy with small sticks. Lila kept asking herself, as she looked up past Beau's shoulder at the vast black expanse of the sky, if this was what she'd come to his camp to find. She couldn't answer that. But she could remove herself as far, almost, as the stars themselves, so that, when it was done, she was too far away to feel it.

Chapter Twenty-Three

There were some eight hundred head of cattle gathered on the east side of the Locknahatchee. They'd been driven from the woods and marshes over the previous weeks and herded to the grazing lands between the river and the holding pens at Hog Hammock. Three major cattlemen - Pennell, Baxter, and Dempsey - and three or four small homesteaders - were there to take a head count of the steers they would send to sale. The cow whips, so prevalent in the hunt, were silent now, as were the dogs that panted beneath the trees around the camp. The drovers were quiet, too, sharp voices and quick movements kept to a minimum. The last thing anybody wanted was a stampede. The cattle milled slowly as the drovers rode among them, parting out steers for the drive to Punta Rassa, and pushing them into the massive pens built years ago for that purpose.

Raymond heard Jack calling him, and followed his frantic gestures. Beau was riding out of the cypress across the river behind a small herd of cattle. Raymond held up a circled forefinger and thumb to Jack, then turned to Dolly.

"Beau's here," he said.

"Good for him," Dolly said, and rode off.

Raymond watched him leave, not knowing whether to laugh at Dolly, or cuss him. That was better than what he'd felt a week ago, when, just for a second, he'd wanted to kill him. He guessed Dolly had seen it in his eyes when he pulled him off Beau, one fist back and ready to slam into his face. Even now, Raymond wasn't sure what made him stop, some little voice in the back of his mind, perhaps, that told him, quicker than thought, that one blow would shatter their friendship beyond repair.

That little moment was uglier than anything Raymond had seen or felt since hanging Vancey. It was frightening, too, to see the rift between himself and Dolly, a rift Raymond knew was due to more than Beau - Jessie, Lupe, Walker's Island, Billy - the substance of their friendship changed over and over again, each time different, less complete, as the boys they had been were lost to the men they had become. At least Jessie hadn't been there. She'd have shot Dolly Baxter where he stood.

Beau and the dogs drove the little bunch of cattle into the water, and crossed behind them. Raymond rubbed his neck as the gray colt trotted toward him, the stiffness there easing for the first time since Beau had left. He'd watched his son ride away after the fight, unable to stop or help him, while Dolly walked off in the opposite direction, returning only after Jack and Fess were asleep. He sat down next to Raymond by the fire, and didn't say anything for so long that Raymond felt obliged to speak first. He cleared his throat, and began. "Dolly..."

But Dolly interrupted him. "I just don't understand it, Ray. Fifteen years, that boy has thought the sun rose in my face and set in my ass. Then one morning he wakes up and decides I'm not worth the dirt he walks on. It made me angry, I guess. Then, when he hit me, my mind went blank. That's when I...did what I did."

The blue eyes across the fire were so full of pain that Raymond had to turn his head away. He had enough pain of his own. "I understand," he said. That was a lie, of course, and Dolly knew it. Raymond stood up and tossed his coffee grounds in the fire. "Beau'll come around, I expect. Best we get some sleep."

No more had been said about it. Raymond had buried his concern, and gone about the business at hand, trusting in luck and time. Now here came the same old Beau, and none the worse for wear. Not even a mark on his neck where Dolly had pinned him to the tree, and a smile on his face like he'd been caught stealing biscuits out of the warmer. Feeling like a fool for all the trouble he'd caused, Raymond guessed, but glad to be back all the same. Raymond grinned with relief and slapped Beau on the shoulder when he rode up. "Right on time," he said.

"Got tired of my own cooking," Beau said.

"I know what that's like," Raymond said. "Run into any problems?"

"Nothing I couldn't handle," Beau said. He paused. "Saw Able Gibbs. He said to take his steers with us, same as always."

"Will do," Raymond said. "All's well with him and his, I suppose."

"Far as I know," Beau said.

Raymond looked past Beau and nodded. "Looky yonder," he said. Dolly was riding toward them.

"I see," Beau said, and waved.

Dolly waved back. When he reached the Pennells, he held out his hand. "Good to have you back," he said.

Beau shook his hand. "Good to be back," he said.

And that was all the discussion the two of them ever had about what happened between them.

They reached the Caloosahatchee twenty-three days later, and pushed the herd across the river to the grazing lands on the south side. Early the next morning, they drove the steers to the head of the corduroy road built across the tidal marsh between the mainland and the port. There the cattle stopped, refusing to go further, though Jack kept moving ahead of them. The men stood in their stirrups and cracked their whips, the sound ricocheting off the flat water like a barrage of rifle fire as the dogs barked and nipped. The cattle stirred reluctantly, bawling in protest and confusion beneath the onslaught, then finally moved like some viscous substance onto the road. Those on the outside pushed toward the middle, instinctively avoiding the quicksand on either side of the road that none of them had ever seen before. Their hooves scrabbled and slipped on the pine logs of the corduroy as they moved across the marsh and into the holding pens on the wharf at Punta Rassa.

From the pens, the steers were driven into the loading chutes, the ones in front shoved up to the very edge of nothing by those in back, where one by one, they were roped and lowered with a block and tackle into the lower holds. Now and then, a steer would panic and jump, and then the screams of wounded animals would mingle with the bellows of those merely frightened. Pine torches waved in the Gulf breezes and lit the faces of the men, black with beards and mud and cow shit, and hollow-eyed with fatigue, and with the incessant bawling of the steers, the Babel of Spanish and English, the dogs, the whips, the thunder of hooves on wood, the creak and luff of schooners, the oily reek of steamships, transformed the docks at night into a version of hell. It was almost two in the morning before the last ship was loaded, its holds packed with three hundred head of cattle. Finally, it pulled anchor and set out for Cuba. Beau stood on the edge of the wharf, an arm hooked around a piling, as mournful as if he'd been abandoned.

"Wish you were going with them?" Raymond asked.

"Yes," Beau said.

"Me, too." Raymond said. "I've always wondered what it was like over there. Maybe one of these days we'll go see." Together, they watched the ship until it disappeared, the pine torches on the wharf snapping like flags in the wind that blew from the sea.

They got into Ft. Myers late that same evening and ate supper without bothering to bathe. Beau got into bed and closed his eyes.

"Oh, by the way," Dolly said. "The desk clerk said Tate Rainey is looking for you. He said Tate wanted you to look him up as soon as you got to town."

Beau opened his eyes. "When did you hear that?" he asked.

Dolly yawned and pulled his overalls off, scratching his belly through a gap where a button on his long johns had popped off. "When we checked in," he said. "Before supper."

"Fine time to tell me," Beau said. His eyelids were as heavy as the meal in his stomach. All he wanted to do was sleep.

Raymond doused the lamp. "There's no hurry," he said. "What's he want with you, anyway?"

"Something about a horse, I think," Beau said. "I'll talk to him in the morning." Then he rolled over and went to sleep.

The morning brought baths, clean clothes, haircuts, and a sit-down breakfast with napkins. Afterwards, everybody but Beau headed for the general store for the annual shopping trip. Beau turned the other direction, toward the stock pens where he figured Tate was waiting. He hadn't gone six steps before Raymond stopped him.

"Where you going?" he asked. "The store is this way."

"I thought I'd go find Tate," Beau said.

"He's waited this long," Raymond said. "You come with me. I need your expert advice."

Raymond approached his procurement duties with great seriousness, determined to please Jessie with the choices he made. In Beau's opinion, his father's anxiety was unwarranted. The list Jessie sent with him was so detailed it left no room for independent thought. The only leeway Raymond had was in the gifts he brought her, and he poured his energies into choosing them, seeking advice from the crew and other customers.

Beau had once enjoyed these excursions, and had laughed to see his father with dresses pressed to his chest, his shoulders festooned with shawls, his brows knit with indecision over various ladies' undergarments. And this year, Dolly was similarly occupied. It should have been funny to see him with a bonnet on his bald white head, frowning with all seriousness into a mirror as he fussed over the angle of the feather. But Beau, petulant with jealousy, decided he'd had enough of their foolishness and headed for the front door. He wouldn't even help Jack pick out things for Bekah and Jonelle. "Get them candy and ribbons," he said. "That's all they ever want."

A clerk stopped him at the front door. "Aren't you Beau Pennell?" he asked.

"Yes," Beau said.

"Tate Rainey is looking for you."

"So I hear," Beau said. He stepped outside, squinting in the bright sunlight, and turned away, walking down the street toward the stock pens. He'd started the trip intending to buy something special for Lupe. But now thoughts of her were crowded out by those of Lila. He could see her too clearly: pulling her dress down over her legs; getting to her feet; picking leaves and twigs out of her hair; and always, her face turned away from him, shadowed by the faint light of the dying fire. Beau guessed he could get her a little something as well. Something to make her feel better, though he didn't know what that would be. Maybe she didn't want anything. Maybe Lila, like him, just wanted to forget what had happened. He was so engrossed in his predicament that he ran slap into Bob Rainey, almost knocking him off the sidewalk.

"Watch where you're going, Pennell," Bob snarled.

"Sorry about that, Bob," Beau said. "I was thinking."

"Do it somewhere else," Bob said. He consulted his watch, pointing at the numerals on the face as he counted, lips moving soundlessly until he figured out the time. He scowled at Beau. "It's already ten-thirty," he said. "Daddy's been waiting all morning."

"Where is he?" Beau asked.

"The stock pens," Bob said. "I'm going there now. You come with me."

They'd not gone half a block when Beau heard footsteps, and turned to see Jack running down the street after them. Bob cursed, but stopped when Beau did, and waited with him for Jack to catch up.

"Daddy wants you," he said.

"What for?" Beau asked.

"He didn't say. He just wanted to know where you were, and I told him you'd gone off with Bob Rainey. He said to come get you, that he wants you for something."

Beau gave the message some thought. He'd discovered that, while he was willing to do any number of things behind his father's back, he was not yet ready to openly defy him, even in something as small as this. He looked at Bob and shrugged.

"Guess I better go see what he wants," he said. "Tell Tate I'll be there as soon as I can."

"He's about tired of waiting on you, Pennell," Bob said. "If you're yellow, just say so."

"I don't know what you're talking about," Beau said. Bob just snorted and walked off.

Beau wished Bob had waited, though, because on the way back to the store, Jack let slip that their father hadn't asked for Beau at all. Instead, Jack had seen Beau leaving with Bob, and fearful for his brother's safety, had brought him back with a lie. Beau was furious. He punched Jack in the arm, forbade him to interfere in his life ever again, and headed for the pens again.

But along the way, something sparkled in a window, shimmering across Beau's eyes. He crossed the street to a watchmaker's shop to see what it was. The display window was full of watches. In a corner of the window, a small glass object dangled from a string, motionless in the quiet air. "It must have been that," he muttered, and stepped into the store. Ignoring the clerk's helpful expression, he walked to the window to look closely at the bauble. It was a small glass bird, no more than two inches long from the tip of its beak to the tip of its tail, the tiny wings outspread. It was clear glass except for the blood red throat, and the rich green head and beak.

"It's a hummingbird," the clerk said.

"I see that," Beau said. He touched the bird with his finger. It whirled around on its string, throwing all the colors of the rainbow against the window. Beau had never seen a thing so pretty. "Look at that," he said.

The clerk came around the counter to stand beside him. "It's a prism," he said. "It breaks light."

Beau was filled with wonder. "I didn't know light was breakable," he said. The hummingbird spun slowly on its string, then stopped. It was so beautiful and rare, so unlike anything Beau had ever seen in his whole life, that it had to be priceless. "How much is it?" he asked.

"Twenty dollars," the clerk said.

"That's it?" Beau demanded. "Twenty dollars?"

"We've had trouble with the wings breaking," the clerk said. "That's the last one, and we won't be ordering any more. They sure are pretty, though."

"I'll take it," Beau said.

The clerk cupped the bird in his hand and snipped the thread that held it to the ceiling with a pair of scissors out of his pocket. The bell over the front door tinkled, and a shadow fell across the counter. The clerk looked past Beau, a helpful expression on his face. "Be with you in a moment, sir," he said. He set the bird down on the counter and smiled at Beau. "Let me see if I can find a box for you." He disappeared into the back of the store and came back carrying a small wooden box with a fitted lid. He slid the lid off and filled the cavity with cotton, set the bird down in it as in a nest, then covered it with more cotton. Snapping the lid shut, he handed the box to Beau. "This for someone special, sir?" he asked.

Beau, flustered at being called 'sir,' felt his face get hot. "Just a girl," he said.

"Bet she's pretty," the clerk said.

Beau handed him two fifteen dollar gold pieces. "She's beautiful," he said. "Take thirty for it. It's worth it."

The clerk winked. "You mean she's worth it," he said, and dropped the coins in the till. "I hope it brings you luck."

Beau put the bird in his pocket and turned around. Dolly was leaning in the doorway, arms crossed over his chest.

"Who's the girl?" he asked.

Beau, caught flatfooted, told the truth. "Lupe," he said.

Dolly stared at Beau, the cobalt blue eyes wide. Beau expected Dolly to hit him then and there, and for the first time, could admit that he deserved it. But to his confusion, Dolly roared with laughter, then threw his arm around Beau's shoulders and pulled him out of the watchmaker's store.

"It's for Lupe, is it?" he asked. "Aw, son, I'm telling you. You are something else again. Let me buy you a drink." Whooping now and then from some inner place of great amusement, Dolly dragged Beau down the street, a prisoner of his vast and inexplicable good will.

Beau walked double-time down a side street in Ft. Myers, Dolly's hand on his shoulder providing speed and direction, and stumbled through the doors of the Red Tail Hawk Saloon with Dolly's thick arm around his neck. That arm dragged him past Raymond, Jack, and Fess at a corner table, and through the men standing six deep at the bar to a place that magically appeared at the counter's very edge. There the grip on his neck eased, and the big hand came up to knuckle Beau's head, knocking his hat off.

"Cut it out, Dolly," Beau complained. He tried to bend down to get his hat, but Dolly's arm came around his neck again, and held him upright.

"Bar keep!" Dolly shouted. "Give my buddy here a drink." A shot glass full of amber fluid plunked down in front of Beau. Dolly hammered him between the shoulder blades with the flat of his hand, and held his own glass in Beau's face. "To you and me," he said solemnly.

Beau lifted his glass. "To us," he said. He put the edge of the glass against his lips, intending to take a very small sip of the whiskey, but Dolly shoved his elbow up and he gulped it, instead. Eyes watering, he patted the edge of the counter, trying to catch his breath.

"You all right there, Beau, ole buddy?" Dolly inquired.

Beau raised his palm in affirmation. By the time he could speak, Dolly was gone, shouldering his way through the crowd to greet some man Beau had never seen before. He blinked the tears away, took a deep breath, lips curled in distaste, and wished whiskey tasted better than it did, so he wouldn't mind drinking it so much. He wished, too, that he knew how it was that he and Dolly had so suddenly become such good friends, now that Dolly knew of Beau's interest in his wife. Beau put his hand in his pocket and fingered the gift he'd bought for Lupe, resentful that his buying it had caused Dolly such amusement, chagrined that he'd been caught buying it in the first place. Beau cupped his hands around the empty glass. He felt stupid, which reminded him of Bob Rainey. He leaned forward, glancing up and down the bar to see if there were any Raineys present, thinking one of them might have followed him to the saloon. He was supposed to have met Tate more than an hour ago, and now here he sat on a bar stool, held in place by forces beyond his control. Distracted with thinking about Tate, Beau tapped his empty glass on the counter. The bartender filled it up again. Beau took a tentative sip, then knocked the rest of it back. The whiskey tasted better now, and his mood improved. He would tell Tate, when he finally met up with him, that the delay had been Dolly's fault.

"You're slowing down, there, buddy," a voice said. Beau jerked around to face Dolly. The blue eyes were very close to his, still bright with merriment. Dolly shoved some coins across the bar. "Bar keep, bring us another!" he said. The empty glass in front of Beau disappeared, and a loaded one took its place. Beau closed his hand around it. A stool slammed into the back of his legs and he sat down.

"Drink up," Dolly commanded.

Beau drank up.

Dolly beamed at him. "You're doing just fine," he said. "Have another."

Beau's glass was full again, and he drank it down without the first sputter. It just took a little getting used to, was all. Like life. And things. Things took a little getting used to. For instance, Lila Gibbs. She was just the same as she'd always been. He'd tell her that, too, first chance he got. Just the same. Hell, it was her idea, anyhow. He wanted to stand up and make an announcement. "It was her idea, folks." Then he'd sit back down. If he could get up the first time, that is, only he couldn't. Something was weighing him down. Dolly was leaning on him, an elbow on Beau's shoulder, telling somebody about the drive.

"Took us four weeks, is all," he said. "Lost six head and a dog on the Caloosahatchee. Current got the steers, 'gator got the dog. Thought we never would get the wagon across. But no stampedes, no snakebites, no bad storms. We hit Punta Rassa right on time. Took us one night to get loaded, and a day to get gone, and here we are, buying dresses. Nothing to it."

Beau agreed. There was nothing to it. He'd take Lila a little something, give Lupe the bird. He put his hand on the box again. He guessed Dolly didn't mind about that, which was all right by Beau. He wouldn't want anybody bringing presents to his wife, if he had one, but it took all kinds, he reckoned. He didn't know what to take Lila, though. A hair ribbon. A postcard of the ocean. He bet she'd never seen the ocean. Something to make her go away was what he wanted. Go away happy, without that hangdog look on her face. Beau took another drink and thought unhappily but from a great distance of Miss Lila Gibbs.

He'd dropped her at the house by the light of a setting half moon, leading the gray colt with her on its back, the smelly old dog laid across the saddle in front of her, worn out by the night's efforts. At her whispered direction, he'd walked wide around the outskirts of the yard to the barn. He'd lifted Soon of the saddle and laid her on the ground, careful not to rattle the chain, then helped Lila down with his hands on her waist, the weight of her heavy in his arms and shoulders. She never said a word, her face averted from his, but Beau felt there was something that needed to be said - something either true or comforting - there didn't seem to be room for both. "You're a nice girl," he mumbled, and tried to stroke her hair.

Lila ducked out from under his hand. "You better go," she said. Her voice was empty.

"Lila..."

She held her hand up as if warding off a blow, and Beau fell quiet. He got on the gray colt and rode it out of the barnyard. He looked back once. Lila was kneeling on the ground, chaining Soon to a stake in the back yard. Beau had turned away and urged the colt into a gallop across the freshly harrowed field, Lila's scent on his lips and clothes and fingers roiling him all over again, the fear of Able Gibbs loping steadily behind, relentless in its pursuit.

The noise in the saloon stepped up a notch. Beau looked anxiously over his shoulder, then relaxed, and took another sip of whiskey. It was silly to worry. Able Gibbs had no business in Ft. Myers.

Raymond's face swam into Beau's field of vision, suspended over the bar. "Want to dance?" he asked.

Beau thought about dancing with his father, and decided he didn't want to. He shook his head. "No," he said. "Do you?"

"I would if your mama was here," Raymond said. "Jack's gone to play down at the hotel, and me and Fess are going to go listen to him. Why don't you come with us?"

The mere thought of Jack's music made Beau feel melancholy. "I don't think so, Daddy," he said. "I'll just stay here."

"From the looks of it," Raymond said. "That's about all you can do. How about you, Dolly?"

"You bet," Dolly said. He slung an arm around Beau's shoulders and squeezed hard. "Sure you won't go?" he asked.

"I'm sure," Beau said.

Dolly patted Beau's shoulder. "One little piece of advice, then, before we part."

"What's that?"

"You ain't got to say everything that's on your mind," Dolly said. "If you take my meaning."

Beau's face was completely numb, or he'd have turned red. "I take it," he said.

"Good." Dolly hugged Beau so hard he pulled him off the stool. Next thing Beau knew, Dolly was helping him up off the floor and slapping the sawdust off his overalls. "Sorry about that, buddy," he said.

"Don't worry about it," Beau said. Dolly settled him back on the stool, then clapped him between the shoulder blades, and left. Beau was alone. He took a swallow of whiskey, and wiped the water out of his eyes. The whiskey was making him sad.

"You Beau Pennell?"

Beau frowned, pulling the face across the bar into focus. It was the bartender. Beau nodded. "Yes," he said. "I am."

"Somebody's looking for you."

Beau choked, then squinted at the door. He couldn't see Able anywhere. "Where?" he asked.

"The other way, stupid," the bartender said.

Beau had to move his head to look the other way. This move could not be made lightly, lest he fall off the stool that seemed to be floating on the floor. Or maybe the stool was solid, only joined somehow to his backside, and the floor itself was floating. Either way, his balance was affected because of the water in his head. Beau knew his head was filled with water because he could feel it sloshing back and forth every time he moved. So, very slowly and with the utmost deliberation, he turned his head the other way and looked to the right side of the room. Tate Rainy was sitting at a corner table, almost hidden by the crowd.

"There's Tate Rainey," Beau said.

"That's who's looking for you," the bartender said.

"And I'm looking for him," Beau said. He stood up, then sank immediately back down on the stool. On the second attempt, he managed to stay upright, and began to walk, one careful step at a time, toward Tate. The floor under Beau's feet was solid, but not fixed, because it tilted at odd angles as he walked across it. This necessitated that he lift his feet a little higher than usual in case some steps appeared. The crowd was tight in front of Tate's table, so Beau moved around the edge of it, to the wall. He put a hand on somebody's shoulder for balance, and made his slow, measured way to the chair next to Tate's table. He carefully pulled out the chair, and sat on the floor. The sudden descent made him dizzy, so he leaned his head against the wall. The stars sparkling inside his closed eyelids were as bright and beautiful as the shards of light through the hummingbird. Their twirling made him feel sick, though, so he opened his eyes again, and took a deep breath. The spinning slowed. "That's better," he said.

Raucous laughter pounded his ears, and Beau looked up to find the crowd staring at him. Tate was standing in front of him, the toe of his boot just touching the heel of Beau's brogan. Bob and Clyde stood on either side of their father and a little behind him, hands in their pockets.

"You don't look better to me," Tate said.

Beau blinked and studied the faces beaming down on him like many-eyed moons. Somebody laughed. Beau flushed, and tried to stand up. It was no use.

"That the boy you been looking for, Tate?" somebody asked.

"That's him," Tate said. He sounded disgusted.

A man Beau had never seen before reached down and hauled him to his feet. "Hey, boy," he said. "I been waiting over a week to meet you. Tate tells me you're a pretty tough rider. But I got a horse can't nobody ride, I don't care how tough he is."

"No such thing," Beau said, "as a horse that can't be rode."

Tate smiled. It didn't suit him. "You tell him, Pennell," he said.

"Think you can ride my horse, boy?" the man asked.

"I know I can," Beau said.

This seemed to please everybody. Even Clyde grinned. For the life of him, Beau couldn't understand why anybody would care either way. It was just a horse.

"Twelve seconds," the man said.

"What?" Beau asked.

"One hundred dollars for twelve seconds."

Beau leaned close to Tate and spoke into his neck. "What's he talking about?" he whispered. Somebody guffawed.

"He can't ride in his condition, Tate," the man said. "Let's get out of here."

Something clicked in Beau's brain. "A hundred says I'll ride him to a standstill."

The man spit a stream of tobacco juice into the sawdust on the floor. "You can wait 'til you're sober," he said. "I don't want it said that I cheated you.."

Beau shook his head, then wished he hadn't. "I have to charge more when I'm sober," he said.

Tate's hand came down on his shoulder. "You come show 'em what you can do, Beau," he said. "I've got money on this one, myself."

The ground still rising and falling beneath him, Beau followed Tate to the stockyards where the stranger's horse was penned. It wasn't a bad looking horse, Beau thought, a smooth-coated roan, taller and wider than the gray colt, but not by much. But it had a nasty ring of white around its eye and a way of baring its teeth that reminded him of a catch dog. When he put his hand on its shoulder, a hind hoof flew out and rang the top board of the cow pens like a brass bell.

"Got a reach, don't he?" Beau said. Tate heaved a saddle over the fence, and Beau shoved it up on the horse's back. The horse immediately threw it off to the other side, and when Beau stepped under its neck to pick it up, tried to bite his head. He elbowed it away and it reared up, pawing at him. Beau grabbed the saddle and backed into the fence. "Is it doing that on purpose?" he asked.

Tate's voice was so soft Beau had to lean forward to hear him. "Were you listening to anything that feller said?" he asked.

"Maybe not everything," Beau said.

"It's trying to take your head off," Tate said.

Beau regarded the horse with more respect, and something niggled a warning in his mind. The men hanging on the fence were silent, no catcalls, no advice, no laughter. Beau approached the horse again, and proceeded to tie it so close to the post that its lips rubbed on the wood. He blindfolded it with his handkerchief and threw the saddle on it again. The horse couldn't buck - it was snubbed too close for that - but the girth was hung on the stirrup on the other side, so Beau reached under the horse to pull it down, and accidentally rubbed its belly. The horse kicked forward and caught his arm, numbing it to the shoulder.

Beau held his arm and bent over to peer under the horse. The girth looked very far away. He decided to go around the other side and untangle it. He ducked under the horse's head and it spooked, almost knocking him down, but he grabbed the halter with both hands and held on, the horse's lips flapping at him and its lower jaw twisting as it tried to bite. Beau's legs were shaking like jelly, but he got a grip on the horse's mane, and walked himself down its neck to the saddle. He jerked the girth loose, then took a long, wide, wobbly stroll around the back end to return to the left side. There he cinched the girth as tight as it would go and pulled his stirrup leathers down. Beau untied the halter rope, climbed up in the saddle, and set his feet hard in the stirrups. Blindfolded, the horse stayed where it was, quivering like a dog passing peach pits.

"Somebody take that blindfold off," Beau said.

The horse's owner climbed up on the fence, and jerked the blindfold off the horse's eyes. Still knotted, it fell down and dangled from the halter rope. The horse just stood there. Beau touched it ever so gently on the sides with his spurs, and the world exploded beneath him.

The roan horse jumped straight up, its back so bowed in the middle that Beau felt like he was balanced on the saddle above a perfect point, then came down on rigid front legs, its back legs kicked out and up so straight that Beau could feel its hindquarters on his shoulders. It rose in great sickening leaps and hit the ground again so hard Beau thought his head would snap off, if his back didn't break first. Beau and the horse both grunted with effort, Beau's stomach lurching nearly out of his mouth. He could see nothing - no pens, no onlookers, no horse - just air. And the whole time, Beau believed he would ride the horse, until it went to spinning, and even then, he believed he could have rode it spinning, if only he could have rode it sober.

But he was drunk, and the horse did go to spinning, whirling Beau around in a circle like Dolly used to do him, spinning around and around by his hands until he lay prone on the air while the world circled madly past him in streaks of color, no sound but the wind rushing by. It was like that now as the horse spun him, except that Beau leaned out from the center from his hips and legs, moving further and further down the horse's side, until he could see the ground twirling like a top beneath him, closer and closer, faster and faster, until he braked his body with his face, and brought himself to a grinding halt.

He hugged the dirt for a minute, feeling it solid and unmoving beneath him, then got to his hands and knees. But the ground wobbled, and he was real dizzy, and he couldn't stand up because something kept knocking him down again while a noise roared around him. He got up on his knees and tried to cover his ears to make the noise stop, but it roared on, and then something hit him in the side and he fell over again and opened his eyes. The roan horse was rearing above him, pawing the air. Beau rolled over and crawled on his elbows and knees toward the fence, grabbed a board, and pulled himself up. There was a loud crack, like a shot being fired. Beau opened his eyes to see if the horse was dead. It was very much alive, but backed into a corner by its owner. Beau sank down on his knees and vomited in the dirt, spitting blood out with the bile and the booze until nothing remained but his heaving stomach. He stood up, one thick leg at a time, and leaned his forehead against a board.

"Get out of the pen, son," the man said.

"I can't," Beau whispered.

"Get out!" the man yelled.

Beau just shook his head. Strong hands grabbed his arms from above, and Beau wanted to cry as they dragged him up over the fence and dropped him, groaning, into the dirt.

"Stop your whining," Tate said.

Something tickled Beau's neck and he scratched at it. When he brought his hand away, it was smeared with blood. Tate jerked the tail of Beau's shirt out of his overalls, ripped it off, and handed it to him.

"Your face is all tore up on one side," he said. "What you feel is the blood trickling down your neck. Wipe it off with this." Beau patted his neck gingerly. Tate took Beau's hand in his own and pressed it into Beau's neck. "Go ahead and wipe it off. That's not where it's skint."

Beau mopped the blood up, amazed that there could be so much of it and him still alive. He shifted and winced. "That's a bad horse," he said.

"You'd of thought he was worse'n that, if that feller hadn't interfered," Tate said. He pushed Beau's lip up and rubbed his two front teeth. "Still got your teeth," he said. He wiped his finger on his pants leg. "You're a mess, all the same. I guess that's something."

A shadow fell over Tate's shoulder, and Beau looked up to see the horse's owner. "Is he broke up anywhere?" he asked.

"Naw," Tate said. "I told you, this boy's tough. Not real smart, but tough."

Beau tried to smile, but felt his lip split, and stopped. Blood trickled inside his mouth, and he swallowed.

"Don't swallow that blood," the man said. "It'll upset your stomach. You got to spit it out, just like it was tobacco juice."

Beau spit, and licked his lips. "That's a bad horse," he said. He couldn't get over how bad a horse it was.

"He's a fool," the man said. "And so are you. You owe me a hundred dollars."

Beau closed his eyes. "It's at the hotel," he said. "I'll have to go get it."

"I'll run into you before you leave town," the man said. "You won't be going anywhere for a day or two. Meanwhile, I reckon I better help you back to your room."

"No need," Tate said. "I'll see to him."

Beau watched the man walk away, then looked at Tate, who was still squatting on his heels beside him. "I'd have rode that horse if I'd been sober," he said.

"You ain't that good," Tate said.

Beau closed his eyes again. He didn't feel like arguing. "Then what's that feller so mad about? He won the bet."

"He wanted a good show," Tate said. "He feels cheated." He took a lock of Beau's hair between his thumb and forefinger, and rubbed it thoughtfully. "Like me."

Beau groaned, then caught himself. He looked at Tate. "If you knew the horse would throw me off, what'd you bet on me for?"

"I bet on the horse," Tate said. "And some broken bones."

A wave of cold washed down Beau's arms, and he shivered. "What are you talking about?" he asked.

Tate laid the lock of hair on Beau's forehead, and smoothed it back, running his fingers through it like a comb until all the tangles were out. "You got a lot of hair," he said. "Bob and Clyde's is thin, like thistle down. Durndest thing. Don't know where they got it. Me and Red, we both got thick hair." He stroked Beau's cheek with the side of his finger, his touch as gentle as Jessie's. "You think my boys are ugly, don't you?"

Beau shook his head.

"There's no need to lie about it," Tate said. "Everybody thinks that way. Red thought that way. Their own mama. It's them teeth, mostly. What do you think caused that?"

Beau shook his head again.

"Ain't your ma ever said? I see her looking at them, now and then. I thought maybe she might have an opinion on it."

"Sugar tits," Beau said.

"What?"

"Sugar tits. She thought it was the sugar tits that done it. Rotted 'em."

"Maybe so," Tate said. "That was their ma. Didn't want to suckle 'em. Said they chewed on her." Tate looked off for a moment, then took a deep breath and returned his attention to Beau. He stroked Beau's face again, following the curve of his eyebrows with his thumb. "You hit my boys," he said. "You remember that?"

Beau's eyes filled with tears. "You said it was a misunderstanding."

Tate wiped the tears away. "It was," he said. "You misunderstood what would happen if you hurt 'em. Their ma, she never could get it straight, right up to the end. You see, it don't matter to me about their teeth. I love 'em just the same. I love 'em like my own life. I can't stand to see 'em hurt. Won't tolerate it. Red never could understand that." Tate took Beau's chin in his hand and held it steady. The black eyes were lifeless, but the voice was as soft as a woman's. "You don't want to end up like Red, now, do you?"

Beau shook his head.

"No," Tate said. "No, you don't. So you need to understand, right here and now, that if you ever touch one of my boys again, I won't just put you on a bad horse. I'll kill you. Do you understand that?"

Beau nodded.

"I didn't hear you."

"Yessir."

"Good boy." Tate's thumb moved slowly, gently, back and forth across Beau's chin, caressing him, studying his eyes. He smiled. "Good boy," he repeated. He let go of Beau's chin and patted his cheek. Then he stood up and walked away.

Beau lay in the dirt outside the pen for what seemed like a long time, dabbing now and then at the blood on his neck. His mind was sluggish, settling for long, unproductive moments on the horse, Tate, Lila. Finally, he thought of Lupe. He slid his hand into his pocket. It was empty. He put his hand into his other pocket. It was empty, too. The bird was gone.

He didn't want to cry because he hurt too much already, but the tears came anyway, trickling down his temples and into his ears. After a while, he rolled over on his stomach and crawled to the fence. He rested there for several minutes, then pulled himself to his feet. He started walking towards town using the fence for a crutch. The roan horse snorted and bucked on the other side until they reached the end of the pens at the edge of the road. From there, Beau had to walk back into town alone.

Chapter Twenty-Four

Jessie, her hands wet with washing collard greens, heard them coming from a long way off, heralded by the dogs that had accompanied them and answered by those that had been left behind. She pictured them plunging across Deep Creek, yelling with anticipation of the cold water and the welcome that awaited them on the island. They would cross with the wagon in the center, mindful of the treasure it held. Jessie smiled through her tears, She had run to meet them the first time they went without her, and stood on the island side holding her breath for fear the wagon would capsize and spill its precious contents in the water. She remembered what it had held, too: salt and baking powder, sacks of flour and coffee, bags of oranges, jugs of cane syrup. She'd made biscuits when they got to the house, biscuits she would remember until the day she died, soaked in butter and cane syrup, the first she'd had since their supplies had run out that August.

And when supper was over and the dishes done, Raymond had pulled a pink satin ribbon out of his shirt pocket and draped it around her neck. Poor Raymond. She'd put her head on his chest and cried like a baby, not knowing until that moment how badly she'd wanted something pretty. She'd excused herself to the bedroom and looked in the mirror, trying to fix the ribbon in her hair, then had put her hands down and really looked at herself, and seen how thin and brown her face was, how rough her hands, how dry and sun-bleached her hair. She'd covered the mirror with one of Raymond's shirts and returned to the kitchen, where she'd asked him to fix the ribbon for her, which he had. He kissed her afterwards, and told her she was beautiful, and she'd determined that night to rub grease on her hands to keep them soft, and to accompany Raymond in public at all times, figuring that should her beauty ever suffer in comparison with another's, she'd at least be there to shoot him before he could follow his eyes away from her.

But such intentions were quickly lost in the fullness of life, and the next year she sent him off to Ft. Myers without her again, trusting in his fidelity as she did her own. Raymond's fiscal prudence was another matter entirely. He neglected practical things in an effort to surprise her, sometimes bringing her such foolishness that she suspected Dolly's influence. She had a chest set aside especially for these gifts: a feather boa, so moth-eaten now it looked like it was molting; six pairs of variously dyed silk stockings with rose-embroidered garters; a fan made of peacock feathers; a hat with a bird-of-paradise nesting in its crown; a blue velvet dress with a matching cape. Jessie shook her head, thinking about that dress. She'd been horrified by its extravagance, and forced by Raymond's delight in her apparent surprise to wear it to church, where the sting of her neighbors' disapproval had been alleviated only by their envy.

Jessie stripped the greens from their stalks, the thick leaves like thin, supple leather in her hands. The cow horns beckoned now, sonorous blasts that called the girls out of the kitchen and down the road to meet them. Jessie stayed in the kitchen, putting off the moment when she would have to tell her husband that Able Gibbs was claiming Beau Pennell had raped his daughter.

She sliced salt pork and put it in a Dutch oven to fry, then wiped her hands on her apron, wishing it were as easy to clean her mind of foul memories. Jonelle had come in from the front porch to tell her the sheriff was there with Able Gibbs and Lila, and the sheriff said would she please come out, because they could not come in right now. No more than curious, Jessie had stepped out on the porch, her smile of welcome fading when she saw their faces.

"Sheriff," she said. "Able. Lila. Is something the matter?"

Able had nodded at her, but did not speak, and Lila stayed as she was, hands folded in her lap, eyes downcast, head half-turned as if looking at something by the right wagon wheel. The sheriff got off his horse and walked to the front steps.

"Raymond's not here, I don't guess," he said.

"He's gone to Punta Rassa," Jessie said. "You know that."

"Yes, ma'am," he said. "I know. I was just hoping." He didn't say what he was hoping for, and Jessie couldn't help him. She waited. Jonelle stirred against her hip. The sheriff seemed to notice her for the first time, and looked alarmed. "Best you send the girls in the house, Miss Jessie."

Jessie let go of Jonelle's hand, and stroked her hair. "Go inside," she said. She turned to Bekah, who was standing in the doorway. "Go to the kitchen. Take your sister with you. No listening at the door."

"Yes, ma'am," Bekah said. She held the door open for Jonelle. When it closed, Jessie turned back to the sheriff. "Now," she said. "What is this about?"

The sheriff cleared his throat. "Mizz Jessie," he said. "You know Mr. Able Gibbs there, and his daughter, Lila."

"You know I do," Jessie said.

"Yes, ma'am. Well, Mr. Gibbs says Lila was raped last night. Says it was your oldest boy, Beau, that done it."

"Mr. Gibbs is mistaken," Jessie said. "Beau would never do such a thing." The words came out of her mouth calmly, in a perfectly normal tone, with utter conviction. For the first time, Lila lifted her head and looked directly at Jessie. A bruise stained the right side of her face, swollen, livid, like a birthmark.

"Beau didn't rape me," she said.

"I told you to shut your whoring mouth," Able said.

Jessie swayed back from his foulness, but Lila appeared unmoved. A carpetbag sat on the wagon seat between them. Able opened it and pulled out a piece of clothing. Lila turned away again, a dark flush staining her neck and lower face.

"Able, there's no call for this," the sheriff said.

Able ignored him. He climbed down out of the wagon and shook the garment out. It was a cotton nightgown. There were stains on it, rust and pale yellow. Able walked up the porch steps and held the nightgown up in front of Jessie. His hand was shaking. "Do you see this?" he asked.

"Yes," Jessie said.

Able pointed at Lila. "It's her nightgown," he said.

"So?" Jessie asked.

That set Able off. "My wife wiped mess off of her with this nightgown," he screamed. "She'd been with your son. This here's her blood and his, his..."

"I talked him out of a posse," the sheriff said. "I told him the Pennells would do the right thing."

"I don't understand," Jessie said, who understood perfectly well.

"I mean that Able's agreed to wait until Raymond and Beau get back from Punta Rassa to get Beau's side of the story," the sheriff said, "and that y'all will do what's right, depending on what the truth is."

Jessie looked at him. "Do you believe this accusation?" she asked.

"I don't know what to believe," the sheriff said. "I have to hear from Beau."

"And until then?" Jessie asked.

"We wait," the sheriff said. He turned to the other man. "All right, Able," he said. "You've had your say. You and Lila go on home now. The Pennells will handle this when Beau gets back."

"By God..." Able began.

"By God nothing," the sheriff said. "You go home and cool off. What's done is done. There'll be no lynching over this, Able, and your daughter is shamed enough as it is. Go home."

And so began the longest four weeks of Jessie's life.

She put the collard greens in a pot with some browned salt pork, covered them with water, put the lid on the pot, and set the pot on the stove. Horses' hooves pounded into the yard, and the cries of men and dogs and mules joined the girls' laughter. Jessie took her apron off and went to the front door, which opened out on a storm whose center was Fess's wagon. Jessie made her way to Raymond and stepped into his arms, holding him fiercely. When he let her go, she stepped back, blinking away her tears.

"What are you crying about?" he asked, wondering at her.

Jessie wiped her eyes and hugged him again. "Later," she said, because the dogs were fighting, and the girls were swarming the wagon. Emptied now of food, it was loaded with presents: dresses and bonnets, shawls and petticoats, mirrors, ribbons, and hard candy; a music box and licorice sticks for Jonelle; a set of combs and a bottle of toilet water for Bekah; an embroidery hoop, thread, needles, and a can of talcum powder for Jessie, in addition to dry goods, seasonings, and bags of flour and salt. It was Christmas and birthdays and wedding anniversaries all at once, with supper invitations extended and declined, and a good hour spent talking, unloading, sorting, and loading again before Dolly and Fess could head back to the crossing and the Baxter house on the other side of Black Hammock. And the whole time, through all the banter and frivolity, Jessie felt as brittle as cracked glass. Finally, Raymond sent Beau and Jack to the barn to feed and water the horses, and followed Jessie and the girls into the house. The kitchen was filled with good smells, and his stomach rumbled so loud that the girls giggled.

"Listen to that," Raymond said. "My poor ole belly wants to know what's for dinner. C'mere and tell me what you're cooking that smells so fine." He pulled out a chair and sat down. Jonelle climbed up in his lap, counting off on her fingers as she told him. "We fixed collard greens, field peas, okra and tomatoes, ham, gravy, spoonbread, and biscuits. Mama said if that weren't enough, you'd just have to go to town and eat at the hotel."

Raymond tweaked her braid. "Is that so?" he said. "Well, I'll try and make do with this here, paltry as it is. Seems a decent meal is the least a man could expect when he got home, but I reckon not."

Jessie tried to smile, and Raymond set Jonelle down on the floor. "Why don't you go try on one of your new dresses," he said. She skipped out of the kitchen, and Raymond got up and hung his hat by the kitchen door, then went out on the back porch. Jessie could hear the creak of the pump and the splash of water in the washbowl. Raymond walked back into the kitchen drying his hands on an old shirt Jessie hung by the pump for that purpose, and gently bumped Jessie with his hip. "You ain't properly joyful to see your husband, woman," he said. "He's mighty troubled by that. Thought you ought to know."

Jessie put the biscuits in the oven and straightened up, sick at heart to bring such news to a man so glad to be home.

"My God, Jessie," Raymond said, and pulled her to him. "What in the world is wrong with you?"

She'd have waited for some better moment, one made for news like hers, had she not borne the weight of knowledge alone for so long. And even now, she could not tell him held in his arms, when what she had to say would hurt him so. She pulled away, then, and held his chair for him, both hands on the back. "Sit down," she said. Raymond sat down. Jessie walked to her own chair, and standing there, the length of the table between them a bulwark and a barrier, Jessie told him about the visit from the sheriff and Able Gibbs.

Raymond wasn't hungry when he finally sat down to eat, but he ate anyway, conscious of Bekah and Jonelle's watchful eyes. He ate all he wanted, then ate some more, since there were two assistant cooks and he had to placate both of them. They were finally satisfied, and rose to clear the table. Beau and Jack patted their bellies and announced they were going fishing. Raymond stopped them.

"Beau," he said. "I need you down at the barn for a minute."

"I'll come with you," Jack said.

"No," Raymond said. "You stay here. We'll be back in a little bit."

Beau shrugged and stood up. Raymond, feeling like an old man, didn't speak until they reached the barn. Everything he felt, or might feel, was held at bay. If asked, he would have said truthfully that he didn't feel anything, because he didn't know anything. But he needed desperately to know, and once they reached the dim silence of the barn, did not wait to find out. He turned and faced his son.

"Your mother says Able Gibbs was here a month ago, claiming you raped his girl. Is that true?"

Beau stared at Raymond with a look of horror on his face. Raymond hoped he knew what his expression meant.

"If she's lying, Beau, we'll fight it," he said. "We'll fight it with everything we've got. No son of mine is going to suffer for another man's wrongdoing."

Beau swallowed hard. "It wasn't rape," he said.

Raymond reached up and peeled a little piece of bark off a stall door, and shredded it between his fingers as the blackest, sickest rage he'd ever known grew in his belly, nudging its way past disbelief and a terrible sadness. "Then tell me this," he said quietly. "What was it?"

Beau wouldn't meet his eyes. "She said she wanted to."

"Did she?"

"Well, she didn't say no."

"She didn't say no. What did you say?"

"Sir?"

"What did you say? You said she didn't say no. What did you say?"

"Well, I didn't say anything much. I, uh,..."

"That's enough."

"Yessir."

It had occurred to Raymond in Ft. Myers, when Beau came staggering through the door of the hotel room, that his son was bent on self-destruction. He'd looked at the torn face, sticky with blood and dirt and gravel, and heard for the first time about the fight with the Rainey twins, and listened with even greater shock to Beau's drunken account of the bet and the ride and Tate's threats. Prepared for any insanity Jack might commit, Raymond had felt blindsided, betrayed, even, by Beau's deceit and stupidity. But that was nothing compared to what he felt now. Were a man to take one of Raymond's daughters as Beau had by his own admission taken Lila Gibbs, he'd call it rape, too. And he would beat that man to death.

Beau must have seen it in his face. "It wasn't like you think, Daddy. She came hunting me. It just got out of hand, is all."

"Got out of hand?" Raymond asked. He did not recognize Beau. He was some stranger that Raymond despised. He hadn't known he could hate like he hated at this moment, or that he could feel so ashamed, so tainted, by his own blood. "It got out of hand, all right. I don't know you, boy. I raised you better than this. I raised you to do right by your family, by your neighbors. You've shamed your mother and me, and you've shamed that girl. Shamed her nigh on to death. Your mama says Able had her with him when he came to the house. Said he'd beaten her, marked the whole side of her face."

Beau's eyes filled with tears, and Raymond shook with renewed fury. "What the hell are you crying about?" he demanded. "You let the women do the crying. You're fixing to have a wife to take care of. Saddle the horses. We're going to the Gibbses."

Beau's face turned ashen. "I never planned on marrying her," he said.

Had Raymond hit Beau then, he'd have killed him. So he took a deep breath and a step backward, and spoke very quietly and carefully. It was the greatest act of self-control he'd ever committed in his life. "You won't walk away from this," he said. "You took what didn't belong to you. Now you're going to pay for it. Saddle the horses. Wait for me here. I'll be back directly."

"Mama..."

"Leave your mother out of this. It's hard enough on her as it is." Raymond stepped past Beau, then stopped. "You hear me on this, boy. Hear me good. Any crying you've got to do, you do it before we leave the island. You blubber in front of Able Gibbs, and I will horsewhip you so bad you'll have to crawl up the aisle on your hands and knees."

Enraged all over again at the very thought of Able Gibbs, Raymond went back to the house to tell Jessie what she already knew. Come the next day or two, she'd have to humble herself and meet with Myrtle Gibbs. There was no help for it. The two of them had a wedding to plan.

A week later, Lila sat on a kitchen chair in Jessie's bedroom, and beheld herself in the mirror. The bruise was almost gone, a faint stain along the side of her face, the merest shadow of her father's contempt. Even the soreness was gone. Lila touched her cheek, and caught Jessie's eyes in the mirror. "Can you see it?" she asked.

"No," Jessie said.

"Pa wanted me to marry with it there," she said. "So everybody would know."

"That's silly," Jessie said. "Everybody knows already. Zeke Mitchell is a good sheriff, but he talks too much."

"He says I deserve to walk down the aisle as a marked woman."

"Lila," Jessie said. "You and I agreed that we would not discuss your family."

Lila smiled. She'd discovered in Jessie Pennell an unlikely ally, one that had scolded, ignored, and bullied her parents until the wedding was as much to Lila's liking as possible. She looked in the mirror again, and caught the reflection of her mother standing in the next room. Myrtle's nostrils were pinched as though she had a bad smell up her nose. Lila cringed every time she saw her mother, aware of the other woman's strength now in a way she'd not been until the morning she came back from Cat Lake.

She'd gone to the house after chaining Soon, walking carefully up the outside of the back steps so they wouldn't creak, and made her way through the kitchen, down the hallways, past her parents' closed door, to her bedroom. She opened the door. Her father was sitting on the edge of her bed. He stood up and leaned over her, the sour odor of sleep rank on his breath.

"Where have you been?" he asked.

"The outhouse."

"I checked there already."

Lila didn't answer. She didn't know what to say.

"You've been to see the Pennell boy, haven't you?"

Lila couldn't speak.

"Answer me!" Able roared. "You've been with him, haven't you?"

Lila shook her head. "No," she whispered.

"Myrtle!"

The door behind Lila opened wider, and her mother stepped into the room, so crowding it with flesh that Lila could hardly breathe.

"Do what I told you," Able said.

"With what?" Myrtle asked.

Able grabbed her nightgown off a nail. "This," he said. He threw the nightgown at Myrtle and walked out, slamming the door behind him. Dread crept over Lila. She looked at her mother, at the nightgown, at her mother again.

"Do what?" she asked.

Myrtle sniffed, her mouth twisted and white. "Check to see if you've been with a man." She thrust the nightgown at Lila. "Here," she said. "Wipe yourself."

"What?"

Myrtle shook the nightgown at her. "Wipe yourself, down there, where he's been."

Aghast, Lila frantically shook her head. "No," she said. "I won't."

"Then I will."

"No. I won't let you."

"Able!" Myrtle yelled. "She won't do it. Come in here and hold her down."

"No!" Lila cried. "No! No. I'll do it."

"Fine," Myrtle said. "Here."

Lila took the nightgown and stood there, waiting for her mother to leave.

"While I watch," Myrtle said.

Lila pulled her skirt up to her knees. Squatting a little, she wiped herself.

"Not like that," Myrtle said. "Pull your drawers down, and wipe right on the place."

"I don't have any drawers on," Lila said. Myrtle's silence struck her like a lash. She gave the nightgown to her mother. Myrtle held it up to the lamp. There was blood on it, and a glistening streak of white.

"Able," Myrtle said.

He came back and stood in the doorway. Myrtle handed him the nightgown. Able looked at it, and gave it back to his wife. "It's the Pennell boy, ain't it?"

"No," Lila said. Her head bounced against the wall when he hit her. "Yes," she said.

"He raped you," Able said.

"No."

"Yes, he did. He raped you."

"No. It was me too."

"You're lying for him," Able said.

"No," Lila said. "It's the truth." And her father could never get her to say other than the truth, though he hit her for a long, hard time.

A brush swept through Lila's hair, startling her from reverie. "I don't know what I'm going to with this hair," Jessie fussed. "Thick as a horse's tail and straight as can be. You wait just a minute. I'll be right back." She returned moments later with Lupe Baxter. "I've got to have some help," Jessie said. "I've never seen such hair."

Lupe took Lila's hair in her hands, and smiled at her in the mirror. "It's beautiful hair," she said. "Thick and full." She held it to her nose. "Smells good, too." She took the brush from Jessie and began to brush Lila's hair in long, slow strokes that pulled her head back and then released it. "I knew somebody once with hair just like this. It's not so hard to fix, once you know how."

"It won't help," Jessie said. "I've about run myself ragged working on it."

"You just hide and watch," Lupe said. "First, a hot iron."

And without a by-your-leave, the amazing Lupe commandeered the bedroom, voicing strong opinions on hairstyles, particularly those for weddings, that surpassed even those of Jessie's. She plundered Jessie's combs and hairpins. Bekah and Jonelle lent ribbons and picked flowers. Under Lupe's direction, Lila's hair was ironed, puffed, pinched, pulled, and ratted in, around, and through innumerable ribbons and blooms. Lila closed her eyes at one point, refusing to look at any longer at the mass of hair that stood out from her head by at least a foot. Not until ordered to do so by Jessie did she open them again, and then was embarrassed by how beautiful it looked. She put a fingertip tenderly on one of the ribbons.

"Will it stay?" she asked.

Lupe, a hairpin clenched between her teeth, tucked a stray piece of hair behind her ear. "Shake your head and see," she said.

Lila shook her head. Nothing moved except the ribbons.

Lupe laughed. "I can fix your hair so nothing will mess it up, and honey, I mean nothing."

Jessie interposed herself between them. "That's enough," she said. "Let's get the dress on." Lupe got Lila into the dress without even touching her hair, and started buttoning it up the back. Raymond knocked on the door.

"Preacher's here," he said. "Y'all about ready in there?"

Everything that had happened, and that which was about to happen, hit Lila like a punch in the gut. "I feel sick," she said. "I think I'm going to faint."

"Nonsense," Jessie said. "Stand up straight. Remember what I told you." She stuck her head out the door. "We're almost done," she said. "Get everybody lined up."

"They've been lined up for fifteen minutes," Raymond said.

"You've probably done it wrong. Check with Myrtle."

Raymond muttered something unintelligible and left.

Five minutes later, they were ready. It was way too soon for Lila, who had changed her mind about marrying. She thought now it would be easier if her father beat her to death. Jessie and Lupe herded her past her mother - who trotted along behind protesting Lila's appearance - to the front yard, where almost every soul in Harris County was gathered. Able and Myrtle had invited no one, which didn't matter, since the Pennells had invited nearly everybody. Only the Raineys and their habitual associates were excluded.

Raymond had divided the crowd in half, forming an aisle down which Lila had to walk. At the other end, atop the porch steps, stood the preacher and Beau. Able was waiting for them by the back door, sullen and stiff. When he saw Lila, he turned positively sour.

"Hold your arm out, Able Gibbs," Jessie said. Able stuck his arm out. Lila put her hand on it. Jessie patted her waist. "I'm proud to have you for a daughter." And with that, Lila walked with her father around the house to the front yard and up the aisle between the guests, to Beau.

It amazed her later, when she had time to think about it, how quickly it was done: ownership of her person transferred from one man to another, troth pledged and received. The ring was hard to get on her finger, the kiss Beau gave her abrupt and clumsy. Then it was over, and she was standing beside her husband while people came by and shook their hands and congratulated them. When that was done, they had to open their gifts on a table in the front room. There were so many that Lila almost started crying again, except that Jessie was watching her with a stern eye, and Lupe was oohhing and ahhing over every little thing. The last gift on the table was a little wooden box with a red ribbon around it and no name. Lupe picked it up and held it over her head.

"Who's this from?" she asked. "There's no note on it. Anybody know who gave this?"

"That's from Beau to Lila," Dolly said. He slipped his arm around Lupe's waist. "He bought it in Ft. Myers."

Lupe handed the box to Lila. She held it in her hand, the import of what Dolly had said slowly growing in her mind as she untied the ribbon and opened the box. Inside was a small glass hummingbird in a nest of cotton. It was the most beautiful thing Lila had ever seen. Joy like she had never known flooded her body and flushed her face, and she groped for words, the right words, any words, to tell Beau so, but none came.

"Take it out of the box," Lupe said. "Let the light shine on it."

"I'm afraid it will break," Lila said.

"Here," Lupe said. "I'll do it." She took the box from Lila. Slipping her finger through the gold string on its back, she lifted the bird from its nest. "Just look at that," she breathed. The hummingbird whirled on its string, streaming colors of every hue. Lupe held her hand out to catch them, and they pooled in her palm and fell through her long fingers to the floor, spilling across her feet. Filled with gladness, Lila looked up at Beau to thank him, and stopped, shattered by what she saw.

Beau was looking at Lupe in a way he had never looked at her and never would, were she to wait a thousand years. The same desperate hunger Lila brought to her own love was reflected in that gaze. She knew then, seeing the light shards sparkle in Lupe's honey brown hand, why Beau had bought the little bird, and she reached for the gift he'd meant for another.

"Please," she said. "Lest it break."

Lupe brought it back to her, twirling it out of the light, and set it in Lila's hand, a little hummingbird of clear glass with a head and beak of rich green, and a blood red throat. With great care, Lila put it back in the box, and covered it with cotton and the wooden lid, where it would be safe, there in the dark.

Beau had lost what little appetite he possessed by dinnertime, and spent the entire wedding supper poking at the food on his plate, waiting for the day to end. He couldn't keep up with all that had happened to him, and kept feeling there ought to be a loose end somewhere that he could pull, one that would unravel his present life all the way back to the place where it first went wrong, at which point he could begin again, and do it right. There was an unreal quality about everything, beginning with the way people treated Lila and him. With the exclusion of her parents, folks acted like there was nothing out of the ordinary, as though the bestowal of his surname on Lila had restored her virtue and his honor, erasing what had happened at Cat Lake. He'd have been content with simple forgiveness, himself.

He sneaked a glance at Lila and wished he hadn't. Except for her hair, which was pretty and smelled of flowers, she looked every bit as miserable as he felt. It wouldn't be so bad if she'd just talk. Other girls talked, ambling from one topic to another like they were on a walk, so that all somebody had to do was amble along beside them and say, "uh, huh." But not Lila. She had to sit there with eyes the size of washtubs in a quiet so deep he couldn't see to the bottom of it. He guessed they'd spend the rest of their natural lives in near total silence, bound to one another close enough to suffocate them both.

He could hear the squeak and twang of tuning instruments on the other side of the house, and looked around for Jack. His place at the table was already empty. Beau's glance intercepted Able's, and Beau dropped his eyes. Things hadn't gone too well since that first meeting. Raymond kept saying that he didn't mind having Lila for a daughter-in-law, but that kinship with Able Gibbs was rubbing him raw. Well, it wasn't bringing Beau any cheer, either.

A hand came down on his shoulder, and Dolly poked his head between Beau and Lila. "You two ain't through eating yet?" he asked.

"I'm stuffed," Beau said, and almost knocked his chair over trying to get up. Dolly set the chair straight and pushed him back in it.

"Settle down," he said. "I'm not rushing you."

"But I'm finished," Beau said. "Can't eat another bite."

"Me, either," Lila said.

Beau looked at her plate. She hadn't bothered to move the food around. Her fork wasn't even dirty. He guessed getting married had ruined her appetite, too. Dolly drew Lila to her feet and tucked her hand in the crook of his arm.

"The band is warming up," he said. "I'm here to claim the third dance." Lila stumbled and would have fallen had Dolly not been holding her arm.

"Who gets the first two?" she asked.

"Well, Beau gets the first one, of course," Dolly said. "And Raymond'll take the second. That is, if your daddy don't take it," he added delicately.

"I don't think he will," Lila said.

Beau thought, not for the first time, that it was sorry luck to be born the child of Able Gibbs.

The side yard had been cleared in a big circle, swept smooth, and a platform built for the band to one side. There was everything needful for a dance: a guitar, a mouth harp, a banjo, two fiddles, and a gathering crowd. Beau followed Dolly to the platform, and waited while he spoke to Jack, who nodded and tucked his fiddle up under his chin. Three strokes of the bow led the band into the "Kentucky Waltz." When Dolly came back, Beau stepped in front of him.

"Dolly?" he asked.

Dolly threw an arm around Beau's shoulders. "What is it, buddy?" he asked.

"How'd you get the hummingbird?"

"I took it out of your pocket in the saloon," Dolly said. "I was afraid it'd get lost or broke, drunk as you were. Go dance with your wife." He tried to shove Beau toward the dance floor, but Beau held his ground.

"I thought it was gone all this time," he said. "Why didn't you give it back before now?"

"Because I thought you should give it to your own wife, instead of mine," Dolly said. "And guess what? That's just what happened. Now everybody's happy. Can't beat that with a stick." He nudged Beau in the side. "Go on, now."

"Go where?"

"Out on the dance floor. That tune's for you and Lila."

"What?" Beau asked.

"Lila," Dolly said. "Your wife. Go dance with her. Everybody's waiting on you."

Beau looked around the circle, and realized that people were staring at him. "Waiting on me?"

"Yep," Dolly said. "Can't nobody else dance until you and Lila take a turn."

"Just her and me? Alone?"

"It'd look pretty funny with the three of us," Dolly said.

Beau felt panicky. He wasn't much of a dancer at the best of times, and the thought of going out there with Lila didn't help any, particularly with everybody watching. He looked at Lila. Her face was pasty white. Beau caught Raymond's eye across the circle. It was all the encouragement he needed.

Beau took Lila's clammy hand in his and led her past the guests to the empty circle, where he faced her, and drew her into his arms. She wouldn't look at him, but her left hand came up to rest on his shoulder, lighter than a leaf fallen from a tree. Her right hand in his trembled very slightly, then grew still. She took a deep breath. Beau faltered, waiting for the right moment to begin, then noticed that Lila was patting his shoulder, her lips moving. He bent his head to listen. She was softly counting, "now, two, three; now, two, three." Beau got a better grip on her hand. She looked him square in the eyes for the first time that day. A second fiddle leaped into the waltz, insisting they move. Lila nodded on "three," Beau stepped out on "now," and they were out on the dance floor together, his hand on her waist, her hand on his shoulder, steady, and still keeping time.

Raymond nodded approval when Beau and Lila started dancing, then noticed with some alarm that dusk was falling rapidly. With the rushed feeling of a late start, he began lighting the wood piles around the dance floor, and had just fired the last one when Dolly approached, hands in his pockets, looking as pleased as though he'd planned everything all by himself. He hunkered down beside the woodpile and held his hands over the small flame.

"You enjoying yourself, Ray?" he asked. Raymond grunted, unable to match Dolly's good humor.

"Well, I'm enjoying myself," Dolly said. "And so is Lupe."

"I didn't know you were so fond of shotgun weddings," Raymond said.

"They're my favorite." Raymond, refusing to be jollied out of his mood, didn't answer. Dolly got up and clapped him on the shoulder. "If you're not going to dance with Jessie, I am." He was an accomplished dancer. It was the only thing about him Jessie liked. It made Raymond jealous, which over the years had delighted Dolly no end.

"Dance with your own wife," Raymond said.

"I can dance with her at home," Dolly said. "The only time I get to dance with Jessie is when you're gone from home."

"Uh, huh," Raymond said.

"Don't say I didn't warn you," Dolly said. Five minutes later, he was weaving through the dancers with Jessie in his arms, her head thrown back, laughing. Raymond left the fire and hunted through the crowd for Lupe. She was leaning against a tree near the musicians' platform, dark eyes watching Dolly and Jessie, a smile playing on her mouth.

"Want to dance?" Raymond asked.

Lupe grinned. "Glad to," she said.

Raymond led her into the circle and turned her around, carefully holding their place in the line. A few measures later and Dolly and Jessie had caught up with them, Jessie's cheeks flushed, her hair curled damply around her face. Dolly winked at Raymond.

"Stay off her feet," he said. "She's got work to do tomorrow." Lupe and Jessie laughed, and Dolly spun Jessie away. Raymond stepped on Lupe's foot. He could feel his face turning red.

"Sorry," he said.

Lupe guffawed. "That's all right," she said. "I'm used to it."

Raymond didn't know quite how to take that, and was glad when the song ended and Dolly came for his wife. Jessie danced with Beau, and Raymond with Lila, then Jack put his fiddle down to dance, first with

Jessie, then with his new sister-in-law, after which the musicians took a break. When they gathered again on the platform, Jessie caught Raymond's arm.

"You should dance with your own wife," she said. "People are starting to talk."

"I reckon they are," Raymond said. "The hussy's been dancing with every man in the place."

"Hush," Jessie said. "Listen." Jack was playing alone, a haunting melody that Raymond had heard before. "It's the song from the cane grinding. Only slower. So the rest of us can keep up." She put her hand on Raymond's shoulder. "Dance with me."

"I thought you'd rather dance with Dolly," he grumbled.

"Don't be silly," Jessie said.

The fiddle played, the tempo and volume building as the other instruments joined in, carefully at first, and then with more confidence, harmonies discovered and held or abandoned and improvised anew, according to the skill and daring of the musicians. It was irresistible, and Raymond found himself smiling. Jessie looked so pretty, all flushed and excited, and the music made him feel like he knew what he was doing. He whirled her around and led her between the dancers and the fires, holding her in his arms, and keeping her close to the light.

Part IV

February – May 1898

Turkey Hammock

Chapter Twenty-Five

Beau walked up to the hog pen with his hands in his pockets, his coat collar pulled up around his ears, and a rifle under his arm. Behind him came twelve-year-old Quincey Baxter, snuffling with the cold and carrying a stout pole. The hogs were lined up inside the pen, peering out through the rails with their little black eyes. Beside the pen was an oak barrel, a long-necked dipper hanging on a nail driven into the side. Quincey threw down the pole and darted to the barrel ahead of Beau.

"I'm gonna do it," he said.

"Go ahead," Beau said.

Quincey pried the lid off the barrel. Inside, corn floated in rancid water white with corn milk. He dipped a gourd full of corn out of the barrel and poured it in the trough. "Sooey," he called, though the hogs were already pushing their way to the trough, squealing and biting.

"I want to shoot one," Quincey said.

"Did you bring a gun?" Beau asked.

"No."

"Then I'll shoot it." A barrow dropped its snout in the trough and managed to keep it there despite the competition. Beau raised the rifle to his shoulder and shot it in the forehead. The hog dropped in the mud and another took its place, scrabbling across the twitching body with small, sharp hooves. Beau helped Quincey drag the hog through the gate, then stuck his pocketknife in its throat, feeling through fat and muscle for the jugular. Beau wiped the blood off his knife, folded it, and put it back in his pocket.

"You got the rope?" he asked.

"Just for me," Quincey said.

"Then carry it alone."

Quincey pulled two lengths of rope out of his coat pocket. He tossed one of them to Beau, who tied the hog's front legs together, while he did the same with the back. That done, Beau reached for the pole and shoved it lengthwise between the hog's trussed legs. "One, two, three," he said.

They lifted the hog off the ground at the same time. Quincey was so much shorter than Beau that he alone could carry the pole on his shoulder. Beau had to carry his end straight-armed. He wished Jack were there to help. They'd been slaughtering hogs since nine that morning - this was the eighth and last of the day - and tomorrow morning they'd get up and do it all again. Beau didn't even want to think about it. The rifle was still laying on the barrel, not six inches from Quincey.

"Get the rifle," Beau said.

"Get it yourself," Quincey replied.

It had been this way between them for years, and only got worse as Quincey got older. Beau had been predisposed to like the boy when he was born. He had two girls by then, and looked forward to a small male presence around the island. But Quincey had been born with a chip on his shoulder. He was a loner, possessed of an odd and irritating proprietary air about the island, quick to scrap and slow to forgive, and promised to be handsome. Beau privately hoped his hair would fall out.

They carried the hog down the path to the Pennells' back yard, where Raymond and Dolly were waiting with ten-year-old July, Dolly's second oldest boy. They stood beside a shallow iron vat, eight feet across, and mounted on four iron legs. Steam rose from the opaque surface of the water within it. A long, heavy table butted against the vat, level with the rim. Dolly tended a fire under the vat, adjusting the depth of the coals to keep the water just below a simmer. He stuck his finger in the water and yanked it back out.

"Just in time," he said. "Dump him in."

Beau and Quincey lowered the hog almost to the ground so July could douse it with buckets of clean water, washing away most of the blood and dirt. Then, with the others' help, they lifted the hog to the level of the vat, pulled the pole out from between its legs, untied the legs, slipped another, longer rope around one of the back legs, and slipped it into the hot water, leaving one end of the rope to dangle over the edge of the vat. Beau shoved the hog under the water with the pole, and the carcass bobbed and swayed, hot steam rising above it heavy with the odor of cooked blood. Every now and then, one of the men would reach in and jerk on the long bristles on the back of the hog's neck. When heated sufficiently, the hair slipped easily from the skin. If left in too long, the skin cooked and sloughed off.

When a clump of hair came away in Raymond's fingers, he nodded. "Good enough," he said. They pulled the carcass out of the vat and onto the table, snatching the hot wet hair from the hide as it came out of the water. Beau came along behind them, scraping the hide with a butcher knife to remove stray hairs. Dolly grasped the heavy jowl and jiggled it.

"This here's a fat one," he said. "We should thank Tate for leaving it for us."

"I'm sure it was an oversight," Raymond said.

"I don't think they're messing much with hogs lately," Beau said. "Too busy with the cattle. I'll bet Tate gives thanks a dozen times a day for the Big Freeze. He'd still be breaking horses and selling 'shine if it weren't for that."

He bore down hard with the knife, the hog's skin waxy and white beneath the blade. The Pennells had lost more than three thousand head of cattle in '95, maybe more, and the Baxters at least that many. Hundreds of people in Harris County had teetered on the edge of bankruptcy, and many went over the edge. A lot of folks moved on, looking for something better. Those that stayed tightened their belts and lived from day to day. Too proud to accept the help offered by their neighbors, the Raineys nearly starved to death. It must have been pure desperation that drove Tate to do what he'd never done before, at least to anyone's knowledge. He took to stealing hogs, and a cow now and then, to feed his family, supplementing the meager living he made trapping and hunting. Through that hard, hard spring, Tate gleaned only what he needed from his neighbors' remaining stock. His neighbors turned a blind eye. Nobody wanted to see Sylla and her children go hungry, though no one would have minded, either, if Tate had moved his raggedy-assed little clan on down the road.

And then things began to get better. Plentiful pasture in the summer of '95 meant fat cows with lots of milk and big calves. Tate continued to take what he needed. Then he took a little more. By the winter of '96, he and the twins were driving stolen cattle to Punta Rassa, the marks cut off along with the ears, and the brands altered, or smeared beyond recognition, with a running iron. Hostilities flared. Men had always carried guns in the woods to kill snakes and other vermin. Now they carried them in hopes of killing Tate Rainey.

But Tate was fast, smart, and impossible to catch. He was making quite a name for himself when disaster struck. A tough young hog farmer - recently arrived from Pennsylvania and unaccustomed to the various ways and personalities of Harris County - caught Bob and Clyde in his hog pen one night literally red-handed, a dead shoat tied to Bob's horse and another on the ground with Clyde's knife in its throat. The farmer, along with his pretty wife and three little children, took the twins at gunpoint to the jail in Elliston, where the sheriff told the farmer he'd best eat the hogs and let the twins go free, seeing as how he hadn't caught their daddy, too. That advice was echoed by a number of people, Beau Pennell among them. But the farmer would have none of it. Stubborn with righteousness, he pressed charges and a week later testified at the trial. Bob and Clyde were convicted of hog stealing and sentenced to eighteen months in the state penitentiary. They went to Raiford, and the farmer went home, where, despite all the warnings, nothing happened. The farmer's stubbornness was vindicated. Even Beau relaxed.

One year to the day after the trial, in the middle of the night, someone coaxed the farmer's hogs out of their pens and into the barn with a bucket of shelled corn, locked them in the stalls, poured a ring of kerosene around the outside walls, and lit it. Within seconds, a stiff breeze had carried the flames to the loft, and carried the scent of smoke and barbecued pork to the farmer, who was already on his feet, snatched from his bed by the ear-splitting screams of burning hogs.

No one was ever arrested for the barn burning. Tate Rainey was not even questioned. He had moved with Sylla and the children to Raiford soon after the trial to be near his boys, and didn't return to Harris County until Christmas of '97, when Bob and Clyde got out of prison. Their stay hadn't done either of them any good. Clyde talked so little he was almost mute, and the rest of Bob's teeth were gone. His sunken mouth aged him thirty years.

Beau wiped his knife on the edge of the table, leaving a wad of gray grease and stiff black hair. He stropped the blade on his boot top before scraping hair out of the black ear, v'd at the tip with the Pennell mark. "Tate's getting greedy, if you ask me," he said. "And arrogant, too. Thinks nobody can catch him."

"So far, he's right," Dolly said.

Beau scraped along the hog's cheek and didn't answer. Tate's rustling enterprise had started up again as soon as the Raineys returned to Harris County. It was now the hottest topic in town, hotter even than cattle prices or the ongoing hostilities with Spain over Cuba. There was tremendous frustration and anger over his depredations, and a lot of hotheaded talk about lynching and shooting. Raymond, Dolly, and Beau were part of a cooler majority. Raymond would have no part of a lynching ever again, and for every child Lupe bore him, Dolly found another reason to stay close to home. Beau refused to move on the Raineys until he had Tate dead to rights, with the emphasis on dead, and he sure wasn't going after the twins by themselves. Like other cattlemen, they had stepped up their patrols and enjoyed some close shots. But Tate stayed perpetually out of reach, almost like a ghost, Dolly said, though only he and the Pennells knew what he meant by that.

"Flip him over," Raymond said.

They turned the carcass over so the could clean the other side, working quickly before the hide cooled and set the hair again. Raymond tugged a hoof off and threw it among the dogs lying in the shade at the edge of the hammock. There was a brief, vicious fight, and one of them trotted off with it into the trees. The hog's bare toes were dainty, shell-pink, and spotlessly clean.

"He's been hauled into court enough times," Beau said. "You'd think by now he'd have spent some time in prison."

"He's quick and he's smart," Dolly said. "And folks don't want to testify against him. Not after what happened to that hog farmer. They're afraid of him."

"I ain't," Quincey said.

Beau pointed a greasy finger at him. "You better be, Mr. Cock o' the Walk. Tate Rainey would just as soon cut your throat as look at you. He's a bad 'un. Bad as they come." Beau heard his own vehemence and looked up to catch a sideways glance between Raymond and Dolly. His neck got hot all the way up to his face. Quincey stared at him with considerable interest, a puzzled frown giving way to a sly smile.

"You're scared of him, ain't you?" he demanded. "You are. You're scared of ole Tate Rainey and his ole ugly boys."

Beau opened his mouth to answer, but shut it again as a clear whistle pierced the crisp afternoon air.

"Jacky's home!" Quincey shouted. He flung a clump of hog hair at a dog and then was gone, July right behind him. They joined a stream of children that tumbled from house and yard and headed toward the road where Jack would be waiting just out of sight of the house, carpetbag in one hand, fiddle in the other, the familiar sweet smile on his face.

Beau looked forward to Jack's visits. His brother was always full of stories, information, and bits of gossip he'd picked up at the galas and parties he played around Tampa, Ft. Myers, and Key West. Jack never turned down an invitation to fiddle, no matter how sorry the company. Grateful for the shift in attention away from himself, Beau looked at his father. Raymond looked like he was having an attack of dyspepsia. Dolly winked at Beau.

"How about Mr. Jacky?" he asked. "Getting here just when the work's done."

"He's good at that," Beau admitted.

"He ought to be," Raymond growled, "with all the practice he's had."

"Aw, Ray, give the boy some time," Dolly said. "He ain't but twenty or thereabouts."

"Twenty-nine," Beau said.

"No matter," Dolly said. "I was thirty-four when I got married. Thirty-nine before I had any young 'uns. Look how I've turned out."

"I'd rather not," Raymond said. Dolly looked offended and Beau grinned. The older those two got, the more crotchety they became. They could pick at each other for hours, criticizing each other's children, horses, dogs, and wives - especially wives - Raymond going on about Lupe's cooking and housekeeping, such as they were, and Dolly quipping every time Jessie had a fit of temper, which was often enough to keep him thinking hard. They both seemed comfortable with their wives in a way Beau was not with his. Maybe it was something that came with age. Lila used to talk a lot, words running out of her mouth about every little thing in the world, like Deep Creek in flood. She'd sing, and play with the girls, and if her approach to housecleaning was less particular than his mother's, then so was her reaction to spilled coffee and boot marks on the kitchen floor. He didn't guess a man could have both, though he still went to his mother's house sometimes, just to rest in the orderliness of it.

Nowadays, though, Lila stayed all closed up inside herself, like a box turtle with the lid shut. Beau missed her like she'd gone off and left him. He had come to love her, if love meant getting used to a particular woman, and needing her. He'd even gotten used to her cooking. He loved her best at night, when he could hold her. It was as close as he ever got to telling her that he loved her. Beau didn't know why that word hung up in his mouth the way it did. He'd always felt before that Lila understood, somehow, what he was unable to say. Now he wasn't so sure. She'd been so distant lately, distracted, unmindful of him. He wished he could talk to her. He wished he knew what to say. Beau ran a hand over the scraped hog, as smooth and white as Dolly's head.

"That's close enough," he said. "Let's hang it. Grab that end, Daddy." Raymond picked the shoulders up off the table, and winched. Beau, a back leg in each hand, eyed his father speculatively. "You all right?"

"Never been better," Raymond said.

Beau didn't believe him for a second, but didn't want anything to be wrong with him, either, so left it alone. He and Raymond carried the carcass to the crossbars with its hanging chains and meat hooks. Beau held the back feet up high, and Dolly cut a slit in the skin of the legs, then shoved the meat hooks in between the tendons and the bone. Raymond let the shoulders down with a look of relief. The carcass hung there upside down, swaying a little in the wind, clean and white save for the gray wounds in its head and throat. The lips were pulled back some, exposing the tushes and two rows of very white, even, human-looking teeth. Dolly pulled out his handkerchief, and rubbed one of the tushes.

"Nice teeth," he said. "Puts me in mind of Bob Rainey."

Beau smiled. Within a month of returning from Raiford, Sylla Rainey had traded her flour bag dresses for taffeta, and Tate was sporting a black silk waistcoat. New furniture and fancy curtains had followed. But the grandest evidence yet of the Rainey's ill-gotten wealth was Bob's teeth.

The first set had come in the mail four months ago, and Tate himself had opened the box, setting them on the bar of the Redman Saloon in Elliston for everyone to see. They'd perched there on the polished counter top in all their glory: glistening white ceramic teeth in gums so pink they rivaled a newborn baby's for health and vigor. The teeth were passed from hand to hand for close inspection. Then Bob, with a considerable amount of grimacing and squirming, put them in his mouth, and grinned. The transformation was remarkable. Bob Rainey was no longer a vision to haunt children in their sleep, but a normal-looking man, one that, with a haircut, shave, and a bath, might even be called handsome. They didn't help Bob's breath any, as Beau discovered when he got up closer to look, but they sure did wonders for his appearance. And they didn't fit just right, either, because eating pickled eggs in the saloon brought tears to Bob's eyes and a certain desperation to his excitement, but by golly, they sure did look fine, and whiskey on the house went a long way to deaden the pain.

“I never saw anybody change so much,” Raymond said. “He looked like a stranger.”

“They made a world of difference, didn’t they?” Dolly said. He had pulled a big washtub beneath the hog and was standing in front of it, stropping a knife on his britches. “I told Bob just the other day that he ought to join a traveling medicine show. Take ‘em out, put ‘em in, watch the monster become a man.”

“What’d Bob say to that?” Raymond asked.

Dolly shrugged and wiped the knife blade on the hog. “He didn’t think it was so funny, but I don’t give much thought to Bob Rainey’s feelings.” He kicked the washtub under the hog and ran a hand down its belly. Then, with a smooth, long motion, he slit it open from tail to throat. Skin, fat, and glistening membrane peeled away behind the knife to expose the intestines, which came spilling out into the washtub in a warm cloud of fetid steam. A cut around the anus set them free from the tail, and a solid jerk on the other end pulled out the heart, lungs, and gullet. Beau lifted the meat saw off the end of the crossbar and sawed the head off. It dropped down on the entrails, where the small eyes looked blandly out on their own remains.

“You better give some thought to Bob’s feelings,” Raymond said. “And Tate’s, too. Leastways as regards them teeth. You don’t want Tate doing to you what he did to Bob.”

“I’d like to see him try,” Dolly said.

Bob hadn’t had his new teeth a week when he threw them in a ‘gator hole, then went home and told his daddy he’d lost them. In a fit of temper over some slight, Clyde told Tate the truth, then screamed like a rabbit as Tate horsewhipped Bob until he fainted. With his back still raw, Bob accompanied his father to Tampa for another set of teeth and a personal fitting. He was taking real good care of that second set.

“Maybe Tate can order him some brains next,” Beau said. “Until then, he’s the stupidest man I know.”

“Second stupidest,” Dolly said. “Don’t forget Clyde.”

Beau set the saw blade beside the curly tail, and started sawing down the middle of the backbone. When the two sides of the carcass swung free from each other, he started on one of the shoulders. As he sawed each quarter free, Dolly or Raymond carried it to the smokehouse. By the time he got down to the last one, the children and Jack had reached the house. Beau lifted the ham from the meat hook and took it to the smokehouse. He could hear Quincey’s voice in the front yard, high and excited.

“I don’t care what anybody says,” Quincey shouted. “I ain’t afraid of no Rainey.”

I ain’t afraid of no Rainey, either, Beau thought. But if he closed his eyes, he could still feel Tate’s finger on his teeth. He remembered Tate’s promise, too, which is why he hadn’t joined in the hunt for Bob and Clyde. Until Tate was dead, Beau would give the twins a wide berth.

Chapter Twenty-Six

Jessie set the hog head on her worktable and split it in two with a hatchet. She scooped the brains out with her hand and set them aside in a bowl, then laid the two sides of the head one on top of the other, and set them down in an empty kettle. She pulled the small intestine out of the tub next, stripping away the membranes that held it in bunches, then running it between her fingers to push the contents out into a bucket. When the intestine was empty, she removed the bucket to the edge of the yard, downwind of the house. She'd have one of the children carry it down to the creek later, and dump it. The child would protest to no avail. Each child, barring the four youngest who were too small, had to take a turn with the bucket.

Returning to the table, Jessie chopped the emptied intestine into small pieces that she dropped in a bucket of fresh water, swirling the contents around with fingers that were dead white and wrinkled from being wet all day. She washed the pieces three times, each time draining them into a bowl and throwing the dirty water across the yard. At another table, Lupe stripped and emptied the large intestine, then turned it inside out to wash, running it up her bare arm and back down itself as she would a stocking. When she was done, it would be sausage casing.

The two women worked in silence, the lively conversations of morning and midday fallen away to afternoon's weary quiet. All ten of the children had run off at Jack's whistle, leaving behind them a stillness, an undisturbed quality of air and space that was almost palpable. It would end soon enough. Before long, the children would return. Quincey would be leading the parade, Jack immediately behind him with two-year-old Nub on his shoulder. And behind Jack, strung out through the palmettos in various states of mind and dress, would be Beau and Lila's daughters and the four remaining Baxter boys. Jessie welcomed the return of the girls. Even little Martha Louise could be a help when she put her mind to it, and Elizabeth, the oldest, was very serious about her responsibilities, though Jack's arrival had, as always, caused her to temporarily backslide.

Jessie felt less sanguine about the Baxter boys. They slid backward, forward, and side-to-side as a matter of course, angels one minute, devils the next, dark-haired, dark-eyed, and beautiful. They were careless of one another's safety, and grief-stricken when disaster struck, as it inevitably did. Quincey and July, the two oldest, were inconsolable for hours when they accidentally cut their baby brother's pinky off while throwing knives at a lizard on the woodpile, mourning the lost digit as if it had been Will himself, and assuring Jessie that they'd learned an important and unforgettable lesson. But by dinnertime they had given Will's finger a soldier's burial - complete with a shotgun salute that barely missed the pallbearers - and changed his name to Nub. The child's tiny stump healed with none of them the wiser. Why any of them had lived this long was a mystery to Jessie.

At least worrying about them kept her mind off Jack, whom she missed with a fierce and ceaseless longing. Reminders of him were everywhere, from the bunch of dried flowers tied in a broken fiddle string and hung beside the kitchen window, to the wind soughing through the hammock. Even her garden spoke to her of his absence. The rows were straight, evenly spaced and uniformly deep, thanks to Raymond and Beau. The two of them hated plowing with every bone in their bodies, and yet, out of duty and with their customary efficiency, achieved a conformity even Able Gibbs couldn't match. Which only caused Jessie to miss Jack the more. He'd made up songs about the creeping and flying things that besieged her seeds and plants, and sung them to the mule as the plow blade dipped and wobbled through the dirt, his high, clear tenor ringing through the kitchen window and setting her heart alight even as she despaired of his abilities. "He can't plow worth a damn," Raymond would say. And Jessie had to agree, because it was true.

Jack couldn't do anything worth a damn, except music. Everything else was a loss. And still Jessie loved him, and felt his absence like a wound.

The children approached the house like shipwrecked sailors, shouting and hallooing, driving the silence they'd left behind them into hiding. Jack's presence had leavened their fatigue with playfulness, as he would lighten Jessie's when she saw him. But even that would fail as evening approached and the time for bed drew near. As tired, almost, as the children, and in the mood for a good shriek herself, Jessie took a deep breath and mentally girded her loins.

"I wish they'd stayed gone a little longer," Lupe said. "I was enjoying the quiet." Lupe, who seemed to thrive on the excitement provided by her unruly sons, rarely made such statements. That she did so now turned Jessie's fatigue to brusque concern.

"You look tired," she said. "Why don't you go in the house?"

Lupe shook her head. "Uh, uh," she said. "I can't stand the smell. You know how it is."

Jessie did indeed. Nothing smelled as bad as chitterlings cooking. To a pregnant woman, it was unbearable. And Lupe was very definitely that way again, a full six months pregnant, though one couldn't tell just to look at her, as heavy as she was. It had taken her five years to catch a baby the first time, but once she got the hang of it, she'd stayed right with it. Starting with Quincey in '86, she'd had one baby each in '88 and '90, twins in '94, one more in '95 - all boys--and now had another one almost ready for delivery. Lupe loved babies, and said she wished they didn't have to grow up. But grow up they did - scrambled up, Jessie said - propelled into a hair-raising self-reliance by the unpredictability of Lupe's moods - one minute holding them to her copious bosom, the next flinging at them whatever came to hand - boot, saucer, button hook, darning egg - with unnerving accuracy. Dolly's discipline, though more consistent, was still too lax to suit Jessie. He rarely struck his sons. They were too beautiful, he said, and it hurt him too much. Lupe stroked her belly now as though it were the baby's head, a thoughtful expression on her face.

"This one is not like the others," she said. "This one is trouble."

Jessie snorted. The one to come couldn't possibly be more trouble than the ones already here. Beau and Lila's four girls were sedate in comparison, though confident, busy, and bossy. They played house and dress-up, scolding like jays or cooing like doves, and every once in a while engaging in a screeching, slapping, hair-pulling fight that Jessie found appalling but which Lupe said was good for their complexions. The girls alternately adored and despised the brothers across the creek, following the example of their Grandma Pennell, who kept peppermints for the Baxter boys in her apron pocket and a yardstick for them over the kitchen door. For her beloved granddaughters, there was a child-sized set of bowls and spoons and pots and pans with which they really cooked, and a child-sized broom and dustpan with which they cleaned up after themselves.

It pleased Jessie to have her granddaughters near by. They almost made up for the loss of her own two girls. Bekah married a local boy and now lived north of Elliston. Two years later, a young cattleman came to Walker's Island to buy horses. He left with four head and Jonelle's heart. They married six months later and went to live in Sanford, where they built a nice house on the St. Johns. Both the girls seemed happy with their lot, but still, Jessie missed them. Lila was respectful and friendly, but made no pretense of daughterly affection. With Jack gone, in fact, Jessie was more lonely than she cared to admit. A sigh escaped her, and Jessie glanced at Lupe to see if she'd noticed.

But Lupe's round face was gray with morning sickness, and hung about with wisps of dulled black hair that had fallen from the thick bun at the nape of her neck. Lupe was even sicker with this baby than she'd been with Nub, and Lord knows, she'd been sick enough with him. Dolly and the boys had eaten three meals a day on the island for four months, moving between, and not necessarily together, Jessie's and Lila's tables. They'd made a habit of it, apparently, because Jessie to this day didn't know from one meal to the next how many she'd be cooking for. There were still many mornings when she looked out on the back porch and see Quincey, a brimming bucket in each hand where he'd already milked the cow, his bright black eyes smiling at her. He wouldn't milk for Lila unless Beau was gone. He and Beau didn't like each other, something to do with the island. Quincey had told her that himself.

"This island should have been mine," he said one morning, handing her the milk pails as he stepped up on the porch.

"Wipe your feet," Jessie said automatically. Then she'd stopped, what Quincey had just said finally registering with her. "What are you talking about, young man?"

"If my daddy had kept that bay mare, he'd have won the horse race. Walker's Island would of been ours, and y'all would be living across the creek in our house."

"Who told you that?" Jessie demanded, old suspicions of Dolly springing back to life.

"Nobody," Quincey said. "I figured it out myself."

Jessie hoped that was true, and prayed that beneath Dolly's loyalty and Lupe's affection, there was no hidden resentment they were passing on to their children. She wondered if Beau had sensed Quincey's covetousness, if that was why he didn't like the child.

Jessie drained the intestines one more time, then set them aside in their bucket and groped around in the washtub for the organs. Her hands moved quickly, competently, and without conscious supervision to find, strip, and clean the kidneys, heart, and maw. Dark blood ran out on the table as Jessie sliced the liver. The voices of the children grew louder. Hurrying now, Jessie and Lupe emptied the blood out of the washtubs, and washed their hands and arms under the pump. The parade was close enough to see now, Jack's curly head bobbing alongside Nub's, flashes of clothing, arms, legs glimpsed through the palmetto fans, weaving along the game trails, bursting into clearings and disappearing again.

"Here they come," Jessie said.

"Hold onto your hat," Lupe answered.

Raymond, Beau, and Dolly came around the side of the house. "Y'all carry these tubs to the house, please," Jessie said. But before they could grasp the handles, Jack was home, and the labor of the moment was set aside until the ruckus of his welcome subsided.

Chapter Twenty-Seven

The wood stove shimmered with heat in the kitchen, where Lila worked alone making chitterlings, crackling, sausage, and hogshead cheese. A pot of chopped intestines and another of maws boiled on the stove, a rank steam escaping from beneath their lids. Pans of hogshead cheese, redolent with bay leaf, pepper, and sage, were cooling in the pie safe. A frying pan full of grease sat to the side, ready to fry the chitterlings when it came time for supper, and crackling, broken pieces of crisp fried fat, drained next to it, waiting for the cornbread batter. Lila stood at the end of the table stuffing handfuls of spiced chopped meat into a sausage casing. A mound of sausages in the pan at her elbow attested to the work she'd already done. She'd been doing something much like this three years before - baking bread, maybe, or canning - she knew her hands had been full of food of some kind - had been married ten years, and had four daughters, when she realized she didn't much care to be a wife or mother anymore.

Water hissed on the stove as the chitterlings boiled over. Lila set a tin colander in the kitchen sink and poured them in it, the scalding water running out beneath the house. Leaving them in the sink to cool, she turned back to the table and picked up the sausage casing she'd been stuffing. She tried to imagine how many sausages she'd made in her relatively short lifetime. This day alone she'd made over a hundred. They'd be hung in the smoke house and smoked, then taken down and cooked and eaten, joining with everything else in her life that went around in a never-ending circle: clothes washed and dried and folded one day and back in the hamper the next; floors swept and mopped after breakfast that required the same again after supper; an endless procession of pots and pans and plates, from cupboard to dinner table to sink and back to the cupboard again, in the service of food the likes of which she'd fixed the day before and would fix again the next.

Lila couldn't understand why the same circumstances didn't affect other women the same way. Jessie's unflagging commitment to orderliness perplexed her, as did Lupe's recurrent good humor in the face of chaos. Despite Jessie's brittleness and Lupe's moods, the two women seemed comfortable in their lives. Why, Lila wondered, did the same life worry her like an ill-fitting dress? And what did other women do who had this problem? Occupied themselves with needlework or good deeds, perhaps, or took up some kind of mental pursuit, ancient history or phrenology. But those pursuits required discipline, and it was discipline she wanted to escape, so she turned inward, instead, to imagine a life where she was beautiful, desirable, free from the demands of marriage and family and home, as independent, self-sufficient, and accountable to no one as Jack Pennell.

Lila could hear welcome rising outside the window, but did not go to join it. She was jealous of Jack, and loved him, too, not like a brother or lover, but as if he were a part of herself that had abandoned her. Raymond's anger toward Jack even reminded Lila of her own father's anger toward her, the rage of a man thwarted by a will as inflexible as his own. Early on, she had let Jack know that she was his friend. In return, he had let her know that he was different. Love worked its wonder and devastation all around him, but left him in peace. Jack enjoyed her friendship, but did not need it. All he needed was his music.

He wandered the country, playing anywhere people would listen. He played at weddings, birthdays, funerals, and political events. He played for low and high alike, for money or for free, and along the way gained a reputation as a drinker and a heartbreaker. Handsome Jack Pennell, he was called, the sweetest, most joyful man ever to draw a bow across a string. Jack's magic, Dolly called it, and he could work it on anybody but his father. And one day, when he'd had all of Raymond and Walker's Island he could stand, Jack picked up his fiddle and walked away. Lila wished that she could go with him. Sometimes she imagined so vividly that she had gone away that her absence felt real to her. It was such a good feeling that she felt guilty, and for a little while tried to turn her heart and mind back to her husband.

And that was hard to do. Beau was like a rusty pump that Lila had to prime, pouring a torrent of words over him in order to get some trickle of conversation in return. More often than not, Beau rewarded her efforts with silence, or else turned his attention to the offerings his daughters brought him - berry pies and broken toys - with an expression of relief on his face, as if grateful for something that made sense to him. But Lila wanted him to make sense of her. She wanted him to look at her in the kitchen the way he touched her in the bedroom. She wanted to feel as close to him with her heart and mind as she did with her body. She wanted and wanted and wanted, and did not get, and wondered how much longer she could bear it.

Lila pulled a knot in the end of the casing, and dropped the sausage in a pan with the others. The children came shrieking onto the porch, Jack in tow. The kitchen door opened, the crowd spilled in, and Lila retreated as far into herself as she could go and slammed the door, while life surged around her like the sea.

Two hours later, the men and children sat down at the kitchen table. They left an empty chair for Lupe between Dolly and Nub, another for Lila between Beau and Jack, and the one at the foot of the table for Jessie. A platter heaped high with chitterlings sat in the center of the table, surrounded by bowls of turnip greens, mashed potatoes, and gravy, two plates of hogshead cheese, and platters of pork chops, baked sweet potatoes, and crackling bread. The women moved around the table, serving the children and refilling dishes. When they had finally taken their seats, those present bowed their heads while Raymond spoke the blessing. A murmured chorus of amens was followed by the clink of forks and knives on china and a minimum of conversation, all of it limited to the meal before them.

When supper was over, the children were excused and the women set about clearing the table. The men stepped out on the back porch to relieve themselves. Raymond came back with his belt unbuckled, but left the top button of his pants done up until he sat back down, in deference to Lila and Lupe. Jessie set an empty Mason jar on the table between him and Dolly for use as a spittoon, and Lila served coffee. Only then, against a background of clatter as the food was put away and the dishes were washed, did they get down to serious talking. The wide-ranging conversation was intended to fill Jack in on all he'd missed since the last time he was home, and included an invitation to go to Turkey Hammock for the hunting trip, which he accepted. The children were bathed and put to bed on pallets in the front room before the women sat down and Jack's turn came to talk.

"What do you hear about the Raineys?" Beau asked.

"Plenty," Jack said. He took a huge bite of chess pie - the third piece he'd had since supper - and swallowed it with a mouthful of coffee. "He's got his own operation now, for one thing."

"I thought he was connected to that bunch down in south Florida," Dolly said.

"He was," Jack said. "But he broke with them. He's got his own gang now. There's eight of them, all told. Tate, the twins, and five other men. I understand he's hell to work for."

"How'd you come to find that out?" Raymond asked.

"Josie Fitch told me," Jack said.

"Who's she?" Jessie asked.

Jack shrugged. "A girl."

"So what does a girl know?" Raymond asked. He didn't try to hide his scorn. It was never far from the surface when Jack was around.

"Well, she's married to Burgess Fitch," Jack said.

"And?"

"And Burgess is one of Tate's men."

"I see," Raymond said. His tone suggested that he didn't see at all. Jack went back to his pie and coffee, apparently oblivious to the people around the table staring at him.

"How well do you know this girl?" Dolly asked. "I'm just curious, is all."

Jack wiped his mouth with his napkin. "Let's just say I used to know her real well, but now I don't know her at all. Not since she married Burgess. I don't know married women. It's bad for my music."

"You mean it's bad for your health," Dolly said.

"That, too." Jack scraped the last of the pie off his plate. "But Burgess stays gone a good part of the time, and Josie likes to talk. She knows I'm good for a listen, if I'm in town." Jack licked the spoon and put it on the plate. "That sure was good," he said.

"What makes Tate so hard to work for?" Beau asked.

"His standards," Jack said.

"His what?" Beau asked.

"His standards. He has high standards. Everybody that works for him has to wear a derby hat and a frock coat and shave every day and take a bath once a week. And they're not allowed to cuss."

"Why is that?" Beau asked.

"Because they're gentlemen," Jack said. There was a moment of silence while this information was digested. Jessie got up and refilled the coffee cups. Dolly lifted his and blew across the surface, then took a sip.

"Gentleman thieves," he said. "You don't see too many of them these days."

"Tate's serious about it, too," Jack said. "He killed a man in Key West for laughing at him. He didn't go to jail, though. Talked his way out of it."

"Said it was a misunderstanding," Beau said.

"That's the exact word Tate used." Jack stretched his arms and cracked his knuckles. "They're peculiar, no doubt it, and Tate most of all. But they're still a bad bunch, mean and hard and dangerous."

"As dangerous as the Spanish?" Lila asked.

Raymond flicked his hand at the table as if brushing away a fly. "The Spanish are aggravating, not dangerous," he said. "I'll tell you one thing. Blowing up the *Maine* was a damn fool thing for them to do. Folks over here won't stand for such as that."

"They've stood it since it happened," Dolly said. "And they can keep on standing it. I don't see any call to go to war. Let Cuba handle its own problems."

Jessie sighed, and folded her hands in her lap. "Listening to you two is like reading the paper: go to war, don't go to war. I say we stay home and mind our own business."

"The *Maine* makes it our business," Raymond said. "Besides, war is good for beef prices."

"No doubt about that," Dolly said.

Jack stared at his father. "So you're ready to go to war."

"Yes, I am," Raymond said.

"Ready enough to start one?" Jack asked.

"We didn't start anything," Raymond said. "Spain did. Besides, why not? So long as it stays over there in Cuba, I don't see the harm in it. Might even pull the country together."

"Unite North and South again, as Hearst says," Jack said.

"That's a man with a head on his shoulders," Raymond said.

"He's a rabble rouser."

"Least ways he ain't a fiddler. He's got that much going for him." Raymond caught and held Jack's eyes, who held Raymond's right back.

"That's enough, you two," Jessie said. She stood up and started collecting the last of the dishes. "It's late and I'm tired and I want me and everybody else to go to bed."

Dolly helped Lupe out of her chair. "I'll get Nub if you'll wake the rest of them," he said.

"Y'all can leave them to sleep here," Jessie said. She lit an extra lantern and handed it to Dolly. "They're plenty warm enough."

"I don't know," Dolly said. "They're likely to miss me."

"They won't even know you're gone," Jessie said.

Lupe took his arm. "Nobody misses you as much as you think they do," she said. "Now quit your fussing and take me home."

Raymond walked with them to the edge of the porch. As they went down the steps, Dolly patted Lupe on the backside and said something to her that Raymond couldn't hear. Lupe laughed softly. The lantern light disappeared in the hammock, and their voices faded. Jack kissed his mother good night and headed for the loft. Beau and Lila left a few minutes later. The children, asleep on their pallets, didn't stir.

Raymond got into bed next to Jessie with a pain in his hip, but, exhausted as he was, fell asleep almost as soon as his head hit the pillow. Deep in the night, he dreamed that he and Dolly were riding the train again to the Cedar Keys. There were cattle in the cars. Their horns poked him through the slats. He tried to push them away, but they kept at it while the train whistle wailed and wailed and wailed. Raymond woke up to find Nub standing by the bed, jabbing Raymond in the side and crying for his daddy. Raymond pulled him up in the bed so Jessie could get him quiet, then drifted back to sleep, hoping to ride the train again, but it was gone.

Chapter Twenty-Eight

The Turkey Hammock hunting camp was a ten-by-twelve pine shack with rawhide windows, a dirt floor, and a cabbage frond roof. The roof had to be replaced with every visit, the fronds having become brittle and leaky in the interim, and infested with palmetto bugs. On clear nights in temperate weather, the hunters went without a roof altogether, and slept beneath the rustling cabbage palms themselves. They didn't sleep on the floor - which was lively with mice, roaches, spiders, ground rattlers, more palmetto bugs, and the occasional foraging gopher tortoise - but in canvas hammocks slung between the support posts. A pit dug some twenty feet from the shack served as a latrine. A hand pump over a shallow well provided water that smelled like hardboiled eggs. Various dented and holed tin cans, shot up boxes, and broken bottles were loosely heaped in a nearby area that served both for target practice and as a dump. A rope tied between two trees for a clothesline and some sawn-off cabbage stumps sunk in the ground around a fire hole completed the basics. The stink, as Fess said, was extra.

There hadn't been any stink at first. It wore off between visits. But five days of warm weather and Fess's beans had combined with unwashed clothes and bodies, the open pit latrine, and the aging carcasses of bear, deer, and turkey to create an odor so potent that one of the dogs tried to roll on Dolly. By the sixth day, it was influencing the taste of the food, and everyone agreed it was time to go home. Six full days of hunting was pretty good, though, considering they'd almost not gone at all.

The second day of butchering had near about done Raymond in. He could hardly walk at the end of it, and by the next morning was suffering from a full-blown sciatica attack. He couldn't even get out of bed to see them off. They'd almost had to go without Dolly, as well. He'd sat on the side of Raymond's bed, unhappy and argumentative, and oblivious to the physical discomfort his weight on the mattress was causing Raymond.

"You and me going was the whole point of the thing," he complained. "I'll just stay here and help Jessie look after you."

"Jessie doesn't need any help," Raymond said. "You go with the rest of 'em, keep 'em out of trouble. You and me, we'll go some other time. And I'd sure appreciate it if you got off this bed. I do better when I lay straight."

So Dolly had gone with the others to Turkey Hammock, but in a poor frame of mind - somewhere between sorrowful and belligerent - that didn't improve for several days into the trip. Even then, he wasn't really himself. All four of them - Fess included - were glad when it was time to go, and not just because they all stank so bad.

To mark the occasion, Fess broke out his jug of 'shine one more time. It was a batch of Fess's own making, and, in Dolly's opinion, as good as any Red Rainey ever made. He had made this announcement their very first night in camp, and thereby created quite a stir. Such a statement was, in fact, blatant heresy in Harris County. Beau and Jack, though too young to have ever tasted Red's whiskey, had refused to countenance this attack on the Moonshine Queen, and Fess had gruffly rejected what was clearly excessive praise. They'd discussed the issue every night after supper, sitting on the cabbage stumps around the fire, drinking hot coffee spiked with judicious dollops of the whiskey in question, mindful of the hour and the need to greet the dawn with a clear head. By the last day - mules harnessed and hitched, wagon loaded, horses saddled - the jug was still nearly a third full, which, Jack opined, seemed a shame, considering the week they'd just been through.

So they built up the fire again and passed the jug around, drinking directly from the lip because the coffee cups were packed away. Dolly's mood was vastly improved with the decision to go home, and he drank deeply from the jug, then proclaimed again, this time with utter conviction, that its contents were clearly equal to Red's. By the time the jug had gone around the circle twice, Beau and Jack were frowning at each other with the critical judgment of men convinced they must have tasted, at least once, the merest sip of Red's 'shine, and Fess was rolling his own product around in his mouth with a faraway look in his eye. By the time it had been around five times, Beau and Jack could recall the Rainey flame going down their infant throats, and by the sixth time around, Fess's humility had surrendered to his honesty, and he could finally admit that, yes, his was clearly as good as Red's, this batch, anyway. Had the jug gone by him another time or two, he might have even said it was better. But an easterly wind stirred the cabbage fronds, and the dogs got to their feet, growling, hackles raised, lips fluttering up and down their teeth. On the edge of the clearing, the horses and mules lifted their heads and whickered.

"Somebody's hereabouts," Dolly said.

Jack raised the jug. "They'll have to hurry if they want any of this," he said, and put the lip to his mouth.

"Let's tell 'em to c'mon," Fess said. He got to his feet and cupped his hands over his mouth like he was going to yell.

Dolly shushed him and stood up. "Don't be hollering until we know who it is," he said. "There's some rascally characters loose in this part of the country, fiddle players and such. Ain't that right, Jacky?"

The names Raymond had called Jack over the years were the stuff of standard island jokes, and he took no offense. "That's right," he said. "Riffraff and other unsavory types."

"I knew you'd understand," Dolly said. "Y'all wait here. I'll go see who it is." In a few minutes, he came back and motioned them to follow him.

"Who...?" Beau asked.

"Come see for yourselves," Dolly said. "But keep your voices down. We don't want to scare them off."

The others followed Dolly along one of several game trails that twisted through the hammock, and ended on the southeastern edge in a mass of cabbage palmettos, within spitting distance of the river. There they parted the fronds and peered out across the water to the wide stretch of prairie between the east bank of the river and Hog Hammock. Bob and Clyde Rainey were riding toward the river from the east.

"I told you these parts was full of riffraff," Dolly whispered.

"That's not riffraff," Jack said. "I'm riffraff. That's trash."

"I wish I'd brought my rifle," Beau said.

"You couldn't hit them from this distance," Dolly said. "Besides, it ain't right to shoot people from ambush, even Raineys."

"I wouldn't shoot directly at them," Beau said. "Just near them."

"Let's call them over here," Dolly said.

"What for?" Beau asked.

"So we can say we did," Dolly said. "Hey, Fess."

"What?"

"Do your gobbler call."

Among Fess Peck's numerous talents was the ability to make animal calls. He could squeal with the ear-splitting shrillness of an outraged hog, and send shivers down a listener's back with a panther's scream. He could mock like a mockingbird, bark like a fox, chirr like a 'coon, and woof like a bear. He could mimic a mourning dove, a gallinule, a quail, a limpkin, and a towhee. But his best call was that of a turkey gobbler, because then he not only sounded like one, but he looked like one, too.

Fess stepped up beside the palmetto, and appeared to cave in on himself. His chin fell down on his chest, his shoulders slumped, his arms hung slackly at his sides. The gobble started at the base of his throat and rose up out of him in a series of bubbles, apparently accompanied by a considerable amount of pain. He stretched his neck out straight, face straining upward, lips loose, eyes closed, head jerking in time with the gobble, Adam's apple jumping in his throat while his shoulders flapped in and out and his arms and hands bowed and fluttered at his sides like a turkey's wings. Across the river, Bob and Clyde stopped where they were. Bob pointed toward the hammock. Fess opened his eyes.

"Did it work?" he asked.

"I think so," Dolly said. "Do it again." Fess did it again, a little longer this time, and louder, his face as red as a turkey's wattles. The twins kicked their horses into a lope.

"They're headed for the crossing," Dolly said.

The crossing was some hundred yards from the edge of the hammock, and at least fifty yards north of where the four hunters were hiding. The Raineys drew their rifles out of the scabbards and held them overhead, then bogged their horses off into the water, swimming in the middle where the channel cut deep. When they came up the other side, Clyde put his rifle away again and turned north, but Bob laid his across the cantle, and waited. Clyde rode back and stopped next to Bob, knee to knee. The discussion that followed was heated.

"I wish I knew what all that was about," Beau said.

Behind him, Jack broke into soft song. "I got a twin at the head of the holler. Hey dee, ho hi, diddle i day. He won't lead and I won't foller. Hey dee, ho di, diddle i day."

"Sing it purty, Handsome Jack," Dolly said. "Maybe they'll dance for us."

Bob grimaced and shrugged. Then Clyde turned back around and the two of them started north again.

"We're losing them, boys," Dolly said. "Fess. Call them again. Get a little closer this time."

Fess trotted north a little ways, alongside the edge of the hammock, then stopped behind an oak tree and gobbled again. As soon as he did, Bob reined his horse around and headed toward them. When Clyde tried to block his way, Bob clubbed him on the shoulder with the rifle butt, and came on. Clyde sat there a minute, rubbing his shoulder, then spat and followed his brother.

"Here they come," Dolly whispered. Fess hunkered down and crept back to the others, and all of them faded back into the dark depths of the hammock.

"What now?" Beau asked.

Dolly pointed southwest. "Fess and Jack, y'all go that way," he said. "Me and Beau will go around the other side, and meet you back at camp. Gobble every once in a while, Fess, but listen close. You may hear a hen talking back at you." He stuck his hand in his pocket and pulled out a frayed stick and the wing bone of a turkey. He cupped the wing bone in his hand and scraped it with the stick, making a soft, drawn out chirruping sound.

Fess drooped, then flung his head up and broke into a passionate gobble. On the outer edge of the hammock, horses' hooves stopped, followed by the creak of saddle leathers, whispers, and a snapping twig. Fess and Jack disappeared behind a cabbage palmetto. Dolly and Beau eased down another game trail that wormed through the oaks, working past the underlying palmettos, briars, and grape vines with infinite caution until the hammock swallowed them up. A cock turkey gobbled, a hen answered, and Bob and Clyde stepped into the hammock.

Had the twins stopped and thought at all, they'd have known something was up. No turkey would have remained in the vicinity with the noise the two of them were making. Besides which, hens and gobblers don't feed together in February. Not until April would the gobblers strut and fight, and the victors gather their harems around them. But Bob and Clyde didn't think. They had other things on their minds, and the calls were too real, too insistent. So they followed the phantom birds all though the hammock, stopping to listen, then moving on again, trying unsuccessfully to be quiet, bemused by the cock's gobble, gobble, gobble, the hen's chirrup, chirrruup, neither bird ever far away, but always in the opposite direction of one another, and always just out of sight. In this way, Fess and Jack made their uneven way around the south end of the hammock, while Dolly and Beau made their way around the north end, and Bob and Clyde went back and forth between them like frantic bird dogs casting for a scent.

Dolly, Beau, Fess, and Jack were sitting sedately around the campfire when Bob and Clyde broke into the clearing, both of them wild-eyed and jittery-looking, and Bob with a rifle in his hand. They stopped dead in their tracks when they saw the clearing was occupied.

"What're y'all doing here?" Bob demanded.

Dolly picked up a jackknife, which was stuck squarely in the middle of an 'x' marked between his feet. "Playing mumblypeg," he said.

"Mumblypeg," Bob repeated. Clyde frowned, his mouth hanging open.

"That's right," Dolly said.

Jack poked a coal out of the fire with a stick, then pointed at it. "Split that coal," he ordered. "From your right ear."

"Easy," Dolly said. Holding the tip of the knife to his ear with the forefinger of his left hand, and the handle between the thumb and forefinger of his right, he flipped the knife at the coal, cutting it neatly in half as the blade sank into the ground. He pulled it out, and drew an 'x' six inches from the toe of Jack's boot. "There's your mark, Beau. From the tip of your nose." Beau pondered the target with a frown. Dolly smiled pleasantly at the Raineys. "What about you boys? What are you doing here? If you don't mind my asking, that is."

"I wish you wouldn't make the target so close to my foot," Jack said. "You know durn well Beau can't hit the broad side of a barn with a knife."

"Don't be squeamish," Dolly said. "It's unmanly. Ain't that right, Bob?"

"We heard turkeys," Bob said. "A gobbler and a bunch of hens. Y'all must of heard them, too."

"I ain't heard nothing," Dolly said. "You fellers heard any turkeys?" Fess and Jack shook their heads.

"Sure haven't," Beau said. He took the proffered knife from Dolly and held the tip of the blade carefully on the end of his nose, positioning his other forefinger with equal care on the handle. Then, with a sharp flick of his wrist, he flipped the knife at the 'x.' The side of the blade hit Jack's boot and spun around, then slid off to one side, on its side and an arm's length from the intended target. "Damn," Beau said.

"You think about it too long," Dolly said. "Just eyeball the target and throw." He looked at Bob as though surprised to see him still standing there. "I swear, Bob, we ain't heard any turkeys."

It was clear Bob didn't believe them, never mind the serenity of their expressions and the innocence in their eyes. On the other hand, he didn't seem ready to call them a bunch of liars, either. Clyde regarded them all, Bob included, with a mixture of confusion and suspicion, then shuffled a little closer to the circle and pointed at the 'x' in front of Jack's boot.

"You missed," he said to Beau.

"He misses all the time," Jack said, and reached for the whiskey jug sitting on the ground beside him.

"Wish I knew where them turkeys went," Bob said. He surveyed the campsite, the garbage heap, the ropes swinging from the oak tree on the edge of the clearing, the wagon beneath the trees. "Y'all been down here hunting."

Dolly picked up the knife, wiped it on his pants leg, and handed it to Beau. "You're a clear sighted young man," he said. "That's exactly what we've been doing. And now we're fixing to go home, just as soon as we beat ole Beau in this here game of mumblypeg, which is so easy to do it almost ain't worth doing. Make your mark, Beau."

"It's hard to believe you didn't hear them turkeys," Bob said. "We followed 'em all the way through this hammock."

"It's a big hammock," Beau said. "Maybe they got lost." He drew a scorched stick out the fire and drew a black circle on the stump beneath Dolly, not an inch from his thigh. Then he handed the knife to Fess. "From the shoulder," he said.

Fess took the knife, and wiped his mouth with the back of his hand. "Hold on, Dolly," he said. "I'm feeling a mite shaky." He laid the tip of the knife on his left shoulder, then hit the end of the handle with one finger. The blade flashed, turned end over end, and landed with a solid thunk, quivering, the tip embedded dead center in the circle. Dolly grinned. Jack elbowed Fess, who bowed sitting down. Beau rolled his eyes.

Bob looked at them all as though the sight pained him. "Bunch of drunks," he said. "And deaf, too." He jerked his head at the hammock. "C'mon, Clyde. We got to be going."

"I told you that back yonder," Clyde said. "Now we're late."

"We ain't late," Bob said. "Now shut up and c'mon."

"We're late," Clyde said.

Bob took his hat off and rubbed his hair until it practically stood on end. "I said we ain't late!" he shouted. He put his hat back on. The gesture seemed to calm him. "We ain't late, Clyde," he said. "So quit your yapping."

"Bye, Bob," Dolly said. "Thank you so much for dropping in."

Bob left without answering. Clyde followed him. They weren't ten feet down the game trail when Dolly winked at Fess, and took the wing bone and stick out of his pocket. "Chirruup," went the flint and stick. "Gobble, gobble, gobble," replied Fess. The twins walked back into the clearing.

"You sons-a-bitches," Bob said.

"Now, now, Bob," Dolly said. "That ain't no way to talk." He 'chirruped' again with the bone and stick. Fess tried to gobble back, but belched, instead.

Beau, elbows on his knees, bent over with his head almost touching his clasped hands, and laughed so hard he cried. Then he sat back up and wiped the tears off his face with his shirtsleeve. "Oh, lord," he said. "I enjoyed that."

Bob shouldered past his brother and walked up to Beau. "I guess you think you're pretty funny," he said.

"Nossir," Beau said. "I think you are." That set everybody off again. The four hunters whooped with laughter. Bob's face got redder and redder, while Clyde looked more and more confused.

"Looky yonder at Clyde," Fess said. "He still ain't caught on." This caused more laughter.

Beau caught his breath. "Bob and Clyde Rainey, turkey hunters," he said. "Hell, the two of you were making so much noise you'd have scared off every turkey within three miles. Hey, lawdy, I can't wait to get to town to tell this one. Chirp, chirp. Gobble, gobble." Beau's gobble was a poor imitation of Fess's, but it was enough to get him tickled again. He was laughing so hard that he didn't see Bob draw his foot back, and by the time he realized what the other man was doing, it was too late to stop him. Bob kicked Beau in the eye and sent him sprawling in the dirt.

The blow seemed to clear Beau's head for a moment. It occurred to him, lying there on the ground, that now would be a good time to back off from all of this, even at the risk of wounding his own pride. That thought stayed with him as the others helped him to his knees, his eye already swelling under a split eyebrow that clouded his vision with blood. It was still with him as he got to his feet, and brushed the hands of his friends away like so many flies. He stood there facing Bob Rainey, clenching and unclenching his hands as though his fingers were tired and wanted stretching, the desire to back off present in the ache of his neck and the throb in his head. He was just about to say 'yes' to the thought, when Bob grinned at him, a big, broad, happy, white-toothed grin that lit up his handsome face and invited the whole world to join him in his mirth.

"Now who's laughing, Pennell?" he asked.

Beau smiled back. "I am," he said, and drove his fist upward from his waist into Bob's mouth with a sound like breaking ice.

Bob staggered backward, dropped the rifle, and bent over, covering his mouth with his hands. He spit and retched and spit again, and dug around in his mouth with his fingers. When he took his fingers away, his mouth was bloody and sunken, and the remains of his teeth were sitting in his palms.

"Your teeth are broke, Bob," Clyde said.

"Don't talk to me, Clyde," Bob said. His voice sounded funny, like he was talking with a mouthful of marbles, and his lips jiggled like calves foot jelly.

"You're in trouble, Bob," Clyde said.

"I'm not listening, Clyde."

"Daddy's going to be mad," Clyde said. "He's going to hurt you again."

Bob turned on him in a rage. "Shut your mouth, you hear me? Shut it!"

Clyde shut his mouth. His brother didn't look so good. Bob's face had gone all peculiar, hollow-cheeked and pouchy around the mouth. His lips were bloody and fat, and trembled like he was going to cry. He poured the broken teeth and shattered pink gums into one hand, and went to messing with them with the other, as though he were trying to fit the pieces back together. One fell through his fingers into the dirt, then another. Bob knelt down beside them, and made a little pile of all the pieces on the ground. Then he spread them apart and tried to put them together again, as if he were working a puzzle. As he worked, he talked to himself in the singsong voice of a small child.

"I'm in big trouble now," he said. "Big, big trouble. I should of listened to Clyde. I can't do nothing right. Goddamn turkeys. Last thing Daddy told me was don't let nothing happen to them teeth. Now they're broke. If I just had some glue, I could fix 'em. Oh, lordy, I wish I could fix 'em. Daddy ain't going to like this one bit. I'm not even supposed to take 'em out of my mouth, and here they are, all over the ground full of goddamn dirt. Daddy's gonna kill me." Bob shoved all the pieces in a pile again, and covered his head with his arms, rocking back and forth on his knees. "Daddy's gonna kill me," he wailed. "Daddy's gonna kill me." Then he hung his head down and sobbed, hitting his own thigh with his fist in a forlorn gesture.

Disgusted and ashamed, Beau bent down and jerked the knife out of the stump where Fess had thrown it. "C'mon, y'all," he said. "I've had all of this I can stand."

Just as suddenly as he'd started, Bob stopped crying. He stared at Beau, his lips loosely together, the mustache above them shiny with tears and the runoff from his nose. He wiped his sleeve across the bottom of his face and grinned, stretching the cut and swollen lips over bare red gums deeply marked where the false teeth had grabbed them. Still grinning, Bob got to his feet. He ground the broken teeth into the dirt with his heel. Then he picked up his rifle, cocked it, and pointed it at Beau. "Laugh at this," he said.

"Whoa, Bob," Dolly said softly.

But Bob just raised the rifle until it lined up with the button on Beau's shirt pocket. A trickle of blood ran down his chin, and he wiped it off with his shoulder. When he did, the rifle barrel moved an inch to the right, and Beau threw the knife. The rifle barrel jerked up and Bob fired, sending the bullet into the trees. Then everyone looked at Bob, even Bob himself. The knife had buried itself, not in his arm where Beau had aimed, but right below his breastbone. Bob dropped the gun and knelt down beside the stump that Dolly had been sitting on. He rested there for a few seconds, leaning on his forearms, careful not to touch the knife handle. Finally, he eased himself to the ground, onto his side, where he lay with his hand hovering over the knife blade as if shielding it from view.

"Oh, my God," Beau said.

"We've got to get him to town," Dolly said. "Fess, throw that meat out of the wagon. Jack, lay the hammocks down for him to lay on. Use the slickers, too. Anything to make a bed. Beau. Clyde. Y'all help me pick him up." Beau squatted down beside Bob and took hold of his shoulders.

Clyde put his hands in his pockets. "Let him walk," he said.

"He can't walk," Dolly snapped. "He's got a knife in his gut."

"Daddy won't like that," Clyde said.

"Daddy can go to hell," Dolly said. "Help your brother."

"No."

"You crazy bastard!" Beau yelled.

"Forget it, Beau," Dolly said. "We'll do it without him."

Bob screamed when they picked him up.

"Get over here, Fess," Dolly said. "Hold him up in the middle so he don't bend."

Bob screamed anyway. They picked their way over the carcasses Fess had thrown out of the wagon, stirring up the flies. The wagon smelled like proud flesh. Jack had put down hammocks, bedrolls and slickers. It was hard getting Bob inside, and before it was over, Dolly was wishing out loud he'd taken the time to make a stretcher. Then it was done, and Bob was covered up with the remaining slicker, folded so as to make a little tent over the knife handle. Fess climbed up on the seat and unwrapped the lines from the brake. Beau, Jack, and Dolly got on their horses. Only Clyde was still afoot.

"Get in the wagon, Clyde," Dolly said. "Ride with Bob."

"No."

"Then walk your sorry ass back through that hammock and get y'all's horses and ride home by yourself."

"No."

"Never mind, Clyde," Dolly said. He sounded tired. "I'm tired of fooling with you. Let's go, Fess."

"Giddup," Fess said.

The mules jerked the wagon into motion. Bob screamed. They pulled it around in a circle, jouncing over tree roots and palmettos. With each jolt, Bob screamed. They started off across the prairie, following the line of the river along the faint wagon track. Every time the wagon bounced or jiggled, which was often, Bob screamed. This went on for what felt like a long, long time, but which really wasn't all that long--maybe a mile or two--because they were still twelve miles from Dolly's house, never mind Elliston itself, when Bob stopped screaming, even when the wagon hit a gopher hole or bull wallow or palmetto stump, which shook it, and him, pretty hard.

In a way, Bob's silence was worse than his screams, though nobody wanted the screams back, either, and had they discussed it, which they didn't, the four men accompanying him would have been hard put to say which they preferred, the silence or the screams, had there been a choice available to them, which there wasn't, which was also why they didn't look in the wagon to see how Bob was doing, because looking wouldn't change anything one way or another, and all there was to see was what they'd seen already, which was Bob Rainey with a knife handle sticking out of his gut, and what they hadn't seen yet, but wouldn't have done them any good to see, or Bob, either, which was more blood than a body could possibly hold, more even than the makeshift linens could hold, so much that it had to find itself a little hole in the back corner of the wagon and let itself out in a thin red stream where it made more noise than Bob Rainey himself as it pitter-pattered across the grass, quick and light, like a mouse.

Chapter Twenty-Nine

Raymond sat on his horse in the shade of a bay myrtle bush. It was the twenty-seventh of April, three months since the killing at Turkey Hammock. The sun was bright and hot. The air was thick. Everything moved slowly. The horse stamped, kicking at flies. A cow and calf trotted out of a stand of pines. They stopped, stared at Raymond, then continued past him, crashing through the palmettos. The yellow dog on the ground beside the horse stood up, ears pricked, and whined.

"Sit down," Raymond said. The dog sat down.

The rains had come early and hard. Eight miles to the southwest, Walker's Island was surrounded by high water. Deep Creek was running at the top of its banks and the lakes had covered the marsh. Here on this sandy pine flat, water glistened in the pine needles that lay atop the hard packed sand like a matted brown carpet. And now, off to the west, a small, dark, anvil-shaped cloud had formed. By mid afternoon it would be a thunderstorm. Raymond wanted to be out of these tall pines by then. He preferred to ride out lightning in the shelter of a hammock. He wished Beau would hurry up.

A twig snapped and a steer trotted by, wooly-headed and pop-eyed. But no sign of Beau. Raymond resisted the urge to go look for him. There had been no shots, no cries, no disturbance of any kind. Nothing but the silence. The horse kicked at the flies on its belly, shifting Raymond in the saddle, then settled back down with a sigh, ears drooping. It was tired of standing there, but Raymond didn't move. He sat watching, listening, waiting.

He'd done a lot of waiting since that February afternoon Jack came pounding up the back steps with a tangled story about the Raineys, some turkeys, and a stabbing. All Raymond really understood was that Dolly and Beau had Bob in the back of Fess's wagon, and were taking him to see a doctor. Raymond met up with them on the road to town, near the cut-off to the Rainey place. He took one look in the wagon and knew that Bob was beyond anybody's help but the undertaker's.

"How'd it happen?" he asked.

"Jack must have told you already," Beau said. "I don't guess there's anything to add." Raymond looked at his son. One eye, purple and weepy, was swollen completely shut. The rest of his face above the dark beard was very pale.

"Tell me again," Raymond said. Beau told him, the words brief, hard, impatient. Raymond listened with his eyes on the ground. He could hear Beau better if he didn't look at him. When he'd finished, Raymond turned to Dolly. "You got anything to add?"

Dolly sucked on a tooth and squinted at Raymond as if he were looking into the sun. Then he spread his hands out, palms up, and shrugged. "We were drunk," he said.

Raymond couldn't tell whether he was making an excuse, offering an explanation, or merely passing on information he thought Raymond didn't have. Whatever he was doing, it wasn't enough, and something in Raymond's expression must have told him so.

Dolly's gaze broke and wandered away - to the wagon, to Beau, to the northwest where Tate Rainey's house lay - but did not return to Raymond. "Beau defended himself, pure and simple," he added. "Bob was going to kill him."

"You'd made a fool of him," Raymond said. "That was your doing."

"Yes, it was," Dolly said. "And I'm sorry. In hindsight, it was a bad idea."

The insufficiency of that statement shook Raymond almost as bad as the sight of Bob's body. He glanced past Dolly at the road to Elliston. "Tell the sheriff I won't be making bail tonight," he said.

"I'm not going to jail!" Beau shouted. "I didn't do anything wrong."

"You sure as hell didn't do anything right," Raymond snapped. He got back on his horse. "Board up the outside window of the cell. Put some extra men on guard. I'll be there as soon as I can."

He gave them an hour to get to town, and another forty minutes to secure the window. The afternoon was old when he rode down the rutted wagon track to the Rainey place. Another wait, while Tate came out on the porch with the cautious air of a man who knows there's trouble, and listened quietly and without comment while Raymond told him what had happened. Raymond waited again, longer this time, while Tate absorbed the information and rubbed the pistol in his hand on his sleeve as a muscle twitched in his cheek and he considered, perhaps, whether to kill the messenger. He might have done so, had not Raymond made his announcement with his rifle drawn and cradled in his arms, a finger resting on the trigger, a wild, bitter desire in his heart that Tate would try something so he could shoot him, a desire so strong that it was all Raymond could do to keep from pulling the trigger when Tate stepped off the porch to go saddle his horse, when Tate rode out of the barn, when Tate loped out ahead of him, his slim, straight back in its white shirt an easy target, a test, a taunt, a dare, a temptation that made Raymond sweat as he followed it into town and evening fell on the road ahead.

To the east, a little bunch of cattle burst out of a myrtle thicket, and seeing Raymond, turned south. Behind them, he could hear a dog barking and the crack of a whip. To the north, though, everything was quiet. The horse shifted beneath him, and switched Raymond's leg with her tail. The dog sighed. Off to the east, a man whooped. There was a crackle of brush and another three head trotted past Raymond.

The woods were full of men and horses and dogs and cattle. Excitement was in the air. The U. S. declaration of war on Spain was expected any day, and the country was mobilizing. A call had gone out for 25,000 volunteers. Troops were already moving into Jacksonville and Key West. But most of the soldiers were coming into Tampa, a mere 240 miles west of Elliston. They needed beef and lots of it. Cattle prices hadn't been this high since the '60s. Every man in Harris County capable of sitting a horse was out shaking the bushes for a cow with his brand on it.

Except Jack Pennell. He was back on the island with Jessie, Lila, and the girls. He'd been a strong right arm while Beau was locked up. Raymond didn't know what he'd have done without him. But he dared not risk both sons to Tate, and he needed some kind of truce with Jessie, besides. The price of peace was Jack. It was a hellish argument, but at the end of it, Jack had stayed behind. Now all Raymond had to worry about was Beau, and the good citizens of Harris County.

Not that there were many to worry about. The Pennells had become outcasts since the killing. Tate Rainey had seen to that. He'd roamed Elliston like a mad man, accosting prospective jurors on the street, haranguing them about Bob's death, swearing that hanging was too good a death for Beau Pennell, and shooting too good an end for anybody who set him free. By the time Tate was finished, no one wanted to serve. Summons after summons was met with tales of inexplicable accidents, strange afflictions, and desperate emergencies. Beau sat in jail for five weeks while a jury was seated. The evidence was heard in one morning. It was a sorry story that edified no one, but one thing was clear: Beau acted in self-defense. Even so, it took the jury six hours to find Beau not guilty, and all twelve men averted their eyes from him as the verdict was read.

A breeze stirred in the pines and died away. A rider came out of the brush and stopped, staring. It was the postmaster, Rufus Billinger. Raymond raised his hand in greeting. Rufus nodded, but did not speak, then rode on, giving Raymond a wide berth. It was like that now. Beau was poison, and so was his family. Raymond had been asked to resign from the bank board; Jessie's invitations to quilting and Bible studies had dried up; people fell silent when Beau walked into a saloon or Lila a store. Excepting the Dempseys, Dolly, and Fess Peck, who stayed too drunk to fear anybody, folks wanted nothing to do with the Pennells. It was too dangerous.

A half mile to the southwest, a whip cracked rapidly three times in a row, paused, then cracked again the same way. That would be Dolly. Nobody else Raymond knew could get that much action out of a cow whip. It was his way of saying everything was all right. Raymond took his hat off, wiped the sweat off his forehead with his arm, and put his hat back on. But he didn't answer. He didn't know what to do about Dolly, what to say to him, or how to treat him. It wasn't possible to avoid him. Dolly prowled the island like a lost soul, keeping an eye on Beau, fearful for his safety. He came to see Raymond once or twice a week, staying long past what little welcome he received. Now that he was over his anger, Raymond visited Dolly, too, and for the same reasons, he guessed: habit, and hope that things would somehow return to the way they'd been before. But relations were just as strained at the Baxter place. Dolly was embarrassingly eager to please, Lupe was smart-mouthed, and the boys were sullen, except for Nub, who was as generous with his affection as he'd always been.

It was partly Nub's sweetness that had enabled Raymond to forgive Dolly for his stupidity, and partly Dolly's broody hen anxiety over Beau. But mostly it was the deep roots of their friendship worn into Raymond's life over thirty plus years like harness marks in the hide of an old mule. It was not something Raymond could explain to Jessie, even if she'd been willing to listen. Not that there was any chance of that happening. To the injury of the deadly foolishness at Turkey Hammock had been added the insult of social exile, and Jessie could not find it in her heart to forgive Dolly for either of them. She'd been cold as a hard freeze the last time she saw him, which was the night before they left to gather cows.

Jessie'd been in a bad mood that night to begin with. Beau and Lila and the girls had come for supper, and the confusion had made her irritable. After supper, the girls had gone outside to play, and were chasing fireflies when Jessie came out on the porch and insisted they come back in the house and go to bed. This had been met with strenuous objections, and Jessie, irate, had called on Raymond for assistance. Raymond was not above sacrificing both reason and fairness for the sake of domestic peace when the occasion warranted it, and he'd made haste to silence the rabble and herd them inside. Then he'd shut the door on the complaints of his house, and walked to the porch rail.

The floorboards were cool under his bare feet, and a damp wind blew from the east, off the lake. He looked northwestward down the wagon track where six miles away Tate Rainey had buried his son and cursed Raymond's. Darkness was falling quickly. The wind rattled through the cabbage palms in the yard, growing in strength and volume into a clamor. Anything could be out there, now, and Raymond would not hear it, nor the dogs smell it. The azaleas on the north side of the porch swayed back and forth, rustling with a sound like bodies brushing against them as the wind riffled through their woody stems.

"Raymond." The voice spoke out of the twilight, barely loud enough to be heard. Raymond jumped, his heart thudding in his throat. Dolly rode around the corner of the house, a broken azalea branch in his hand. "Sorry," he said. "Didn't mean to scare you."

Raymond sat one haunch on the porch rail and tried to look relaxed. "I'm kind of jumpy tonight," he said. "Must be the weather."

"We're all jumpy," Dolly said. He reined his horse in at the bottom of the steps. "Who'd you think it was? Tate?"

"I guess," Raymond said.

"Or Vancey, maybe?"

"Maybe."

A dog scratched underneath the porch, thumping the floorboards with a back leg. The front door slammed, and Jessie walked outside. "When are you coming in?" she asked. Then she stopped. "Who's out there?"

"Me," Dolly said.

Jessie walked to the top step. "What do you want?"

"I'm looking for Beau," he said. "He's not home. Nobody is."

"They're sleeping here tonight," Jessie said.

"I figured as much, but just wanted to check," Dolly said. "I was worried about him."

"It's a little late for that," Jessie said. She went back in the house and slammed the door.

The two men said nothing for a while. Then there was a soft passage of air, a sigh from Dolly or wind under the eaves, Raymond couldn't tell which.

"I wonder if she'll ever let this pass," Dolly said.

"I don't know," Raymond said. "Maybe. When it's been over a while."

"It's got to end first."

"That's right."

Dolly reined the horse around, then stopped. "Ray?"

"What?"

"Are you scared?"

Raymond gripped the porch rail so hard he could feel the raised grain of the weathered boards through the callouses on his hands. "Some," he said. "Tate's not the forgiving sort."

"No," Dolly said. "He's not."

Raymond stared out into the night. There was rain in the air. The wind soughed through the cabbage palms as slow and regular as the breath of someone sleeping.

"He's coming after Beau," Dolly said. "We can count on it."

"I know," Raymond said.

"Like we came after Vancey." The words seemed to hang in the air, as if waiting to be recalled. Then the wind caught them, and carried them out into the darkness. When Dolly spoke again, it was in a voice so low that Raymond could barely hear him. "I wish we'd buried Vancey on his face," he said.

"I do, too," Raymond replied.

"Maybe next time, you'll listen to me."

"Maybe." Raymond walked down the steps to Dolly, and put his hand on the horse's shoulder. "It's getting late. Lupe will be worried."

"I'm sorry, Ray. I'm real sorry. About everything."

"I know. I am too."

"Good night, Ray."

"Good night, Dolly."

Dolly turned and left. The thud of hooves faded and died. The wind rattled in the cabbage palms, then rose and gusted across the porch, cool and clammy, heavy with the stink of water, rotted wool, old bones. Raymond stood it as long as he could, then went back inside his house and bolted the door against it.

In response to some signal only they recognized, frogs burst into song, a raucous, nerve-wracking chorus. It would rain soon. The dog sat up and barked, its stump of a tail wagging its whole back end as Beau rode into sight. A stone's throw behind him rode Dolly. Raymond waved and reined his horse around to the south. For a while, the three of them rode nearly parallel and in sight of one another, until Beau disappeared once more in the brush, then Dolly, and the waiting settled on Raymond again, drawing around him like a noose.

Tate Rainey was the last thing on Beau's mind. First there was Lila to think about, and then the girls, all four of them, one by one. Then there were the colts he was breaking, two belonging to Able Gibbs, one of his own, and the corner of the barn that needed replacing because dry rot had set in. Then there was the drive to Tampa and a list of things Lila and the girls wanted when he got there. The list was in his pocket, but he was carefully committing the items on it to memory, in case he lost the list, or it was destroyed somehow. Then there was the task to hand, which was to gather cows, which sometimes required his full attention and so went to the top of the list, but most of the time didn't require much attention at all. So he also thought about the new barn he wanted to build. There was a sketch of the barn on the back of the shopping list, but he didn't refer to it much. He referred instead to the sketch in his mind, because that one had the measurements written on it. He could see them quite clearly: thin, scratchy-looking numbers and x's beneath straight, clean lines, giving the width and length and height of the barn. Another mental sketch showed the completed barn. Various other plans showed individual stalls, along with the tack room, feed room, and tool room. Sometimes he pictured himself building the barn: cutting, skinning, and sinking the posts; measuring and sawing the boards; nailing the boards to the posts; building and hanging the gates. But mostly, he just looked at the measurements.

He'd begun the barn in jail and had done the whole thing - from the initial sketches to putting horses in the finished stalls - more times than he could count since February, and had become so proficient at it that those other images, the ones that frightened him, hardly intruded at all. Every once in a while, something would surprise him - a quail exploding in flight; a branch catching his sleeve; a squirrel chattering ahead of him; a cabbage frond rustling behind his back - then more unwelcome images and sounds would intrude: Bob's ruined mouth; the knife handle sticking out beneath his breastbone; Tate's finger clawing through the boarded-up window of the jail; Tate's fixed, lusterless black eyes at the trial; Tate walking out of the courtroom when the verdict was announced; Tate standing at the end of his road that evening, old-looking and stoop-shouldered, staring at Beau with those flat, dead eyes, and mouthing curses as he passed; the Rainey house and barn two days later, empty except for the raw mound of Bob's grave, and empty ever since, with no word from anybody about the whole family, as though the Raineys had stepped off the face of the earth, which was the worst of all, because it meant Tate could be anywhere.

That kind of thinking was enough to drive a man crazy, which is why Beau thought so much about that new barn and the list of things for Lila and the girls. Not that it had been easy at first to think about those things consistently. Lila, particularly, had wanted to talk about the other. Beau hadn't wanted to yell at her, had not yelled at her, in fact, had only spoken strongly to her, about the need to leave all that alone, to leave unsaid things that didn't have to be said, that were bad enough already. It had taken her a little while to understand that talking didn't help those things any. On the other hand, he talked more to her than he ever had before. In fact, he had explained in great detail just how this barn was put together, and he'd insisted she describe every single item on her list, until he could picture it exactly, which was absolutely necessary since she wouldn't be going on the drive with him, and so wouldn't be in Tampa to pick out what she wanted. She'd never been to Tampa, and couldn't go on a cattle drive, because women didn't do that sort of thing, but he wished she could go, all the same. He would miss her, sorely. Because when he wasn't talking to her about the barn, or listening to her about her list, it was nighttime and they were making love, or fooling around, as Beau called it. It was better than either the barn or the list, burying his mind with his body in Lila's flesh, her heat burning away thoughts of Tate and Bob and the stupid, careless, drunken thing he'd done, that they'd all done, teasing Bob Rainey when they knew, every one of them, that it was just like poking a stick at a shedding rattler. Damn Bob Rainey and his stupid brother, damn Dolly and Jack and Fess and himself and damn Tate Rainey most of all, wherever he was, which was someplace close, Beau knew, because he could come and go at will, like a haunt, worse than ole Vancey Adams. Vancey had merely haunted Beau's childhood dreams. Tate drove past Dolly's house and then past Beau's, no more than the width of the creek away, in the middle of the night in a wagon with a massive headstone in it and riders alongside, and no one knew until the next morning that he had come so close, not even the dogs.

Beau had discovered the tracks himself a month ago, those of the wagon cut into the sand like plow furrows, all along the west edge of Black Hammock, dipping down to the north crossing to the very water's edge, then pulling away again. Beau followed the tracks in the strong morning light to the road that led to the Rainey place. He couldn't go any further from that point, couldn't breathe, hardly, for the fear that pressed on his lungs. He nearly fainted when someone spoke behind him.

"What do you think about it?"

All but choking with terror, Beau had turned around. His father, Dolly, and Jack were standing there, the horses beneath them wet with sweat, their faces unreadable. Beau was surprised to see Raymond, and relieved to see his brother, but he should have known that Dolly would be close. He'd been close ever since Beau got out of jail, showing up at all hours of the day and night, uninvited and unannounced, scaring Lila and the girls half out of their wits. Beau didn't mind, felt it was owed him, in fact, in some vague way he could not explain or defend.

"It's Tate," Beau said.

"I imagine so," Dolly said.

"That wagon sure was loaded heavy," Jack said. "I wonder what he had in it."

"Let's go see," Raymond said.

The Rainey place was deserted. Johnson grass had gown up around the porch, and lantana was blooming in between the porch steps. A weather-bleached sofa with a broken leg sat in the yard. There were holes in the upholstery where mice had made their nests. The front door hung crazily on one hinge; the other had broken off. Save for the wind in the oaks, it was quiet, even peaceful. There was nothing to suggest human use or habitation, barring the tracks in the yard. The wagon wheels had cut deep into the sod, and the grass was still bent down.

"We didn't miss him by much," Raymond said.

Jack rode around the side of the house. "Look at this," he called.

On the east side of the house, Bob's grave had a massive granite tombstone on it, carved with Bob's name and the date of death. The stone was taller than Beau, and wider than Dolly.

"Look at the size of that thing," Raymond said.

"He could have put Bob's birth date on there, at least," Jack said.

"That's not the date he cares about," Raymond said.

Someone had tried to mow the grave by hand. The grass was ragged where it had been torn off. In places, clumps of sod had been pulled out and stuffed back in.

"That stone's too big for Tate and Clyde to move by themselves," Dolly said. "I wonder how many men were with him."

Beau looked beyond the house, to the outlying hammocks and the road off in the distance cutting a straight line toward Elliston. There was plenty of cover for many men. He reined his horse around. "I'll check the house," he said.

The front door wobbled on its one hinge, then broke off and fell to the floor. Beau picked it up and stood it against the wall, turned back to the doorway, and stopped. The dust that lay thick on the floor was traced with boot prints. He counted seven different pairs. "Tate had lots of company," he said, and stood back to let the others look.

"Probably that bunch that rides with him," Jack said.

"They're gravediggers, are they?" Dolly asked.

"They're killers," Jack said.

Beau stepped through the doorway and walked across the front room to the kitchen. Soot had fallen from the stovepipe onto the vacant fireboard. Tin cans were piled in the corner. He picked one up. The lid was ridged and bent where it had been cut open with a knife. "Ate right out of the cans," he said. "Didn't want to risk building a fire, I guess." He looked aimlessly around the kitchen as if he expected Tate to somehow materialize.

"He's gone, Beau," Raymond said.

"He feels close, though," Beau said. "Maybe he's in the barn."

"I looked in the barn," Dolly said. "Nobody's there."

"He's got to be somewhere," Beau said. "He can't just disappear."

"We'll find him, Beau," Raymond said. "Just not right now."

"That's right," Dolly said. "Tate ain't lost. He knows where he is. When he's ready, he'll let us know. One thing's for certain, he ain't here."

Only Beau hadn't been so sure of that, anymore than he was sure of it now. Wherever 'here' was at the moment, it felt like Tate was there as well. Beau could feel him, sometimes, could almost hear him breathing, and squirmed in the saddle just thinking about him. He searched the woods with eyes grown tired from searching, and wished that Lila was with him right now. He needed her, needed something, needed that piece of paper out of his pocket so he could study those plans for the barn and read Lila's list, the paper shaking in his hand and hard to read with its wrinkles and smudges. He held it close to his face, squinting in the sun, the lines swimming up and down because the bright light was making his eyes water. That happened sometimes when he thought too much, about how he couldn't sleep at night, and about how tired he was, and about how three months was too long for Tate Rainey to come for his revenge, and about things he wanted to forget, such as that moment in Turkey Hammock when he'd had the chance to back away, to let it drop, to eat crow, and didn't, and the moment after when everything went bad, the moment he'd give anything he had, just about, to undo.

Beau smoothed the paper out on his thigh and read the list again, out loud, going all the way through it twice, from hair ribbons to stays to horehound candy. Then he turned it over and started reciting the measurements of the barn, the horse beneath him quick stepping to the rhythm of its construction.

Chapter Thirty

Jessie was alone a great deal after the drive started. Raymond and Beau were gone. Jack, angry at having been left behind, rarely made it home for supper and always slept through breakfast. He didn't play his fiddle much at the house, and when he did, all the tunes were sad. Lila and the girls came over every day, but they never stayed long. Other than that, she didn't have company. There was no one in town she wanted to see, and no one who wanted to see her. As for Lupe, well, she and Jessie weren't speaking much nowadays.

There was a time Jessie had enjoyed quiet, and been grateful for it. But there'd been too much of it since the killing. Raymond had shared with her only the bare bones of the incident, and Jack would say nothing except to confirm what his father had said. Beau wouldn't talk to her at all, and flew into a terrible rage the one time she pressed him about it. She hadn't mentioned it in front of him since. Lila was too close to Lupe, who was too close to Dolly, and Dolly, well, had it not been for him, this dreadful business would never have happened in the first place. She knew that from what the children said.

The children, led by Quincey, had made up a play about the killing and the events that followed. Where Quincey got his facts, Jessie didn't know. She supposed Dolly and Lupe told him, or else he'd overheard conversations about it. Quincey was good at that sort of thing. He was quiet, and nosy about other people's business. Even the way the play was first revealed to her - with partly averted faces and lines spoken just within earshot so that she had to strain to hear them - suggested slyness on Quincey's part. It was not a trait in him that she'd appreciated before.

But she'd been so hungry for details that she soon became his audience and accomplice, pretending she could neither see the actors nor hear their lines, thereby giving them tacit permission to continue. In return, Quincey moved the drama closer to her. It followed her outside as she went about her chores, and played beneath the open windows of the house. The boys took their turns in the men's' parts. They made turkey calls, pretended to hit and stab each other, took their time dying, then jumped to their feet, exchanged parts, and did it all again. The girls played Jessie, Lupe, Lila, and Sylla Rainey. They wrung their hands and remonstrated with their men, weeping and wailing over the dead and threatened. Sometimes they fainted, though they had to fall into each other's arms, since the boys tended to drop them in the excitement. Besides, the fainting was an embellishment. To Quincey's knowledge, none of the females involved had been so silly.

And Quincey was a stickler for details. Everything - every gesture, every move, every expression, every word - had to be just so, or the actor couldn't play the part. He was a tyrant. Because he couldn't control them, he told the girls they could do whatever they wanted, so long as they didn't get in the way. Nub, who had a hard time remembering his lines, was only allowed to play Clyde.

In this way, Jessie learned that Beau was barely in his cell before Tate and Raymond rode into town, that the sheriff was hammering boards over the window when Tate dismounted, that Tate howled like a dog when he saw Bob's body, and probed Bob's face and the pockets of his pants searching for those teeth, then crawled back out of the wagon when he found out they were destroyed, and walked up to Beau's window to whisper obscene threats through the cracks in the boards and scrape the wood with his fingernails like a panther sharpening its claws, until he sank to the ground, his slender body shaking with sobs, his face twisted with grief into a grotesque likeness of his son's.

The trial she had seen for herself, but she watched Quincey's version of it, anyhow, as a way to check the accuracy of his earlier information. Certainly he got the trial right: the four hunters - first Dolly, then Fess, then Jack, and finally Beau - all of them clean and sober and neatly dressed, came forward one at a time to tell essentially the same wretched story of a drunken joke gone terribly wrong. One of the girls, now playing a member of the Ladies' Auxiliary, fanned herself, raised her eyebrows, and sent long, pointed looks at the ones playing Jessie, Lila, and Lupe, who all three looked stoically to the front. Nub was always last. He'd stand in the witness box, his small, sweet face frowning with concentration, and insist over and over again, just as Clyde had done, that Bob had Beau Pennell dead to rights, and would have killed him, too, had Beau not thrown that knife. The judge of the moment pounded his gavel - a hammer on a block of wood - and directed the jury to reach its verdict. After a brief wait - less than a minute - in real life, the hours had crept by like days - the foreman pronounced Beau Pennell not guilty of the murder of Robert Wood Rainey.

Tate - Quincey always played the part of Tate - would then get up from his seat on the ground, square his shoulders, and stalk from the courtroom, head high, looking neither right nor left. He'd step over the line in the dirt that marked the courtroom door and walk to the chicken coop, which served as the Rainey homestead. There he gathered up the rest of his family - the girls now playing Sylla and her daughters - loaded them and their goods onto a sled, and dragged them around the corner of the house and away from Harris County. Over and over, Jessie watched the little drama, and every time, she grieved for poor, wretched Bob Rainey, who had died so horribly, and for her son, who'd killed him. And every time, there at the center of it all, stood Dolly Baxter and his deadly prank.

She could not forgive Dolly for it. Raymond said she was unreasonable, to hold Dolly accountable for the whole thing, what with Beau a grown man and just as responsible as Dolly, never mind Fess and Jack. They were in on it, too, don't forget. Blame it on all of them, he said, or don't blame it on any of them, but don't go singling Dolly out. But Raymond was wrong, like he'd always been wrong about Dolly. Dolly had never grown up. Like a child, he could never see beyond his actions to their consequences.

The little play should have ended with the Raineys' departure. However many times those children went over the same ground, there was no more ground to be gone over once Tate was gone. The children seemed to feel the same way, because by the end of March, they had all resumed their usual games. Yet Jessie did not relax. Who but children could relax, knowing what had happened to the young hog farmer? Any day, the Pennells' houses or the barns might burn, or Beau might be shot dead. Tate's unseen presence was all about them, all the time. There was no rest from it. But no one spoke of it, and the children knew nothing of it.

Or that's what Jessie believed, anyway, until one morning in early April. Something had set her behind that day, she couldn't remember what, and she was gathering eggs after dinner instead of mid-morning, like she usually did. She had just stepped back out of the open door with her basket when a body hurtled past her head and hit someone on the ground. Quincey had jumped off the roof onto Matt's shoulders. They froze when Jessie screamed, the knife in Quincey's hand still pressed against his brother's throat.

"What are you doing?" she demanded

"Just playing," Quincey said.

"Playing? That's not playing. Put that knife away. What are you playing?"

Quincey stuck the knife in his belt. "Nothing," he said.

"Matt," Jessie said. "What are you playing?"

"Don't tell her, Matt," Quincey said.

"Matt." Jessie's voice was firmer than her jaw, which wanted to chatter as though with cold. Even the eggs in the basket were trembling, her hands were shaking so hard.

"I'm Beau," Matt muttered. "Quincey, he's Tate. He always gets to play Tate. It ain't fair."

"But Mr. Rainey never jumped on Beau," Jessie said.

"It's what happens next," Matt said. He got up and dusted himself off. "Tate jumps on Beau one day when he's not looking, and kills him."

"Who told you that?" Jessie whispered.

"It's what Tate told Beau through the boards," Quincey said sulkily. "He said, 'I'm gonna get you when you're not looking, boy. I'm gonna do you like you done Bob."

"We don't know that Mr. Rainey is going to try such a thing," Jessie said, feeling faint. "People say things when they're upset that they don't mean."

"We told Quincey that already," Matt said. "But he won't listen. He's got to have it all his own way. I'm tired of getting jumped on, I can tell you that."

"Do the girls play this, too?" Jessie asked. She was horrified at the thought of the girls acting out their father's death.

"No, ma'am," Quincey said. "We didn't tell 'em about this part. We was afraid it'd upset 'em."

"That ain't why, Miss Jessie," Matt said. "Quincey said they'd tattle on us."

Quincey gave Matt a look, and Jessie knew the younger boy would pay dearly for his honesty. "He was right," she said. "They would have tattled on you." She looked Quincey in the eyes, and under her gaze his honey brown skin diffused with red. "This is wrong," she told him. "Bad wrong. You've got to stop it."

Quincey shoved Matt in the chest, knocking him to the ground. "That's what traitors get," he said. "That and worse."

"That's enough, Quincey," Jessie said.

"Leave me alone," Quincey said. Jessie, hardly believing her ears, tried to catch him by the arm. He dodged her and ran off down the path into the hammock. Matt scrambled to his feet and followed him.

"Quincey, hold up," Matt called. "I'm sorry. Wait for me."

Since then, none of the boys had come to see her, and neither had Lupe. Raymond and Dolly wanted peace again between the two families. Lila felt the same way, Jessie knew, and maybe Beau did, too. Maybe even Lupe, as well, though Jessie doubted it. Certainly the girls wanted things to be as they had been. But the past could not be put back together again, and maybe it had never been what they thought it was. Either way, it was too late now, and bitter comfort to know that Jessie had an ally in Quincey, whose heart was as single and unrelenting as her own.

A storm gathered in the afternoon, plunging Lila's kitchen into an early dusk. She got up from the table where the girls were making cinnamon rolls, and lit the lamp on the sideboard. Then she opened the back door and stared out at the sky over the clearing. It was low and heavy, almost black with rain. A low growl of thunder rattled the plates in the cabinet. Coolness eddied across the porch, and Lila held her head up so she could feel it on her face and neck. Then it died away. Just for a moment, she leaned against the door jamb and closed her eyes.

Nights had been pure misery since the rains started. Mosquitoes were so thick she had to keep the shutters closed and burn smudge pots under the windows. She lay on her back in the bed in the pitch black dark, sweat trickling like little fingers down her breasts and between her thighs, until she fell asleep from sheer exhaustion. She woke up several times each night, the mattress soaked beneath her, her nightgown damp with sweat. What woke her up were the noises - rustlings and stirrings, coughs, the barks of dogs and foxes, the shrieks of screech owls and dying rabbits, the lowing of cattle, the moaning of the wind, what seemed like men's voices in the kitchen and the yard - muttered, secretive, low-pitched - but weren't. The least little sound was magnified a thousand times and shaded with meaning. She'd learned not to say anything to Beau, whose anger was more immediate and more frightening than any imagined threat. Instead, she just moved closer to him and lay silent, rigid with terror, and listened until the skin grew tight at her temples, and the sound stopped or dissolved into something trivial and familiar.

Things weren't much better during the day. Tate Rainey stayed just outside her field of vision, and was always gone by the time she glanced around. He crawled in the girls' window in the small hours of the morning, followed Lila to the garden and the outhouse, and stalked Beau as he went to the barn. He was everywhere and nowhere. Now he was gone, drawn away by Beau's departure, and Lila was heartsick with worry.

"Mama," Elizabeth said.

"What?"

"Look what Martha Louise is doing."

Three of the girls had rolled the dough up with brown sugar, cinnamon and raisins on the inside, and were cutting biscuits off the ends and laying them in pans. The youngest, however, was pinching off one little piece of dough at a time, which she covered with butter and smashed in a bowl of sugar and cinnamon before rolling it into a ball. Her pan was dotted with these little balls, most of them no bigger than an acorn.

"They'll burn and be harder than rocks," Elizabeth said.

"I like them that way," Martha Louise said. She smashed another pinch of dough into the sugar bowl with her thumb, then took it out, rolled it into a ball between her palms, and dropped it on the sheet.

"Granny doesn't let her do that when we make cinnamon rolls at her house," Elizabeth said. "She says it's a waste of time and sugar." Of all her daughters, Elizabeth reminded Lila most of Jessie. She had the same effortless competence and unrelenting good sense. Lila hadn't found those virtues very helpful lately.

"Leave her be," she said, and turned back to the doorway.

A roll of thunder shook the house and the rain began to fall, sighing across the yard in the windless heat of the afternoon, picking up speed and volume on its way. Raindrops fell on the back porch eaves like a handful of acorns thrown on the roof. They bounced and skittered over the shingles, those behind coming faster and harder until the house drummed with rain and the hammock disappeared behind a pewter sheet of water.

In the beginning, Lila hadn't worried about Beau. She'd tried to see him the day after the killing, though he'd sent a message to Lila through Raymond that he wanted her to stay on the island, where she'd be safe. Lila, however, had felt a compelling sense of propriety, not of danger, and so had put on her next best dress and bonnet, and driven to town with a jar of syrup and a pan of buttered cornbread wrapped so careful and close it was still warm when she reached the jail. Beau refused to see her. Wouldn't even speak to her. Had the sheriff walk her right back out the door to her wagon - the man's hand on her elbow like she might fall over or run off or faint - with instructions from her husband to return to Walker's Island and stay there like she'd been told. Lila had climbed high-headed into the wagon, face burning, hands fumbling with the lines and the brake, so clumsy and blitherated that the horses went skittish and backed the wagon up onto the sidewalk, knocking the cross bar off the hitching rail. She heard later that the sheriff made Beau come out and fix it.

She'd stayed on the island after that - wouldn't even go into town for groceries - but only so she wouldn't be humiliated again. She thought it wrong of Beau to treat her so badly. He sent no more messages and asked nothing of her. By the time the trial came around, resentment almost prevented her from attending. Certainly she was unprepared for the man she saw there.

Five weeks had left Beau pale and sickly-looking, the skin of his face beneath the shadow of his beard almost as pearly white as Lila knew his buttocks and legs and feet to be. And he had an unpleasant odor, stale, like mildew. She breathed through her mouth as he rocked her in his arms, her eyes almost level with the seam of his shirtsleeve which had fallen off his shoulder to the top of his arm, as though he'd shrunk. He kept talking into her hair, about how much he'd missed her, needed her, wanted her, and even as she recoiled from the sourness of his breath, felt him growing hard against her belly. She got flustered, then, and pushed him away, then thought about his need all during the trial, until the very end, when something else caught her attention.

Lila shoved herself off the doorjamb and went back in the kitchen. The heat almost snatched her breath away. Sweat popped out on her forehead and ran down into her eyes. "Do you think you've got enough wood in that stove?" she asked.

"Granny says it's got to be hot to make good biscuits," Elizabeth said.

"Well, hurry up and put them in, then, so we can damp it down," Lila said.

Elizabeth opened the oven door and shoved her pan in, followed by her two sisters. Martha Louise came last, her pan covered with small, sugary balls.

"Y'all keep an eye on those, now," Lila said. "They'll cook faster than the rest."

"We will," Adele said, and promptly left the kitchen.

"There she goes," Sadie said. "Leaving us to watch her biscuits, just like always."

"Well, I'm not doing it," Elizabeth said.

"Me, neither," the other two chorused.

"All right, then," Lila said. "I will. Now quit your fussing. It's too hot to argue."

She turned back to the open doorway again, drawn to the coolness on the other side. A flash of lightning lit the yard with a weird blue glow. Lila counted to three before she heard the rumble of thunder that followed. The storm was already three miles on its way, moving east. Soon it would reach Hog Hammock, where they were holding the herd until it was big enough to drive to Tampa. Beau was there, but he was still here, too, in this place, with her. She could smell him, feel him, remember his flesh in her own, the knowledge of him deep in her body where he'd touched her, as if for the very first time, the night he returned to the island after the trial. The rain before her dissolved into the bedroom where his hands and tongue and teeth, tentative and wary, had explored her as if she were a food he'd never eaten before, her form and textures and tastes strange to him, a fruit that ripened at his touch.

After that night, any excuse would do, any time of day or night there was time and privacy enough, at night when they went to bed and again in the morning before she got up to fix breakfast, when he woke up from a dream or a nightmare, or came in from working around the house. She'd learned early on not to ask him anything about that day at Turkey Hammock, or Bob Rainey, or Tate, because those subjects sent him into a terrifying rage, after which he'd send the girls to Raymond and Jessie's and take Lila so savagely that she ached for hours afterwards. She didn't mind, though, because she knew she mattered. No one could do for him what she did. She missed him, now that he was gone, in a way she had not missed him when he was in jail, and wondered, not if he loved her - she knew better than that - but how long his need would last, and what she would do when it burned itself out.

"Mama!" Martha Louise screeched. "The biscuits!"

Lila whirled around and ran to the stove. Black smoke was seeping around the edges of the oven door. Using her apron as a potholder, Lila took the pans out. Three of them were fine, the rolls baked gold on top with rings of dark brown where the sugar had caramelized. Martha Louise's, however, were completely scorched. Lila pried them loose from the bottom of the pan with a pancake turner, then set the pan down on the counter. Martha Louise eyed her ruined biscuits disconsolately.

"You said you'd watch," she said.

"I know," Lila said. "I got to thinking about something else."

"You do that a lot," Sadie said.

"Do I?" Lila asked. "I hadn't noticed." She got cups and plates out of the cupboard and set them on the table, along with a bowl of butter that had melted from the heat in the kitchen, and an empty jug. "One of you take that jug and go get some milk, please. Smelling these biscuits is making me hungry."

"They smell burnt," Martha Louise said.

"Go get some milk," Lila said.

Elizabeth picked up the jug. "Granny Gibbs says it's because you're worried about Daddy."

Lila dipped a biscuit in the butter, and remembered why she seldom took her children to visit their maternal grandmother. "Why would I be worried about him?" she asked.

"Granny says you're afraid Tate Rainey is going to kill him."

Lila took a bite of biscuit. It tasted like sweetened sawdust. She looked at her daughters. Their faces were pinched and anxious. "I am not afraid," she said. "Your daddy is a smart, strong man. He has family and friends who stand by him and protect him. Tate Rainey is the one who is afraid. He ran away. He won't hurt your daddy. He can't." The words were rhythmic in her mouth, almost a chant, a spell against terror.

"Granny Gibbs says..." Elizabeth began.

"Sometimes Granny Gibbs is wrong and doesn't know it," Lila said. The girls looked doubtful. "There's still no milk on this table," she added.

"Do you swear you're not afraid?" Sadie asked.

"No, because swearing is wrong," Lila said.

"Then promise."

"I promise."

"Do it again."

Lila looked her daughters square in the eye, one by one. "I promise that I am not afraid. Tate Rainey cannot harm your daddy." She took another bite of biscuit. "Now please go get some milk. My mouth is drying up."

The girls looked at one another. Finally, Elizabeth shrugged and left, Sadie and Adele behind her. Lila followed them to the door. The rain had slacked off to a drizzle and the late afternoon sun was driving away what remained of the clouds. Steam rose in tendrils from the earth, drifted through the grass, and disappeared. Miles away, the ceaseless lowing of distressed cattle rose and fell and rose again like distant horns. That sound had been growing for days as the holding pens at Hog Hammock filled. In another day or two, the drive to Tampa would begin. Somewhere along that trip, either going or coming home, Tate Rainey would make his move. Lila was sure of it. Because there at the end of the trial, as the jury foreman read the not guilty verdict, she'd looked, not at Beau - looking at Beau made her blush - but at Tate Rainey. He was sitting alone at the end of the second bench on the left hand side of the courtroom, facing the judge. Tate had looked almost frail during the trial, he was so thin and seemed so tired. His hollowed cheeks were clean-shaven, though, his mouth stern and beautiful, his gray hair neatly combed, and he wore a shirt so dazzling white that it shone in the sun coming through the windows. He'd appeared impassive during the trial, but at the reading of the verdict, he'd looked at Beau with a lingering intensity that she hadn't recognized until now. It was desire. With all his heart, Tate Rainey wanted Beau's life.

"Mama?"

Lila looked around. Martha Louise was standing there with the pan of burnt biscuits in her hand.

"I'm real sorry," Lila said. "We'll try again tomorrow, and take more care."

"I'm scared," Martha Louise said.

"Don't be silly," Lila said. She patted her knee. "Come sit on my lap."

"Granny says I'm too big."

"No disrespect to Granny," Lila said, "but I'm just about tired of her opinions."

Martha Louise, still clutching the pan of biscuits, got up on Lila's lap. Once in place, she turned halfway around and looked hard at her mother. "I'm believing you," she warned.

Lila kissed her forehead. "Good," she said. "Because I'm telling you true." But when she hugged her daughter, she hit the pan with her elbow, spilling its contents. The little biscuits rolled across the kitchen floor, hard and shiny and black, and clicking together like bullets.

Chapter Thirty-One

On May twelfth, a week after pushing three hundred forty-eight head of cattle out of Hog Hammock, the herd was still eight days from Tampa. It was just past suppertime, and night was falling on the dark of the moon. There was no wind. Frogs croaked and trilled and thrummed. Mosquitoes rose in maddening swarms from the wet grass, and heat lightning jittered on the horizon. The steers, tormented by the mosquitoes, were restless and hard to hold. Beau was riding the perimeter of the herd. The cattle stared at him as he went by, then dropped their heads to snatch at the grass or trotted away, high-headed and white-eyed. Beau and the other riders moved slowly and spoke quietly.

The night deepened. Shadows and the things that cast them ran together until both disappeared. There were no sounds but night sounds: frogs, mosquitoes, teeth tearing grass, the click of horns, the belch of a cud coming up. Beau's horse flung its head up and down and snorted. He swiped its neck and brought his hand away filled with a pulp of mosquitoes and blood, then flung the mess on the ground and wiped his palm on his britches. Two riders loomed up out of the dark, and he grabbed the gun in his waistband.

"It's just us," Raymond said.

"That's a good way to get shot," Beau said.

"Gunfire would scatter these cattle to kingdom come," Raymond said.

"That's better than sitting still for whatever Tate offers," Beau said.

"He won't try anything tonight," Dolly said. "It's too damn dark."

"You don't know what he'll do," Raymond said.

It was an ongoing discussion, and so far, purely speculative. Except for the unease of the herd - cause enough for concern all by itself - the drive to this point had been without incident. There were six men - seven including Fess Peck - and their dogs: Raymond, Dolly, and Beau, and George Dempsey and his two oldest sons, Seth and Jacob. No one else would send their cattle with Raymond, or ride with him. They were too afraid of Tate Rainey. Raymond didn't blame them. Tonight, especially, the herd seemed infected with restlessness. It moved with a pervasive unease, a taut waiting, as though the cattle sensed something beneath the clamor of the frogs.

"I wonder where Tate is," Beau said.

"He could be anywhere," Raymond said. "Back in Elliston, or waiting for us in Tampa. There's just no telling."

"I think he's right here," Beau said.

"Where?" Raymond asked.

"Close," Beau said. "Waiting. Taking his time. He's here."

"Beau, you don't need Tate to shoot you," Dolly said. "You can scare yourself to death."

"Even the cows can feel him," Beau said.

"What they feel is the skeeters sucking them dry," Dolly said. "And if they could talk, they'd tell you so."

"Go get some sleep, son," Raymond said. "Me and Dolly will watch 'til morning. And try not to think so much."

"I'd rather stay here," Beau said. "I don't feel like sleeping."

"Do it anyway," Raymond said. "And stay close to the wagon, so I know where to find you."

Beau dozed on his bedroll behind the wagon. A smudge fire smoldered beside him. When the choking brown smoke blew over him, it chased the mosquitoes away. When it blew the other direction, he breathed fresh air and mosquitoes. Fess snored nearby, his lanky frame sprawled like a clothed collection of loose sticks beneath the wagon. The hobbled mules stood on the other side of Beau, downwind from the smudge fire, each with a hind hoof cocked and resting on its tip. Now and then one of them would switch its tail and sigh. Fireflies glowed fitfully in the trees, and beyond them, far, far away, the stars burned bright and steady, as if to show the fireflies how it was done.

On the edge of the herd, Raymond, Dolly, and George Dempsey watched the darkness, their ears straining to hear above the frogs and insects. Farther out, Seth and Jacob rode lookout, stopping to listen, then moving on again. Hour followed hour as the night settled into utter blackness that paled with agonizing slowness to charcoal, then to the dull gray of the predawn sky. Steam rose from the grass in thin wisps, and hung shoulder-high around the horses. The exhausted sentinels were to slow to notice the cattle stir as if blown by a strong wind, and slower still to see the black-cloaked riders bearing down on them.

They came through the swirling mist in total silence, mounted figures dressed in black and carrying torches in both hands that they windmilled like flaming wheels on either side of their horses before flinging them into the cattle that were already bawling in panic. Then a weird, piercing shriek from one of the attacking riders caused the herd to become one animal that whirled around toward the west and ran with all its might, flanked by the attackers whose black dusters flapped like wings, their high, freakish screams audible even over the crash and thunder of cattle stampeding through brush and palmettos and caroming into Fess's wagon. Mules and horses added their screams to those of the attackers and the cow hunters stretched low over their horses' necks, riding for their lives with the cattle through the camp, the sleepers lost to sight beneath a deadly rain of hooves. Crouched behind Fess's overturned wagon, Beau got a shot off at one of the black-caped riders before something big hit him, and darkness fell again.

When he came to, he was laying on a saddle blanket beside the fire. Jacob Dempsey was sitting on the ground beside him, a dirty cloth wrapped around his head. Blood had seeped through the shirt and dried in a black streak down the side of his face.

"Hey, Jacob," Beau said.

Jacob jumped, and his long-lashed, bloodshot eyes grew wide. He grinned sheepishly at Beau. "You scared me," he said.

"Why?"

"I thought you were dead."

"Oh," Beau said. He thought about that awhile, then took a deep breath. "Where's Daddy?"

"Hunting cows," Jacob said.

"They scattered bad?"

"Over hell and half of Georgia."

Beau closed his eyes. He didn't want to think about it. "How's everybody else?" he asked.

"Shook up," Jacob said. "Especially Fess."

Beau raised himself up on one elbow to look. Fess was sitting with his back against a tree, skinny knees drawn up to his chest, head resting on his crossed arms.

"What's wrong with him?" Beau asked.

"One of his mules was killed."

Beau stared at Fess for a moment, then laid back down. "I'm sorry to hear that," he said. He thought some more, trying to figure the time of day, then gave up. "How long have I been out?"

"Most of the day," Jacob said. "You've got a big ole knot on the back of your head." He nodded his head at something off to Beau's right. "Fess's mule fell on you. The cows went over it."

Beau followed Jacob's gaze. Fess's mule lay on its side, legs stuck stiffly out. Its whole side was sliced and pulpy-looking. Beau closed his eyes. "That's bad," he said.

"It saved your life," Jacob said.

Beau felt the back of his head. There was a bump there the size of an orange. "We lose any other stock?" he asked.

"A horse and two dogs," Jacob said.

"It could have been worse, I guess," Beau said.

"Uh, huh."

"I guess the others are cow hunting, too. Dolly and your daddy and Seth."

"Uh, huh."

There didn't seem to be much else to say. Beau faded off to sleep. When he woke up again, it was nearly dark. Jacob was lying down. "They back yet?" Beau asked.

`"No," Jacob said.

"I wish they'd come on."

Jacob yawned and rubbed his beard. "Them cows was some kind of scattered," he said. "It'll take a while to catch 'em, I expect."

It took three days, at the end of which they were still shy sixty-eight head. Raymond, Dolly, and George went looking for them, riding a shotgun pattern to the west until the tracks turned back to the center and headed off in a bunch toward Tampa, bounded on either side by the hoof prints of several horses. The three men returned to camp where the others were waiting. No one was watching the herd, which grazed quietly, too worn out to go anywhere. The crew sat around a fire drinking gritty coffee. The beans had spilled when the wagon went over, and Fess had raked them out of the dirt with his fingers, then ground them up with the sand that covered them and boiled the results in a leaky pot that dripped in the fire and made it hiss and spit and smoke. Dolly took a careful sip.

"Hey, Raymond," he said.

"Hmmm?"

"What are we going to do about them cows?"

Raymond swirled the sandy dregs around in his cup and tossed them into the fire. "We're going after 'em," he said.

"Who's 'we'?" Seth asked.

"Me and whoever else wants to go," Raymond said.

"I'm going," Dolly said.

"Me, too," Beau said.

"Count me and my boys in," George said. He pulled the revolver out of his belt, broke the barrel open, gave it a spin, and clicked it shut again. "We've got a little something for Tate."

"Who's going to watch the herd?" Jacob asked.

"Fess, if he wants to," Raymond said. "Otherwise, just let 'em sit. They're too tired to go far."

"What if Tate swings around and comes back for them?" Beau asked.

"We'll have to take that chance," Raymond said. "My guess is he'll head straight for Tampa, and then come back on us." He set his coffee cup beside the fire. "Let's get some sleep. We leave at first light."

The trail headed due west over trampled brush and torn earth, as straight and wide as a cleared road. Raymond led the way, his quick-stepping little bay mare the pacesetter for the other horses. Stopping seldom and briefly, they covered a good twenty miles a day, and caught up with Tate three days after the attack, guided by the lowing of unseen cattle. Beau saw them first, and halted the others with an upraised hand.

"There they are," he said.

A lone man rode out of a cabbage hammock into an early morning fog bank that stretched like a milky sea over the prairie. The rider was invisible from the waist down, and followed a wide patch of horned heads that filled the thick gray air with the ceaseless complaint of driven cattle. Raymond could see another man to the first one's left. One by one, four others rode out of the hammock.

"I count six," George said. "How about you, Raymond?" There was no need to whisper. Words dropped like lead weights in the thick air.

"That's all I see," Raymond said. "There could be more, though. We'll have to just follow along until this fog dries out."

They rode slowly, keeping to hammocks when they could, allowing the man in front of them to ride out of sight when they had to break cover. As the fog burned away to swirling mist, they dropped further back, and followed the sound of the cattle. When the full sun burned through, they swung wide to the south, then turned back to the northwest, riding hard for the cover of a hammock two miles west of the slow moving herd.

Raymond pulled up behind a clump of cabbage palms and got down off his horse. He tied the mare to a myrtle bush and pulled his shotgun out of the scabbard. With the gun on his shoulder, he walked along the edge of the hammock until he found a cleared space, then got down on one knee. The others followed him, forming a line in the shadows of the palms, Raymond first, then Beau, Dolly, Seth, George, and Jacob.

Behind them, mist still tied tree to tree in the hammock and beaded the spider webs in the branches. In front of them, the prairie shimmered under a ten o'clock sun so bright it made their eyes water. Men whistled and yelled. Cattle bawled. Whips cracked. The voices of the rustlers grew clear, and then their faces. Clyde Rainey was riding point. Two men rode on each side, all four of them strangers to Raymond. Jack would have known who they were, and just for a second, Raymond regretted leaving him behind. Then he saw Tate in the back, riding alone, and cast regret away like a dirty rag.

"Pick your man," he said.

"I've got Tate," Beau said.

"Let me take him," Dolly said. "I'm a better shot."

"Even Beau can't miss at this range," Seth said.

"Let me take him," Dolly repeated.

"No," Beau said. "He's mine."

"See to it you don't miss him, then," Dolly said. Beau cast a sharp glance at him. The older man was staring out at the approaching men. "I'll take the one in the southeast corner."

"I've got the man ahead of him," George said. "Seth. Able. Y'all take the ones to the north."

"That leaves Clyde," Dolly said. "You reckon you can hit him, Raymond?"

"I'll do my best," Raymond said.

"This is gonna run them steers off again," Seth said.

"They won't go far," George said. "That's a wore out bunch of cattle."

The herd drew closer. When he could see the kerchief around Clyde's throat, Raymond raised his hand. "Ready. Aim," he said.

"Wait one more second," Dolly said. Raymond waited. It was one second too long. Clyde's horse shied, nearly throwing him to the ground, then whickered. Raymond's horse neighed in answer. Clyde opened his mouth to yell, but it wasn't necessary. Tate and the other four men had already whirled their horses around, headed for the hammock on the east side of the clearing.

"Fire!" Raymond yelled. He threw the shotgun to his shoulder and pulled the trigger. Five shots echoed his with a deafening blast. Clyde reeled in the saddle, fell to the ground, and lay still. One of the rustlers pitched forward over his horse's shoulder, flopped in the saddle for a few strides, then fell off. Another arched his back, but held on. Seth fired again. The man dropped to the ground like a sack of feed. The third one clutched his side. George fired again. The man let go of his side and grabbed his neck. With the other hand, he pulled his horse to a halt, then got down off the horse and sat down in a patch of grass, one hand still on the back of his neck. When the horse walked off, the man didn't move. Jacob missed his man entirely, hitting the horse instead. The horse screamed and pitched forward onto its shoulder, pinning the rider beneath as it jerked and thrashed and kicked. There was a lot of cursing and yelling as the rider extricated himself. Using the horse for a shield, he fired back at the drovers. A bullet whopped the tree over Raymond's head. Unscathed, Tate had nearly made it to the far hammock. Ignoring the periodic shots of the downed rustler, Beau stood up and fired again. Tate fell to one side.

"Got him," Beau said.

"Get him again," Dolly said.

Beau fired a third time, and Tate fell a little further, then slipped off his horse into the palmettos. The fronds waved, then grew still. The rustler hiding behind the dead horse had stopped firing and was watching the patch of palmettos where Tate had gone down.

"You reckon he's dead?" Jacob asked.

"Hang on a second," Raymond said.

They waited. Nothing moved. The cattle, scattered through the clearing, had been watching the activity around them. Now that it was quiet, they dropped their heads and went to grazing. A hand appeared behind the dead horse, waving a blue handkerchief.

"Don't shoot," the rustler yelled. "I'm unarmed." A revolver flew over the body of the horse, tumbled end over end through the air, and landed not ten feet in front of George. "I'm coming out now."

"Come on ahead," Raymond yelled.

The man stood up and put his hands in the air, then stepped around the horse and started walking toward the waiting gunmen. He hadn't taken three steps when a shot rang out from the palmettos where Tate had gone down. The man grabbed his arm and fell to the ground. "Son-of-a-bitch!" he shrieked. "Mean, sorry, low down son-of-a-bitch!" He lay in the dirt, crying and moaning.

Dolly fired at the palmettos. Buckshot pattered on the distant fronds like a brief rain. The palmettos didn't move. Raymond stood up and fired, then ducked back down. More rain. Still no movement. Then a breeze set everything on the prairie into motion. Fifteen minutes had passed since the shooting began, maybe twenty. The sun beat down, nearly blinding them. Raymond shaded his eyes with his hand, but couldn't see anything. The cattle grazed unperturbed. The breeze died down and the palmettos stilled. No one moved. Even the wounded rustler was quiet.

"How long do we wait?" Jacob asked.

"As long as it takes," George said.

Beau got down on his hands and knees. "Maybe I can get a little closer," he said.

"Better stay where you are," Dolly said.

"I can't," Beau said. "I've got to see where he is." He crawled out beyond the cabbage palms to crouch beneath a big palmetto, then stood up, slowly, as if working the cramps out of his legs. Finally, he stood up straight. Nothing happened. He squinted, trying to see beneath the palmetto fronds where Tate had gone down. There was nothing. Beau turned around and grinned at the others. "It's all right," he said. "We got him." A rifle shot rang out and his hat flew off. Beau dropped to the ground and scrambled back on his elbows to the safety of the palms, grabbing his hat along the way. It had a hole through the crown. Beau could feel a draft when he put it on.

"That was close enough," Dolly said.

"Everybody load," Raymond said. Bolts snapped open, shells clicked, bolts snapped shut. "On the count of three, stand and fire. One. Two. Three."

As one, the six men stood up, stepped forward, and fired. There was a terrible scream. The palmettos thrashed and waved, then grew still again. Cattle grazed. Bees droned in the purple spike. Dragonflies flitted and darted in the sun. Ten minutes went by, each of them an hour long.

Raymond thumbed another shell into the shotgun and stood up. "Let's go see what we got," he said, and headed for the palmettos.

Chapter Thirty-Two

Tate was gone. They rode back and forth through the palmettos where he'd fallen, and in and out of the hammocks on either side of the clearing, but there was no sign of him, no blood, no tracks, nothing. All they had were three dead rustlers and two wounded ones: Clyde, and a sixteen-year-old boy who said he was from Arcadia. The boy was nervous and talkative.

"How about that Tate, shooting me in the arm?" he asked. "What kind of man would do a thing like that, do you reckon?"

"One like Tate," Raymond said.

"He couldn't stand it, I reckon, me giving myself up." The boy wiped his nose on the back of his hand. "That's a bad man, a mean man. I wouldn't be in your shoes for nothing. Tate Rainey hates your guts. He's going to get you for this. I'm going to enjoy it when he does, too, you see if I don't."

"What makes you think you'll live to see it?" Raymond asked.

The boy's eyes traveled to Seth, who had taken the rope off his saddle and was tying a noose in one end. "There ain't no call for that there," the boy said. "I done wrong and I know it, but I don't mind taking my chances in court. Nossir, I don't." He wiped his nose again, though he wasn't sniffling. Raymond supposed it was a nervous habit.

"Friend of mine says prison's not too bad. Two meals a day and a bed." The boy laughed, then winced when the movement jiggled his arm. The shirtsleeve was dark and wet with blood.

"You won't make it," Dolly said. "Prison is hard enough on men with two arms."

Seth threw the other end of the rope to Jacob, who was sitting on an oak limb on the edge of the hammock, long legs dangling on each side. He caught the rope and tied it to the limb, then let himself down the rope, hand over hand, to the ground. He picked up the noose end and started walking toward the boy. Raymond rode between them.

"Climb back up that rope and untie it," he said. "We're taking these two to Tampa." Jacob stopped and looked at his father.

"These men are rustlers," George said. "And rustling's a hanging offense."

"Then I expect they'll hang," Raymond said. "But not here."

"You are a merciful man," the boy said. "I swear, you have moved my soul. I'm going to take my punishment like the repentant sinner I am and never, ever do this kind of thing again, you have my solemn word on it."

"If you don't get quiet," Raymond said. "I'm going to tie that knot around your neck myself."

"Aw, you couldn't do that," the boy said.

"I've done it before," Raymond said. "It's not as hard as you might think."

"I don't know what you're going so soft for," George said. "Look at that arm. He'll die of lead poisoning before we can get him to Tampa. We'd be doing him a favor to hang him."

"Don't put yourself out on my account," the boy said. "I'll take my chances with the lead. I don't mind."

Dolly nudged Clyde, who was sitting lumpishly in his saddle. A red streak between two ribs showed through a tear in his shirt. "You're awful quiet, Possum," Dolly said. Clyde had stayed on the ground throughout the fight, and was still lying there with his eyes shut when they came to get his body. He didn't open them until Dolly dug into his side with the butt of a cow whip. Dolly had been calling him 'Possum' ever since. Clyde hadn't responded, except to cut his eyes over at Dolly every time he said it, as if trying to figure out what he meant.

"Tell me something, 'Possum," Dolly said. "Did the young'un talk as much around your daddy?"

Clyde shook his head.

"Don't let your mouth run away with you, 'Possum," Dolly said. He turned back to the others. "Well, we got to make a decision here. Hang 'em, or drag their sorry butts to Tampa. Which will it be?"

"I say Tampa, hands down," the boy said.

"Hang 'em," Clyde said.

Everybody looked at him.

"This is you we're talking about," Dolly said.

Clyde nodded. "I know," he said. "Hang 'em."

"Don't listen to him," the boy said. His face was glistening with sweat. "He's crazy."

"I'd rather be dead than go back to prison," Clyde said. "It's a bad place."

"Ray," Dolly said. "'Possum thinks hanging would be an act of mercy. I say we oblige him."

"He's going to Tampa," Raymond said.

"All right, boys," Dolly said. "The young 'un here and Raymond have voted for Tampa. 'Possum and me say hang 'em. What about the rest of you?"

"Hang them," Beau said. He looked defiantly at his father. Raymond returned the gaze until Beau dropped his eyes.

"Two for Tampa, three for hanging," Dolly said. He winked at Seth and Jacob. "Let me guess what you boys will say."

"Ask Daddy," Seth said. "We stand with him."

"George?"

But George was thinking a slow thought, and it was a while before he spoke. "You say prison's pretty bad, huh, Clyde?"

"Real bad," Clyde said.

George thought some more. "Maybe you're just trying to buy time," he said, "so your daddy can come after you."

"He won't come after me." Clyde spoke with such sadness that it had to be true.

For a moment, even George seemed moved. Then he went back to his thought, and his expression hardened again. "Tampa," he said. Clyde gave him an anguished look, but George would have none of it. "You go ahead and look sorry, see what good it does you. I've got two hundred head of steers in that herd, and you rascals have run 'em half to death. I hope the pair of you serve a year for every pound they've lost."

"You're a vengeful man, George Dempsey," Dolly said. "Either that, or Clyde's smarter than he looks. Tampa it is."

"Tampa!" the boy cried. "That is sweet to hear." He walked up to Clyde's horse, his eyes like slits. "You keep your fool opinions to yourself from now on," he added. "Or I'll make you wish your mama had strangled you when you were born. Stupid, ugly bastard. No wonder that fella calls you 'Possum."

They buried the three bodies in the sand of the prairie, and left the cattle to graze. As they were making camp, Beau showed Dolly the hole in his hat.

"You'll have to get another one in Tampa," Dolly said. "If Lila was to see this one, she'd never let you leave the house again. Ain't that right, Ray?"

But Raymond was watching a brilliant green lizard and didn't hear him. It scampered down the length of a myrtle branch and turned dark brown, then flicked beneath a leaf. Only the very tip of its tail, now palest green, betrayed its position.

"Raymond," Dolly said.

"What?"

"Look at Beau's hat."

Raymond looked at the hat. "He'll need a new one," he said.

"Or else Lila won't let him play posse like this anymore, ain't that right?"

"That's right," Raymond said. He turned back to the lizard. It had sidled to the top of a dead twig and turned the color of straw. A thin red flare of skin bulged out of its throat, like a warning. Raymond gazed out over the palmettos. Nothing moved in them. He turned back to the group. Everyone was staring at him. "Beau. I want you to take care of Clyde. Keep close to him. I don't want anything happening to him before we get to Tampa."

"What about me?" the boy asked.

"I don't care about you," Raymond said. He turned back to the myrtle branch. The lizard was still there, its delicate ribs pulsing with life. Raymond made a gun of his finger and pointed at the lizard. "Pow," he whispered. The lizard crouched down, looked about with quick darts of its head, and jumped. The thick leaves of the myrtle bush rustled, then grew quiet. Somewhere beneath them waited the little lizard, watchful, patient, and still.

The sentry on duty at the edge of the encampment was sweating like a stewed chicken in a thick blue woolen uniform, and carried a black powder gun older than the one Raymond had used in '65. The young private was also fighting a case of dysentery. Raymond had no sooner given his name than the boy doubled over and hobbled off into the bushes.

"Go wherever the hell you want," he yelled. "Just leave me alone. God have mercy and let me die, my ass is sore."

Raymond led the herd through sandspurs and scrub past tents, campfires, makeshift clotheslines, and latrines under the relentless Florida sun with only the occasional pine tree for shade. He passed men marching in close order drill, some with muskets, others with sticks and broom handles, like boys playing war. All of them wore the same heavy woolen blue uniforms. Set off from the other tents at regular intervals were those flying yellow quarantine flags. They were the first thing the drovers asked about when they found the quartermaster.

"You bet we've got fever," he said. "Typhoid, Yellow Jack, malaria, dysentery. You name it, we've got it. Hell, we're going to kill these boys off before they ever see a Spaniard." The quartermaster was a grizzled veteran of two wars and none too pleased about the way this latest one was being handled. He tallied cattle between caustic jokes about the military and civic insanities that, along with heat, humidity, sand, and insects, abounded in Tampa: inadequate sanitation, inefficient transportation, rampant disease, woolen uniforms, antique munitions, spoiled food, overpriced whores, and the ineptitude, venality, and plain stupidity of the people in charge.

"That kind of talk is going to get you court marshaled," George warned.

"Who's to hear me?" the quartermaster shot back. "The powers that be are all sitting on their butts down at the Tampa Hotel. Can't say as I blame them. I'd be sitting there, too, only my butt ain't refined enough." He waved off their inquiries about Tate like a man shooing flies. "Slender silver-haired man. What kind of description is that? There's hundreds of men around here like that, and half of them are thieves and murderers." He handed Raymond a receipt. "Take this to the paymaster. He'll give you your money. Nice doing business with you."

"Where's the paymaster?" Raymond asked.

The quartermaster gestured toward town. "Up there, in all that mess. Sign's on the door."

Tampa was in chaos. Shanties lined a bewildering arrangement of sand and shell streets, lanes, alleys, and cul-de-sacs between the encampment and town. Raw pine buildings - Army offices, mercantile stores, hotels, saloons, and whorehouses - butted up against one another, clamoring for business. Mules, horses, and wagons jostled each other as their riders and drivers hollered threats and abuse, while paperboys hawked the latest headlines and dodged in and out of the traffic, seeking customers. The frantic paymaster waved off Raymond's questions with the rudeness of the overtaxed.

"Never seen him, never heard of him. Sheriff's up the road a piece. Go ask him. Here's your money. Next!"

They put the canvas moneybags in the back of Fess's wagon - the little outlaw, his arm already stinking, almost salivated when he saw them - and continued up the road to the jail.

"Yes, sir, I know Tate Rainey," the sheriff said. "I know these boys, too. Howdy, Clyde. Brad."

The two young men nodded back. "Morning, Sheriff," Brad said. "I'd shake your hand, but my arm's kind of messed up."

"I see that," the sheriff said. He grabbed Brad by the back of the shirt and dragged him out of the wagon. "We better get you in here so a doctor can look at it."

"Get a good one, Sheriff," Brad said.

"You bet I will," the sheriff said. "A quality doctor for a quality cow thief. Get down off that horse, Clyde, and stay a while." He turned to his deputy. "Put these two in a cell, Tom, then go get Doc Jones."

"Doc Jones!" Brad squawked. "He's a damn horse doctor!"

"Yeah, well, we don't have any snake doctors around here, so he'll have to do. Now you go in there with Tom and sit quiet until Jones gets here. Any noise or unseemly behavior, and I'll shoot your other arm." Brad rubbed his nose like he was trying to rub it off his face, but followed Tom without further comment. The sheriff turned back to Raymond. "Where's the old man?" he asked.

"We were hoping you'd seen him," Raymond said. He put his hand out. "I'm Raymond Pennell." He made the other introductions, ending with Beau.

The sheriff shook Beau's hand harder than he had the others. "I've heard about you," he said. "You're the man who killed Bob Rainey. I'm going to buy you a whiskey."

"As soon as Tate's dead," Beau said.

The sheriff clapped Beau on the shoulder and let go of his hand. "That sounds good to me," he said. He looked up and down the street, and shook his head. "I wish I could stop everything and help you look for him, but I can't. This town has gone slap crazy."

"We can find him ourselves," Raymond said. "If that's all right with you."

"You bet," the sheriff said. He winked at Jacob. "Consider yourselves deputized. That way, if you track the rascal down, you can go ahead and plug him. Save me the aggravation of a trial."

They left the money at the jail for safekeeping. Fess went back to look for the quartermaster, with whom he meant to dicker for another mule. The others fanned out to begin the search.

It was an interesting and eye-opening experience for them all. Jacob stood in line for hours at various fancy houses - as Dolly insisted they be called - enduring boredom, heat, and hunger to speak with the women inside. There he paid good Spanish gold to sit on the edge of rumpled beds in hot little rooms as the ladies of the night, morning, and noon waved lace fans at their bared breasts and said with lips redder than nature ever intended that they had never met Tate Rainey, so far as they knew, and did not know where he might be. One of the ladies was so young and pretty, and spoke so softly and with such elegance, that Jacob returned four times, putting a twenty-dollar gold piece in her little hand each time. It was, she told him, the easiest money she had ever earned in her whole life, from the sweetest boy she'd ever met. He'd have gone to see her a fifth time, had not Seth dragged him from her bedroom by threatening to tell their mother where all that money had gone. Thereafter, Jacob had to content himself with standing drinks for soldiers in the numerous saloons around Tampa, in between which he interviewed gamblers, bartenders and piano players. Seth, a solidly married man and staunch churchgoer, questioned the fancy women himself, but learned no more from them than Jacob had, and enjoyed himself far less.

Raymond, Dolly, Beau, and George rode and walked through streets mired with rain and mud and manure to the Tampa Hotel. There they stood in the street out front with enlisted men and tourists to gawk at its silver minarets and sparkling fountains, moving aside to allow its guests - Yankee millionaires, industry tycoons, European royalty, military officers, high government officials, and press barons - to stroll unimpeded up and down the sidewalk. Or they walked around to the servants' entrance, and watched Theodore Roosevelt put his Rough Riders through close order drills on the back lawns, their horses' hooves cutting the manicured grass to shreds while hotel patrons applauded from balconies and patios.

From the Tampa Hotel they went to Ybor City, which was another world. They looked in fragrant, high-ceilinged factories where rows of silent men rolled Cuban tobacco into expensive cigars as another man sat at an elevated podium and read to them in melodious Spanish. Raymond, remembering the lizard, led them through every church he could find, some of them austere, with bare white walls, others painted and gilded and redolent with incense. But they never saw Tate Rainey, and no one they questioned had heard of him. It was as though the earth had swallowed him up, and the pursuers began to hope, if not yet to believe, that he was dead. And on the morning of May 21, 1895, as the sun rose over the pines, Raymond, Beau, and Dolly followed the Dempsey men and Fess's wagon out of Tampa, headed home.

Chapter Thirty-Three

They traveled slowly east, suffering heat, rain, mosquitoes, and one another's company with the stolid endurance of men accustomed to such burdens. What really wore on them was the threat - or not - of Tate Rainey. Opinions were voiced on the subject, positions taken, explained, staked out, defended, abandoned. Heated arguments sprang up among them regarding the likelihood of Tate's death or survival; his condition, if alive, and possible whereabouts. Unsettled even further by these exchanges, the men would fall silent again, searching earth and sky for signs of danger, poised for an attack that did not come from an enemy they could not see, that perhaps did not even exist. There were no bets either way. Nor was there any sign of Tate. Only, every now and then, a flock of birds would rise up from the south in startled flight, or squirrels in a nearby hammock bark. Then the hackles would rise on the dogs' necks, and the riders would wonder if someone was out there, keeping pace with them.

Days were long and hot, and every afternoon brought a thunderstorm that drove them to the nearest cover. Nights, however, were sheer torture. Homesick, bored, alternately complacent and afraid, tired in mind and body, they lay down to restless sleep and bad dreams, or stood watch against a bogeyman. Each man watched alone until the night Beau spooked and fired at a noise in the woods, waking the others who emptied their revolvers into the same vicinity before thinking to ask what it was they were shooting at. It was Dolly, finally, who stomped into the woods with a palm frond torch, returning five minutes and four torches later with the bullet-blasted carcass of a raccoon. That's when they decided to watch in teams: first Fess and Jacob, then George and Seth; and finally Raymond, Beau, and Dolly, who, because there were three of them, took the long watch from midnight to dawn. It was agreed that the sentries would stay within earshot of one another, so there would be no mistaking friend for foe. As George pointed out, none of them wanted to end up like that 'coon.

It didn't take long for the last watch to fall into a pattern. George would get Raymond up, then head for his bedroll. Raymond would build up the fire and put a fresh pot of coffee on before waking Dolly and Beau. The three of them would drink a cup of coffee each - standing, not sitting, by the fire - then toss the grounds in the bushes, bank the fire, and begin their patrol, a single-file, continuous stop-and-start walk around and through whatever pine island or oak hammock they were camped in. Other than the usual night sounds - frogs, crickets, owls, and the like - and the occasional terse question and answer, these walks and pauses were conducted in silence. Come first light they returned to camp, Dolly to put wood on the fire, Raymond to start the coffee, Beau to wake the others. Night after night went by like this, and routine had become ritual, when one night Dolly broke with their short-lived tradition by sitting down to drink his coffee, then refusing to damp the fire or get up for the patrol. His stubbornness clearly infuriated Raymond, but Dolly didn't seem to care. Beau got up and walked off to relieve himself, staying away longer than necessary in hopes that the tension between the two men would die down. He was disappointed, however, because they were clearly still at odds when he returned.

They were silhouetted against the fire, Raymond standing behind Dolly and a little to the side, one hand on the tree trunk Dolly was leaning against, arm outstretched, head bent as if to listen more closely; Dolly seated on a log, facing the fire, coffee cup in his hands. Every now and then he'd nod, take a sip of coffee, nod again, shrug, but always facing the fire, never Raymond, who did not sit or move to face Dolly, but remained at his back, looking down at him. Beau lingered at the edge of camp, feeling like an intruder. Curiosity finally got the better of him, however, and he walked up to the fire. The two older men ignored him, so Beau got a cup off the wagon, filled it with coffee, and sat down. He may as well have been a piece of firewood for all the difference his presence made.

"I told you, I don't believe Tate's out there," Dolly said. "And if he was, he'd get around us easy enough. All we do is walk around in circles. He'd just wait for us to make a pass, then slip on by. We'd never know the difference. This way, I can keep an eye on all our sleeping beauties." He poured another cup of coffee, and took a reflective sip. "Anyway," he added. "We're not walking around out there because it does any good. We're doing it because you're restless and it makes you feel like you're doing something."

"So instead," Raymond said, "we're just going to sit down next to a fire that says, 'Here we are, Tate. Come and get us.' That makes a lot of sense."

"If that's what's bothering you, I'll put the fire out." Dolly kicked a log off the fire, then shoved dirt over top of the coals, making little ruts in the sand with the heel of his boot. Within moments, the flames were gone and the campsite was shrouded in darkness.

Beau blinked, and waited for his eyes to adjust. Little by little, identifiable objects came back into focus: the wagon, the low mounds that were the sleeping drovers, Raymond's long form, Dolly's bulk. He located the coffee pot in the sand. Using his handkerchief as a potholder, he grasped the handle, intending to fill his cup again.

"Take it easy on the coffee," Dolly said. "It's got to last until your daddy thinks it's safe to build another fire."

Beau let go of the handle and put the handkerchief back in his pocket. "Sorry," he said. Nobody answered him.

After a while, Dolly spoke again. "We ought to be facing outwards," he said. "In a circle, so we can see the woods."

"I don't want to sit down," Raymond said.

"Fine," Dolly said. "But you don't have to be standing over me, either."

Raymond shoved off the tree, walked around to the other side of the fire, and stopped at another tree. He kicked the needles and cones from the base of it, then set the heel of his boot about three feet up the trunk, pushed his hat back on his head, and leaned back, almost sitting on the calf of his leg. Beau watched him do all this, then looked at Dolly. He could just make out his face. The blue eyes, though, were hidden.

"What are you looking at?" Dolly asked.

"You," Beau said.

"Stop it."

Beau turned around and sat with his back to the fire. When he spoke, his words fell into the darkness in front of him, directionless and spreading, like water poured out on the ground.

"That better?" he asked.

"Some." Dolly's voice sounded distant and unformed, and Beau knew that he, too, was now facing outward. The arrangement did not lend itself to conversation, and Beau figured they'd gotten down to serious watching. He couldn't see worth a damn, so closed his eyes and listened, instead, sorting out the various sounds: an owl, a whippoorwill, a dog sighing, a horse grinding its teeth, one of the sleepers snoring. There was a thud, a mumble, and the snoring stopped. The wagon creaked in the cooling air, a coal snapped beneath the sand. Beau's attention wandered away from the sounds and settled on his own back, which was beginning to ache. He wished he'd chosen a tree to lean against, as his father and Dolly had done, and was considering getting up and doing just that when Dolly spoke.

"I wish we'd done this back in '64," Dolly said. "Then Billy and them might not have died."

The comment was stunning in its unexpectedness. Beau felt transported. Like a picture book opening before him, the stories of his childhood appeared in his mind. There, asleep on the ground, were those who died: young Billy; fatherly Ben Monroe; childlike Lucas Walker; Everett Asbell with his notched stick; Wallace Turner with his wooden woman. Behind the hickory tree, the cards in their hands, were his father, looking as he did now, only younger; Dolly, also the same, only with something like a black mop on his head, because Beau had always had difficulty imagining him with hair; and Hebron Wilkes, who was short and thin and hazy around the edges. And there, too, was the coward Vancey Adams, a pale figure gibbering at the fierce Union captain, sealing his comrades' fates with his lies. This is what the story had looked like since he first heard it, a story given to him like an heirloom, unchanging and unchangeable.

But with Dolly's statement, the picture in Beau's mind did change. Raymond, Dolly, and Hebron rearranged themselves around the ashes of a dead campfire where before there had been no fire at all, and sat facing outward as sentries where there had only been one sentry, and he a traitor. Instead of Billy being off by himself, he was with the others, within sight of his brother and protected. The Union soldiers came, there were shots fired, or not; people died, or not. Only, if they didn't die, then nothing that happened later made any sense. They had to die. The vengeance that followed, and the prize that came with it, was Beau's heritage. There was no changing it, no wishing now, after all these years, that things had been different. It was too late for that.

"Good Lord, Dolly," Raymond said. "What's that got to do with anything? Leave the past lay."

"That's hard to do," Dolly said. "It seems to just follow me around, sometimes. I can't get rid of it."

Their voices had that same empty, shapeless quality. It occurred to Beau that this was what dead people would sound like, if they could talk. The hair prickled on the back of his neck, and he looked quickly at his father and Dolly. Raymond was still sitting against the tree. All Beau could see of Dolly was his wide back, leaned forward. Probably he was resting his elbows on his knees. Beau faced around again and wiped the sweat from his forehead. He hated hot, sticky nights like this, and wished a breeze would kick up.

"There were times I thought the past would eat me alive," Dolly said. "The only thing worse was the future. I used to wake up scared that the day in front of me would be just like the one behind me. When Billy was alive, I'd wake up in the night and feel around for him, just to make sure he was there. After he died, I'd do the same thing, only he wouldn't be there, so I looked for you, instead. I didn't touch you, of course, but I looked for you. And as soon as I saw you, I'd know I wasn't alone. Then I'd go back to sleep. That's why I got so mad at Jessie back there in Debussy. I knew I couldn't stay, that I had to go, but I didn't know what I'd do in the night, without somebody there. Going to Summerlin's afterwards, I didn't sleep all that good at night. There was nobody there, you see, and I was alone. Sometimes, I was so scared of being alone that I thought about dying, on purpose-like. Only thing that kept me from it, I guess, was knowing there'd be nobody to find me. And I didn't want that, because it don't get no lonelier than that."

"Dolly..." Raymond said.

"I know you're not interested in hearing this," Dolly said. "But it's on my mind, and you'd be doing me a favor to listen. I don't think it's too much to ask, after thirty years of friendship, that you at least listen."

The quality of his voice changed, and Beau knew that Dolly had turned around and was facing the fire again. He didn't know what to do, whether to turn around himself, or keep facing the trees. He split the difference and came around halfway. From there he could see both Dolly and Raymond, who still had his back to the tree. He had an intent look on his face, as if he were indeed listening, but to something far away. Dolly sat with his hands clasped between his widespread knees, his head bowed as if praying. Beau couldn't imagine Dolly praying. He didn't know that he'd ever seen him inside a church.

"Then I came back to Debussy," Dolly said. "And there you were, sitting on the porch of that store. I was so glad to see you, I wanted to hug you, like I would have done if you'd been Billy. I didn't, of course." He shrugged. "I mean, you weren't Billy. You weren't my brother. I wasn't even sure if you were still my friend. I knew you'd go with me, because you'd given me your word, and because I knew you wanted that island for your own. I know we talked all the time about how we were going to share it, how we would settle and build it together, but I knew all along you wanted it just for yourself. I knew you'd go for yourself, if not for me or any of the others. I guess somehow I always knew that about you, that in the end, you'd always do what was best for you."

"There's no call to say such as that to me," Raymond said.

"I don't know if there is or there isn't," Dolly said. "I just know it's true. And it's all right. I don't mind that you're that way. I used to mind, but I don't anymore." He filled his coffee cup and took a sip. "Anyhow, we went to the island, and we did what we did, and we went back to Debussy and got your wife and your baby and your household goods, and we came back to the island again, and I helped you build your house. And when that was done, and we'd gathered our first herd and taken it down to Punta Gorda, and come back, then you helped me build my house on the other side of the creek. And that's where I stayed, for a long time, alone."

"I didn't mean for you to be alone," Raymond said.

"I know that," Dolly said. "You never gave it a thought. Most people wouldn't. You didn't even wonder why I spent so much time on the island. Jessie did. She wondered, but she never figured it out. But you just expected me to be there. Hell, you'd have built me a room in your house, if I'd asked for it, and if Jessie could have stood it. Only Jessie didn't like having me around. There was no place for me in her mind. Everything has its place with Jessie, and everything best be in it, but there was no place for me. I wasn't kin nor hired help nor visitor nor passer-through. I was just somebody who wouldn't leave. She tried her best to get rid of me, but I wouldn't go. My fear was stronger than her stubbornness, and that's saying something. She wanted to be happy. I wanted to survive. You and your young'uns, most especially Beau, were all I had in the world, Raymond. I wasn't about to let go."

"Jessie didn't mind as much as you think she did," Raymond said.

"You don't have to say that, Raymond," Dolly said. "I been living with the truth so long I've got callouses. You want some coffee?"

"No."

"How about you, Beau?"

"I'll have some more."

"Here." Beau held his cup out. Dolly filled it to the brim. "Do you remember the first time you had coffee?" he asked.

"I thought I'd been drinking it forever," Beau said.

"Uh, uh," Dolly said. "Your mama didn't hold with babies drinking coffee. But I fixed it for you one morning, down on the island. Put enough milk in it to turn it white, and poured some syrup in it, and stirred it up and gave it to you to drink. You squinted at me like you thought I might be playing a joke on you, then put your mouth on the cup in that cautious way you always have with new things, and took a swallow. You looked at me and grinned, smacked your lips, put both hands on the cup, and sucked that coffee down like you was a yearling calf. So I fixed you some more. By the time you'd had three cups, you were jumping around the kitchen like a flea. Lord, your mama was mad. But I didn't care. I just picked you up and carried you off for the rest of the day."

Dolly stopped and rubbed the back of his neck. "I held you every chance I got," he said. "I didn't know why for a long time, just that you felt good to me, and smelled good, especially when you were little and full of kisses and patty cakes and couldn't go far without being carried. There came a time, though, when all I could do was hold your hand, and later, I couldn't touch you at all, except to show you how to hold a whip or a gun. Finally, I lost even that, and that's when I understood that nobody ever touched me except you and Jack and the girls. In time, I lost them, too. I remember the last time Bekah hugged my neck. I'd brought her a bracelet back from Ft. Myers. It was made of baby conch shells strung together on a piece of hempen string. I put that bracelet on her wrist and she jingled it and laughed and jumped in my arms. I whirled her around the front porch like we were dancing, her laughing and giggling, until Jessie stepped up and said, 'that's enough, Bekah,' and Bekah turned red and started wiggling, so I set her down and she ran off. Nobody touched me like that again for the next eight years. If I'd seen those years coming, I believe I'd have held her a little longer."

"But I needed to be touched, and I found a way to have it. There's women in this world that'll touch you most any way you want, if you pay them enough. I never wanted anything ugly or nasty, didn't want to be hurt or shamed, any more than I already was by the asking, and never wanted to hurt or shame anybody else. I just wanted to be with a woman the way a man's supposed to be, wanted somebody beside me in the dark, somebody there when first light came. I never envied anything you had, Raymond, but that. You could have owned every cow in the world, and a thousand Walker's Islands, and sat on the board of every bank that ever was, and you'd have been no richer than me, sitting there in that empty house by myself. It was the woman by your side and the babies in your arms that made you a wealthy man, and the lack of them that made me a poor one.

"And no amount of money could make up for it. I can't tell you the gold pieces I gave in exchange for a woman's tenderness. I was drunk most of the time, and don't know how much I gave them, or how much they stole. I can't even tell you their names. They all looked the same, smelled the same, felt the same, all did the same things in pretty much the same way. I had to get drunk to be with one of them, and get drunk again when it was over, so I could forget. I didn't want it to be that way, and I guess sometimes that showed. There's this old Bible I've got. A madam gave it to me when I first started going to Tampa. Said she thought it might comfort me, give me hope. When I got it home and opened it up, the back was broken in the middle, so that it fell open every time to the Song of Songs. Every page of the Song had fingerprints on it, and smelled of cheap perfume. I'd sit there in the kitchen night after night, holding a whore's Bible and reading about a man's love for a woman and hers for him, and I'd ask God, whoever and wherever He was, to please give me a woman like that, and let me be a man like that to her. And every few months, I'd ride down to Tampa to look for her, knowing the whole time that a whorehouse wasn't the best place to be looking, but knowing, too, that there wasn't anyplace else for a man like me to look. I did that for eight years. And then I met Lupe."

Dolly put his head in his hands, his shoulders shaking. Beau thought he was crying. It wasn't until Dolly lifted his head with a little whoop that Beau realized he was laughing.

"I'm sorry," he said. "But that woman beats all I ever seen. And beautiful. After all these years, I still can't believe how beautiful she is, like she stepped right out of Solomon's life and into mine."

This really was too much for Beau. He thought of the woman Lupe had become, the heavy flesh, the shining black hair gone gray and dull-looking, the long hands coarsened, the bold gaze replaced by that remote, faintly irritated expression common to most of the mothers Beau had ever known. He could see nothing of the woman Dolly was describing, no likeness to pearly dawns or fiery sunsets, to the delicate orchids that hung in the cypress trees, to the resurrection fern growing along the oak limbs, that withered in dry spells then burst into life again, fragile and green, when the rains came, to queens and gazelle fawns and bowls of wheat and mounds of lilies. Who was this woman? Where did she live? Beau was so taken aback by Dolly's descriptions of Lupe that he turned to his father, expecting to see amusement, disdain, contempt, compassion - something, anything - to help Beau judge the meaning and value of Dolly's confession. But he could see nothing more than Raymond's temple and the line of his jaw. All else was hidden in shadow. For all Beau could tell, his father hadn't even heard what Dolly said.

Dolly's talking spell ended with the dawn, but picked up again the next night, and every night thereafter. Hour after hour, Dolly sat beside the fire and examined his life and loves and losses, ranging back and forth across thirty-odd years of living like a man rummaging through a trunk, holding up for inspection images and memories Beau had forgotten, or never known, or misunderstood, or ignored because they were so ordinary, so unremarkable, or so long ago, the everyday transformed by Dolly's telling into something beautiful and terrible and strange. And through it all, though Dolly often spoke his name, and Beau kept looking to him for some kind of reaction or response, Raymond stood alone, his face turned toward the darkness, away from the fire, and Dolly.

Raymond never knew that Beau was looking at him, either that first night, or the nights that followed. He was too engrossed in what Dolly was saying. Weeks later, he would remember a man he'd met one time, who said he'd been hit on the head and spent five years lying unconscious on a bed. When he finally came to, he didn't know who he was, or where he was, or where he'd been. But he sure knew he'd been somewhere. "I went places I can't describe to you," he told Raymond. "Places like you never seen in your life. I don't remember them now. Only that there was some I wish I could go back to, and others I don't ever want to see again. But every one of them was more real than where I am right now." That's how Raymond felt once Dolly started talking: that he'd returned to a past he'd never known before, where everything he saw was more real than here and now, and another's account more accurate than Raymond's own experience. Perhaps he was just tired, or the watch was too long, or maybe it was the way the stars caught in the treetops, and the air stirred and the frogs sang and the whippoorwills cried and the crickets chirped in the grass. Or maybe he was just worn out with worrying, or Dolly had caught him off-guard, and he just never recovered his balance. Whatever happened, Raymond Pennell went somewhere that night, and didn't come back until the world within and around him had been shattered beyond all hope of restoration.

Nothing bad happened, at first. Dolly's voice drifted past Raymond as if in a dream, conjuring memories that rose up in his mind like fireflies through the branches of the pine trees. These memories winked on and off, each one slow enough to catch and study, were it not for the others appearing nearby, distracting him. Each one was so vivid that it captured his entire attention, piercing him with powerful emotions he could never immediately identify: grief, perhaps, or desire, or yearning, or sorrow, or wonder, or overwhelming gratitude. There was a continuous sense of loss that he was so slow to recognize these visitors, which kept fading beyond recognition, yet lingered in his mind the way light remains in the eye when one moves suddenly out of bright sunlight into a dark room. These emotions - which presented themselves not just as qualities of mental light that seemed to affect his perceptions, but as feelings he actually experienced in his body - accompanied images that followed so quickly one on another that he could not tell if what he saw and felt were the dying light and feelings of the image he had just abandoned, or the expanding light and feelings of the one immediately before him.

There were so many images, all very clear, with distinct lines and bright colors, and each of them evoked these sensory responses, as though they were stored, not just in Raymond's mind, but in his flesh, as well. He heard the raucous laughter of the other cow hunters as Billy wet his pants, felt Vancey's nose crumble under his fist, looked square and unflinching into Dolly's cobalt blue eyes, and shook Ben Monroe's hand when the fight was over. He heard Lucas Walker's nightmare cries, held Dolly's face in the dirt, saw the blood well up in Billy's mouth, smelled the sweat-soaked belly of the chestnut horse as it jumped the fallen hickory tree, heard the flies buzz as they crawled on the bodies in the clearing. The bloody white shards of Vancey's knee gleamed in front of him, Vancey's body jerked at the end of the rope, and the bay mare rose beneath him and carried him across Deep Creek while Dolly's anguished cry of loss echoed behind him. The flesh of Jessie's thighs jerked against his hands and her screams followed him into the kitchen as she labored with Jack. His throat burned with the fiery taste of Red Rainey's whiskey, and he smelled again as if for the first time the scent of wild limes blooming on Walker's Island. His blood raced with excitement, his belly growled with hunger, his hands held rifles and reins and children and hammers and horses. Sorrow filled him, confusion, anger, exultation, expectation, and the bone-deep satisfaction of good work done well. Dolly's words fell like yarn from a bobbin, shuttled back and forth between him and Raymond, spun their past into unexpected patterns, the strands of his and Dolly's lives woven together in a rough, sturdy cloth bordered by Walker's Island and Raymond's marriage. And everything was one piece for a long time in Raymond's mind, until he heard Dolly's pain, and faced its source, and acknowledged, finally, what he was saying.

This understanding came slowly to Raymond. He had to get past indignation first, then disbelief. Only then did he let himself remember, with that shock of recognition peculiar to dreams, things he would have sworn he'd never seen or heard before, that had gone on for years: Dolly standing like a beggar at Raymond's door; Dolly wandering the docks on Tampa Bay, seeking gifts to delight Raymond's children; Dolly sitting alone in his empty kitchen, reading the Song of Songs by candlelight; Dolly yearning for respect from Beau, kindness from Jessie, affection from their children, comfort from whores, forgetfulness from whiskey and carousing and sleep. This, Raymond had to finally admit, was the other side of Deep Creek. Dolly's revelations were shocking, not because of Raymond's ignorance, but because of his knowledge: that he'd willfully and deliberately left Dolly standing on the threshold of his life for all those years, that he'd be standing there yet, were it not for Lupe.

Sweet Lupe, Dolly called her, sweeter than honey, even than the honeycomb. He'd held the golden flesh of his young wife in his hands like ripe fruit and tasted her, warm and satisfying, with his mouth. Sweet Lupe, generous and luxuriant, as unpredictable as summer weather. She cooked his meals and washed his clothes and cleaned his house, flew in anger and laughed with abandon, threw tantrums and pot lids and pillows, cursed like a sailor and sang like one, too, and held Dolly in her arms without reluctance or complaint, her body pleasure and comfort and healing, all at once. Bit by bit, the loneliness ebbed out of him, and the anger, and the fear. And then Lupe caught a baby inside.

If Lupe was a gift beyond all hope, a baby was a gift beyond all comprehension. Dolly watched with wonder as it grew, laying his face on Lupe's satin belly, grown round and taut as a muskmelon, to feel it roll and kick and butt against his cheek. And when her time came, Dolly sent for no midwife, but knelt between his wife's legs and received into his own hands the body of his newborn son, and felt what God must have felt when He formed Adam out of the dust, the same fierce, exultant, all-consuming love.

"And it was right then," Dolly said quietly, "when everything I'd ever wanted was there in my hands, that I started thinking about Vancey and what we'd done to him."

That comment broke the spell. Raymond came back to the present like a man swimming up out of deep water. The gray light of dawn was rising on the last day of their journey, and Dolly's trailing voice mingled in Raymond's awareness with the twittering of the birds as they awoke from their night's rest. Raymond yawned and rubbed his face and smiled to himself. Dolly had talked the last few nights like a man drunk on moonshine, so full of life and living he'd made Raymond feel stingy and prissy and small. It felt good to Raymond to step back into a more familiar way of seeing things, of being the wiser of the two, the one who took careful thought and planned ahead and kept his mind on the business at hand, who didn't have foolish notions about ghosts or curses or whether somebody was buried on his back or his face down in the mud. He turned around to start the fire. Dolly was looking at him.

"You remember Vancey," Dolly said.

Raymond picked up a log and tossed it on the fire. "Yes," he said. "A bully, a coward, and a murderer. What about him?"

"We hanged him," Dolly said.

"We could have shot him," Raymond said. "Or drowned him, or burned him at the stake, or tied him up and fed him to the 'gators. I don't see what was so special about hanging."

"It wasn't how we killed him," Dolly said. "It was that we killed him. You and me. On purpose."

"That's what we went there for," Raymond said. "To make it up to Billy and Ben and the rest of them, as best we could. It seemed right then, and it still seems right."

"The island was supposed to be a safe place," Dolly said. "For all of us."

"Vancey didn't deserve safety," Raymond said. "He ruined that for himself."

"But that was never part of it," Dolly said. "Ben never said we had to deserve it or earn it or anything like that. Just that if we made it there, if we found it, we would be safe. That's what Ben said, what he promised. That's what the island did. It kept whoever went there safe. That's why Vancey went there, and why he didn't leave."

"I wasn't thinking about that at the time," Raymond said.

"Yes, you were," Dolly said. "It's why you took so long to put that rope around his neck, and why I wanted you to do it, because I'd lost Billy and you had Jessie and a baby and a picture in your head of what you wanted out of life and how to get it, and I had nothing. And when you put that rope on Vancey, I knew you'd done something you couldn't walk away from or fix, and somehow, that made you just like me, even if you didn't know it. Whatever Vancey said to you, I wish I'd said it, because it made you do something bad, and I was glad. I'd have done more than that, pulled you in even deeper, if I'd known how. I tried, too. You know that horse you rode in the race, the one I brought you from Summerlin's?"

"Yes."

"She wasn't as good as the one I kept for myself. She wasn't as fast or as smart. That's why I gave her to you, so I'd have a good horse and you'd have a sorry one. That's why I thought a horse race was such a fine contest. I thought I'd win it. I didn't count on the bay mare having more heart, that when it came time to jump the creek, she would risk it and my horse would balk."

Raymond felt like the ground had opened up in front of him. He took a step backwards to get away from the hole, and backed right into a pine tree. But he couldn't get away from Dolly. Those blue eyes held him like chains. Worse still, he'd gotten up and was walking toward him, still talking, still telling Raymond things he didn't want to know, and could have gone the whole rest of his life without hearing.

"I bet you don't remember this," Dolly said. "But one day, you were standing in one of those big holes we dug for the pilings, and thinking about Vancey's grave - I know, because I was thinking about the same thing - and you asked me if I thought he could poison the island somehow, from down there under the ground. You remember that? I started to say, hell yes, he can do anything he wants to, that a curse like the one he made don't just up and go away. But it dawned on me right then, that I was the one in trouble if he came back, because you would always come out on top, no matter what happened, but I'd be lost to the end of my days."

"So I told you not to fret, and put that silly thinking behind me, and turned the whole sorry mess into a bedtime story about heroes and villains, and told it to Beau in such a way that he grew up believing that you and me were both better men than we are, and when he got too old for stories, I put them away like worn out toys and didn't think about Vancey again, or what we'd done to him, for years and years."

"He can't hurt us," Raymond said. "No matter what we did, Vancey can't hurt us."

"I know that's what you tell yourself," Dolly said. "I told myself the same thing after Quincey was born. 'Look at Raymond,' I'd say to myself. 'His land has prospered and his babies have lived and his wife is faithful and keeps a clean house. It's all worked out for him and it's working out for me and even if something goes wrong, it won't be about Vancey. It'll be because there's them that's naturally lucky and them that's not, and Raymond's the first kind and I'm the second, only now I'm telling you there's more to it than that."

Dolly took another step toward Raymond, his face worn and gray in the pale dawn light. But Raymond couldn't bear his gaze any longer. What Dolly had just said was too big, too shocking. Raymond walked over to the wagon and pulled out the coffee grinder. He filled the hopper with beans and turned the handle as hard and fast as he could, hoping that Dolly would shut his mouth, or that the noise of the grinder would drown him out. But Dolly's voice carried too well for that.

"I know you can hear me, so you listen to this. Something bad is fixing to happen, because what we did to Vancey was wrong, and it's coming back to us, one way or another. Whatever you believe about the island protecting you is a lie. It's just a piece of dirt, and we didn't betray a piece of dirt. We betrayed ourselves and each other. And nobody gets away with that. Nobody."

Raymond and Dolly didn't speak to one another the rest of the day. By four o'clock in the afternoon, the riders could see the cypress on the south end of Walker's Island, and the outskirts of Black Hammock to the northeast. And still there was no sign of Tate. Safety was almost close enough to touch, and the usual afternoon thunderstorm was on its way. Jaundiced sunlight tinted the world a dull yellow. The air was thick, sulfurous, hard to breathe. Another mile and they'd reach the hammock; a quarter mile further still, and they'd be standing at the south crossing. The Pennell and Baxter horses pulled at the bit and whickered at the scent of familiar pasture. Given their heads, they'd have made it home before the first drop of rain fell. But the wagon was as slow as ever, lurching over bull wallows and grass tussocks, and could not be left behind.

So they continued as they'd begun, riding in time with the mules as the storm bore down upon them in a boil of violet and black. The bruised sky lit with a bolt of brilliant white lightning. Thunder shook the ground. St. Elmo's fire rolled around the brim of George's hat in balls of blue flame the size of silver dollars. Birds flailed against the rising wind, then surrendered to it and swept past them, over the hammock and out of sight. Dolly reined his horse in and held a hand up. The others, hats pulled down hard to keep them from blowing away, came to a stop around him.

"It's coming a bad one," he said. "Y'all best come to my house and get out of it."

"I was thinking the same thing," George said.

"Me and Beau are going to the island," Raymond said. "It's safer there."

"That's what Vancey thought," Dolly said.

Raymond's head jerked like he'd been slapped. George frowned, clearly aggravated.

"I don't know what you two are talking about," he said. "But we're fixing to get cooked."

"I'm going to the island," Raymond said. "And Beau is coming with me."

"Fine," Dolly said. He reined his horse around to the east and spoke to Fess. "Tell Lupe I'll be home in time for supper."

"You're crazy," Fess said. "I'd take Tate on before I'd face this storm. C'mon, boys and girls, we're going to Dolly's." He slapped the mules with the lines, and they jerked forward into motion.

"We're with you, Fess," George said. "Seth. Jacob. Let's go." He spurred his horse forward, and his sons followed him. Lightning cracked so close the men could smell it. St. Elmo's fire danced blue-white from mule to mule, and rolled down their backs in glittering orbs. It flickered between the horses' ears and spun the rowels on Dolly's spurs. A raindrop as big as a baby's fist struck the corner of Raymond's mouth. Another hit Beau's neck, another Dolly's jaw, then there were too many to count, running greasily off their soiled ponchos and over their boots. Lightning branched with an ear-splitting crack. Thunder boomed. The wagon kept rolling away, the Dempsey men beside it. Raymond, Beau, and Dolly faced each other in a tight circle, yelling above the storm.

"What are we waiting on?" Dolly shouted. "Let's go to the island."

"Not you," Raymond said.

"What do you mean, not me?" Dolly asked.

"I don't want your company," Raymond said.

"Too bad," Dolly said. "I'm coming anyway. That's what friends are for."

Raymond leaned forward in the saddle, both hands on the cantle, and squinted at Dolly from under his hat. "You've never been anything but trouble," he said. "I don't want your friendship. I don't want you anywhere near me, or my family, or the island. You got that?"

Dark as it was, Beau could see the flush come up on Dolly's face. Beau himself felt such shame at his father's words that he didn't know what to do with his eyes.

"You don't mean that," Dolly said.

"I mean every word of it," Raymond said. "Now get the hell away from me, and take your lies and daydreams along with you, and your careless ways and foolish notions. I should have let you die with your brother like you wanted to."

"Daddy, what are you doing?" Beau cried.

"You stay out of things you don't understand," Raymond said. But his eyes had never left Dolly, and when he spoke again, the loathing in his voice was sheer poison. "I'm going now. You follow me, and I swear I'll shoot you down. Then you won't have to worry about Tate or Vancey, either one." He jerked the mare around, popped her with his spurs, and struck a lope toward the south crossing.

Dolly stared after him with his mouth half-open. It made him look stupid, and Beau felt sorry for him. Worse yet, the water in his eyes was more than rain. Beau had never seen Dolly cry in his life, and wasn't about to watch now. He tugged the brim of his hat in farewell, as he would for an acquaintance or a stranger, and followed Raymond. He looked back just one time. Dolly had turned north, and was headed for Black Hammock and Lupe.

Chapter Thirty-Four

The storm echoed in the hammock as in a cavern. Treetops thrashed and swayed and lightning cast shadows across the path. Leaves and twigs and Spanish moss pressed close. The passage of a body would sound like wind rustling through the fox grape vines, the crack of a rifle like a branch breaking. But Raymond kept going, the mare splashing through water up to her fetlocks. The light changed from blue-green to pewter. Then the oaks and cabbage palms were behind him, and he could see clearly for the first time. Deep Creek had disappeared. There was nothing but water.

Beau rode up beside him. "I know you're not thinking about swimming that," he said.

"I might be," Raymond said.

"Let's go back to Dolly's," Beau said.

"Don't talk to me about him," Raymond said.

"I don't understand what happened back there."

"It doesn't concern you."

A tree limb swept past, a tin can stuck to one branch. Raymond nudged the bay mare forward.

"What are you doing?" Beau asked.

"I want to know where the edge is."

"Why? What difference does it make?"

"I just want to know where it is."

"It's too dangerous," Beau said. "Look how fast that water's traveling."

Raymond popped the mare with his spurs. She took three steps, then stopped. "C'mon, horse," he snapped.

In his mind was a map of the south crossing, with its narrow path and steep sides. The creek itself was roughly fifteen feet across at this point, measuring from the cypress tree just ahead to the opposite bank. The mare could walk up even with that tree and still be on solid ground. Beau was ranting behind him, his voice joining the other sounds in Raymond's ears: the creek rushing past, wind, thunder, rain popping on the water like hot grease. But in his mind, everything was quiet. This was Deep Creek. On the other side was Walker's Island. Nothing here would hurt him. He nudged the mare again, gentling her with voice and hands. She stumbled - a cypress knee, or a root. Two more steps brought her head nearly even with the tree. She stopped again. Water surged over Raymond's knees. He figured they were standing some two or three feet from the edge of the creek. Across the current, he could see a narrow stream cutting through the trees: the submerged game trail. Raymond eyed the distance from the cypress tree to that stream, and addressed himself to the mare.

"You could swim across if you tried," he said. "Your great grandma would have done it on a dare." The mare took a step backward.

"Coward," Raymond said.

He laid a rein against her neck. But even as the two of them turned, the cypress tree on their right began to shrink. It took Raymond a full second to realize the creek bank was caving in. The mare rose up on her hind legs and twisted around. For a moment she hung in the air, weightless over deep water. Then Raymond felt her weight return and the two of them were falling upside down through the sky.

The water was dark and cold and deep. The mare writhed as if her back were broken, and Raymond could not get away from her. He kicked free of the stirrups, and felt the creek bed under his feet. The mare lurched upwards. She was swimming. Raymond caught a stirrup with both hands and held on. The horse crawled up the bank on her knees then staggered to her feet, dragging Raymond with her to level ground. She stood spraddle-legged above him, his hands still clenched on the stirrup. Finger by finger, Raymond let go of the stirrup. Creek water filled his mouth. Legs appeared in front of him.

"Daddy?"

"Help me," he whispered.

A hand grabbed his arm and half-lifted, half-dragged him to his feet. Raymond hung both arms across the saddle and rested his head on the seat. He could feel the mare trembling through the leather. His own legs were shaking so bad he could hardly stand on them, and his hand, when he took up the reins, fluttered in her mane. But when he tried to put his leg in the stirrup, he found he couldn't lift his leg high enough. He tried again. It was no use. All he could do was hold onto the saddle, and quiver. "Help me up," he said. The act of speaking left him breathless, and he rested his head on the saddle again.

"What?" Beau asked.

Listen, Raymond wanted to say. Pay attention. Don't be stupid. But he didn't have enough breath for all that. He had to ration it, so it would be there for the important words, the words that were absolutely necessary. "Help me up," he said again, louder this time.

"Let me take you back to Dolly's," Beau said.

Raymond waited, then said it again. "Help me up."

Beau shoved him into the saddle. Raymond concentrated on staying in the saddle. If he fell off, Beau would take him to the Baxters', or leave him on the ground and go there for help.

"Where are we going?" Beau asked.

"To the bridge," Raymond said.

"Why?" Beau asked. "We won't be able to cross there, either."

Raymond pressed the mare with his knees, the muscles in his thighs spasming. She took two steps, then gave so hard on her left back leg that Raymond thought she might fall. He figured she must be hurt pretty bad. He wouldn't get down to see how bad, though. It was too hard to get back up, and he was too tired. It didn't matter, anyway. He couldn't walk - his legs were jelly - so she had to carry him.

"Get up, girl," he whispered. Unbelievably, she kept walking. Beau passed them, his horse moving smooth and easy. Raymond didn't care. He only cared that the bay mare was moving, however slowly and with whatever pain, toward the bridge to Walker's Island.

Beau navigated slowly down the hidden path, shoving himself away from tree trunks and fending off grape vines as his horse picked its way between the lines of underbrush. Every now and then, he looked back at his father. Lightning still flickered like silver on Raymond's drawn face, but when it receded, his features remained visible. The rain had slackened, the vibrating booms of thunder were further off, the wind had died down. The storm was passing. Water was still high in the hammock, but Beau knew from experience that it would recede quickly. Within the hour, probably, the path would be exposed. Before long, he could see the middle crossing through the trees. All that showed were the handrails.

"Look yonder," Beau said. "The bridge is under water. We can't use it." His voice was big in the silence of the world after the rain. The weird yellow light that had preceded the storm returned, faded, then disappeared completely. The sun came out. It sparkled on the storm waters, dirty and full of debris, that raced over the bridge. The wind rustled in the branches of the oak. Raindrops pattered and thrummed on cabbage palms and palmetto fronds with every gust. Beau looked back at his father. Raymond was peering through the trees at the bridge.

"Maybe we can use it," he said. "We'll wait and see."

"The foundations are liable to be washed out," Beau said. "If getting to the island is that important to you, let's just go on to the north crossing. It won't take much longer."

"All right," Raymond said. "We can do that."

"You're sure you don't want to go back to Dolly's?"

"I'm sure."

Beau watched him a moment, hoping he would change his mind. Then he cussed his father's stubbornness under his breath, and continued on to the bridge.

Raymond saw Beau's lips move, and guessed what he was saying. He didn't care what Beau thought of him right now. He didn't even have the strength to concern himself with the whereabouts of Tate Rainey. Right now, he had enough to do to stay upright in the saddle, knowing he still had to make it back to Walker's Island. Even the north crossing would be high in water like this, and he and the mare both had to conserve their strength to make it across. Raymond bowed his head - it was too heavy to hold up, anyway - and spoke again to the bay mare.

"There's all kinds of races to run," he said. "This one here is yours and mine." The mare jerked an ear back when he spoke. Steam rose from her neck. Raymond laid his hand on her shoulder. It was hot, and slick with rain and sweat.

"You're a good horse," he said. "I'm sorry if I ever said otherwise." The bay mare waggled an ear back and forth, and seemed to move a little easier. It comforted Raymond that she was listening. He was silent for a moment, then shared something else with her.

"That back there was an otter den washing out, most likely." Otters dug holes up under the tree roots, above the high water mark. It was not unusual for the banks to give out at these points, especially in fast water. That one had given way directly beneath Raymond and the mare, nearly killing them both, was just a coincidence. There was no other explanation. Dolly, Raymond knew, would blame it on Vancey Adams.

"Vancey's like the devil," Raymond said. "He catches hell for a lot that ain't his fault." The mare bobbed her head, and Raymond took it for agreement. "Besides," he added. "If it was Vancey, he'd have gone ahead and killed us. It'll probably grieve the Baxters that such didn't happen." He paused, then added, "And it couldn't have been Tate, because he couldn't know we'd ride out to that spot." The thought crossed Raymond's mind that Dolly, Tate, and Vancey all three would assume Raymond would have more sense, but he pushed it aside. "It had to have been an otter den," he said. Comforted by the logic of his own thinking, Raymond went to shove his hat back on his head for emphasis. It wasn't there. "My hat's gone," he said.

He tried twisting around to look back the way he'd come, but couldn't. The muscles in his neck were too stiff. He gave up, and faced forward again. The movement had caused a sharp pain between his shoulder blades, and his hip was aching. Tonight would find him in bed with a sciatica attack. But Raymond was used to physical discomfort. What worried him now was his hat. He never went anywhere without it, and never took it off except in the house and in church. He even wore it to the outhouse, along with his boots. He'd as soon ride around in his birthday suit as ride without his hat. Raymond wondered what else was missing. He patted his pockets and around the saddle, and discovered he still owned a pocketknife, but his rope and saddlebags were gone, along with the leather tie downs that had held them on the saddle. He reached down to grasp the butt of his rifle, and closed his hand on air. He looked down at the scabbard. It was empty.

Raymond raised his eyes to the path ahead of him, as if to inquire of someone how this could be. Perhaps it was merely the loss of the gun, but something felt seriously different, out of kilter. It wasn't the weather, though he noticed that it was quickly changing. Patches of blue showed through the storm clouds, and the wind was almost gone. The cloying heat of summer was returning, wisps of steam already rising off the receding water. The sunlight was so bright it hurt his eyes. The only thing missing was bird song. Birds usually filled the hammock with their calls after a rain, but now they were quiet. The whole hammock was quiet, except for the squirrels barking frantically across the creek.

"Something's over there," Raymond said. "It's got them squirrels all upset."

Sweat trickled down his back and into the waistband of his britches. Leaving one hand on the saddle horn, he reached up with the other and unbuttoned his collar, still searching for trouble. Beau was ahead of him, sitting motionless on his horse where the trail intersected the path from Dolly's house to the bridge. He was facing the bridge, and seemed to be staring at something on the other side of it. Raymond waved. "Hey, Beau," he yelled. "What is it?"

Beau didn't answer or show that he'd heard. Whatever he was looking at had his full attention. Maybe the bridge was going out, Raymond thought. If so, then all Beau had to do was keep riding north. There was no call for him to just sit there like that. Raymond peered through the trees on both sides of the creek. The path was clear in both directions as far as he could see. Everything appeared to be all right. But the squirrels would not stop barking, and the expression on Beau's face was not a good one. He looked like someone seeing a ghost, or staring down the barrel of a gun.

Raymond cursed his lost rifle and kicked the bay mare. She broke into a clumsy, lopsided trot. He kicked her again, gouging her sides with his spurs, and she struggled into a lope, her left hind leg giving way beneath her each time it hit the ground. The resulting gait threw Raymond from side to side, banging him into trees and nearly slinging him out of the saddle. To his left, the hammock was dark and full of steam. To his right, broken in his field of vision by trees, were the creek, the bridge, and the path leading to his and Jessie's house. They were all empty, as far as Raymond could see. Beau was just ahead of him now, so still he seemed frozen in the saddle.

"Beau!" Raymond yelled. "Beau!"

Beau did not answer, but his hand came slowly up, palm out in front of him as if in warning or supplication. Raymond held tight with both hands to the saddle horn and stared through the trees at the bridge until his eyes hurt, while the squirrels barked and scolded and chattered, and jumped from tree to tree with alarm. Then the squirrels on the west side of the creek began barking as well. Raymond, his body in agony from the joint-wrenching motion of the mare's broken stride, tried to see the west end of the path, but couldn't because of the trees. He couldn't see anything but Beau, and couldn't hear anything but his own wheezing, whimpering breath. And then, coming down the path toward the bridge, Raymond finally saw what Beau was looking at.

The earth felt heavy and soft after the fury of the storm, and it made Beau sleepy. The light around him still pulsed now and then with distant lightning, and the air quivered with the growl of departing thunder, but all that truly remained was water. It hung in the air and dripped from the trees. It glistened in hoary veils of Spanish moss and pooled in orchids and ferns. Leaves and fronds and bark were slick and silvery with it in the blue-green light. Tendrils of steam rose slowly from the ground, and seeped out from underneath piles of leafy trash with a rich, fecund odor. Soon both riders and horses would be wet all over again, basted like roasting chickens in an oven. Still, the heat felt good at the moment, like a warm, wet blanket, and Beau's head was nodding on his chest by the time he reached the bridge. A moment later he was almost thrown to the ground when his horse shied to the left. It came to a complete standstill, legs stiff, blowing, ears pricked toward the crossing. Then it gave a long, rattling snort and took a step back. Beau righted himself in the saddle and followed the horse's gaze, past the bridge, up the path that led into the hammock on Walker's Island.

A figure had stepped out of the hammock and onto the path leading to the bridge. It wore black, sodden clothes, and a ragged woolen poncho over its shoulders. Long silver hair plastered its head and stuck to a skull-thin face the dead white of a toadstool. The thing had one good leg, while the other stuck out like a stick of wood. There was a wound in it, right above the knee. The wrapping had come off the wound and the bone showed through, jagged and gray. The stench of rotten flesh carried on the breeze. Under its left arm, the figure held a crutch made from a forked tree branch. Its right arm hung down by its side.

It came down the path toward the bridge, dragging its bad leg. It did not look at the ground, but at Beau, staring at him with black eyes like dead coals. Water ran down its face and into the beard that silvered its gaunt chin and cheeks. Steam swirled around its feet and legs as it came down the path, humping and lurching, soundless except for an occasional grunt as of pain or concentration. As it approached, it raised a stiff black arm and pointed at Beau. The arm jiggled with each step, then stiffened again, but always returned to Beau.

Beau's attention was fully on the thing coming down the path. But he wanted someone to tell him what it was and why it was pointing at him, singling him out, and why it was on the island. Tate, the man they'd all been waiting for, was not supposed to be on the island. Beau had envisioned him everywhere and anywhere but there. But this thing was not Tate. It was not even a man. It was a monster. He thought he heard someone call his name, but could not turn his head to answer. He could not look anywhere but at the thing on the path. Indeed, the whole hammock seemed focused on it. Through the cloying thickness of the steam and the heat, the trees and vines bore down as though straining to speak, to say the name of the thing on the path, the name that had come to them from the roots of the hanging tree, that had seeped through the dirt and under the creek and up through the sap of the witnesses in the hammock. Other voices called Beau's name and barked commands, told him to run, to stay, to take cover, to break it. He wanted them to make up their minds and turned to tell them so. His father and Dolly were riding side by side down the path to the bridge, both of them shouting at him. Then there was only Dolly, the wooden grip of a cow whip in his right hand. He dropped the grip to his side, swept it along the flank of his horse to its hip, brought it up over his head, then flipped it sharply forward from the wrist, the whip following in a straight, black, hissing line past Dolly's hat and the horse's ear, straight for Beau. Beau tried to get away, and turned in the saddle to charge the bridge, only to see the monster before him dissolve into a man with a shotgun, its muzzle rising from the ground to point at Beau. Then the whip wrapped around his shoulders and jerked him off his horse. The ground rose to meet him, slamming into his shoulder and side with a force that knocked the wind out of Beau's lungs and made his mouth gape soundlessly, helplessly open and shut like that of a landed fish. Even then, all he could think of was the way the man had smiled when he pulled the trigger.

Raymond, flung back and forth on the laboring mare, stared in horror at the rotting scarecrow making its tortured way down the path, at the filthy poncho that covered its arms and chest, and the dirty bone sticking out of the injured leg where a knee should have been. The face was a skull with skin and beard stuck to it, and hair fell to its shoulders in greasy gray ropes. It held a shotgun in its right hand that rose and fell with each step, dipping and swaying as if following a trail through the air.

"Vancey," Raymond whispered. As if it had read his mind and found the contents amusing, the thing smiled. Only then did Raymond recognize Tate Rainey. "Move, Beau!" he screamed. But Beau just sat there on his horse, his eyes as wide as a child's, staring at Tate.

The muffled hoof beats of a running horse pounded down the path leading from the Baxter place, and Dolly rode up beside Raymond as the bay mare turned the corner. For a moment they were close enough to touch, then Dolly was past him, his whip trailing through the air as Tate raised the shotgun and fired.

Raymond sawed on the reins but the mare could not stop. She gained the bridge just as Tate fired a second time. The blast caught the mare square in the chest, and she went down on her face and knees, skidding along the boards in a spray of water. Then she fell over on her left side, pinning Raymond to the bridge. She grunted a few times, and her legs paddled hard as if she were still trying to run, until they slowed, and finally came to rest.

Chapter Thirty-Five

Raymond was not particularly uncomfortable. Creek water was running past his ear, but he was not drowning, and his leg didn't hurt. He was in an awkward position, though, and his left leg was caught under the horse. He heard a clicking noise, and got up on his elbow to see what it was. Tate was standing on the island side of the bridge, talking to himself. Breathing heavily, he pried the spent shells out of the shotgun, then thumbed two more into the breech. He snapped it shut and pointed it at Raymond.

"Your turn, Pennell," he said. The end of the shotgun wandered away, then came back. Tate smelled like rotten meat. Bone showed through his trouser leg. Raymond gagged. Tate dragged his leg through the water until his shattered knee was touching Raymond's cheek. "You like that smell?" he asked.

Raymond turned his head. Leaning against the handrail on the other end of the bridge, a rifle in the crook of his arm, was Dolly. Behind him, stretched out on the ground but clearly alive, was Beau. Raymond opened his mouth to speak. Beau put a finger to his lips. Raymond closed his mouth. Something poked the nape of his neck. He rolled his head over again, and found himself staring at the shotgun. Tate tapped his chin with the barrel.

"Open your mouth," he said.

Raymond clamped his mouth shut and shook his head.

"Open your mouth," Tate said. He opened his mouth so wide the molars showed, then shut it again. "Like that. So I can break your teeth."

Raymond wondered if Tate had mistaken him for Beau, or if he just had a grudge against anybody with teeth.

"C'mon," Tate said. "Show me your teeth."

"Hey, Tate," Dolly said.

Tate looked up with an irritated expression. "What is it, Baxter?" he asked.

"This," Dolly said. The rifle cracked. Tate spun around, the shotgun flying from his grasp. He fell to his hands and knees on the bridge, a hole in his back where the bullet had come out. He crawled toward the shotgun, then pitched forward and lay still.

Raymond felt dizzy. He put his head down and listened to the creek. Water splashed beside him. Dolly sat down on the mare. He seemed to have something on his mind.

"He's dead," Raymond said.

"Yes," Dolly said.

"It's Tate. Not Vancey."

"He was on the island."

Raymond couldn't argue with that. "I guess we were both right," he said. He thought that Dolly would notice his predicament and offer to help him. When that didn't happen, he thought maybe Dolly was waiting on an apology. It took him a while to work up to it, but his leg started cramping, and that moved things along.

"I reckon I should have stayed with you," he said. "Maybe we could have avoided some of this."

"Maybe," Dolly said.

"It doesn't matter," Raymond said. "I mean, everything's turned out all right. That's all that really matters." Dolly looked at him, but didn't say anything. Raymond decided he owed Dolly more than an apology. "You saved my life," he said. "And Beau's, too." Dolly, still silent, watched Raymond.

"It was generous of you, considering the way I acted back yonder." Raymond pointed with his chin in the general direction of the prairie. "I don't know what got into me."

"I said some things," Dolly said.

Raymond was glad to hear Dolly take some responsibility. It made it easier to shoulder his own. "I made a mess of things. Lost my rifle at the south crossing. My hat, too. I fell in, if you can believe that."

"It's all right," Dolly said.

"Hell, it ain't all right, neither," Raymond said, irritated. "I damn near drowned." He got up on his elbow again, and slapped Dolly on the shin. "Help me out from under this horse. You ain't even noticed that I'm stuck."

Dolly was sitting up very straight, the rifle across his knees. With both hands, he shoved the gun slowly off his lap. It fell in the water. Raymond fished around for it, picked it up, and propped it against the mare's belly. "What'd you do that for?" he demanded.

"It's heavy," Dolly said.

"You beat all I ever seen," Raymond said. "Help me out from under this horse."

"No," Dolly said.

"Go to hell," Raymond said. He looked around for Beau, but couldn't see him. "Hey, Beau!" he called. "What are you doing?"

"Catching these horses," Beau said.

"Hurry up," Raymond said. "My leg is caught."

"I'm going as fast as I can," Beau said. "Get Dolly to help you."

"Damn the both of you," Raymond muttered. He pushed against the saddle with his free foot and pulled on the trapped one, and was gratified to feel it move a couple of inches. It was hard work, especially with Dolly sitting on the horse. Raymond didn't appreciate his attitude one bit.

"Your extra two hundred pounds on my leg ain't helping any," he said.

"I'm shot," Dolly said.

Raymond stared at him. The water suddenly felt a lot colder. "Where?" he asked.

Dolly unbuttoned his shirt and pulled it open. A loop of filmy blue intestine the size of Raymond's thumb was poking out through a hole in his belly. The skin at the top of the hole was turning purple; the skin below it was already black. Around the wound were smaller holes, some with the dull gray sheen of a pellet in them. Stunned, Raymond watched as a thin drizzle of blood leaked past the intestine and ran down into Dolly's waistband. He looked from the wound into Dolly's eyes. He didn't think he'd ever seen them so blue, and they were watching Raymond very intently.

"Is it bad?" Dolly asked.

"Yes," Raymond said.

"I thought so," Dolly said. He pulled his shirt back over the wound, then rested his hands, palms down, on his thighs. He looked patient and resigned, like an old man waiting for a train.

Raymond's hands were twitching. He tried holding them together, but that just made his arms shake. Then the shaking was all the way through him, into his organs and veins and bones. Even his throat was trembling.

"C'mon, Beau," he said.

"Just a minute," Beau said.

"We ain't got a minute," Raymond muttered. He rolled over on his belly, wincing as his leg twisted. He grabbed the side of the bridge with both hands, put his other foot back on the saddle, and jerked until his leg came free. He pulled himself upright using the handrails, and leaned there for a moment, trying to think. Finally, he turned around. Dolly was watching him.

"There you go," he said.

"Yep," Raymond said. Muscle spasms ran up and down his arms and legs, and his hands flailed on his wrists. He stuck them under his arms to keep them still and looked around. Dolly's horse was tied to a tree. Beau was nowhere to be seen. Raymond led Dolly's horse to the end of the bridge and tied it to the rail.

"I'm cold," Dolly said.

"You can warm up at home," Raymond said. He took the rope off the saddle and set it down on the ground, then untied Dolly's poncho and laid it over the handrail of the bridge."

"I'm late," Dolly said. "Lupe will be mad."

"I know how that is," Raymond said. He paused. "Did Lupe know you were coming down here?"

"No," Dolly said.

"We better get you home, then, before she comes looking for you." Raymond opened his pocketknife and started cutting Dolly's poncho into strips.

"That's mine," Dolly said.

"I'll get you another one," Raymond said. "I need this one to cover that sore spot on your belly. Then I'm going to put you on this horse and take you home."

"I don't feel up to riding a horse," Dolly said.

"You have to," Raymond said. "That's the plan."

"It's no good," Dolly said.

Raymond felt his temper rising. It was uncontrollable, like the palsy afflicting his limbs. "If you don't like my plan, make your own."

"It's no good," Dolly said again.

Raymond couldn't stop his head from nodding or his voice from rising or change the words that came out of his mouth. "It's as good as any plan of yours," he said. "You came down here where you weren't wanted and got yourself gut shot. You made that plan. And you didn't tell Lupe besides, so she wouldn't know where you were or what might happen to you. You made that plan. So why don't you come up with a plan to fix the mess you made with the first two?"

"I'm sorry, Ray."

"Well, sorry ain't enough, is it? Hell, I'm sorry. I'm so sorry that if sorry was enough, I'd have enough sorry for the whole goddamn world. But it ain't enough." Raymond's body started jerking as if he were having a seizure. He heard a noise behind him and whirled around.

Beau was walking down the path, leading his horse. He grinned sheepishly at Raymond. "I had to chase him halfway to Dolly's," he said. "I guess he's hungry." He stopped then, and peered anxiously at his father. "You cold, Daddy?"

"It's Dolly," Raymond said.

"What's wrong with him?"

Raymond pulled Dolly's shirt away. The piece of intestine had turned greenish black, and the abdomen was dark and splotched.

"God in heaven," Beau said.

"It's bad," Dolly said.

"No," Beau said quickly. "Not all that bad."

"He knows," Raymond said.

"Oh," Beau said.

"I want to sit down," Dolly said.

"You're already sitting down," Raymond said.

"All the way down," Dolly said. He put his hand on the mare. "Against this here."

Raymond and Beau knelt down on either side of him. Making a sling with their arms, they eased him down into the water. By the time they were done, Dolly's face had turned gray. He leaned against the mare and closed his eyes.

"That's better," he said.

"That water'll make the swelling go down," Raymond said. He put a strip of the poncho on the wound.

Dolly shuddered. "Don't," he said.

Raymond stopped. "I've got to do something, Dolly," he said.

"I'm cold."

"Let me take you home. It's warm there."

"Listen," Dolly said.

"I'm listening," Raymond said.

"There's a box. In the barn. Find it. Tell Quincey.,."

"You tell him," Raymond said.

"I made it for…because…didn't mean to…"

"What are you talking about? What box?"

"Tell Lupe…"

"Tell her what?" Dolly didn't answer, and Raymond patted his cheek. "Tell her what?" he asked. Dolly did not respond. Raymond patted harder. "Tell Lupe what?" No answer. Raymond took Dolly's face in his hands "Wake up," he said. "Open your eyes. I need your help. I can't get you home without your help." Dolly still didn't answer. Raymond grabbed him by the shoulders "Wake up, you bastard!" he screamed. "Don't you die! Goddamn you, Baxter, don't you die. You son-of-a-bitch. You sorry, stupid, interfering son-of-a-bitch, don't you die!" Dolly's breathing changed, became a throaty snore.

"I've got to tell Lupe something," Raymond shouted. "Tell me what to say to Lupe, Dolly, tell me what to say!" A long, slow breath rattled out of Dolly's throat. Raymond held him upright and waited for him to take another. When that didn't happen, Raymond sat down in the water next to him. "Tell me what to say to Lupe," he muttered. The body was so very quiet. Something in Raymond wanted to lie face down in the water and never get up again. Something else wanted to run away. Something between the two pushed him to his feet. Beau was watching him.

"Good," Raymond said. "You're still here. Let's get him home before things get any worse."

Beau stared at his father. "He's dead, Daddy," he said.

Raymond grabbed Beau by the shirtfront and slammed him against the handrail. "I know that," he said.

Beau swallowed hard. "I'll help you, Daddy. Just let me go."

Raymond let go of Beau's shirt and took a step back. His head and hands were trembling again. "Fine," he said. "Let's get him on the horse."

They tied the body across Dolly's saddle with his rope and covered it with Beau's poncho. When it was done, Raymond looked around. He had a feeling he'd forgotten something.

There was a buzzing sound, and he followed it with his eyes across the bridge. He'd forgotten about Tate. He couldn't remember why he had ever been important, or why him laying there looked so familiar.

Even the sun was the same, hot and bright and hurtful to the eyes. And there were so many flies. Raymond leaned over and was sick

"Daddy?"

"It ain't nothing," Raymond said. He wiped his mouth with the back of his hand. "Go get your mother. Lupe will need her."

Beau swung up on his horse. "Daddy?"

"What is it?"

"I'm sorry. About everything."

"Yes. Well. You go on now. Take the north crossing. I don't want Jessie to see this."

Raymond waited until Beau had left, then untied the horse. "C'mon," he said. The horse started walking, then snorted and shied. The body shifted to one side, and Raymond made a grab for it. He held it up with both hands and followed the horse around in a circle, yelling "Whoa! Whoa!" until the animal sidled into a tree and stopped. Raymond worked Dolly's body back up on the saddle and tightened the ropes again. He was drenched with sweat by the time he finished and so weak he could barely stand.

"I can't do this," he said, and put his head down on his arm. There, right under his feet, was the biggest snake he'd ever seen in his life. A spasm convulsed his body. The horse blew and backed away, trampling the snake, which did not move. Raymond gave a shaky little laugh, and picked up Dolly's cow whip.

"That's a good one, Dolly," he said. "I'll remember it." He coiled the whip and hung it on the saddle horn. Then he took Dolly home to Lupe.

Part V

Thursday evening, May 28 – Friday morning, May 29

Bridge Over Deep Creek

Chapter Thirty-Six

One lantern burned on the chest-of-drawers in front of the mirror, so that it looked like there were two of them. One lantern burned on each of the small tables on either side of the bed. The shutters were closed on both windows. The light from the lanterns was steady but not very strong. Its weakness was both a difficulty and a blessing.

Beside the bed were two buckets of clean water, a pile of rags, a bar of lye soap, and a bar of soap that smelled like lilies-of-the-valley. When Jessie first got there, the bedroom smelled of that soap. Then they'd brought the body in, and other odors had overwhelmed it. The scent of the soap still hung about Lupe, though, who smelled, very faintly, of that and something else, some perfume, delicate and unfamiliar. Someday Jessie meant to ask her what that perfume was called. But not now.

Now there was the body on the bed. Jessie believed that it was Lupe's right and duty to care for her husband in death as in life. But when Lupe did not move, did not even speak, Jessie picked up the scissors to cut away the clothes.

The body sickened Lila. It smelled bad, and the wound smelled bad in a special way. She'd have fainted when she saw the face, only Jessie shoved a chair beneath her, then shoved her head down between her knees. Lila cried for a while, then a thought came to her. She stopped crying and sat up straight. Jessie had covered the face with a cloth.

"Do we have to take his boots off?" she asked.

"No," Jessie said. "They won't come off. I've already tried."

That made things easier. Still, it was hard work. Sweat rolled down their faces and dropped on Dolly's naked skin. Lila did not wipe it off. She would not have touched the body with hers at all, had not disgust made her clumsy.

Jessie was not disgusted by the body. Touching Dolly by lantern light in places she'd only touched her own husband in the dark, she asked his forgiveness, forgiving in advance those who would someday handle her own abandoned flesh. At best, it would be withered and dry. At worst, well, whatever could happen to a body in this life was what those still living had to deal with when it was dead.

"I got to do that one time," Lupe said. Her eyes were open, and she was watching Jessie.

"So how come you're not doing it now?" Jessie asked.

"'Cause it's an unlucky day," Lupe said. "For me. Not for you. It's lucky for you."

Jessie stuffed Dolly's soiled britches in the empty bucket. "I don't feel lucky," she said.

Lupe smiled. "You don't at first," she said. "But you learn. No taking turns, either. It's all in the chance. That's a house rule."

"What house?" Lila asked.

The smile on Lupe's face turned sly. "You know what house."

"Tell me again," Jessie said. "I've forgotten."

"I will never forget," Lupe said. "Not as long as I live." Her mouth softened, her gazed on the lantern in the mirror. The girl Lupe once had been appeared beside it, beautiful and content. The odor of that strange and lovely perfume grew stronger. Gooseflesh rose on Jessie's arms and on the back of her neck, and Lila's eyes got big. Jessie picked up the bar of lye soap.

"Use that other soap," Lupe said. "He likes the smell of it." Her voice was low-pitched and slow and full of effort, as if coming from that place between love and sleep. "I heard about Dolly before I ever met him," she said. "He was coming to our house regular by then. The madam had taken a shine to him, because he said yes, ma'am, and no, ma'am like he meant it, and was clean, and had the prettiest blue eyes she'd ever seen. So she wouldn't let her girls rob him when he got drunk, and dump him out in the street, but made them take him upstairs, and clean him up when he got sick from the drink and passed out, and serve him when he came to. Oh, she was a smart woman, because it turned out Dolly was a grateful man and a generous one. Kindness was not wasted on him, but came back tenfold. Why, he'd pay every girl who took care of him whatever she asked just to stay there beside him when he was done with her, and sleep."

Jessie washed the last of the dirt from the body's neck and chest, while Lila looked through the wardrobe for the black suit that Dolly always wore to funerals.

"Sleep," Lupe said again. "Lord, them girls had been asked to do a lot of things, but never that. They thought Dolly a fool. They thought he didn't know that they'd have done for the kind of money he paid. However much business a girl said she was losing - two, three, four men - that's what he'd pay to keep her there beside him when it was over, just to sleep. He came every six months to the day, and they took to marking him on the calendar, the one in the back room where they kept track of their monthlies, and as the time approached, they'd argue and fuss and fight so bad over who was getting him next that the madam got tired of the ruckus and started giving him to any girl that was free at the moment, whether she'd had him before or not. That became a house rule and nobody fought over him again. He turned into a plain ole piece of good luck. They knew all about luck, and how hard the good kind was to come by. That's why nobody minded when the chance fell on me. It didn't matter that I was younger than them and new and still pretty, because it was just some good luck coming my way. 'Oh, look at that,' they said when my name came out of the hat, 'Lupe is lucky tonight.'

"Only I didn't feel lucky, not at first. I mean, here was this drunk in my room with a head like a boiled egg, puking and crying and apologizing for the mess he was making until I figured a line of cow hunters stretching around the block would be less aggravation than him. But taking care of him was a house rule, so that's what I did. I wrassled him onto the bed when he passed out, and got his clothes off of him, and scrubbed him with hot water and some of that soap, there, and dried him with my own towel. He was sound asleep the whole time, and didn't feel me pushing and pulling on that wide, hard ole body with its big shoulders and bowed legs, or see me sniffing him when I was done, my nose right down there on his skin because he smelled so good, and I started to understand what the others had meant by lucky.

Jessie picked the last clean rag up off the floor and laid it over the shotgun wound, which did not smell good at all. Then she went back to washing the body, turned the color of ivory in the lantern light.

"When Dolly woke up," Lupe said, he wanted to do it, and it was what it was, no better, no worse, except that he was clean and talked decent. When he asked me what he owed me, I said - I knew I was pushing my luck, but I said it anyway - I said ten, I'm missing ten - and he said, that's a lot of men, and I said, I don't waste time, and he laughed and said, all right, said it so easy it made me sick I hadn't said twenty, but then I thought, what the heck, he's paying me to sleep and I never get enough of that. So I laid back in his arms and closed my eyes and tried to go to sleep, only I couldn't because of his snoring, which was the godawfullest I ever heard."

Lupe laughed out loud. The sound was startling, and made Lila jump so hard she banged her head on the wardrobe, and Jessie dropped the washcloth. She picked it up again and washed carefully around the wound as though touching it could hurt, and then down the belly to the genitals and the heavy, thick-muscled thighs and bowed legs to the top of the boots.

"He kept going back to sleep and snoring," Lupe said. "And I kept jabbing him in the side to make him hush. Finally, he grabbed my arm and said he was paying me to sleep with him, not beat him up. I told him I couldn't sleep for all the noise he was making and I'd sleep with him for free if he'd just be quiet. Then he looked at me with those eyes," Lupe sobbed then, as suddenly as she'd laughed.

"Lord God in Heaven," she said. "Those eyes. I'd never seen anything so blue. He looked at me with 'em and said he'd be quiet for the whole rest of the night if I'd marry him." She grew quiet and was quiet for a long time. Jessie finished the one leg and had begun on the other before she spoke again. "Nobody had ever asked me to marry them before," she said. "I thought he was joking. When he kept on, I decided he was crazy. It sounded too good to be true, that I'd never have to do anything I didn't want to, except what I was used to doing already, and I could sleep afterwards, every time. I figured him for a fool, but a rich one, so I said yes, because all that sleeping sounded so good, and because the whole thing felt like a streak of good luck the likes of which I'd never seen before and most likely would never see again, and I figured to run it all the way to the end."

"And I think the end must be here!" she cried. "Or else another woman would not be washing my man!" Lupe made a sound in her throat, the first whining notes of that dreadful wailing she'd been doing down by the path.

"I've found his best suit," Lila said. "Now he's got something to wear." There was an edge of hysteria in her voice, and either that or what she'd said stopped Lupe cold. She opened her eyes and looked at the black suit hung over Lila's arm. Then she closed her eyes again, and went back to rocking.

"That ain't his best one," she said.

"Where is his best one?" Lila asked.

"In the cedar chest," Lupe said.

It was at the bottom of the chest, beneath layers of beautiful fabrics of blue and crimson, a black silk suit, greenish and shiny with age. It smelled of cedar, and was clearly too small for the body on the bed.

"It's his wedding suit," Lupe said. "Nobody's ever seen him wear it. Not even me."

"Why not?" Lila asked.

"Because he's never had it on," Lupe said. She sounded irritated, as if she were telling Lila something she should already know. "He didn't have it with him when we met, and we didn't have a regular wedding, anyhow. Could be, we never really married at all."

Jessie was vexed. Of all the things that had ever issued from the mouth of Lupe Baxter, this was the worst. But her tightly pursed mouth was wasted on Lupe, who had closed her eyes again and was rocking, rocking, rocking, arms crossed over her breasts. Now and then, the material of her skirt would move as the baby in her belly rolled and kicked. Lupe took up her story again, her voice as rich and warm and soft as the lantern light, the unfamiliar perfume stronger, now, around her person.

"When we stopped that first day out from Tampa, Dolly went all prim and proper, said we couldn't do it again until we were man and wife. I thought it was funny, him getting religion all of a sudden, but didn't argue with him, thinking it was pure pleasure to be resting from all that. I left him fixing supper to wash in the river, and I got back to camp, there was a man standing by the fire, a tall, stringy fellow in a cutaway coat and slouch hat. He smelled like a skunk and talked like a professor and claimed - but not until after we told him our story - to be a traveling preacher. He said he was hungry as a sparrow God had forgot, and offered to marry us for a share of our rations. It seemed a fair enough deal, though that preacher talked more than he ate, and ate most everything we had. But he said the marriage words over us, and preached a sermon so's the words would take. It was the first sermon I'd ever heard and right hard to follow, all about people I didn't know - barring Adam and Eve - everybody's heard of them - such as Abraham and Sarah and Jacob and Rachel and Boab and Ruth and a bunch of other folks the preacher had married on his travels. He'd have kept on preaching until daylight, I guess, except Dolly gave him five dollars to quit and another five dollars to go away. By the time he was gone, though, me and Dolly was either married or as good as, and I was obliged to do for free what up 'til then I'd been paid good money for."

Jessie felt sorry for Lupe but this was going too far. She gestured sharply at Lila, who handed her the old suit. Jessie shook her head, and held her hand out for the newer one. Lila gave it to her with reluctance. Jessie picked up the scissors again and cut down the middle of the white shirt. Lupe kept talking.

"I took my dress off and hung it on a tree limb and laid down on the bedroll and pulled my shift up to my chin, expecting Dolly to climb on and get it over with. Instead, he pulled my shift back down and started talking. I thought at first it'd be nasty. Some men like that, I don't know why. After a while, though, I could tell it wasn't nasty, but wasn't like any talk I'd ever heard before, either."

Her voice hushed, as though she were telling a fairy tale to children. "'My love, my fair one,' he said. 'Rise and come away, for the winter is past and the rain is gone, the flowers have appeared on the earth, the time of singing had come, and the voice of the turtle is heard in our land.' I stopped him right there. 'Wait a minute," I said. 'Heard doing what?' 'Singing,' he said. 'That's stupid,' I said. 'Turtles don't sing.' 'Shush,' he said. He kissed my hair. Nobody ever did that before. 'If you'll be still and listen,' he said. 'I promise that someday you'll hear the turtle sing. Oh, it's the sweetest sound there ever was.' I asked him, 'Can you hear it?' And he said, 'Yes, I can hear it right now.' I listened hard, but I didn't hear it, just frogs and owls and such. I was still listening when he started taking off my shift. 'Well,' I thought. 'Here it comes.' But he just pulled away from me. Then he touched my feet with his hands."

Lupe, her eyes closed and the scent of that elusive perfume grown very strong, lifted her hands to her hair and pulled the pins out, one by one, and her words fell on the women by the bed like scented oil, as Dolly's words had fallen on her so many years ago, when he'd called her a queenly maiden, and kissed her feet, for they were graceful; her thighs, for they were jewels; her navel, for it was a bowl of wine; her belly, for it was a bowl of wheat encircled with lilies; her breasts, for they were two fawns; then laid his body on top of hers and tangled his fingers in her long black hair that was like purple and pulled her mouth to his, a king held captive in her tresses. The long hair fell over her shoulders and around her face, a shimmering veil of silver and black, and Lupe's voice faded to a whisper and then to silence and the odor of lilies returned as the strange perfume lingered, faded, and was gone.

Jessie had stopped cutting long ago to listen. In the silence, she looked down at the funeral suit in her hands, the sleeves ruined for having been cut. She set it down.

"Give me the other one," she said. Lila handed her the wedding suit. Jessie cut the jacket and pants down the back and laid them over Dolly's body. Lupe rose and walked heavily across the room. She stopped at the bed and laid her hand on Dolly's.

"He's cold," she said.

"Yes," Jessie said.

Lupe straightened the collar of the suit. "He bought this a long time before he met me," she said. "With money he made from those first cows y'all took to Punta Rassa. He kept it for all those years he was by himself, there in that chest. He called it his hope chest. I never had a hope chest. I never had anything or anybody until I met him. Even then, I didn't care about him. Not at first. But after awhile, I came to need him, and then one night I wanted him, and a long time after that - it was after Nub was born - I woke up one morning and looked at him snoring in the bed beside me, and I knew that I loved him. It was just like finding a new penny, and I knew I'd got lucky all over again. But I never heard the turtle singing in our land. Silly, I called it, right up to this afternoon. Before he left, he walked up behind me in the kitchen and kissed me on the ear and said, 'Can you hear the turtle singing?'

'Turtles don't sing,' I said.

'Someday you'll hear it,' he said. 'I know you will.'

"Now here he is, gone away, and I know that I was hearing it all along, because it was him loving me. I was hearing it all that time, and didn't know that's what he was talking about, and I wish more than anything in the world that he could hear me just one more time, just long enough for me to tell him that I finally heard it sing." She seemed to break in the middle then, sinking down on the floor to hide her face in her arms, her back heaving.

Jessie walked around the bed and stood beside her, pulling her hair back and stroking it as she would a child's. "Go tell them we're done," she said.

Lila went to the door and turned around, wishing she could say something of comfort. But Lupe's face was still buried in her own arms, and Jessie was looking at Dolly as if she'd never seen him before.

Chapter Thirty-Seven

Beau couldn't find the box Dolly mentioned. He'd spent a good twenty minutes looking in and around the barn, from alley to loft to alley again, with no success. He decided it must be much smaller than he first believed, and so began a new, more intensive search as he gathered tools and lumber to build a coffin. That was his job, to build the coffin. His, because everybody else who could do it was gone: George and Seth for their wives, Jacob to feed the Dempsey stock, Jack to town for the sheriff and the preacher, Raymond to dig a grave. Raymond hadn't said that's where he was going. He hadn't said anything. But Beau had seen him with shovel and ax walking southeast toward what Dolly had always called his burying ground. Every time they rode that way, Dolly would say, "This here's where I want to be buried," and Raymond would say, "I'll see to it," unless he wasn't there, in which case Beau would say, "We'll see to it." Then Dolly would say, "I want a fancy coffin, too, and some good music," and Raymond, if he was there, would say, "all right," and if he wasn't there, Beau would say, "will do." Then they'd go on about their business as if such a time would never come. Only now that time had come, and there would be no fancy coffin, only a cypress box lined with one of Jessie's quilts that was sitting on a chair in the Baxter's front room, waiting for the coffin that Beau had come to the barn to build.

First, though, he wanted to find that box. He didn't know anything about it except what Dolly had told him, that he'd built it himself. Beau was reminded of the humor of that statement when he opened the door to the tool room and held the lantern up. Tools were scattered carelessly over the worktable, and some had fallen to the floor. Dolly didn't care for his tools any better than he used them. Beau ran his hand over the doorframe. It was only an inch thick, but he felt along it carefully. He had no idea how big the box was, or what it was made of, wood, most likely, though horn was a possibility, as was leather. There was nothing on top of the frame, and he turned to the table, looking on it, behind it, to either side of it. Then he looked in and under and behind several buckets of nails and piles of scrap lumber, a box of hinges and another of latches. He poked in all four corners and rummaged through both toolboxes. He even looked behind the saws hanging on the wall, though how anyone could hide a box there he didn't really know. He didn't worry about messing things up. It was hard to mess up what was already a mess. Finally, he took a hammer, a saw, a rule, and a bucket of nails into the barn alley, and shut the door.

Late afternoon sunlight poured over the gates at both ends of the alley, but illuminated little within the barn itself. Beau held the lantern up again, following its yellow light down the stalls, first one side, then the other. The boards were straight on the stalls and fit just right. Raymond had cut and nailed them. Beau ran his hand along the tops of the stalls and looked into the feed boxes. Most of them were sturdy and level. Raymond had made those. A few, though, were lopsided, with cracks in them where the boards weren't flush. Those were the ones Dolly had made. Any box he'd made, large or small, would look like them: clumsy and ill-fitted. It was the only concrete aspect of the picture in Beau's mind of the box Dolly had told him to find.

Beau hung the lantern on an iron bar sunk into a post by the feed room, and walked out the back gate. A pile of cypress lumber was stacked against the outside wall of the barn. Beside the lumber were two sawhorses. A rusted saw lay on the ground nearby. Beau would have put it away, but it was so far gone that there didn't seem to be any point in it.

Instead, he pulled the weeds away from the siding and looked along the ground on both sides of the gate. He climbed the ladder to the outside door of the loft, flipped the big iron hook out of its eye, and swung the door open. A pile of old hay blocked the opening. There was no way to get over it from the outside. Beau stuck his arm under the hay as far as he could reach and felt along the wall and floor. Nothing. He pulled his arm out, shut the door, dropped the hook in the eye, and went back down the ladder. Then he brought in eight boards and stacked them beside the sawhorses. That done, he took the lantern off the wall, and went to the feed room.

A complicated odor made up of molasses, hay, corn, and mouse musk hung in the air like dust. Beau opened the feed barrel, sunk his arm down in the kernels and stirred them around, holding his breath against the chaff. He put the lid back on the barrel and pulled it away from the wall. A rat snake butted the wall until it found a hole and eased its way out of the room. Beau moved a stack of hay from one wall to another, disturbing a nest of baby mice. They fell like pink peanuts to the floor. Beau held the lantern up and studied the walls and beams, then shut the door on their squeaking.

Between the feed room and the tack room were the stairs to the loft. Beau started to go up there again, then changed his mind. It made more sense to finish looking downstairs first. He opened the door to the tack room, and held the lantern up. One wall, studded with wooden pegs, held bridles in various stages of repair, rusted bits and curb chains, cracked reins, and dusty halters. A wide shelf ran the length of the facing wall. Smaller shelves and stacks of drawers rose from its surface to the ceiling. Beau set the lantern down on the wide shelf, and opened one of the drawers.

He was looking for a small box that Dolly had made. It had to be small. If it was big, he'd have seen it already. He continued to open drawers and rifle through their contents. The only box he found, though, was ordinary and full of rivets. Beau thought Dolly might have decorated the box in some way, glued beads to it, or shells, or painted it some bright color. He'd known him to do things like that. Or it might be just a plain box - wooden, badly made - but with something special inside it, something that Dolly thought not only pretty, but important. Dolly hadn't said why it was important. Beau figured he'd know that when he saw it.

He slammed the last drawer shut and turned around, gripping the edge of the shelf behind him with both hands. Attached to the wall at the far end of the room was a row of saddle racks. Dolly's saddle was hanging on one of them. And on the saddle, tied to the skirt right where it belonged, was Dolly's cow whip.

Evening approached. Shadows lengthened in the barn. The floor creaked as Beau walked across the room and untied the whip from the saddle. Foot by foot, he let it drop to the floor until all he held was the handle. It was one of the few things Dolly had ever cared enough about to take his time with, cutting it out of a seasoned hickory log with a hatchet, discovering its shape in the heartwood like a long lost friend. He'd shaped and smoothed it with a plane until it fit his hand, then rubbed it with oil and a pumice stone. But the deep patina came from long use, and the plaited leather woven to the end was the third whip it had held.

Beau rubbed the leather with his thumb. The deer hide strips slipped over and under one another in a diamond pattern, the leather supple with oil and sweat and age. Twelve feet from the handle butt to the popper, the leather so dark brown it was almost black. The popper stung cruelly and raised a welt, even cut, when it hit flesh. Higher up its length, the whip struck like a cudgel, and bruised. Beau had a black and blue stripe on his arm where it had landed. The rest of it had followed, wrapping around him like thread on a bobbin, pinning his arms to his sides and dragging him out of the saddle. It was a helpless feeling. So was lying on the ground like a trussed pig, squirming and grunting as he tried to escape. Then Dolly was there, a hand on Beau's mouth, blue eyes intense and unsmiling. He put the whip handle in Beau's right hand and a revolver in his left. Then he walked to the bridge, spoke to Tate, and shot him. And then...well, then all that other had happened, the events that Beau kept walking around and looking at sideways, afraid to face them head on because Dolly's death was still so new and raw, and because they might show him things about himself he didn't want to see.

Beau coiled the whip, shaking it out between wraps to keep it from twisting. He had picked the whip up off the ground beside the bridge, coiled it just like he was doing here, and put it on the saddle seat. It must have fallen off, though, because it wasn't there when he and Raymond put Dolly's body on the horse. Raymond must have found it and tied it on the saddle. Beau wished he'd tied it on to begin with. He was in a hurry to catch his horse. He couldn't remember now why that horse had seemed so important. He could have walked home quicker than it took to catch it.

Beau got to the end of the whip. The popper was frayed. It would need replacing soon. He would teach Dolly's sons how to do that, the way Dolly had taught him. He remembered it as if it were yesterday, Dolly's big hands patiently guiding his small fingers as together they plaited eight strips of leather into a boy-sized whip. He could feel Dolly's unshaven cheek against his own, and smell the tobacco on his breath.

There was a sound behind him. Beau spun around, a wild hope leaping his heart. Quincey was standing in the doorway, staring at him.

Beau rubbed the tears off his face with the flat of his hand, and nodded, formally, as if they'd just met on the street. "Quincey," he said.

"What are you doing here?" Quincey asked.

Beau held the whip up. "I was looking for something," he said. "Saw this on the saddle. Got to looking at it, and thinking about your daddy." He smiled at Quincey, trying to be friendly, to be gentle with this boy who had just lost his father.

"He's the one taught me to make a whip. I bet you didn't know that. I was about eight, I guess, maybe a little younger. It took me a while to catch on. I never knew a man so patient." He offered the whip to Quincey. "You ought to take this up to the house. There will never be another like it."

Quincey glanced at the whip, then looked at Beau. "I don't want it," he said.

"Maybe you'll give it to me, then," Beau said. "As a remembrance of your daddy."

Quincey just looked at him.

Beau turned his back and tied the whip to the saddle. "Maybe later," he said. He turned around again. Quincey was still watching him. "What's on your mind?" he asked.

"What were you looking for?" Quincey asked.

Beau didn't want Quincey finding for him what he couldn't find himself. "Nothing important," he said. He picked the lantern up off the shelf and walked with it past Quincey to the alley. It was later than he thought. Night would fall before he finished the coffin. He hung the lantern on the iron bar again, picked up a two by six from the pile on the ground, and set it on the sawhorses.

Quincey climbed up on the top rail and sat down. "What are you making?" he asked.

"A coffin," Beau said.

"What's a coffin?" Quincey asked.

"A box to put a body in," Beau said.

"To hold this mortal flesh," Quincey said. "Until that great day cometh."

This solemn utterance caught Beau off guard, and he smiled in spite of himself. "You sound like a preacher," he said. "I wouldn't have thought it of you."

"Daddy told me that," Quincey said.

"I wouldn't have thought it of him, either," Beau said. He unfolded the rule, laid it on the board, and marked off six feet with a nail.

Then he folded the rule again, set it in the tool bucket, and picked up the saw.

"Who's this coffin for?" Quincey asked.

The question set Beau's teeth on edge. He put his knee on the board and drew the saw teeth across the mark. He was in no mood for Quincey's games. "Your daddy," he said.

"He's already got one," Quincey said.

Beau stopped, his knee still on the board, and looked Quincey in the eyes for the first time. "Where?" he asked.

Quincey pointed to the loft.

"I've been up there already," Beau said. "I didn't see any such thing."

"You didn't know where to look," Quincey said. He jumped down off the stall. "C'mon. I'll show you."

Beau took the lantern off the bar and followed Quincey up the stairs. When he reached the top, he saw the same thing he'd seen the first time: a pile of harness sitting on the floor on one end, and a big pile of hay on the other. Quincey headed directly for the hay and started digging in it. Soon he uncovered the end of a wooden box, gray with age. He pushed hay to one side until an entire coffin was revealed, its lid fastened down with screws.

Quincey shimmied up a post to the rafter it was attached to, and came back down with a screwdriver. "You look at the outside real good," he said. "Then I'll show you the rest."

Beau squatted down beside the coffin and held the light up. The dovetails were irregular at best, and the boards were scarred by saw teeth. But every scratch and crack and split had been shimmed with slivers of wood and sawdust mixed with glue and sanded smooth until the faults were the loveliest things about it. It reminded Beau of parquet, except there was no pattern, and he knew he was looking at the box Dolly had sent him to find.

"What do you think?" Quincey asked.

"I don't know," Beau said. It was the truth. He hadn't been looking for a coffin, and wasn't sure how he felt about finding one. Tricked, maybe. He had expected to find something pretty. Coffins weren't pretty. A man could fashion a coffin out of solid gold, and it wouldn't be pretty. Beau felt lied to. Not tricked, like Dolly had played a joke on him. Lied to. He rubbed the back of his neck. The tendons felt like cables. "I don't know what to say."

"Wait 'til you see inside," Quincey said.

"I don't want to see inside," Beau said.

Quincey ignored him. "Hold on," he said. "I'm getting there." It took him nearly forever to get all the way around the lid with the screwdriver, he was so careful not to scratch the wood or drop any of the screws. Finally, he put the screwdriver down. "That's got it," he said. "Don't help me pick it up, and don't look until I tell you to."

Beau, who had not offered to help and had no desire to look, held the lantern and watched Quincey's shadow on the wall.

Quincey pried one edge of the lid up with the screwdriver, got his fingers under it, then lifted it until it rested against the wall. "Now you can look," he whispered.

"I don't want to," Beau said.

"Look," Quincey demanded. He took the lantern out of Beau's hand and held it over the coffin. "Look inside."

Beau looked.

The inside of the coffin, and the lid, too, was upholstered in a rich brocade of a blue so dark it looked black. The material was puffed out - Beau guessed it had cotton batten underneath it - and covered with silver netting that sparkled in the light.

"Them sparklers are glass," Quincey said. "But they're as pretty as real diamonds. You can touch 'em if you want to. I don't mind."

"No thanks," Beau said.

Quincey put a finger on one of the glass beads. "Stars in the night sky," he said reverently. "Only this sky ain't black. It's dark blue, like Daddy's eyes. You can tell it better in the daylight. Daddy always called this the pretty box, and it sure is."

Beau could not stifle the outrage he felt any longer. "I can't believe this," he said. "What was he thinking?"

"Hard to tell," Quincey said. He looked pensive all of a sudden. "The only time Daddy ever hit me was because of this here."

"Why was that?" Beau asked dully.

"He caught me sleeping in it," Quincey said.

Beau stared at him. "Sleeping in it?" he asked. "What for?"

"He didn't know I knew about it," Quincey said. "Sometimes, when he wasn't around, I'd come up here and lie in it. It was so soft, I wouldn't have minded staying there for a long time. One day, I laid down in it and fell asleep. He came upstairs and found me and started yelling at me. 'What are you doing? What are you doing?' I tried to tell him. I said, 'I'm practicing! I'm practicing!' But he wouldn't listen. He hit me exactly five times before he stopped."

"You kept count?" Beau asked.

"I always keep count," Quincey said. "Of everything. Anyway, he stopped hitting me and said, 'What do you mean, practicing?' 'Being dead,' I told him. 'Only I fell asleep.' Quincey's expression turned stony. "He started crying then, just like you are now. He said he was sorry that he hit me, and sad that I was playing dead, but I didn't care. I didn't talk to him for a long time. He had to let me help with the other one, to make it up to me."

"What other one?" Beau asked.

"I'll show you," Quincey said. He set the lid back down on Dolly's coffin. "Daddy says we've got to be careful with it, lest we get it dirty."

Quincey returned to the hay pile and started clearing out another section. Sooner than before, another coffin was exposed. This one was wider than Dolly's, and a good six inches longer. It, too, was screwed shut. When Quincey got the lid off, Beau held the lantern up. The lining was scarlet satin. Green cut glass beads like emeralds rimmed the edges and glimmered in the tufts of the upholstery. On one end was a pillow made of the dark blue brocade. Someone had embroidered in gold thread: Lupe Baxter Beloved Wife Of Dolly Baxter. The stitches were uneven but the gold thread was clean and the material was spotless and unwrinkled. The needle worker had taken great care with it.

"Daddy did that ole pillow by himself," Quincey said. "But I got to put all the jewels in." He licked his forefinger and polished one of the beads. "Pretty, isn't it?"

Beau felt sick to his stomach and didn't answer.

There were footsteps in the alley below. Quincey hunched down beside the coffin as if whoever it was might see him. "Shhh," he whispered.

"Beau?" Jack called.

Beau started to answer, but Quincey shook his head, frowning.

The footsteps walked back out of the barn. Quincey hastily closed the lid on Lupe's coffin and started putting the screws back in like somebody who'd had a lot of practice. When he finished, he scuttled over to Dolly's. "You cover that one up with hay while I tighten this one down," he said. He dug down in his pants pocket where he'd put the screws, and noticed that Beau wasn't moving. "Hurry up."

"What are you doing?" Beau asked. "I can see screwing the lid down on your mama's, but that one you may as well leave loose."

"Be quiet," Quincey said. "Jack will hear you."

Footsteps came back in the barn.

"Beau?" Jack called again.

"Up here," Beau said.

Quincey grabbed him by the arm, his face wrathful. "He's going to see it," he hissed.

Beau shook his hand off. "So are a lot of other people," he said.

Jack's head appeared at the top of the stairs. "You haven't got much done," he said. He glanced past Beau. "Hey, Quincey."

Quincey stared over Jack's head and didn't answer. He was sitting on the very end of the coffin, knees together, hands stretched out and clamped to either side as if, by sitting on the narrow edge and spreading himself wide, he could hide the coffin with his body.

Jack didn't seem to think there was anything odd about Quincey's behavior. "What are y'all doing up here?" he asked.

"Dolly's already built a coffin," Beau said. "Quincey's sitting on it."

Jack came the rest of the way up the stairs. "Let me see it," he said.

Quincey stood up and crossed his arms. "Get away," he said.

Beau grimaced, disgusted with Quincey and Dolly both. "Never mind," he told Jack. "You can look at it when we get to the house." He looked over the edge of the loft opening, judging distances. "We better take it down on its side. That way we'll have plenty of clearance."

"You ain't taking this anywhere," Quincey said.

"We need it for the funeral," Beau said.

"There ain't going to be a funeral," Quincey said.

"Yes there is," Jack said. "In the morning. For your daddy."

Quincey shook his head with the confidence of someone absolutely sure of his facts. "Nossir," he said. "Daddy don't want a funeral. He's just going to rest eternal here in this coffin."

"Just what do you think rest eternal is?" Beau asked.

"It's a long nap," Quincey said. "When you wake up from it, your family is standing around waiting for you to get up, so you do, and things go on just like before."

"Oh, Dolly," Beau said. "What have you done? Quincey..." He couldn't go any further. "You tell him, Jack."

Jack squatted down in front of the coffin's guardian. "Your daddy's dead, Quincey," he said.

"Not for long," Quincey said. "Us Baxters has got too much living to do to die for long. Daddy told me so."

"Quincey," Jack pleaded. "You're daddy isn't coming back."

"Yes he is," Quincey said. "And you ain't telling me different. I won't listen. And you won't take this coffin, neither. I'm sorry I showed it to you."

"But your daddy would want us to take it," Jack said. "He even told Beau to look for it so we could use it."

Quincey squinted at him suspiciously. "Use it for what?" he asked.

"To put your daddy's body in," Jack said.

"You ain't got to take it anywhere to do that," Quincey said. "You can just bring Daddy up here and put him in it. This is his resting place."

"Son," Jack said gently. "After we put him in it, we've got to bury it."

"WHAT?" Quincey's voice quivered with outrage. "Bury it? In the dirt? You ain't putting this box or my daddy in the dirt, neither one. Me and Mama will take care of things here. You ain't wanted. Just go on home."

Jack stood up. "I've done the best I know to do," he told Beau. "You try it."

Beau took a deep breath and blew it out again. "Quincey," he said. "We've got to bury your daddy's body because..." He paused. "Because pretty soon it's going to stink. Flesh is just a fancy word for meat, and in hot weather, meat..."

"You're lying!" Quincey screamed. "My daddy is going to rise with a shout of acclamation! He said so! He promised!"

"Can't you understand anything?" Beau yelled back. "I don't care what your daddy told you, or what he promised you, he is dead! He is dead and he ain't ever coming back and his body is going to rot in the ground!"

"That's a lie!" Quincey shrieked. "You're a liar! You're both liars! I hate you! I hate you forever!" He threw the screwdriver at Beau. It went wide, bounced off a post, and clattered down the steps with Quincey right behind it.

Beau waited at the head of the stairs, prepared to fight him off if he came back up, but there was nothing: no name-calling, no threats, no throwing anything. Beau couldn't even hear him moving in the barn. Heartsick and exhausted, he leaned against the wall and closed his eyes.

"Quincey's taking it hard," Jack said.

"Seems to be," Beau said. He couldn't think about Quincey. It was too confusing, and he was too tired. Given half a chance, he'd lie down and sleep the rest of his life away. The thought of sleep, and the dreams that might attend it, acted like a spring on his eyelids, jerking them open. Jack was watching him. Beau changed the subject. "Did you find everybody you went looking for?"

"All but the preacher," Jack said. "He'd gone fishing. His wife said it might be morning before he got here."

"The sheriff?"

"Down at the bridge with the rest of them."

"Who all's there?"

"Dr. Webb, Fess, George, your daddy-in-law, five or six other men. More are on their way."

"Word gets around pretty fast," Beau said. He cleared his throat. "What about Tate?"

"His leg was black all the way to the groin with gangrene," Jack said. "Dr. Webb said he should have been dead a week ago."

"What are they doing with him?" Beau asked.

"Taking him to the Rainey place, to bury him next to Bob. The sheriff went to town for a wagon."

"Fess wouldn't do it?"

Jack shook his head. "He says he's a trail cook, not a garbage hauler."

Beau nodded, but didn't say anything. Whatever Tate had been, it wasn't garbage. He had been, and still was, too powerful. Even dead, he was a shadow in Beau's mind, like the stain a nightmare leaves on the morning. It made going to sleep a scary thought.

"Beau," Jack said.

"What?"

"The wick needs trimming."

Beau picked up the lantern and gave it a shake. "It's almost out of oil," he said. "There's more in the tool room." He turned to leave.

"What about this here?" Jack asked.

Beau held the lantern up and looked at the coffin one more time. Death had met him on the bridge. He'd mistaken it for Vancey at first, and then for Tate, but in the end, he'd known it for what it was. He'd turned coward when he saw it, and that cowardice had cost Dolly his life. Beau would live with that shame to the end of his days. But he knew he'd only put Death off for a while. He hadn't escaped it, and he hadn't dressed it up and pretended it was something else, and he wouldn't be party to that now. Not even for Dolly.

"Leave it," he said. "I'll make another one. This one belongs to Quincey."

There was a noise downstairs. Somebody was chopping wood. The blows hit over and over again, jerky and without rhythm.

"Quincey," Jack said.

"Let's get out of here before he sets the barn on fire and burns us both alive," Beau said. As soon as his foot hit the top step, the chopping stopped and footsteps ran out of the barn. When they reached the alley, no one was there.

"He's been up to something," Beau said. "You can count on that."

Jack pointed to the stall across the alley. "What's that over there?" he asked.

Beau held the lantern up. Its feeble light showed the pile of lumber, the tools and nail bucket, the sawhorses, the two by six. Dolly's whip lay on the two by six. It had been chopped into pieces, and the handle nailed to the board with a hatchet.

Chapter Thirty-Eight

Raymond carried a shovel and an ax along the creek to the Baxter cemetery. His boots felt heavy. His legs ached with the effort of picking them up and setting them back down. His steps felt dreamlike. The trees on either side of him were dreamlike, too, as if he were seeing them through the wrong end of a telescope, and the birds sounded as if they sang from inside a barrel.

It had been the same when he met up with the Dempseys on his way to Dolly's house. They and their horses looked small and far away, and when George asked, "How did this happen?" he sounded as if he were speaking under water. Maybe he sounded the same way to himself, because he allowed Raymond to pass even though he hadn't answered the question.

The three men fell in behind Dolly's horse like a posse. They were far enough back, though, that Raymond was alone when he walked into the sunlight of the Baxter's yard. He had hoped to see Jessie there, waiting for him. What he saw instead was Dolly's youngest boy playing on a swing.

Nub had the same distant quality as the Dempseys. He clung to a rope Dolly had hung from an oak limb, his head almost upside down, fists clenched on the rope, arms extended, eyes closed, laughing, whirling around so fast it made Raymond sick at his stomach to watch. Suddenly, without any warning or sign from Nub that it should be so, the rope jerked back and forth and came to a stop. That's when Raymond noticed the other boy. It was one of the twins. He let go of the rope as soon as Raymond looked at him and ran, yelling for his mother and Quincey.

Nub slipped down the rope to the ground, and staggered toward the house. He had not taken three steps when the kitchen door opened. Lupe stood in the doorway for a moment, then came down the steps and across the yard, the boys straggling behind her like puppies. Lupe walked with the wide-legged stance of a pregnant woman approaching her time. She passed Nub and his outstretched arms as if he weren't there, and looked at Raymond as if he were an obstacle of some kind. He moved out of her way. Lupe walked up to the horse, pulled the poncho off, and exposed the body. The boys moaned but did not cry out. Lupe untied the ropes that held her husband and pulled him to the ground. Then she got down on her knees, gathered Dolly in her arms, and screamed.

If a voice could rend, then Lupe's was claws and fangs. It threw her head back and gaped her mouth with its keening. The boys screamed with her. They climbed on top of her. They hit her with their fists and begged her to stop. She paid them no mind, and paid none to the men who tried to silence her. Raymond said nothing. He did nothing. Then Jessie came. She dragged the children off their mother and shoved them at the Dempseys.

"Take them to the house and keep them there," she said. "Tie them up if you have to." She got down in the dirt beside Lupe. Her voice was flat and steady.

"Listen to me," she said. "Listen. The heat. His body. There is no time for this. Because it's too hot. Listen. Lupe, the heat. Lupe. For his sake, listen. You know what this heat is doing to him. Listen."

The wailing stopped. Jessie helped Lupe to her feet and the two of them walked to the house. Beau and Jack came with a door and took the body away. Raymond took Dolly's horse to the barn, unsaddled it, and turned it out to pasture. There was a shovel in the feed room and an ax behind the barn. The blades on both were dull. He took them to the tool shed to sharpen them, but the grinding wheel had come off its mount. He used his whetstone instead. It didn't work very well, and he put it back in his pocket. Then he walked around the house to the edge of the hammock, and chose from among five trails the one that led to the Baxter cemetery.

Dolly had started on it after Quincey was born. Standing in the center and looking due east across Deep Creek, a man could see the whole southern end of Walker's Island, a pie-shaped wedge bordered by the swamp and hanging tree to the south, the hammock to the north and the wide blue line of Lake Locknahatchee straight ahead. West of the clearing, the land fell away in a gentle slope along the edge of the hammock to the prairie.

"It drains good," Dolly said. "I like that in a burying ground. And I can keep an eye on you and Vancey."

"We don't want you spying on us," Raymond said.

"I've done it for years," Dolly said. "It keeps you two from fussing."

Raymond had laughed when Dolly said that. Now it wasn't funny. He felt light-headed and his belly ached. He could have asked for help, but didn't want it. Digging this grave was Raymond's last gift to Dolly. It would be difficult, as such a gift should be, but not impossible. Dolly himself had seen to that. He'd spent the last twelve years clearing the plot of trees and brush. Only sand and grass and wildflowers remained. Only a hole was required. Six feet long. Six feet deep. Three feet wide. That was a fair amount of sand. But it could be done. And Raymond would do it. For Dolly. As a gift. A private farewell.

Carefully, Raymond bent over and laid the ax on the ground. He stuck the shovel in the dirt, set his foot on the lip, and pushed. The shovel went in about three inches and stopped. Raymond waggled the tip in the dirt. There was something hard beneath it. He pulled the shovel out and scraped away at the ground with his boot. A tree stump was cut off so close to the surface that sand and grass had covered it. Raymond picked the shovel up, moved over two steps, and jabbed the blade into the ground again. Again, he hit something hard. He scraped the dirt away again and found the same thing: a tree stump level with the ground and overgrown with grass. He walked to the other side of the first stump. This would put the grave off center and a little too close to the path, but Raymond didn't care. He just wanted to get the grave dug before dark fell. He jabbed the shovel at the ground. The blade rang. He scraped the sand away again and found another hidden stump.

"What in the world?" Raymond muttered. He stepped three feet to the right and jabbed the shovel at the ground. It bounced back up. A root was lying on top of the ground. At the thick end of it, hidden in the grass, was a stump.

"Listen here, Baxter," Raymond said. "I know you didn't leave these stumps here for me to pull out." As soon as he spoke, however, he knew that Dolly had done exactly that. Raymond briefly lost his mind. He kicked roots and fell over stumps and stabbed at the ground with the shovel blade only to find the same thing over and over again: that under the lush pasture and dainty wildflowers of Dolly's so-called burying ground was Black Hammock itself. Before he could dig Dolly's grave, Raymond would have to pull an oak tree out of the ground.

The terrible clarity that had afflicted Raymond earlier in the day now returned, with this difference: the world was no longer far away, but so close he could scarcely breathe. The grass crowded him, each blade as sharp as broken glass and paired with something different from itself. One dangled a drop of water, another bowed under a cricket, another swayed in a wind only it could feel. Each one was so brightly lit that Raymond had to squint to look at it. A bumblebee perched on a blue flower, bending it nearly to the ground. The two of them were held in an orb of light. The three of them together - the bee, the flower, the orb of light - were a glass paperweight hanging on the end of a stem. Everything Raymond looked at was distinct in this way, as though the falling dusk were a blanket with holes in it that light shone through, revealing small objects in its path. And each object - animal or plant - was perfect and different from all others of its kind, and each was touching, in some special way, another thing that was equally perfect and different from all others of its kind, and every pairing was held in the light that came through the blanket.

Watching this, a feeling of excitement came over Raymond. He stood up straight, his hand barely touching the shovel handle. The darkness that had followed him for months, that had gathered and deepened around him the entire day, until even the sun had shadowed, this darkness was torn, and light was shining through it into his mind, so that he finally understood why he had come to this place. He had not come here to hide from Lupe Baxter or from her children. He had not come here to escape his neighbors' accusations, or Jessie's pity, or Beau's shame. He had not come here because he was so broken that he didn't know who he was and so lost that he didn't know where to turn. He had come here to give his strength in exchange for Dolly's life. By honoring Dolly's desire to be buried in this place, by finishing the task begun here but not completed, by doing the greater part of it, the harder part of it, here, now, alone, at the end of this long and dreadful day, by sacrificing the strength - not of his body, for that was gone - but of his heart, a heart filled to breaking with gratitude for the gift that had been given - a gift unasked for, unnecessary, perhaps even pointless, but given all the same - Raymond would rid himself of obligation to the giver. He would pull a tree out of this ground and dig a grave, and thereby free himself, and Beau, of Dolly's death.

Raymond went back to the path to get the ax. It was hard to find because it was hidden in the grass and not exactly where he remembered leaving it. But he found it eventually, not far from a stump he didn't see until he fell over it. He got a good feel for the thing, however, groping around it until he knew where the roots were and how wide the trunk was and where to put his feet so he wouldn't lose his balance when he stood up, which he finally did with the help of the shovel. And it wasn't particularly hard to lift the ax, except that he had to put the shovel down because he couldn't hold it and the ax at the same time. It was hard, too, to keep his balance, but he finally managed to raise the ax and bring it down on the root.

The blade went in fairly deep, though Raymond couldn't see all that well because the twilight was so thick, close to night, really, and the light that had held the bumblebee and the flower and the other partnered things did not touch the ax and the root, though in his mind they were partners of a sort and some light would have helped. Still, he knew the blade had gone in because it didn't want to come out again, even when he went down on one knee and then the other to pull on the handle. So he pressed down. The blade gave a little. He pulled up again. It gave a little more. He pushed down again, then pulled up. Up and down, up and down, little by little, the blade loosened in the wood until he could pull it out.

Then he had to get to his feet again, which took some time, and he had to raise the ax again, which knocked him off balance. The weight of it was such that he could not swing it down, but had to drop it. The blade bounced so hard off the root that Raymond felt the vibrations in his underarms. He rested a moment, then lifted the ax again. This time he swung it up and brought it down in a long, smooth, uninterrupted arc, his back and hips and thighs in line behind the swing, the motion strong and sure to the very end, when he felt in his bones the blade sink deep into the root.

It was a satisfying feeling, the kind he got when his mind was clear and his judgment sound. The last few months he'd been a stranger to himself. Today should not have happened, would not have happened, had Dolly not dredged up the past, then interfered in someone else's business. Given the chance, Beau might have overcome his terror, Raymond and the bay mare might have crossed Deep Creek. Together and against great odds, the three of them might have won through to Walker's Island. And if they'd failed, if their various weaknesses of mind and heart and body had not only betrayed, but defeated them, then they'd be dead, leaving no one the wiser.

But Dolly had interfered. He'd left his wife and children and charged the bridge and died a hero's death with all its glory and honor and unsullied sorrow. From now until the day of his own death, only Raymond would know the truth: that Dolly had simply been ashamed for what he'd said and done, and that his death at the bridge was no more than an apology gone wrong. It was just another one of Dolly's mistakes, another one of his messes that Raymond had to clean up.

"Ain't that right, Dolly?" Raymond said. "You left your mess with the better man, didn't you? It ain't many that would take this trouble just because you asked them to, and you dead with no way to hold them to their promise. You're lucky it's me made you that promise. You're lucky it's me."

Self-justification warmed Raymond like a hot meal as he hauled back on the ax. It didn't move. "Don't you be aggravating me, Baxter," he said. "It's way past time for me to be done." He jerked on the handle again. "I might have known you'd do something like this." He tugged again, pulled up, pushed down. Nothing happened.

Raymond peered into the dark. "This ax is stuck," he called. "I need this ax. I've got work to do." No one answered. He raised his voice until he was shouting. "Hey, you hear me? I've got work to do and I can't do it because of this ax. This ain't right. It's wrong to do me this way. I've been done wrong once today already. Ain't that right, Dolly? You tell them. Tell them what you've done. You know what he's done? He's gone off and left me with a mess. He's torn something up and left me to fix it. It happens all the time, don't it, Dolly? Tell them how you do this kind of thing all the time, how you mess something up, then want me to fix it. Well this time you can just fix it your own damn self. I didn't ask for this. I didn't ask you to help me with Tate. I didn't ask you to butt in. It was my business and I was handling it my way, and if I wanted to be stupid and prideful and near about drown in the creek and ruin a good horse and get Beau killed, what was that to you? Why couldn't you just mind your own damn business, Dolly? What the hell was the matter with you anyway, that you couldn't just leave me alone?"

Raymond stopped shouting as suddenly as he'd begun, and tightened his grip on the ax handle. "Never you mind," he said. "I'll just do this my own damn self." He jerked with all his might on the ax, but it didn't move. He pulled it, pushed it, pounded on it with his fist, to no avail. No matter what he did, the handle jutted up from the root as fixed as iron. Finally, Raymond got down on his knees so he could see the problem. There it was. The blade was nearly buried in the root.

Somehow, he had sunk the ax too deep in the wood. It would not come out, because it could not.

Raymond's attention wandered, then returned to the ax and the root. The two of them were so perfectly joined that he half-expected the light he'd seen earlier to form around them. But it was too late for that now. He'd driven the light away with his arrogance, as he had driven so many things away. Or maybe there wasn't a need for it any longer. Maybe it had already shown him what to look for: the details of things, and how they fit together. He could see through the ax and the root those partnered things within himself. Desiring greatness, he'd become mean; desiring safety, he'd provoked danger; desiring wholeness, he'd broken beyond repair his life and the lives of those he loved. And Dolly had died a little bit with every gift of himself to those who didn't want it, until he'd given them all he had. Raymond could cling to his pride and refuse that final gift, or humble himself and accept it. He knelt beside the root and considered his options, then, because he was tired, and because it was all he had to give in return, chose the second.

At that moment, the darkness in his mind was torn and the light shone through so clear and pure and bright that Raymond had to shut his eyes to keep from going blind. He kept them shut as long as he could, even after they'd found him - Beau and Jack and George Dempsey - though he was neither lost nor witless, as they seemed to think. He was just full of light, and he wanted to tell them about it, about what he'd learned from it, only they wouldn't listen. They kept telling him to calm down when he wasn't excited, only grateful and unwilling to lose the light.

But he lost it, anyway, in the glare of their fatwood torches and the darkness of their ignorance, lost it so completely it was as if he'd never seen it at all, and the truth it had revealed about him and Dolly was hidden again as they told him that George and Seth and Jacob had dug a grave already, one closer to the Baxter house; that Beau and Jack had built a coffin and it was in the house with the body in it; that the funeral was set for in the morning and all the preparations made and the work done; that there was nothing left for him to do but go on home to Walker's Island and get some rest.

Chapter Thirty-Nine

The coffin rested on two sawhorses in the middle of the front room. Jessie stood by the coffin. Lupe and the five youngest boys sat in chairs against the long wall. The pallbearers - George, Seth, and Jacob Dempsey, the sheriff, Fess Peck, and Quincey - stood with the preacher against the short wall opposite the fireplace. Raymond and Beau sat on chairs near the front door. No one spoke to them. Everyone spoke to the pallbearers and the preacher, and to Jessie, and most of them offered to shake Lupe's hand, but she did not respond. Condolences fell like stones into her silence. Children brought her flowers. When she did not take them, they put them in her lap. Jessie took the flowers and put them in the coffin. The pile of flowers grew. They covered the gifts in the coffin: a tin whistle, a dog-eared Bible, a turtle's egg. They covered Dolly's hands and the cloth over his face. Their sweetness mingled with the odors of his body to form one scent that strengthened as the morning passed. At ten o'clock, Jessie took a breath and tasted bile.

"It's time," she said.

Raymond heard her, but did not raise his eyes. He had not shaved, not just because his hands were so unsteady, but because his hair and beard had turned to silver overnight and he could not bear to look at himself. The eyes in the mirror were so helpless he had to turn away. He was not alone in this. Others, too, looked once at him and turned away, even his own family. Only Jessie looked at him, and Quincey, the one with such pity and the other with such hatred that he could not bear either gaze.

"Raymond." Raymond looked up. Fess Peck was standing in front of him, hat in hand.

"Jessie says it's time," he said.

"All right," Raymond said. He stood up, took his hat off - the one he wore to church and funerals and weddings - and walked across the room to Lupe.

"It's time," he said.

She nodded, but did not speak or move. Seth and Jack set the lid on the coffin. Seth and Jacob nailed it down. Beau wanted to help them, but didn't. He wanted to be a pallbearer, too, but Quincey had said no. He turned to the preacher.

"Pastor Winslow," he said. "You go first, and they'll follow with the coffin. Moe and Moe here, they'll walk with you to show you the way."

The twins stepped up, one on each side of the preacher. The pastor, a short, chubby man with small boys of his own, tried to take their hands, but they eyed him suspiciously and stuck them in their pockets. "It's easy walking," one of them said. "You won't need no help."

Raymond put a hand on Lupe's shoulder and said again, "It's time."

Lupe looked at him as if she actually saw him for the first time since he'd brought Dolly home. Her eyes were sunken, the skin around them so bruised it looked like she'd been beaten. "I can't," she said.

"I'll help you," Raymond said. He put one hand under her elbow and another her waist. "Come on, now. I've got you."

Lupe put a hand on each widespread knee and with Raymond's help got to her feet. She groaned when she stood, as much with the burden of the child she carried, it seemed, as with sorrow. Once up, she turned pale. Sweat broke out on her forehead. "God help me," she said. "I've got no strength."

"Lean on me," Raymond said. And she did, putting her weight on him as if he were a rock. Raymond bowed his head in gratitude. Her dependency quickened hope that all was not lost, that something of Dolly's friendship might remain to him, if only in such small favors. He took a deep breath, and felt something ease inside.

Then Quincey was beside him, yapping like a feist. "Let go of her!" he yelled. "Don't let him touch you, Mama!"

Raymond could have struck the boy for his cruelty. Perhaps he even raised his hand, because George was very suddenly there, his bulk shielding Quincey. He caught Raymond's eyes and held them. Raymond's anger ebbed. There was a time when no man would have challenged his place at Lupe's side, but now, that too, was changed. Grief clawed at his belly. He dropped his eyes, and patted Lupe's arm. "George will help you," he said.

Lupe took her hand off Raymond's arm. "That's best," she said. George took her arm, and Able Gibbs took his place. The six pallbearers lifted the coffin using the rope handles along the side and carried it as far as the door, then had to stop. The door wasn't wide enough for them all to pass through at one time.

"Get under it until you're out of the house," Beau said.

"Let me help," Quincey said. The men ignored him, lifting the coffin overhead, out of his reach, and carrying it through the front door, across the porch, and down the steps. Only then did they lower it again so Quincey could catch hold of one of the handles. People made two lines around the east side of the house, forming an aisle. The preacher walked down the aisle between the twins, followed by the pallbearers and the coffin. Lupe came next on George's arm, and after them the rest of the Baxter boys but one, and that was Nub. He came next, riding on Jessie's hip. Jack walked with Lila. He carried a chair off the porch. Lila held his fiddle case. Raymond and Beau walked behind them. Beau carried two stout ropes. The aisle closed in behind them as they passed, and soon Dolly's funeral procession was winding through the oak trees behind the Baxter house.

Black Hammock was green and sweet-smelling from the rain. Wild orchids clung to the oaks, rain drops dangling from the lips of their spidery leaves, and resurrection fern rose like a mane on the tops of the rough limbs. Palmetto fronds heavy with water spilled their contents on people as they walked by. A woodpecker hammered on a tree and frogs sang in the grass, their high-pitched voices falling away as the coffin approached, then rising up again, urgent and shrill, as it passed.

The morning was heating up by the time the procession reached the gravesite, with that heaviness in the air that warned of rain to come. Everyone was hot and sweaty, and a number of men had stopped to cut palmetto fans for their wives. The pallbearers set the coffin down beside the hole, and Beau handed them the ropes. Jacob and Seth looped one length under the front of the coffin, and Quincey, with Fess and Able's help, put the other length under the back. Then they lowered the coffin into the grave. It thumped to the ground and the ropes went slack, and thumped again as the Dempseys pulled the ropes back up. Jack set the chair down by the grave.

"For you, Lupe," he said.

Lupe nodded her thanks and sat down. The front legs sank into the ground until it seemed as if she might pitch into the hole after Dolly, and George had to help her get it square. Quincey stood behind her with his hand on her shoulder as if he could hold her in place.

Pastor Winslow cleared his throat. "Dearly beloved," he said. "We are gathered here to commend Dolly Baxter's soul to God and his body to the earth." He paused for a moment. Dolly had not been a church-going man. As far Winslow knew, Dolly had never even been inside one. He'd been a likeable man, more so than many of the preacher's flock. Likeability, however, was not a redemptive quality. The preacher, so accustomed to public speaking, found himself at a loss for words, his natural expansiveness of heart at odds with his theology. He looked around for help.

"I expect his boys would like to say something," George said.

The preacher looked at Quincey. "Young man..."

"My name's Quincey."

"Quincey," Pastor Winslow amended. "Would you like to say something in honor of your father?"

"I would." Hat clenched in his hands and a fierce scowl on his face, Quincey stepped up to the grave and spoke loud and clear. "My daddy was a good man," he said. "He was good to his family. He provided for us. He was proud of us, and proud to call us his own. He was better than God, because he didn't take a man from his family less'n he had to. He didn't go to church. He didn't need to. Church is for sorry folks, and my daddy weren't sorry. There was no meanness in him. He was a good man and a good daddy. There was no call for him dying, and us Baxters won't forget it." He paused for a moment, then said, "Amen."

There was a rustle of movement, a collective sigh, a whispered amen. There were also a few smiles and a number of grim expressions. The preacher regretted surrendering control of the eulogy, and had opened his mouth to reclaim it when Quincey pushed one of his brothers in the back.

"Your turn," he said.

The boy shoved him back. "You ain't my daddy," he said. Then he started crying.

Pastor Winslow opened his mouth again, but Lupe raised her hand. "You want to say something, Mizz Baxter?" he asked.

"No," Lupe said. "There's been enough said. George?"

"What is it, Lupe?"

"Help me up."

George put his arm under hers and helped her to her feet. She stood there, breathing hard, the baby in her belly rolling and kicking beneath her dress.

"The shovel," she said.

A shovel passed through the crowd to Lupe. She leaned on it for a moment, then stuck it in the pile of dirt and dropped a blade full in the grave. The dirt fell on the coffin with a dull thud. She offered the shovel to George. He held it with one hand and helped her into the chair with the other. She sat down, arranged her skirt around her feet, and folded her hands in her lap.

"Jacky?"

"Yes, Lupe?"

"I'd like you to play something."

"Here, Jack." Lila handed him the fiddle case.

Jack opened the case and took out his fiddle and bow, then handed the case back to Lila. He put the fiddle under his chin and plucked the strings, tightening the pegs until it was tuned. He drew the bow across a string in one high, clear, steady note. George dropped a shovelful of dirt on the coffin and handed the shovel to Quincey. Quincey shoveled a clod into the hole and handed the shovel to July. The shovel passed from child to child, Jessie helping Nub when it came his turn because it was so heavy.

"Is there anything particular you want me to play?" Jack asked.

"Something he could dance to," Lupe said.

Winslow opened his mouth again. Fess handed him the shovel. "Your turn, Preacher," he said. Maybe it was the smell of whiskey on Fess's breath, or the powerful presence of a man who'd been better than a month without bathing, but Pastor Winslow shut his mouth, backed up, and stuck the shovel in the dirt.

"Here we go," Jack said. He settled his chin on the fiddle, pulled the bow across the strings, and began to play.

The notes were soft at first, almost inaudible, as though they were waking from a deep sleep. They shook themselves, circled and spiraled, spun apart and came back together again, chased one another, turned this way and that as if pondering their reflections in a mirror before sliding away to bow and curtsy into a tune, a familiar one that dipped and bobbed between partnered things, a fern in the rain, a bough in the wind, a crane courting its mate, a girl with long black hair who danced in the arms of a blue-eyed man, the two of them turning so close to Lila that she reached out to catch the colors that flew from them like light through a bird made of glass, shards of green and ruby and gold and blue and violet and white that sparkled in her hands and fell through her fingers and bathed her feet as they danced away.

The man circled Beau through sunlight and shadows, now hero, now coward, now wise man, now clown, the woman in his arms first beauty, then crone, then beauty again, the two of them laughing then weeping and dancing away and taking the music with them, leaving Beau with the echo and then with a silence that was louder than any music he'd ever heard in his life or would ever hear again.

The notes spun apart and came together again as a man and a woman came waltzing past Jessie, the flames of their passion burned down to gray ash and red coals, the woman at a stove and supper on the table and children sitting in their chairs down either side, the man at the head, solid and warm and smelling of tobacco and whiskey, who faded and was gone, leaving an empty chair, an empty bed, his phantom lips on the woman's mouth, his phantom hand on her breast, his phantom arm around her waist as she danced alone to a tune in a minor key.

Then the woman spun out of sight and Raymond was left with the notes that dissolved into rhythms of wind and sky and earth and rain that woke the dead who rose speaking their names in clear single notes: Billy Baxter, Ben Monroe, Lucas Walker, Everett Asbell, Wallace Turner, Edward Fitz, Vancey Adams, each looking past Raymond with such yearning and wonder that Raymond was sure they were looking at Dolly, so that were Raymond to turn, he, too, would see him, and the abandoned flesh, the coffin, the grave, all would be gone, burned away like a fog by the bright cry of greeting that leaped from the fiddle, so full of glad recognition that Raymond did turn, the grave behind him now, his heel on its edge and Dolly at his shoulder, and he could finally see - past the hammock and the house and the wandering paths - what the light had been trying to show him, what the music had known since music began, that Walker's Island was still there and would always be there, just over the creek, and forever just out of reach.

Acknowledgements

I am grateful to and for the following communities and people:

1992-94 Miami University graduate fiction workshop professors Eric Goodman, Stephen Bauer, and Constance Pearce;

1994-95 graduate fiction workshop members Kelly Bahmer-Brouse, Scott Berg, Christopher Coake, Pierce Johnston, Greg Kauffman, Catherine Pinckert, Beth Slattery, Andrew Tonn, and Bill Willard;

My thesis committee members, Eric Goodman, Stephen Bauer, and Mary Jean Corbett;

Those gracious readers of many revisions, Eric Goodman and Scott Berg;

My NLP and Self-Relations communities, particularly Tom and Bobbi Best, Linda Moore, Stephen Gilligan, Neda Gluhajic, Randall Fulton, Jenny Schipper, Dvorah Simons, and Selene Vega;

My teachers, readers, neighbors, helpers, friends Helen Adams, Willie Mae Beckham, Karen Borglum, Virginia Brodie, the Carrasquillo family, Cathy Carignan, Barbara Chasteen, Marnay Coleman, Corinne Eaker, Archie and Doris Whalen, Keith Fail, Paula Garber, Jo Gillibrand, Risa Gorelick, Dean Halfacre, Devin Hastings, the Ianes family, Hank Laurence, Karen Liebenguth, Helen Lombardy, Sis Nagle, Jen and JoAnn Overstreet, Catherine Parrill, Katie Raver, Bob and Kay Riggs, the Rutherfords, Brett Yeager, and Tom and Jackie Young;

Beloved family members Jim and Joy Radebaugh, Gran, Phyll, Lee, Anita, Ken, Jenn, Larry, Mary, Bingo, Kennan, Katie, Jessie, Nettie, Candra, Beau, Justin, Mike, Sam, Vinny, Hank, Kalee, Jacob, Riley, Bennett, Niko, and all the rest on both sides as far back and out as they go;

And again, and finally, and most especially, those two small boys who made the journey with me. I here commend them to the care of the men they have become and those they are becoming, confidant that with them, as Dame Julian says, all shall be well, and all shall be well, and all manner of thing shall be well.

About the Author

K. J. Radebaugh currently lives and writes in Austin, Texas, where she also facilitates workshops on the creative process. Interested readers will find more of Ms. Radebaugh's writing at www.westernnovel.com. She may be contacted at kradebaugh@gmail.com.

About the Artist

Jenn Spurlock spends many hours traveling country roads in Florida and Tennessee, where she looks for old homesteads and barns. In this age of concrete and chrome, she hopes that her art will remind people of a simpler time. Ms. Spurlock may be contacted at jradspur@hotmail.com.

3244489

Made in the USA